THE PRIEST AND THE SEÑORITA . . .

María moved closer to him. Their bodies almost touched. Juan held the candle to one side. He could feel the heat radiating from her, hear her breathing, see deeply into her eyes that seemed clouded over with love and life.

"And now?" María asked.

"And now I no longer hide, María, from life and," he had to say it, ". . . and from you."

THE EAGLE AND THE SERPENT

LEE JACKSON

A JOVE BOOK

THE EAGLE AND THE SERPENT

Requests for permission to make copies of any part of the work should be mailed to: Permissions, Jove Publications, Inc., 200 Madison Avenue, New York, New York 10016

First Jove edition published March 1982

First printing

Printed in the United States of America

Jove books are published by Jove Publications, Inc., 200 Madison Avenue, New York, NY 10016

Book One

CHAPTER ONE

May 1803

Father Juan de Soltura stood in front of the church and looked out over a small public plaza in the town of Nuestra Señora de los Dolores, in the Mexican province of Michoacán. It was noon. The May sun was at its zenith, and at its hottest.

Father Soltura was not bothered by the heat on that day, so consumed was he with the activity in the plaza. A hundred Spanish soldiers were busy constructing a wooden hitching post in the center of the square. Tripods of short, thick logs supported a twenty-foot-long horizontal bar which was being lashed to them.

The commandant shook the long bar. Satisfied that it was sturdy enough for its task, he barked orders to his men. They moved away, some going to a wagon twenty feet from the hitching post, others disappearing around the corner of a two-story government building that was directly across the plaza from the church.

Father Soltura was joined by another Catholic priest. The second priest was older, and bald except for a fringe of white hair that rippled in a breeze that suddenly blew up.

"They intend to go through with it," Soltura said to his older colleague.

"Yes, and apparently with relish. Our Spanish friends approach these things as sport."

"And we are to be spectators," said Soltura. He shook his head and sighed.

The older priest, Father Miguel Hidalgo, placed his hand upon Soltura's shoulder. "My son, I realize that you would prefer to go inside and avoid witnessing such barbarity. But now that you have entered the priesthood, there are many unpleasant things you must witness if the meaning of your calling is to be clear to you. Our Lord watches and cries, and so must we.''

The Spanish commandant of Dolores ordered two buglers and a snare drummer to begin playing. The discordant sounds of the instruments cut through the swirling dust of the plaza and caused Father Soltura to wince. He turned to Hidalgo. ''Father,'' he said, ''is there nothing we can do to stop this?''

Hidalgo shook his head. ''No, my son, it is condoned by the government, by *gachupínes* and *criollos* alike.

Soltura's face hardened. ''Not by *all* criollos, Father Hidalgo. I come from a criollo family, and no one in my family would condone such punishment for anyone, including these poor unfortunate Indians.''

Hidalgo managed a smile. ''Of course, my son. I, too, am criollo. Because I was born in Mexico, I am not considered a Spaniard, just as you are not. Our *pure* Spanish friends, the gachupines, detect a difference between those of us born here and those born in Spain.''

''Foolishness.''

''Of course. Excuse me, Father Soltura, but I must tend to my brother.''

Soltura looked into the dark recesses of the church. ''How is he today?''

''He is doing poorly. I suspect the end is near.''

''And you will replace him here in Dolores as parish priest?''

''Yes. It will be my last parish. I will die here.''

Hidalgo turned and entered the church. He said over his shoulder, ''I will be back before it begins. I will stand with you.''

Father Soltura returned his attention to the plaza. Some of the soldiers removed three large tree stumps from the wagon and spaced them five feet apart, near the hitching post.

A crowd of civilians had begun to gather. The buglers and drummer repeated their ragged march melody, this time with more volume and conviction.

Father Soltura felt the heat for the first time that day. He closed his eyes and was cooled by thoughts of his home that he would soon visit again. It was located in Valladolid, at the other end of the province, closer to Mexico City. His father, Manuel, was a *ranchero* there. The farm and ranch spanned eighty acres of green fields and clumps of mimosa and ocote pine trees. A cool, clear stream of water ran through the property, and Manuel de Soltura had devised irrigation canals from it to feed the more arid portions of the farm.

Juan thought back to lying naked in that stream, as he had done as a small boy. Often, while a theology student at San Nicolás Obispo, he'd thought of the stream and its coolness upon his body. Now, within a few days, he would be there once again, an ordained member of Mexico's Catholic clergy, a source of pride to his mother and father.

But he was no longer a boy. He was a man, and that realization gave him courage. He opened his eyes and again observed the soldiers at work.

The commandant was a short, pudgy Mexican with baggy pants, whose thick black hair hung down in clumps beneath a nine-inch-tall, dull black leather shako. His chinstrap and shield were brass. A crimson pompom stood above a tricolor cockade. His pants were crimson, although dirt had dulled their vividness. He wore a tan shirt beneath a soiled and wrinkled dark blue coat. Brass buttons lined the front of the coat. The collar was red, as were the cuffs.

The other soldiers were dressed similarly, except that their hats were two-sided blue barracks caps with red tassels.

The three-piece military band had just begun a third chorus of the march they'd been playing when the commandant raised his hands and shouted, *"Alto!"*

The band ceased playing as ordered.

The commandant barked further orders. A group of onlookers in front of the government building stepped back to allow a dozen soldiers to lead three Indian prisoners to the center of the plaza. The Indians' hands were bound behind their backs with leather straps. Manacles on their ankles allowed them only enough freedom to shuffle along the ground. Tiny clouds of yellow dust kicked up from their feet.

Father Hidalgo rejoined Father Soltura in front of the church. They watched another heavily armed contingent of soldiers appear from behind the government building. In their midst were twenty Indians, who were also tied and manacled.

"They will kill them all?" Soltura asked Hidalgo.

The older priest shook his head. "No. Those three in the center are accused of being the leaders of the so-called revolt. They will die. The others will be flogged."

"Was there a trial?"

"Of course not. There are never trials for mestizos and

sambos and mulattoes." He was referring to the distinctions that people made among the children of mixed marriages. The child of an Indian and European marriage produced a mestizo; Indian and Negro produced a sambo; Indian and white created a mulatto.

"And what does the church say?" asked Soltura.

Father Hidalgo drew a deep breath, almost as though to dismiss the question by his action.

Soltura noticed that Hidalgo's lip trembled. "Forgive me, Father," he said, "for questioning the church of our Lord."

"Forgive *you*, Father Soltura? It is the church that should ask forgiveness. You ask what the church does in this matter? It does nothing. Our church here in New Spain conducts itself like the government that grants it power. Our church leaders are all members of the privileged gachupine class, or criollos who aspire to such privileged position. There are few who see their calling as a cry to liberate the wretched Indians and black men. Too few, Father Soltura." His voice trailed off. "Too few."

Upon orders from the commandant, the twenty Indian prisoners were positioned along the length of the hitching post. Their hands were untied from behind their backs and refastened to the crossbar. While a contingent of soldiers drew their *escopetas* and trained them upon the Indians, twenty other soldiers drew *cuartas* from the nearby wagon, short heavy whips with iron stocks and lashes made of three loose leather thongs. These troops removed their blue coats and tossed them onto the wagon. There was much joking and laughter among the soldiers.

"What of those to be executed?" Soltura asked.

Father Hidalgo pointed to a far corner of the plaza. Three tall and powerfully built Negroes stood silently together, long, gleaming swords in their hands. They were stripped to the waist. Their heads were shaven.

"Without a trial," Father Soltura muttered.

Hidalgo did not reply. He prayed silently for the souls of the three men about to be executed.

Father Soltura did not join him in prayer. Instead, he asked, "What of the men to be flogged? Who will care for them?"

Hidalgo was annoyed for the moment at the interruption. "Their families, *if* they survive the beating."

5

"We could administer to them in the church, couldn't we?"

"Are you a physician as well as a priest, Father Soltura?"

"No, but perhaps the simple act of offering to help will ease the guilt I feel."

Father Hidalgo said nothing.

"Well?" asked Soltura. "Shall we offer to tend to them in the church?"

Hidalgo smiled at the younger priest's fire. He considered telling him of all the times he had ministered to the sick and beaten, of the poor and impoverished he had taken into his churches against vehement objections of the more conservative clergy, his battles with the gachupine ruling class and of his own beating at the hands of a military commander in Mexico City when he, Miguel Hidalgo, had led a small band of mestizos in a protest march against working conditions on the ranches and farms.

Instead, he shrugged. "Do what your conscience tells you, my son. Do what you must."

Soltura left the shade of the church and walked directly to the Mexican commandant who, at that moment, was calling his troops into a semblance of order.

"Señor," Father Soltura said. "May I speak with you for a moment?"

The commandant turned and glared at the young priest. "*Qué*?" he asked.

"Señor, I wish to offer the church as a place where these Indians, who are to be punished, might have their wounds tended to."

The commandant screwed up his face into an exaggerated question. "Who are you? This is not your parish."

"I am Father Juan de Soltura. I am a *vallesoletano*. I visit here with Father Hidalgo."

The commandant looked across the plaza at Hidalgo. He snorted, then broke into a twisted grin that exposed gold in his front teeth. "That old meddler? You visit with him? A fine young man like you, a priest, a vallesoletano? You should stay in Valladolid. That's a nice place. This is not your place. Here, in Dolores, we do not use the church to help revolutionaries. Be gone now. Go into your church and be quiet." He dismissed Soltura with a wave of his hand and took a few steps toward the hitching post.

Soltura followed him. "Señor," he said, "I ask in the

name of Our Father that I be allowed to treat those you will punish.''

There was no smile this time on the commandant's face. He spun around and snarled, *"No quiero hablar con usted!* Be gone, father, before I am forced to make a scene here with you.''

Father Soltura knew it was hopeless to pursue the matter any further. He walked past the row of Indians tied to the crossbar and muttered a prayer that their pain would be of short duration. He stopped in front of the three men condemned to die, placed his hand upon the naked shoulder of one of them and said, ''Peace be with you, my brother. You go to a better life.''

The Indian's eyes were filled with terror. Soltura avoided them and returned to the front of the church.

''I feel better having tried,'' Soltura said to Hidalgo.

Hidalgo nodded.

The first sickening sounds of leather slashing into flesh assaulted the two priests. Then, the first screams. Again and again the soldiers wielded their quirts. The cries of pain and anguish eventually reduced to moans, then to silence.

After each prisoner had received two hundred blows, their bonds were cut and all of them slumped to the ground, their backs shredded clear through to the bones of their shoulder blades, their blood forming pasty pools in the yellow sand of the plaza.

The commandant immediately beckoned the three Negro executioners, *verdugos* in Spanish. The condemned prisoners, who'd stood silently as their brothers received their lashes, were brought to their knees, their hands still tied behind their backs. Their heads were forced forward until they rested on the tree stumps. Not one of them moved. No one cried out. The only sound in the plaza came from the wife of one of the condemned. She uttered a long, anguished cry that ricocheted off the stone walls of the buildings surrounding the plaza.

The verdugos approached. As they took their positions next to each tree stump, a soldier poked a stick into the spine of each prisoner, which caused their heads to jerk forward, like the heads of turtles. In a flash, the swords were raised. The brilliant sunlight caught the steel and flashed in wild patterns on the buildings. Suddenly, the Negroes wielded the swords. The Indians' heads flew from their trunks and rolled across the ground. A gust of wind swept around the corner of the church and covered the blood with a layer of Mexican soil. A woman's screams were drowned out by the blare of the bugles and the roll of the drum.

Later that afternoon, Father Miguel Hidalgo's brother died inside the church.

At six, after receiving Communion from Hidalgo, Father Juan de Soltura mounted his horse and began the final portion of his journey to his home in Valladolid. As he passed through the plaza and found the narrow dirt road leading from the town of Dolores, he looked up at pikestaffs that had been erected atop three huts in which the executed prisoners had lived with their families. Jammed onto each pike was the severed head of the executed. Their heads would remain there until the commandant decided the lesson had been learned.

Father Soltura stopped his horse and looked back at the now quiet town of Nuestra Señora de los Dolores. *How apt,* he thought, *that this town should be called Our Lady of the Sorrows.*

The church bell chimed. He prodded his horse forward and headed for home, his handsome young face heavy with anger and despair.

CHAPTER TWO

Two Days Later

Valladolid

María de Jardinero entered a small paddock and closed the gate behind her. The Indian in charge of the Jardinero family horses had seen her approaching and had quickly begun saddling María's favorite steed, a black and white stallion bred from Arabian and Spanish stock. María had named him Tormenta, the Spanish word for storm. Of all the horses in the Jardinero stable, Tormenta was the most volatile, the most spirited. "He's stormy," María had said upon first seeing him. "I like his rage."

The Indian completed cinching the saddle and greeted María, *"Buenos días, señorita."*

"Buenos días," she replied. "The day is beautiful."

"Sí."

The sky was a brilliant blue, unmarked by clouds. The air was hot but dry. A pleasant breeze blew from the north and ruffled a field of pink sweet william just outside the paddock.

María patted Tormenta on the neck and smiled as the horse whinnied and nuzzled her with his head.

"He is pleased to see you, señorita. He always is."

"No more pleased than I am to see him, and to ride him," she said.

The stablehand offered his hand but, as usual, María shook him off. She placed her booted foot in the silver stirrup and pulled herself up onto the animal.

The Indian appreciated the sixteen-year-old girl's independence. She never allowed anyone to help her mount, nor would she shirk the responsibility of rubbing down and brushing the horse after the ride. She had as much spirit as Tormenta, spirit that at once frustrated and pleased her parents.

María leaned left and twisted her left hand so that the leather reins were lifted slightly off Tormenta's neck. The horse responded to this gentle direction by throwing its head to the left and moving that way. María never used the heavy and cruel "Spanish bit" to control Tormenta. She used her knees, side-shifted her body and slapped the reins to control the stallion.

Tiny bells on the silver rowel of María's spurs tinkled as she held Tormenta in a steady canter from the paddock and into an open field separating the stables from the main house. She saw her mother come through the door from the kitchen and stand on the shaded porch. María waved and her mother returned it.

Her father, José de Jardinero suddenly appeared from around the rear of the house. He'd been inspecting the southernmost corner of his hacienda and had returned for breakfast. The horse he rode was a dappled mare that had been his for ten years.

"Aquí, aquí," he called to María, motioning for her to join him.

María guided Tormenta to where her father had dismounted and was wiping perspiration from his lean, lined face.

"A donde va usted?" asked her father.

"For a ride, papa. Nowhere special."

"You have eaten?"

"Yes."

José Jardinero ran his hand through coarse gray hair. *"Bueno."*

He smiled at his daughter. She looked especially beautiful to him that morning. The sun lighted her face like a search-light. Her large, round brown eyes were filled with a life of their own that threatened to burst forth at any moment. Her carriage in the saddle was perfection, ramrod straight and yet feminine. That morning, María wore a new riding outfit that had recently arrived from Spain. So much of Spain's fashion was being influenced by the French, and the riding outfit was no exception. A long, loose, pale green skirt accented with elaborate needlework of trailing vines and flowers hung above the tops of her shiny black boots. A white, lacy chemisette scooped gently beneath her collarbone and stretched tightly across the mounds of her breasts. Had María chosen to use an elaborate system of loops and catches to close the darker green gilet over the chemisette, the protrusion of her breasts would not have been as evident. But she'd chosen to let the gilet, which was fashioned of Saxon cloth and featured a two-inch arabesque border of white lace, to remain open. Although the sleeves of the gilet were puffed and ornamented with needlework, the overall effect of the jacket was that of an old Continental waistcoat, rounded at the bottom and resting on María's thighs.

A hat had accompanied the new outfit from Spain, but María discarded it immediately. Women's riding hats, which were made of straw or fine leghorn, tended to be small-rimmed and overly decorated with ribbon and feathers. Instead, María wore her favorite hat, a broad-brimmed, white felt range hat used by the *vaqueros* who worked her father's cattle. María's only modification of the hat was replacing the heavy leather band with a strip of bright yellow cloth. One side of the brim was held up against the crown by a leather thong.

"You will be careful," said her father.

"Of course, papa."

"They say that renegade Indians are attacking again."

"So I have heard."

"And María," her father said as she made a move to turn Tormenta toward the open spaces, "remember that you promised Juan's mother you would help her prepare the welcoming feast."

"I will be only a few hours, papa." A broad smile broke over her face. "Isn't it exciting that Juan will be home at last?"

Her father nodded. "Yes, my daughter, but remember that it is Father Juan de Soltura. He is now a priest."

"I will remember."

María leaned to the left and clicked her tongue against her teeth. Tormenta responded and was soon galloping toward the hills that defined the eastern edge of the fertile valley in which the Jardinero family lived.

A well-worn trail led rider and horse past the house of their neighbors, the Soltura family. Manuel Soltura was more of a farmer than was José Jardinero, although he, too, derived income from ranching. Both men had inherited their lands from their fathers, who, in turn, had been recipients of it from others in the family lineage.

As María drew abreast of the Soltura house, she saw the younger of the two Soltura brothers, Gordo, directing a group of Indian laborers as they erected a welcome sign for Gordo's brother, Juan. Gordo heard María approach and yelled for her to join them. She ignored him and urged Tormenta to speed up.

She looked back and saw that Gordo had leaped upon an unsaddled buff-and-black horse and was in pursuit of her.

"Fool," she yelled into the wind, a smile upon her lips. Of all the young men she knew in the valley, Gordo excited her the most. Although she did not have the maturity to fully recognize the cruel and insensitive streak within the younger Soltura brother, she did sense that Gordo probably would cause trouble and grief to any girl who succumbed to his wickedly handsome and virile appearance.

No one in the Michoacán valley was stronger than Gordo Soltura. He proved it at every festival by beating all the other men and boys in contests that measured strength and endurance. Gordo stood over six feet tall. He was an expert horseman, but was known to mistreat the animals on his father's hacienda. He enjoyed working in the sun with his shirt off, heavy muscles glistening with perspiration. And he was always aware of the furtive glances of nearby women as he flexed his powerful body.

María saw that Gordo was gaining on her. She veered to the right and through a clump of superb *ahuehuete* trees that flourished on the lower slopes of the hills. A short span of tall grass separated the ahuehuetes from fruit trees that grew halfway up the hillside. María brought Tormenta to a halt, leaped off and led him into the midst of the fruit trees, where a heavy scent of orange mingled with the cool, shaded air.

Once she was safely hidden by the foliage, she peered out upon the plain of grass. Gordo's steed burst through the ahuehuete clump and reached the middle of the grassy area before Gordo stopped him. A grin broke over Gordo's face. He looked down and saw the swath Tormenta had cut through the grass.

"María," he called. "Why do you play these games?"

María continued to peer at him from her hiding place. He was naked from the waist up. He wore heavy, tight blue pants and tightly fitted brown boots with narrow soles and small, high heels. A bright red silk kerchief with a hard knot in front was tied around his neck. His torso and face were golden

12

brown from the sun. There wasn't an ounce of excess flesh on him. Each muscle was clearly defined as his chest rose and fell with his breathing.

"María! If you do not end this game, it shall be ended by my rules."

Tormenta suddenly snorted and tugged against his reins.

"See?" Gordo yelled, advancing toward the fruit trees. "Even your horse wants to end the game."

María stifled a laugh. She leaped up into the heavy saddle decorated with pure silver, dug her spurs into Tormenta's sides and burst through the trees, directly at Gordo. He reached for her but she was past him in an instant. He roared with laughter and pursued her again, back through the ahuehuetes, to the trail and across it into a vast field of wheat that stretched for miles until confronting another range of hills to the north. Beyond those hills stretched a line of mountains etched against the blue sky.

The wind whipped into María's face as she leaned forward and urged Tormenta to go faster. Gordo was not far behind, but just as he was about to overtake her, María executed a caracole. Tormenta seemed to reverse direction instantly, his pivot so sharp and precise that Gordo could do nothing but bring his steed to a halt and shake his head at María's skill.

A hundred yards away, María brought Tormenta to a halt and turned in her saddle. Gordo hadn't moved from where he'd stopped. He sat bareback on his horse and shook his head. Then, he raised his arms and shouted, "You win, María. You win."

María was pleased. She patted Tormenta's neck as the younger Soltura brother joined her.

"*Buenos días,* María."

"*Buenos días,* Gordo."

"You could have killed your horse making such a turn."

She looked down at Tormenta. "He seems fine to me."

Gordo shrugged. "Where are you going?"

"For a ride. I didn't expect company."

"Do you mind if I ride with you? I won't accompany you far. There is still much to do to prepare for my brother's arrival."

María allowed herself to relax in the saddle and sighed deeply. "Imagine," she said, "to have your brother a priest. It's very wonderful."

Gordo broke into a toothy grin. "That depends. It would

not be wonderful for me. To never enjoy a pretty lady would make me unhappy."

María's laugh was scornful. "Do you enjoy that many pretty ladies, Gordo?"

"None as pretty as you, María."

She looked directly into his eyes. "Nor will you, Gordo de Soltura. I've heard all about your whores in the town."

The comment angered Gordo. He looked at the ground when he said, "Don't believe all you hear, María. There are women who are jealous and will say anything to get even."

"You flatter yourself too much," said María. She'd wanted to hurt him with her remark but knew she'd said it without conviction. Inside, she did not feel scornful or disdainful toward her neighbor. On the contrary, she felt, at that moment, an intense passion for him. The feeling was not new. Often, when she saw him working about the hacienda, there was a powerful and discomforting heat in her loins, a fluttering of the heart, even a light-headedness that could not be explained away by the sun's heat. María had often wondered what it would be like to touch him, to run her fingertips over the sculptured strength of his body, to kiss his full lips.

To make love.

Their horses were so close they touched. María felt Gordo's leg against hers. She turned to look at him. He closed the gap between them and brushed her lips with a kiss. When she didn't move, he pressed harder against her mouth. Her right hand moved involuntarily to him. Her fingers stroked the curly black hair on his chest.

Gordo twisted in his saddle and wrapped his arms about her.

"No," she said, pulling away.

"Why? My kiss does not please you?"

"Please, Gordo. Someone will see us."

Gordo sat up straight and laughed. "Who will see us? Indians? So what?" He grabbed Tormenta's reins. "Come, María, to the ahuehuetes. No one will see us there."

María shook her head. She was confused. Gordo's kiss had pleased her. The familiar feelings of lust for him had returned, lust that could now be realized. Yet, she balked. It would be wrong to accompany Gordo Soltura into the trees. It was a matter of time and place. Not on the morning of the day that his brother would return from his clerical studies. Not when María's father expected her to be riding alone. Most of all, it must not happen so quickly, so easily. If Gordo wanted her, he could pursue her, court her, legitimize the process as was only proper between men and women.

The confusion remained, however, and was heightened by the intense yearning within her to be one with him. Her heart pulled her in the direction of the trees. Her head told her something else.

In the end, her head prevailed.

"I must go home," she said.

Gordo sneered, "That's not what you really want to do, María. Look, you tremble."

"I do not tremble."

He laughed. "Yes, you do."

María urged Tormenta into a slow trot. Gordo's horse matched her pace. When they reached the trail heading to their homes, Gordo looked at her, then at the ahuehuetes. For a moment, María almost decided to turn toward the trees. At that moment in her young life she wanted more than anything to strip away her clothing and be naked against Gordo Soltura. Instead, she slapped the reins on Tormenta's neck and galloped toward the houses.

When they reached the Soltura house, María brought Tormenta to a halt, turned and said to Gordo, "I am not as easy as the rest, Gordo."

Gordo shook his head and smiled. "Then I must work hard to achieve the difficult, María. May I begin my efforts tonight, at the feast?"

"Begin? How will you begin?"

"Be with me tonight. Be my woman at the feast. Dance with me, sit with me. That is how we will begin."

María's hat had slipped off her head and hung from her neck by a long strap. She replaced it on her head and secured it by tugging at the front and rear of the broad brim. "I don't think I shall be with anyone tonight, Gordo," she said. "I think I shall be free to enjoy the evening with whomever I choose."

"Suit yourself, María." Gordo's tone had changed. It was hard, matter-of-fact. His mouth had tightened into a thin line. "But remember one thing. If you tease me, I shall respond. And you do tease me, María."

Her reply was to slap the reins on Tormenta's neck and race for home.

CHAPTER THREE

Father Juan de Soltura's ride from Dolores had been uneventful, although a band of thirty Indians had given him a few moments of concern. They'd swept down from the hills on horseback and blocked his passage along a road that paralleled the now dried-up Cuitzed River. Juan had spoken to them in an Indian dialect they evidently understood because, without a word, they departed, leaving him free to continue his journey. Perhaps his black Jesuit robe had dissuaded them from robbing, and possibly killing him. If so, Juan had mused after continuing his ride along the Cuitzed, they had been very forgiving. The Indians of New Spain had little reason to forgive the Catholic clergy. The atrocities committed against them in the name of Christian conversion were, it seemed to the new priest, cause enough to warrant the slaughter of anyone wearing a clerical robe, be it Jesuit black or Franciscan brown.

As Juan had approached his home in Valladolid, he tried to shake off his somber mood and buoyed himself for the warm reception that would be forthcoming from his family and friends. It had been four years since he'd gone away to study for the priesthood, and he had remained away for that entire length of time. His father and mother had visited him twice at the university. Friends had also visited him. But he had not initiated the visits, nor had he ever considered finding time to return to the Valladolid hacienda. He'd wanted only to lose himself in his religion, bathe himself in its power, shroud himself with its mystery. Most of all, he wanted to escape the secular life in which he saw such cruelty and greed. Each day in the seminary found him praying for forgiveness for loathing his own father's aspirations to achieve the sort of power reserved for the Spanish-born gachupines. He asked also to be forgiven for the scorn and envy he felt toward his brother, Gordo, whose bravado and masculine strutting disgusted him.

But now, on the occasion of his return to his home, he felt differently. He'd come to know that were he to find a true happiness as a messenger of Christ it would mean becoming involved with his fellowman, the good and the evil, the greedy and the humble. As Father Hidalgo had told him just before Juan had departed Dolores, "You were right in offering the church for the tortured, my son. In all the world, the greatest sin is for good men to stand by and witness evil and not take action against it."

Juan de Soltura was now committed to action. It could be no other way.

As it turned out, the outpouring of greetings and warmth from Juan's family did away with any need for him to consciously lift his spirits. They were elevated naturally on a rising current of family love, and by six that evening the young priest was glowing in the festive air of the Soltura hacienda.

"Well, my son," Manuel Soltura, Juan's father, said after he and Juan had shared a glass of wine, "we must talk of the world before the party begins. Once the music plays, serious talk is impossible."

Juan laughed. "Perhaps it is best, father, to simply laugh and sing. To talk seriously of this world is not especially pleasant."

Manuel Soltura slapped his hand upon the table and shook his head. "No, no, my son, we shall have none of that dreary conversation on this day."

The elder Soltura sat back in his chair and focused upon his son's face. "You look good, Juan. Older, wiser, healthy."

"I feel good, father. When I left here I was not the sort of son a father boasts of." He held up his hand to silence his father's objection. "No, wait, father, let me finish. I left here a sour, moody, spoiled young boy, frail of body, soft of mind."

"And look at you now," said his father.

Juan chuckled. "Don't be too expansive in your words, father. I am not, nor could I ever be as strong as Gordo. I will never be the horseman he is, nor the help to you that he has been. But yes, I have changed. I am no longer *afraid*."

17

"Afraid of what?"

"Life. I walk with my God now, and together, we fear no one, nor anything."

Manuel Soltura was becoming uncomfortable with the tenor of the conversation. He sensed the distance between him and his son and was anxious to close it. He leaned on the table and said, "Gordo begins to cause me much trouble and grief."

"How so?"

"He is too spirited, too anxious to taste all of life in too short a time."

"He is young." Juan was twenty-one, Gordo was eighteen.

"Young and rambunctious."

"Which is good." Juan stood and went to the kitchen window. Outside, six musicians had arrived and were carrying their instruments into the *sala,* a spacious hall that had been constructed twenty years earlier to house the area's numerous festivals and dances. The Soltura sala served forty families in the valley, and it was in that same hall that Juan had been given his going-away party four years ago.

Juan shifted focus to his reflection in the windowpane. He recalled the evening of his departure party as vividly as though it were happening right now. That night, four years ago, while everyone from the valley sang and danced to celebrate his entrance into the priesthood, Juan had slipped away and sat by himself in the cellar of his house. There, by the light of a candle, he'd peered into a small mirror at a face that disgusted him. It was a weak face, pale from too many days spent indoors instead of in the glorious sun of New Spain. Those quiet days alone inside the cool house had been spent reading every book in the Soltura library. But as the music and laughter had carried across the field from the sala and into the cellar, Juan had cursed himself and his mirror-image. What good was knowledge if it didn't show? What woman would respond to his pale, delicate features? Knowledge? It was only an escape from life, he decided that night, an escape he would welcome in the safety of the church and his service to it.

"Juan," his father said, breaking his son's reverie at the window.

"Oh, yes, father. I was daydreaming."

"You were always good at that."

"I know. Do you know what I would like, father?"

"What?"

"More wine."

Manuel Soltura laughed and poured more of the valley's own wine into Juan's glass. He handed his son his glass, raised his own and said, "To you, my son, who make me proud."

Juan nodded. "That pleases me, father."

They drained their glasses and went to the living room where Juan's mother, Margarita, was putting the finishing touches on the dress she would wear that evening. Two female Indian servants who'd been polishing a massive mahogany table scurried from the room when the men entered.

Juan's mother looked up and said to Juan, "You should eat more. You're skin and bones."

Manuel shook his head and smiled at his son. Juan went to his mother and kissed her. "I have never been fatter," he said, "and if I listen to you, I'll be as . . ."

"As fat as I am?" his father said good-naturedly.

An old Indian servant, who'd been with the family for years, answered a knock on the door. He escorted the visitor, José Jardinero, María's father, to the living room.

"Welcome, José," Manuel said as he shook his next-door neighbor's hand. The physical differences between the two family heads were striking. José Jardinero was tall and lean. Dark blue eyes sparkled beneath salt and pepper eyebrows. He wore a workman's blue shirt and a pair of faded goatskin trousers. Iron-gray hair the consistency of steel wool twisted up from his scalp in no regular pattern.

José turned to Juan and extended a rough, calloused hand. Juan shook it and said how pleased he was to see José.

"It is good to have you home in Valladolid," said José. "We are all very proud of you, father."

"You embarrass me," Juan said. "Please, it is still Juan."

"I am pleased to hear that," José said. He grinned, looked at Manuel, and added, "We don't need additional pomposity here in the valley."

Manuel grunted. "You, a gachupin, speak of pomposity?"

Juan had to smile. Nothing had changed between his father and José Jardinero. They'd been arguing about politics and their respective social classes ever since José had arrived from Spain to take over his family's hacienda. By virtue of having been Spanish-born, José held a privileged position in the valley. As a gachupin, he was appointed *regidor,* or council-

19

man to the valley's *cabildo*. That local council was supposed to work in concert with other councils of Michoacán Province to establish the laws for the citizens. But it was no different from all the other provincial councils of New Spain. Bickering was the rule rather than the exception. As José often said, "New Spain will fall not at the hands of a foreign conqueror, but at the hands of its own government."

As the two men continued their political discussion, Juan was aware, however, of one change. It had to do with José's feelings about the new Spanish viceroy. New Spain was ruled by viceroys appointed by Ferdinand III, King of Spain. They came and went with regularity, depending upon Ferdinand's latest whim. The viceroy now in power was Iturrigaray who, it appeared, was the most liberal of all the viceroys. Because of his liberal stance on certain issues, Iturrigaray was not trusted by the gachupine ruling class, nor by the criollos who aspired to the gachupine rung on the social ladder.

What interested Juan was that José, a gachupin, spoke in positive terms about the liberal Iturrigaray. It was Juan's father, the criollo, who condemned the viceroy for expressing certain liberal views, as modest as they were.

The debate between José and Manuel was heating up. Margarita Soltura put down the dress she was sewing and said gaily, "Enough of this on Juan's day of return. What does it matter what a viceroy thinks or what a king does? All that matters is that my son, who has blessed me by becoming a priest, is safe and is home with us." She pulled her large body up from the chair and gave Juan a smothering hug.

"Margarita is right," said José as he walked to the door. "Tonight, we salute you, Juan. We dance and sing in your honor."

"I look forward to it," Juan said.

Manuel walked José to the front door. "By the way, José, have you received any further word of the plans to open the north territory to the Yankees?"

José shook his head. "Only what the last correspondence indicated. The murder of that Anglo, Nolan, did not help. He was the first into the territory and was killed. The Yankee president, Jefferson, still pushes for compensation in the Nolan matter."

"No other news?"

"No, Manuel. Now that France has sold all of the Louisiana to the Yankees, things might change suddenly. I was told, although it is not official, that President Jefferson plans to send explorers into the new territories." José laughed. "He calls them explorers. Spies would be more accurate."

José turned serious. He looked at his neighbor and friend, Manuel, and asked, "Are you still serious about applying for a position as *empresario* in the north territory?"

"Yes," Manuel replied. "I believe that to be a land agent in the undeveloped territory will mean great wealth one day. More than that, it means to me that . . ."

"That a fat criollo has achieved status." José said it warmly. "You know something, Manuel? If I could do it I would gladly give to you my gachupine credentials. It would make you so happy."

"And then what would you have, my friend?"

"Peace of mind. That is all I look for now. Peace. Well, Manuel, as usual it was pleasant to visit in your home. Oh, I almost forgot. María is ready to help Margarita with whatever she needs. Tell her that, will you?"

"Yes, of course. Your daughter is a fine girl."

"Yes. She is that. And, I fear at times, *too* beautiful. To have such a beautiful daughter does not contribute to my quest for peace of mind. Perhaps if María were not so pretty, I would worry less about her."

Manuel nodded his understanding.

"I will see you at the sala, my friend."

"At the sala. Enjoy your siesta."

"I will."

They shook hands, and José departed through the huge iron-studded doors.

The party for Juan began at ten. Everyone was rested from their siestas and was in high spirits.

Large kegs of local wine were manned by Indian men who kept glasses filled for the more than two hundred guests. Indian women, who'd worked all day in the kitchens, served a vast variety of food on silver plates. Whole roast stuffed pigeons were carved at each table. An *olla,* a rich, hearty and heavily spiced mutton stew with red beans and tender, small peas was ladled onto plates from large silver urns. The supply of tamales and enchiladas seemed endless.

The sala was decorated with richly colored rugs that had been woven by local Indians, and with broad Chinese silk wall hangings that had been brought into New Spain from the Philippines.

The orchestra consisted of three violinists, two guitarists and a flutist. The spirited triple-time rhythms of the fandango, with its uniquely Moorish harmonies, had everyone up on their feet.

Because the party was in his honor, Juan found himself occupied with a procession of handshaking neighbors who welcomed him home and wished him success and happiness in the priesthood. His father stood next to him and served as an intermediary in the informal reception line that stretched from the door of the sala to its farthest corner.

Juan was pleased to see so many familiar faces from his youth. But he soon became distracted and his eyes wandered over the hall until they fixed upon María Jardinero. She was twelve when he'd left for school. Even then, he recalled, she was a beautiful child. Now, she was a beautiful young woman, and he wanted very much to leave his corner and go to her.

He continued to watch her from across the room, but his attention was constantly brought back to the business of greeting still another guest and engaging in conversation about how school had been, what plans had been made for him by the church's hierarchy, how long he would remain in Valladolid and whether he had any privileged information that would put the spate of political rumors into perspective.

Juan tried his best to respond to each inquiry with a fresh and enthusiastic answer but it became increasingly difficult. He looked across the sala and saw his brother, Gordo, who was dressed in form-fitting black velvet pants and jacket. A brilliant yellow and red serape hung stylishly from his broad shoulders. He was the true *caballero,* dashing and self-assured.

As Juan watched, Gordo went to María, took her hand and led her to the dance floor. They made a very handsome couple, Juan had to admit to himself. María wore a flowing red silk skirt. Her blouse was white and frilly, and was cut low, revealing the upper softness of breasts that were already full and mature, under a tight black cotton jacket embroidered with vivid red designs. Her hair was pulled up. A tall, hand-carved tortoiseshell comb rose from her thick auburn tresses and supported a flowing black lace mantilla that swept behind her as she and Gordo spiritedly danced the fandango.

When Juan was finally able to break away from the greet-ers, he went to the wine table and had his glass refilled. He sipped from it and turned to face the dance floor. Directly behind him, holding her empty glass, was María.

"*Buenas noches,* María."

"*Buenas noches,* Juan. Or should I call you 'father'?"

"Juan. I insist. As your father says, we have enough pomposity in the valley."

María smiled, and the brilliance of it caused Juan's heart to trip. Her teeth were two rows of perfect pearls, their whiteness made all the more so against the radiant bronze of her skin.

"It's a wonderful party," Juan said. He couldn't think of anything else to say.

"Yes, it is. I'm sorry I didn't greet you formally with the others but I knew we could find time to talk like this. I prefer it to all the . . ."

"Formality?"

"Pomposity."

They laughed.

As they continued to talk, María became aware of Juan's furtive glances at the rise and fall of her bosom. While such masculine interest in her was pleasing, it was accompanied by a vague twinge of guilt for provoking a man of the cloth.

María was also aware of how her perception of Juan Soltura had changed over the past five years. She remembered him as a pale, frail boy living on the next hacienda, who preferred to remain by himself and read books. That image of him was gone now. He'd become an extremely handsome young man. His blue eyes sparkled, and yet spoke eloquently of a worldly sadness that she found appealing. His face was fuller than she'd remembered, although it was still lean. A deep tan had replaced the pasty skin of youth, and lines in his forehead and around his mouth gave his face definition and character. Juan's hair was lighter in color than that of anyone else in his family. It was also cut shorter, which tended to give him a look of humility, an image enhanced by the simple black robe he wore. *Christlike.* A manly, sensuous, attractive Christ.

"Do you dance?"

Her question took him by surprise.

"Would you dance with me, father?"

"Oh, María, I'm afraid dancing was not one of my stronger subjects at school."

"I could be your teacher."

Juan raised his eyebrows and grinned. "I don't really think that . . ."

"Please."

He looked into her eyes and experienced an alien sensation. Over the past four years there had been general sexual yearnings that were dealt with by the rules of his chosen profession, vague lustful urges brought on by an attractive female.

But this was different. And much better.

"I'll try," he said.

María tentatively took his hand and led him to the floor, where dozens of couples had just finished dancing. The orchestra had intended to take a short intermission, but when its leader saw that the guest of honor, and a young priest to boot, was about to dance, he turned to the other musicians and called for another song to be played. It, too, was a fandango, but the tempo was slower than previous songs had been. The orchestra leader felt that slower tempos were more respectful to the clergy.

Much to Juan's embarrassment, and to María's inner amusement, everyone else formed a circle around them. The guests began clapping to the fandango's rhythm. For an instant, Juan considered stopping. But it was as though an unseen, irrefutable force had taken over his body and mind. He was slightly light-headed. The wine seemed to replace his blood and to pulsate throughout his body, pumped by a heart that was, by now, pounding.

Across from him was the most beautiful woman he'd ever seen.

The intensity of his feelings increased. The clapping and the music blended into one driving force. He saw his mother and father in the crowd, their faces lighted up with smiles as they watched their son let down his defenses and join in the simple secular act of dancing, of having fun.

He also saw that María's eyes never left him. She moved to the music like a wild horse, strong, proud, in love with the moment she was living.

And so did Juan. The faces around him were no longer identifiable, nor important. He became aware of his own body beneath the robe, a body that could proudly interpret the pulse and passion of the music. It was as though four years of pent-up energy had suddenly been released.

He had never been happier.

His basic lack of knowledge of the fandango caught up

with him, however, and in a moment of awkwardness he tripped and almost knocked María over. They both stopped dancing and she wrapped her arms about him. She was breathing hard and laughing.

The crowd laughed, too, and applauded.

The feel of María against him caused a rush of passion that startled him. He realized that the manifestation of that passion was evident beneath his robe. He pulled away from her and looked at his father, who came to him and wrapped his arms around him.

"Bravo, Father Juan," someone yelled. It became a chorus.

"Bravo, bravo."

Juan looked over at María. She smiled and nodded. "Welcome home," she said. Then, Gordo broke through the crowd. He stood next to María and motioned for the band to begin playing again. The leader waved his arms and another song echoed throughout the sala.

Juan's father led him to the wine tables. Juan's last glance at the dance floor saw María and Gordo dancing. Gordo was looking intently into her eyes, but María's eyes were upon Juan.

"You dance well for a priest, my son," Manuel Soltura said as they toasted each other.

"Not well enough, father, but thank you."

"Well, what do you think of that little girl who lived next door?"

"Pardon?"

"María. Isn't she a beauty?"

"Oh, yes," Juan said.

Manuel Soltura had had a lot to drink. Had he not, he probably wouldn't have said what he did. He looked at his son, winked and said, "See what you miss, son, by becoming a priest?"

Juan took a moment to respond to his father's comment. In that silence, Manuel realized the inappropriateness of his remark. He added quickly, "But your life will bring much greater glory than simple worldly pleasures."

Juan drew a deep breath and looked into his father's heavy eyes. "All man's glory is the same, father. To have dignity is to have all the glory of the kingdom."

His father did not quite understand but he nodded, slapped his son on the arm and went in search of Margarita. Juan placed his glass upon the table and left the sala. He walked across the broad field that separated the sala from the house. He climbed onto the porch of the house and looked out over the vast land that comprised his father's hacienda, and that of other citizens of New Spain. The sky was inky black. Stars were strung across it like pearls against a Negro's neck.

He looked back at the sala and a wave of fatigue washed over him. He'd returned to the house to escape from the vibrancy of life within the sala, just as he'd done five years earlier. He considered going to the cool cellar and, perhaps, even finding the same mirror and candle.

Instead, he leaned on a stone pillar at a corner of the porch and listened intently to the music and laughter coming from the sala. It was pleasant to the ear, and he found his right foot tapping to the rhythms of the orchestra.

The pleasantness was replaced, but only momentarily, by the vision of the heads of the Dolores Indians who'd been executed. Those heads, so grotesquely displayed on the pike-staffs, were replaced by another vision—the face of María Jardinero. It was her face he saw as he retraced his steps across the field, toward the sala. He realized as he walked that to be a servant of God was to represent Him in the midst of life, *all of life,* and not only in the dark, cool sanctity of His churches.

With that thought firmly entrenched within him, he climbed the stairs to the sala's front door, opened it and rejoined the guests at his party.

CHAPTER FOUR

By the time the members of the Soltura household sat down for breakfast, two hours' work had been accomplished. The wine and late hour of the party the night before had slowed everyone down a bit, but a buoyancy of spirit made up for the physical fatigue and nagging headaches.

Gordo attacked a mound of corncakes with enthusiasm. Juan sat across from him and enjoyed the sweet succulence of melon with honey. Señora Soltura scolded one of the Indian kitchen help for being sloppy. Manuel Soltura sipped his coffee and perused a prospectus that had been given him regarding the opening of the northern territory to state-appointed land agents.

"Foolishness," Margarita said after she'd dismissed the servant from the kitchen.

"What is?" asked Manuel.

"What you're reading there. Why can't you be content with what you have here? To become an empresario in the godforsaken land to the north is foolishness."

"Quiet, woman!"

"Perhaps she is right," Juan offered.

"No, papa is right," Gordo said. "The future is in the undeveloped region."

Juan smiled and took another bite of melon. "You love the vision of a wilderness to be tamed, Gordo." He'd meant it as a compliment. His brother took it as an insult and grumbled into his plate.

"It makes no difference what any of you think," Manuel said. "If I decide to expand my success, you will come with me."

Margarita knew it was true and returned to arranging flowers in a copper vase.

The family was about to leave the table when someone knocked at the door. Juan went to it and was greeted by a small boy from the village.

"Father Soltura?" the boy asked.

"Yes."

"For you." He handed Juan an envelope.

"Who sends this to me?" Juan asked.

"Father Gomez, from the church."

"*Gracias.*"

The boy bowed and ran off.

Juan returned to the kitchen table and opened the envelope. He read the note silently, then aloud to his family.

> *Dear Father Soltura—I have received a communication from the Bishop of Michoacán. You are to remain in Valladolid and assist me in this parish. Would you be so kind as to visit with me this evening so that we might talk of the work that is to be done here.*
>
> *I welcome you to the brotherhood of Christ, and trust you will find your assignment here to be fruitful and rewarding. Yours in Christ, Father José Gomez.*

Juan's mother let out a shriek of joy and hugged him from behind his chair. "My prayers are answered," she said. "Both my sons will be with me now."

Juan managed to smile, although his reaction to the note did not match his mother's response. He'd hoped to be assigned away from home, preferably in some remote village where he could work with the impoverished. There were, at that time in New Spain, over 1,700 parishes, overseen by eight bishops and one archbishop. Certainly, Juan mused, out of 1,700 possibilities for assignment he could have received one other than Valladolid.

As Juan wondered what influence he might have with the bishop, and what effect a successful request for reassignment might have upon his mother, Gordo broke into his thoughts by announcing that he had requested an evening with María Jardinero.

"Tonight?" asked his mother.

"Yes. I will visit her at her home."

Manuel Soltura laughed and slapped his son on the back.

"I knew you would pursue her eventually, Gordo. Enough of the village . . ." he hesitated and looked at Juan before adding, ". . , village *ladies*."

Gordo laughed heartily and rose. "Well, Juan," he said, "what will you do today? There is much to be done in the fields, if that sort of work is permissible for a priest."

Juan looked up at his brother, shrugged and placed the note from Father Gomez in his robe. "Of course it is permissible, brother. In fact, our Lord blesses those of us who use body *and* mind."

Gordo missed the point of Juan's comment. "Good," he said. "Come with me then. Half of our Indian labor will begin work today on the field to the west. I can use all the help I can get to keep the lazy louts moving."

Juan winced at what his brother said but curbed his inclination to challenge him. Instead, he went to his room and changed from his clerical robe into faded brown work pants, a workshirt that belonged to Gordo and which was too big for him, and a pair of tan riding boots.

Gordo was waiting outside the house. He looked very much the typical Mexican vaquero. His hat was black and wide and covered with a layer of range dust. His chaps were made of goatskin and had been tanned with the hair on them to better turn away cactus plants through which he might ride. Juan noticed the bulk of his brother's arms as they strained against the tight fabric of his blue shirt. His thighs, too, threatened to burst the material of his pants.

"Well, brother," Gordo said, "you look ready for a hard day."

"I look forward to it."

"Then let us begin."

One of the Indian stablehands had brought two horses to the front of the house. Juan and Gordo mounted them and trotted to the west, past a barn and toolhouse, past an Indian labor group at work in a field of maize.

"Shall we race?" Gordo asked.

"Why not?" Juan replied.

Juan's horse was smaller and leaner than Gordo's, naturally faster. But it had been years since Juan had urged an animal to a gallop. At first, fear gripped his chest. But it was fleeting. Within seconds he felt one with the horse. The warm air whipped his face and billowed his shirt. They raced neck and neck until Juan inched ahead, then led by two lengths. He looked over his shoulder and saw Gordo bring his horse to a stop. Juan did, too. "Are you all right?" he yelled.

"There is something wrong with my horse," Gordo answered, bringing a short whip down viciously on his animal's neck.

"Perhaps he's lame," Juan said. "No sense in beating him for being lame."

Gordo's answer was to dig his spurs into the horse's flesh and burst past his brother. Juan shook his head as he watched his brother gallop into the distance until he reached the west field. Juan trotted after him. By the time Juan reached him, Gordo had dismounted and was yelling at a dozen Indians, three of whom were women. Two children stood next to their mothers, large, round brown eyes filled with terror as they looked up at Gordo.

"What have you done all morning?" Gordo screamed at a man who appeared to be the leader of the group. The Indian answered in his native language. Gordo lashed out at him with his whip and screamed obscenities. "When you speak to me, you heathen devil, you speak in my language."

"Sí, Sí," the Indian said as he pressed his hand against where the whip had stung his chest.

"Come on, then, let's get to work. No standing around. We give you homes and food and you show your gratitude by shirking your work." He raised the whip menacingly. The Indians moved away to where they'd been breaking ground with primitive hoes and rakes. One of the Indian mothers handed her seven-year-old daughter a hoe, and the child began working earnestly alongside her.

Juan was sickened by his brother's display of anger. His comment about the Indians having been provided housing and food was absurd, he thought. They lived in the most squalid of conditions. The houses provided by Juan's father were nothing more than huts made of reeds and dried mud. Each family was allowed a tiny patch of land on which to grow its own food. Actually, Manuel Soltura was more generous than most holders of large tracts of land. He paid his Indian and mestizo help a small monthly wage. The few sambos and mulattoes he owned did not receive any money, which placed them even lower on the labor scale.

Gordo turned to his brother and told him to take six of the laborers to the far corner where a ditch was to be dug linking the remote field with the main irrigation system. Juan found it difficult to issue even a gentle order to the workers, but he did it to avoid embarrassment in front of his brother. After instructing them in what was to be done, he stripped off his shirt, picked up a shovel and began digging alongside them. The intense sun on his back sent shivers through him. Perspiration formed on his face and neck and dripped onto his shovel. The flow of blood to his muscles cleared his brain of all thought except the simple act of forcing the tool into the soil, breaking it free and tossing it to another spot where it would eventually find its level and disappear. *Ashes to ashes. Dust to dust.* Juan straightened up and looked into the sun. Its brilliance dazzled his senses, made him faint. He looked at the Indians who continued to dig, their backs arched over like prehistoric monsters, silent, their only concession to the backbreaking labor the regular exhalation of breath.

Gordo stood across the field, the whip in his hand. His expression was quizzical as he watched his brother labor with the Indians. "Fool," he muttered to himself.

Juan looked at Gordo and nodded. Gordo turned his attention to the laborers under his direction. The older worker had straightened up from his task and was wiping his brow with a red handkerchief. He stretched to relieve the stiffness in his back.

"Come on, now, back to work," Gordo told him.

"Puede traerme agua potable, por favor? Está demasiado caliente."

"You'll have water later," Gordo said. "And if it's not too hot for me, it's not too hot for you. Get back to work."

"Sí, señor."

The Indian resumed the work. Juan had heard the exchange between Gordo and the Indian but decided not to interfere. He went back to his own labors.

An hour later, Gordo called for a break. A small barrel of water had been hauled to the work site and the Indians cupped their hands and drank from it. Juan, too, used his cupped hands as a vessel. Gordo used a wooden ladle that hung from the barrel.

Five minutes later, Gordo called for work to resume. The older worker had sat down after his drink, and rested against a tree. He attempted to get up but his legs wouldn't support him.

"Back to work," Gordo told him.

The old man extended his hand to the youngest Soltura brother. *"Por favor, gracias, Señor Gordo, pero yo enfermo."*

"Like hell you're sick," Gordo yelled. "You're lazy, that's what you are. Goddamn lazy Indian bastards." He kicked the Indian in the leg with his boot. "Get up, damn you." When the old man didn't respond, Gordo brought the whip squarely across his cheek. A thin trickle of blood ran from it. The man said nothing, but his eyes spoke eloquently of his hatred for his master.

Juan looked around at the others. They seemed ready to strike at Gordo, but he knew they wouldn't. Fear would keep their hatred bottled up inside them.

"Gordo," Juan said, "the old man is sick. Let him go home."

Gordo shook his head. "He works like the rest. This one has done this before. Of course, you wouldn't know that, Juan. You've been away learning to save their black souls. Don't interfere." He struck the old man again with his whip.

"Stop it," Juan said. He reached out and caught Gordo's wrist as he was about to strike the Indian again.

Gordo was momentarily shocked by his brother's bold action. He turned and gaped at him. What he saw was a face hardened by determination. It was a look he'd not seen on his brother before, and it was disconcerting. He realized that the eyes of every Indian in the field were upon him. He shook loose of Juan's grip and returned his attention to the older Indian who, by this time, had managed to pull himself to his feet.

Gordo shook with rage. His right hand instinctively tightened on the whip's stock and his arm came back to deliver another blow.

"Don't," Juan said. His voice was like the hardest of minerals. Its tone left no doubt that he was ready to act should Gordo not heed his warning.

Gordo's body relaxed. His shoulders sagged, the whip hung lifelessly at his side. He forced a grin as he looked at the workers in the field. "All right," he said, raising his hands, "back to work." He looked at the old man and said, "Go to your home. You're finished for the day."

"Gracias, señor," the old man said to Juan. Juan simply nodded.

When everyone was back at work, Gordo moved close to his brother and snarled, "You go home, too, my brother, and do not ever again come into the fields. You do not understand the real world here. You hide in your sacred church where it is cool and where your hands never become soiled. That is your decision, your life. You have chosen it. But do not ever again interfere with my life. If you do, I will not be responsible for what happens.''

Juan watched his brother throw the ladle into the water barrel and walk to where his horse was tied to a tree. He climbed up into the saddle and sat ramrod straight, his eyes upon the Indians in the field. Juan slowly walked to where he'd been digging, picked up his shirt, put it on and went to his horse. He mounted and turned the animal in the direction of the house. Before he left, he said to Gordo, ''I will leave you alone with your fields and your slaves, Gordo. But there will come a day when these people will no longer suffer the indignity of your words and your whip. That day approaches rapidly, my young brother, and when it comes, God help you.''

CHAPTER FIVE

That Night

The parish of Valladolid was centered around a small, yellow church of mortar and stone. Some thought it looked more like a fortress than a house of worship. Actually, it was two structures joined together. On one side was the church itself. A narrow, simple doorway was its entrance. A steeple and belfry rose above it. Atop the steeple was a tall, slender cross made of gold.

The adjoining structure was not quite as tall as the church portion. It was squared off on top. Arched openings in its walls provided gunports that could be manned on the roof. It had, in fact, been designed with a dual use in mind. Its architect had patterned it after the mission of San José, in San Antonio, in the Texas Province of New Spain. Like most churches in developing areas of the nation, it served not only as a place of prayer but as a sanctuary of safety against frequent Indian raids.

In Valladolid, Indian raids had become so infrequent that no one saw the need for a church to be anything but a church. That didn't deter its founder, however, and the fortress was built into the original plan. The roof was used as a gathering place for members of a nearby convent, one of 250 in New Spain. There the nuns could enjoy the sun, talk, laugh and escape the rigors of convent life. The gunports served only as convenient peepholes through which the activity of the village of Valladolid could be observed by those on the roof.

Juan Soltura rode into town on the same horse he'd ridden that morning. He'd bathed, shaved and put on a robe that had been freshly laundered by one of his mother's household help.

34

He arrived just as night became final and shrouded the village in a cool, peaceful darkness.

He paused before entering the church and looked out over the town plaza. *They're all the same,* he thought. Every town and village in New Spain revolved around a plaza. And, he reminded himself, around a church.

The cafes were ablaze with candlelight and life. Horses were hitched to posts in front of the cafes and their owners came and went, those going in walking steadily, those coming out of the establishments not so steadily. Juan would have enjoyed a bottle of good wine at that moment. The company and affection of women might be denied those of his persuasion, but not wine. Some of the best drinkers he knew were priests.

He debated whether to enter through the narrow door that led into the church, or through a larger set of doors that led into the secular portion of the building. He chose the narrow door, decided not to knock and pushed it open.

Inside a dozen people prayed in the pews. A heavy scent of incense stung his nostrils. The church was dark except for offering candles that flickered upon the altar. An old lady left a pew and paused when she saw Juan standing by the door. She moved to him, went almost to her knees and kissed his hand.

"Peace be with you," Juan said.

"Gracias, padre. Gracias. And with you, too."

Once Juan's eyes had become accustomed to the gloom he saw the shadow of a man in the far left corner, where the confessional booths were located. Juan began to walk toward him but was stopped by a voice from behind a curtain.

"Father Soltura?" the voice asked.

"Sí."

The curtain parted and a short, rotund priest stepped from behind it. "Greetings, father," the other priest said. "I am José Gomez, the new priest in Valladolid. I see my note was delivered."

"Yes. I was surprised at my assignment to Valladolid."

"Why?"

"I suppose it is more a case of wanting something else rather than surprise. I had thought that . . ."

Father Gomez looked at the scattering of people praying in the pews. He turned to Juan and said, "Come with me."

Juan followed him through the curtains and into the adjoining building. They walked through a dimly lighted room with stone walls until they came to a narrow stairway against a wall. Juan followed Father Gomez up the stairs and to a hallway that was lighted by a single candelabra. Halfway down the hall they entered a room with a window that overlooked the Valladolid plaza. A cot was under the window. A small wooden desk occupied a corner. Two hooks on the wall next to the desk held a few items of clothing. A kerosene lamp cast an orange glow over the room.

"Here," said Father Gomez as he pulled a chair from beneath the desk. "Sit, father."

Instead of sitting, Juan went to the window and looked down at the plaza. Activity had picked up since he'd entered the church. A drunken woman staggered out of one of the cafes, her arm around an equally drunken man. They crossed the plaza and entered the only hotel in the town.

Juan turned from the window. He said, "I came to this parish as a child. At that time Father Montoya was parish priest. He inspired me to the priesthood."

"I did not know him, although I have heard many wonderful things about him," Gomez said. "You do know, do you not, that he was excommunicated for heretical teaching?"

"Yes. I heard that the charges were never proved but that the punishment was inflicted nonetheless."

"That is what I hear, too."

Juan drew a deep sigh and sat on the edge of the cot. Father Gomez took the chair. After a few moments of silence, Juan asked, "My assignment here, father. It is definite?"

"Yes."

"Then I accept it in the name of God. I will serve where He sends me."

A tiny smile crossed Gomez's cherubic face. "I have a confession to make, Father Soltura."

Juan thought at first that he meant confession in the religious sense. He quickly realized that that was not the case. Father Gomez said, "You are here because someone has requested that you be here."

"Someone? Who?"

"Someone who has faith in your motives. Someone who has faith in *you.*"

Juan was confused. Was Gomez speaking of the bishop of Michoacán who'd assigned him to Valladolid? He didn't have to ask.

"You are here at the request of Father Miguel Hidalgo, of Dolores."

Juan sat forward on the cot. "Father Hidalgo? What does he have to do with this?"

Father Gomez held out his hands in a calming gesture. "Perhaps it would be best if he told you himself. He was in the church when you arrived."

"Near the confessional. I saw someone."

"Yes, that was Father Hidalgo." Gomez cocked an ear to the door. "Before I ask him to come in and explain to you, I must ask whether your commitment to social reform remains as firm as it was in the university."

Juan felt ill at ease for the first time. He'd been reprimanded more than once by the faculty and administrators of the university for reading certain literature that was considered inflammatory to the state. The United States Declaration of Independence and Constitution had been translated into Spanish and smuggled into New Spain. So had literature describing the process of democratization of the states of Virginia and Massachusetts. Once, Juan had been threatened with dismissal from the university for openly reading a translation of the French philosopher, Diderot.

Was this, he wondered, a trap? Was Father Gomez attempting to ferret out revolutionary ideology from him on behalf of the church bureaucracy?

Gomez sensed Juan's concern. He smiled and said, "You have nothing to fear here, Father Soltura. You are among friends."

With that, he went to the door and opened it. He motioned to someone in the hallway. Moments later Father Miguel Hidalgo stepped through the door.

Juan got up from the cot and shook the older priest's hand.

"It is good to see you again so soon," Hidalgo said.

"Yes," Juan said. "It has been only three days since the slaughter in Dolores."

"That day is past, father. It is now time to look to the future." Hidalgo turned to Gomez. "Wine?"

"Of course."

When the wine had been poured and the three men were seated, Hidalgo on the chair, Juan and Gomez on the cot, Juan asked simply and directly, "Why am I here?"

Hidalgo cocked his head and looked at the young priest. His search for just the right words was almost visible in the

room's dimness. Finally, he said, "The time has come for th
revolution."

Juan was speechless.

Hidalgo filled the gap. "For years now I have worked wit
those who suffer under Spanish oppression here in New Spain
As a child, I watched such oppression imposed by my ow
father on our hacienda. Since those early days I have ha
bored a precious dream that one day all men would be free i
New Spain. I have waited for it patiently as I've nursed th
wounds inflicted on the oppressed. But it has not happened
Today, I continue to nurse wounds and bury the dead, instea
of eradicating the source of the wounds and the killing. I ar
fifty years old. If I do not act now, my time will be past.
cannot wait any longer. The time is now."

"For revolution?" Juan asked.

"Exactly."

Juan let out a long, slow breath. He got up and stood b
the window. "Why me?" he asked, not looking at the othe
men.

"Your reputation precedes you, Father Soltura," said Gomez

"That's true," Hidalgo said. "Did it ever occur to yo
why you were told to visit me in Dolores prior to returning t
your home?"

"Yes, of course. I knew why. Father Ojinaga at the uni
versity told me that because of your brother's illness, yo
might need my help for a day or two. As it turned out, m
help was not needed."

Hidalgo stood. His tone was flat, matter-of-fact. "Yo
were told to visit me so that I could evaluate you for myself.'

"Evaluate?"

"Yes. Father Ojinaga at the university is one of us. Whe
the revolution begins, he will be at our side."

Juan nodded. He understood. "I see," he said. "Becaus
of my activities at the university, I have been recruited b
you."

"You sound angry," Gomez said.

"No, not angry. But I wonder about the need for all thi
secrecy. Couldn't you have simply asked whether I wished t
join the cause?"

"And risk *our* exposure?" Gomez asked. "Certainly, yo
must know what happens to priests who plot revolutions."

"I suppose my disappointment has to do with being so sur
of my own motivations." Juan stood and paced the smal

38

room. "It has occurred to me—and I pray for forgiveness each day for the thought—it has occurred to me that my calling to be a servant of God is rendered meaningless unless it is coupled with some concrete action to free the people of New Spain. Each day I see their slavery and suffering and I cry for them."

Father Hidalgo muttered, "Yes."

Juan looked at the older priest and saw something he hadn't noticed in him in Dolores. There, perhaps because of Hidalgo's brother's impending death, perhaps because Juan wasn't looking for it, Hidalgo seemed a weary, resigned priest. Nothing special in his face, no remarkable fire in his words. Just an older man with a fringe of white hair and a ruddy complexion who'd grown fatigued and resigned.

He was different now. Juan observed a bold intensity in his blue eyes that would not be extinguished. And as the young priest looked into those eyes, he was overwhelmed with the realization that he was sitting with someone destined to change the face of his land and people.

Nothing was said for a moment or two. Juan then asked, "How many are with us?"

"Few," Hidalgo answered. "Perhaps ten. But more will join. I do not look for too many leaders. That could weaken our cause. No, I look for just enough dedicated men like those of us in this room. Our army will swell as the oppressed raise their hearts and minds as one."

"With our Lord as our commander-in-chief," Gomez said.

"What do you want me to do?" Juan asked.

Hidalgo stood and placed his hands upon Juan's shoulders. "Work here with Father Gomez, my son. I will return to Dolores where I will begin building an army. I am establishing a porcelain factory there where the Indians and mestizos can work. It is from that work force that our first soldiers will be recruited. You, Father Soltura, will do much of the normal parish work in Valladolid while Father Gomez travels on my behalf. He, too, will be recruiting those who will eventually fight side by side with us."

Juan was disappointed at what seemed an insignificant role in the plan. "Is there nothing else I can do?" he asked.

"At this moment, no. It was not easy arranging for you to be assigned here. The bishop balked. He said that Valladolid was too small for two priests."

"What changed his mind?" Juan asked.

Gomez smiled. "We have a friend."

"Who?"

"Better that you do not know this, at least as yet."

Father Hidalgo walked to the door, turned and said to Juan, "Your time will come to take a more direct role in this, father. Until then, be patient. Take comfort in the fact that everything you do each day will contribute to our cause."

"I will, father," Juan said. "I have one other question, however."

"Yes?"

"When will the revolution take place?"

"In the future," replied Hidalgo. "There is much to be done in preparation for it. To launch it too soon would be to insure its defeat. I must be certain that when we do rise up we will be able to maintain our thrust for whatever time it takes to achieve total victory."

Hidalgo left the room.

"More wine, father?" Gomez asked.

"Yes, please."

CHAPTER SIX

March 1804
New York City

"Gentlemen, Mr. Burr will see you now," a young man announced to Robert Barrigan and to Barrigan's twenty-year-old son, John.

"It's about time," the elder Barrigan murmured as he stood and motioned for John to do the same. They'd been waiting to see Burr for almost an hour, and if there was anything that riled Bob Barrigan it was being kept waiting.

John Barrigan stood and stretched. He was as tall as his father, and as lean. It had been said that they could pass for brothers if his father's hair hadn't turned steely gray. Aside from his hair, age hadn't diminished Robert Barrigan's physical strength, his youthful gait or his love of adventure. He often said, "The minute a man stops seekin', he stops livin'."

Aside from being annoyed at the wait, neither Barrigan liked the young aide who'd originally greeted them when they'd arrived at Aaron Burr's New York campaign headquarters, and who now had been sent to fetch them. He was slight and pasty-faced. Soft red curls fell over his forehead. "Looks like a girl," John had said to his father as they waited. Now, as they followed the aide along a hallway, father and son looked at each other and smiled. The aide's fleshy buttocks moved beneath his velvet breeches like a female's rear end.

The aide opened a door at the end of the corridor and stepped aside to allow the Barrigans to enter a spacious study. Sunlight streamed in through wide windows covered with delicate white lace curtains. The walls were painted a pastel yellow that was rendered even more cheerful by the sunshine.

Two large hooked rugs of yellow and green covered much of the highly polished oak floor. A massive oak desk inlaid with French leather dominated the room and made the small man standing behind it seem even smaller.

"Gentlemen, welcome to New York," the man behind the desk said.

Both Barrigans scrutinized the gentleman they'd waited an hour to see, Aaron Burr, who had recently decided not to seek another term as vice-president of the United States in order that he might run for the governorship of New York State. The waspish, slender Burr arched his eyebrows. A smile smacking of contempt crossed his wide, thin mouth.

"I'm Robert Barrigan. This here is my son, John."

Burr extended his hand across the desk. Father and son shook it.

"Well, gentlemen, please sit down. Since I'm no longer the vice-president there's no need for formality."

The Barrigans took chairs directly in front of the desk. They were spindly chairs upholstered in pale green velvet, and Robert Barrigan thought, for a moment, that his chair might give way beneath him.

Burr slid his eyeglasses up to the top of his balding head and quickly perused a solitary piece of paper on the desk. He sighed and rubbed his eyes as he sat in a wingback chair behind the desk. "Well, gentlemen, you were told, I assume, why I wished to see you."

"Just that there was some sort of work that John here and me could do for you. At least that's what they said up in Massachusetts."

"You're referring to Harold Sims?" Burr asked.

"That's right," said John. "Mr. Harold Sims. He said he was authorized to speak for you."

"That's true. Did Mr. Sims indicate to you the sort of work I had in mind?"

"Nope," said Robert. "He just said that John and me would like it fine. He said it was the sort of work we'd be good at and happy with. And, he said we'd be doin' a real service to our government." Robert Barrigan didn't add the fact that neither he nor his son had much faith or love for the present government of the United States. President Jefferson had begun to act more like a Federalist than a political philosopher. The elder Barrigan, like many citizens, had thought that Jefferson's strict constitutionalist views would lead the nation on a path of appropriate isolationism. Instead, the third president of the United States had entered into agreements with France to purchase an empire. It was gravel in Bob Barrigan's craw, and he was quick to express his views.

Obviously, Aaron Burr was aware of Barrigan's disappointment with Thomas Jefferson. "Mr. Barrigan," said Burr, "I understand that you are not especially pleased with the direction our president is taking."

"That's right," Barrigan said. He felt a twinge of discomfort at saying it to the man who'd served, until recently, as the nation's second-ranking leader. He needn't have been concerned. Burr's dislike for Jefferson, politically and personally, was common knowledge.

In the election of 1800, Jefferson and Burr had each received seventy-three electoral votes. The decision was rightfully tossed to the House of Representatives where, after an all-night session, Jefferson was elected president, Burr vice-president. It was an open secret that Burr's enemy, Alexander Hamilton, had worked hard to sway the members of the House to Jefferson, and was currently working just as diligently to keep the New York governorship from Burr.

Burr smiled. He found Robert Barrigan amusing. Burr always smiled when confronted with an "honest man." It wasn't a matter of disliking honesty. It had more to do with responding to a style that was alien to him. He shifted his gaze to the younger Barrigan. "Like father, like son," he thought. Frontiersmen. Physical. Born of hearty stock and uncomfortable in drawing rooms and the conservative clothing they'd obviously donned for the occasion. Both men wore frilly white silk shirts and homemade versions of English dress coats that were popular among the middle class. Their breeches were long, the bottoms of them disappearing into boots that came up to their knees. The overall picture, thought Burr, was of two ruffians forced to attend a state dinner. Amusing fellows. But not to be trifled with. The steel in their eyes warned of that.

Burr was about to discuss the reason for the visit when his redheaded aide knocked, entered and whispered something to the gubernatorial candidate.

"Excuse me," Burr said, rising quickly and leaving the room.

While he was gone, Robert Barrigan turned to his son and said, "Arrogant little fella, ain't he?"

John nodded.

"I wouldn't be liking him any better as president than Jefferson."

"I don't trust him, pa."

"No?"

"No. I say we get out of here and back home. There's lots of work we can be doin' there."

Robert nodded and rubbed the stubble of his prominent chin. "Tell you what, John. Let's hear the man out. Then, we can tell him we'll go home and think about it. After all, he did pay our way down here."

"Whatever you say, only I'm beginnin' to itch sittin' here. It don't make sense sitting here with the vice-president of the country. Hell, he can go and hire anybody he wants to for any job. What's so special about us?"

Robert Barrigan laughed. "We're about to find out, my boy."

When Aaron Burr returned he was frowning. He angrily picked up the paper from the desk, read it, tossed it down and said, "Let me be quick, gentlemen. Something has come up that demands my attention. As you may know, President Jefferson has dispatched his friend and secretary, Meriwether Lewis, to explore the newly acquired Louisiana Territory. Mr. Lewis is now in St. Louis ready to proceed with the exploration. With him is a close friend of his, George Rogers Clark. Are you aware of this?"

Both Barrigans shook their heads.

"It is my opinion that there is a far greater benefit to this nation to explore the region presently known as New Spain. The Spanish province of Mexico offers us a region of untold wealth and strategic importance. Coupled with the Mississippi and Orleans territories, Mexico holds the key, I believe, to the future of America. I'm not alone in this belief. Harman Blennerhassett and General James Wilkinson share my feelings in this matter."

"So?" Robert Barrigan asked.

Burr leaned forward, his chin in his hands. "I am offering the two of you financing and the opportunity to join the first official explorers of this new territory."

Father and son looked at each other, their eyebrows raised.

"Well?" Burr asked. "What is your response?"

Robert Barrigan spoke. "Well now, Mr. Burr, this is the sort of thing a man has to mull over a bit."

"How long will you need?"

The older Barrigan shrugged.

"I'll give you two weeks. You must let me know your decision by then."

John Barrigan said, "Sir, I think my father and I would have a few questions about this. I mean, after all, this here seems to be a pretty big order to just toss at us."

"You can ask all the questions you wish," Burr said, taking the paper from the desk and standing. "Mr. Blenner-hassett is in the building and knows as much as I know about it. He has my full power to discuss any aspect of it, including finances. You'll have to excuse me now. This campaign is becoming unnecessarily nasty, thanks to Mr. Hamilton. Two weeks, gentlemen. Thank you for coming."

Burr was almost out the door when Bob Barrigan stopped him by asking, "I got one question for you, sir. Why us?"

Burr turned and smiled. "Because people I trust have told me that *you* can be trusted. Besides, you come with quite a good reputation, Mr. Barrigan, as an explorer. Unafraid, daring, rugged, hearty, resourceful, all those things that shape a great nation. Good day." He was gone.

Robert Barrigan slapped his knee and shook his head. "Well, John, how's that strike you?"

"You'd really like to know?"

"Yup."

"I think we've just been talkin' with a fella who's got pretty good taste in people."

His father laughed. "It's up to you, boy. Should we stay and talk to this Blennerhassett fella, or should we get rid of these silly damn shirts and head for Massachusetts?"

"Since we're wearin' them, pa, we might as well stay."

CHAPTER SEVEN

While the Barrigans waited to be summoned to the next meeting, Harman Blennerhassett sat with General James Wilkinson and with Zebulon Pike.

Blennerhassett, an Englishman, had migrated to the new land and had amassed a small fortune through a variety of business ventures, many of them illegal or, at best, resulting in someone losing a life's savings to one of his schemes. Always sensitive to the favors one could gain from political connections, he managed to work himself into Aaron Burr's inner circle of confidants. Like Burr, he saw wealth to the west, and had recently purchased his own island in the Ohio River.

Pike, twenty-five years old, had recently been raised in rank to captain, First U.S. Infantry. Thick-lipped, eyes always threatening to close under heavy, sensuous lids, he had the air of a wary, weary saloon brawler. Yet, beneath a head of thick, wavy black hair, there was a gentleness about him that was almost poetic.

General Wilkinson stood with his back to the other men. He was dressed in full military dress uniform reflecting his rank as commander-in-chief of the army. It was rumored that President Jefferson planned to appoint Wilkinson to the governorship of one of two political divisions to be created under the newly acquired Louisiana Territory. The official transfer of the territory from France to the United States was to take place five days hence, March 9, in ceremonies to be held in St. Louis. Congress was currently considering how the division of the territory would be handled. The plan most popular with a majority of members of Congress mirrored Jefferson's thinking, that the Louisiana Purchase should be divided into one region to be known as the Territory of Orleans, and another to be known as the District of Louisiana, with eventual political control of the latter to fall under the jurisdiction of the Territory of Indiana.

"Well," Wilkinson said, without turning his attention from the garden outside the window, "the grand march west appears to have begun."

Blennerhassett, who enjoyed retaining English flavoring in his dress, fiddled with ivory buttons on his green, double-breasted, silk English riding coat and looked at Pike. The young officer raised his eyebrows and waited for the general to say something else.

Wilkinson turned from the window and clasped his hands behind his back. He rocked up and down and said, "The Spanish aren't going to like us poking around in their territory one damn bit."

"They really shouldn't be too upset, sir," Pike offered. "After all, there isn't any military objective behind it, is there?"

Wilkinson hesitated before answering. "None that I'm aware of," he finally said.

Harman Blennerhassett ran his hand over a close-cropped salt-and-pepper beard and flicked a speck of lint from his brown linen breeches. "We should see the Barrigans now," he said.

"I don't see any sense in my being here when they come in," Wilkinson said. He looked at Pike. "Since you're to be in charge of the mission, captain, you might as well interview them."

"As you wish, sir."

Wilkinson took his hat from the desk and strode to the door, returning Captain Pike's casual salute. "I'll be leaving for Washington in the morning," he said. "Then, if things go as the rumormongers say they will, St. Louis will be my next stop. If you have any reservations about these Barrigans, don't hesitate to dismiss them, captain. They come highly recommended by Sims and Warbuckle in Massachusetts, but be certain about them."

"Yes, sir."

"Mr. Blennerhassett, could I see you outside for a moment?"

Blennerhassett followed Wilkinson from the room. They walked halfway up a corridor leading to the front door before

Wilkinson stopped, fixed Blennerhassett in a stony stare and said, "I just want you to know for the record, sir, that I am becoming disenchanted with this whole affair."

"Why?"

"Why? To begin with, it won't be long before people will begin asking why such an important mission, to be taken on behalf of our president, is under the control of his *former* vice-president. Second, my dear Mr. Blennerhassett, launching an exploratory thrust into a foreign territory is not an easy matter, especially when the motives for it are not exactly as stated by this government. And third, sir, should the president gain any knowledge of Mr. Burr's real interest in exploring the Spanish frontier, we'll all be in line for charges of treason."

"Why would anyone have to know, general? There are only three of us involved."

Wilkinson snorted and drew a deep, troubled breath. "These Barrigans, Mr. Blennerhassett. Why are they being recruited? I'd prefer to see no one but our own military involved."

Blennerhassett's annoyance with the conversation became apparent. "I must go back, general. And I suggest you calm down and begin thinking clearly. The exploratory force cannot be made up only of military. That should be obvious, especially to the commander-in-chief of our army. We'll meet tonight as planned. Good day." He turned, straightened a lace cuff protruding four inches from the sleeve of his riding coat and returned to where Captain Pike had just been introduced to Robert and John Barrigan by Burr's redheaded aide.

"I'm sorry, Mr. Blennerhassett," Pike said. "We would have waited for you but these gentlemen were about to leave."

"Leave?" Blennerhassett asked. "Why?"

"We began to think that everybody else had left," Bob Barrigan said. "No sense sittin' around in an empty house. Name's Robert Barrigan, sir. This here is my son, John." The father extended his hand to Blennerhassett, who took it tentatively, as though not sure of its cleanliness.

"Pleased to meet you, sir," said John, also shaking hands.

Harman Blennerhassett perched on the edge of a desk and played with his shirt cuff. The Barrigans stood awkwardly until Captain Pike suggested they take seats.

"Much obliged," Bob Barrigan said, casting a scornful look at Blennerhassett.

After a period of silence, Blennerhassett cleared his throat and said, "Well, so you are the rather infamous Barrigans. Your reputations certainly do precede you."

Bob Barrigan had to stifle a growing dislike for the foppish Blennerhassett. He'd been through too much hardship in his fifty years, seen too much trouble and lost too much, to have patience with pretty talk. He'd lost two wives, one to an Indian attack, another to influenza. Of three sons born to him, only John had survived. He looked over at his handsome son and felt immense pride.

Captain Pike said, "I assume Mr. Burr has told you something of the proposed exploration into the Spanish territories."

John Barrigan nodded. "That he did, but my father and I have a few questions."

"Of course," said Pike. "Would anyone like tea?"

"I wouldn't turn down a whiskey," Bob said.

"Sounds good to me," John said.

"Whiskey?" asked Blennerhassett. "At this hour?"

"I was about to say the same thing about tea," Bob Barrigan said. "Awful late in the day for tea."

Zebulon Pike laughed. "I'll see what I can do about some whiskey, Mr. Barrigan."

Blennerhassett had little to say during Pike's brief absence from the room. He answered the one question the elder Barrigan asked, which was how long a period of time was estimated for the exploration. "Undetermined," was the reply. "Probably a year, maybe longer."

The redheaded aide brought two water glasses filled with dark whiskey. "Much obliged," John Barrigan said. He tipped his glass to his father and took a long, deliberate swig. "Real good whiskey," he said.

"Damn good," his father said.

"Well, now," Pike said, "let's get down to hard facts. As you know, it is planned to explore the regions of New Spain. Mr. Burr has advocated this for a considerable period of time now. It was his intention as vice-president to make this a top priority. Then, as you know, he decided to run for governor of this state, which meant resigning as vice-president. But President Jefferson holds him in such high esteem that he's urged him to continue putting together the plans to enter Spanish territory on behalf of commerce and trade."

Bob Barrigan laughed and took another drink from his glass. "Commerce and trade? I figured there was more to it than that."

Blennerhassett waved his hand in a gesture of annoyance. "No, no," he said from his perch on the desk, "there is absolutely no political or military significance to this project. The president realizes the potentials of commerce to the west, and feels it is in the nation's best interests to investigate them. Financing will come from both the government and from private sectors. It will truly be an apolitical exploration."

Captain Pike noted a quizzical expression on John Barrigan's face. "A problem, Mr. Barrigan?"

"No," said John. "It's just that I don't understand why Mr. Burr is in charge. It would seem to me—and I'll be the first to admit I'm not too familiar with how folks in high places work—it seems to me that somebody down there in Washington would be in charge."

Blennerhassett forced a smile. "As Captain Pike has already said, Mr. Barrigan, Mr. Burr is held in the highest regard by President Jefferson. Mr. Burr is also a very public-minded citizen. Even with the demands of being governor of New York, he is determined to find time for this project. And he will. I can assure you of that."

"If he wins," said Bob Barrigan.

"Pardon?" asked Blennerhassett.

"Oh, nothin'. It's just that we hear up in Massachusetts that things look pretty close down here in New York."

Blennerhassett sighed and picked lint from his jacket sleeve.

Pike said to Bob Barrigan, "I'd like to ask you a question if I might, sir."

"Go right ahead, son," Barrigan responded. John smiled at his father's calling the captain son. He knew that it meant that his father had taken a liking to Pike. Those who did not please Robert Barrigan were never called son.

"As you can see, I'm considerably younger than you," said Pike. "I obviously don't have your breadth of experience in the wilderness, or your knowledge of the Indians we might encounter in our journey. But I'm not without experience, Mr. Barrigan. My military duties have taken me into very rugged and dangerous country. What I'm trying to say is . . ."

Barrigan grinned. "What you're trying to say is that you're in command of this expedition, and you're wondering how a crusty old bastard like me will take to havin' you give me orders."

Pike sighed and smiled.

"Well, son, let me tell you how I feel about that. I always said that a good leader should be a good follower. If you can't follow, you can't lead. I'll take orders from any man just so long as that man cares about me and has a head on his shoulders. I think I could live with you givin' out an order now and then."

"I appreciate that, Mr. Barrigan."

Blennerhassett had grown impatient with the conversation. He paced the room as he said, "I think we've said enough here for today, Mr. Barrigan. It now remains for you and your son to decide whether you will join Captain Pike on the project. If so, you'll each receive twenty dollars a month. In addition to that, you'll be granted certain trapping rights. Fur is plentiful in the west. You could come back a rich man."

"Just so long as I come back a live one." Bob and John Barrigan stood. "We'll let you know within two weeks like we promised Mr. Burr."

"Good," said Blennerhassett. "We'll be expecting to hear from you."

Captain Pike escorted the Barrigans to the door of the house. "Where are you staying?" he asked.

"A room over by Eighth Street run by a nice woman named Murray," John said. "She makes delicious cakes. And serves wine with them, too."

"I was wondering if you gentlemen would join me this evening," Pike said. "I thought I'd take advantage of what New York has to offer. Now that the White House has moved from here to Washington, the city seems to have opened up considerably."

"I never will understand movin' the official place of government from one city to another," Bob Barrigan said. "Just because the new president turns out to be a southern gentleman doesn't seem cause to move a government."

Pike agreed. He then said, "Well, I'd be very pleased to have you join me this evening."

"Thanks, son, but not me. I'm damn tired. I think I'll sip a little whiskey in a tavern over there near Mrs. Murray's place and get me to bed early."

"I think I'd like to see a little of New York," John Barrigan said.

"Good," said Pike. "Meet me back here at six. We'll have dinner and spend a little time seeing what New York has to offer. Everyone talks about Fraunces Tavern. We could go there.''

"Whatever you say," John said. "Do I have to wear these fancy clothes?''

Pike laughed and slapped John on the arm. "Absolutely not. Wear whatever is comfortable. Six? Here?''

"I'll be here.''

CHAPTER EIGHT

When John Barrigan arrived at Burr's campaign headquarters at six he was met by a Zebulon Pike out of uniform. The young officer had changed into blue linen pantaloons and a carmagnole, or short jacket, the working man's garb. He held in his hand a red galley-slave cap which had become popular in New York.

John wore his homemade English dress coat, but had abandoned the frilly shirt for one of plain cotton. He wore the same breeches and boots he'd worn that afternoon. Pike wore flat shoes and knee stockings.

"Ready?" asked Pike.

"I think so," John responded. "Where are we headin'?"

"The famed Fraunces Tavern," Pike replied as they left the house and hailed a horse-drawn carriage.

After they'd climbed into the carriage, John said, "I wonder whether you'd mind us goin' someplace else first."

Pike looked over and shrugged. "Where?"

"I might never get to see New York City again, captain. I figured maybe you wouldn't mind havin' the driver take us on a little tour."

Pike smiled. Although only twenty-five, he'd been exposed to a variety of life experiences because of his officer status. John Barrigan's straightforward request pleased him. One of the reasons Pike looked forward to the mission to New Spain was to escape the glitter and pretension of big-city life. The wilderness appealed to him, as did adventure.

"I think it's a good idea," Pike replied. "But from now on it's Zeb. No more Captain Pike."

John nodded and slapped his knee. "That sets right with me, Zeb."

Pike instructed the driver to give them a tour of New York. The driver was a little taken back. He'd given tours before, but always for a couple, the man wanting to impress his lady with his knowledge of the city. He looked back, said he was the best tour guide in New York and urged his aging gray mare ahead with a flick of his whip.

Pike and Barrigan sat back and took in the sights of the nation's largest city. The driver, who spoke with a thick Irish brogue, first pointed out the Blooming Dale section of the city, on its western perimeter. "The Dutch call it that," he added, trying to pronounce the Dutch word *Bloemendaal*.

As the carriage traveled south, it passed street vendors hawking their daily catch from the Hudson River; huge lobsters, sturgeon, shad, oysters and giant crabs. They cried, "Fresh sturgeon—a penny a pound." On the river itself barges loaded with fish moved upriver. They would stop at a succession of wharfs where anxious customers would be ready to buy.

"That's a pretty one," John Barrigan said, tapping Pike on the arm and pointing to a clipper ship that had recently returned from China with a cargo of exotic teas.

The sky slowly darkened and the sun slipped lower in the horizon, a ball of orange ice melting into the land. A sprawling grove of fruit and elm trees seemed to soak up the darkness. A bear was visible on the fringe of the woods. A fox darted across the avenue and disappeared into a lush garden.

Eventually, the carriage driver took Pike and Barrigan to the site of what had been the nation's White House, more popularly known as "The Place" to native New Yorkers. "That was it," said the driver, pointing to a building at number three Cherry Street. "President Washington moved it uptown to Broadway. Then along comes Mr. Hamilton who connives a deal with the southerner, Mr. Jefferson, and we lose it to Washington."

Pike and Barrigan sensed the Irishman's pique over seeing his adopted city lose the nation's capital. His pride in New York, so evident during the tour, was refreshing in the face of the city's well-known problems.

"How long have you been in New York?" Pike asked the driver.

"Two years now, sir."

"You certainly seem to like it," Barrigan said.

"My mother would curse you, sir, for suggestin' such a vile thing. It's a bad city. They'll hit you over the head for a loaf of bread you're carryin'. Go down to the wharfs and you'll end up shanghaied on some vermin-infested ship bound for the ends of the earth. The women are wicked, the niggers filthier than hogs and the politicians as crooked as my dear daddy's shillelagh. *Like* this hellhole?" He was becoming increasingly animated. He stopped the horse and turned to face his passengers. "You want to see what this city is really like, gentlemen? I'll take you to Paradise Square, over by Five Points. Then you can *really* see New York."

Zebulon Pike threw up his hands. "Please, sir, I think you'd best take us to Fraunces Tavern straight on."

The driver snorted. "Of course. That's the way it'll be. A couple of fine-lookin' young fellas like yourselves only want to see the good, never the bad. You only want to believe how wonderful and free this city is compared to where I come from." He inhaled with gusto and spat on the ground. "Did you know, gentlemen, that a man can't even vote in this city? That's your freedom for you."

Pike knew the driver was right. Only the rich and powerful were allowed to vote in New York City. A bill pending before the city council would allow those paying at least twenty-five dollars a year in rent to vote for an alderman, but not for any elected position higher than that.

Pike was growing bored with the diatribe. His voice had an edge to it when he said, "Enough of this. On to Fraunces Tavern immediately."

But John Barrigan looked at Pike and asked, with squinted eyes and a cocking of his head, that the driver not be shut off.

Pike shrugged and smiled. "Whatever you say, John."

Barrigan looked up at the driver. "Take us to this Paradise Square."

The driver looked aghast. "I wasn't suggestin' that the likes of you go there," he said. "You'll not come out with your lives."

"Just drive us," John said. "We can take care of ourselves, I believe." He looked at Pike for confirmation.

"He's right," Pike said to the driver. "Paradise Square it is."

"As you say, only don't forget you've been warned by one who knows."

It took twenty minutes to reach the Five Points section of the city. It was formed by the intersection of Cross, Little Water, Mulberry, Orange and Anthony Streets. In the center of where the streets converged was a park, Paradise Square. Surrounding the park was a picket fence upon which laundry had been hung to dry. Small boys armed with brickbats and with pickets broken off from the fence stood guard over the family wash.

Unlike areas further uptown, Five Points was bustling with activity. It was as though with the coming of night, the bowels of the decrepit buildings had been emptied onto the streets. Longshoremen, sailors, oystermen, laborers and an assortment of unclassifiable men moved through the choked streets, along the edge of the tiny park and in and out of alleys between buildings. The largest of these buildings was Coulter's Brewery, which sat on the edge of a pond known as the Collect. A stream at its northernmost end wound through Lispenard's Meadows until it connected with the Hudson River. In the center of the Collect was a small island on which Negroes had been hanged and burned, or broken upon the wheel, following an unsuccessful slave revolt in 1741 during which they rose against their owners and attempted to burn and loot the city.

"Well, gents, this will be it," the carriage driver said. He nervously looked about. "If you're getting off be quick about it. I've no desire to linger here." Pike paid the fare and he and John hopped down to the ground.

"Thank you," John called after the driver, who'd wasted no time in flicking his whip across the gray mare's rump.

Zeb Pike looked around at the milling crowd of men. There were few women on the street. Those who were appeared to be prostitutes.

"Well, here we are," said Pike. "What do we do now?"

"Damned if I know," Barrigan said. "But the man was right. It certainly looks different than those other places we've seen."

A passing prostitute openly admired John's rugged good looks. The twenty-year-old son of Robert Barrigan stood three inches taller than Pike, which put him at six feet, four inches. Pike recalled John's father's eyes from that afternoon's meeting, eyes that had seen much and had hardened

56

against what they'd seen. John's eyes, too, had the steely temper of his father's. They narrowed against the vision of poverty that was represented in Five Points, and against the stench that suddenly filled his nostrils, an odor that seemed to come from every doorway, every alley. John found himself breathing shallowly in order to minimize the potency of it.

"You look like you just smelled a very old fish," Pike said.

"I believe I have," said Barrigan. He brushed aside a lock of brown hair that usually hung over his forehead and looked up at the roof of a three-story red brick building. A vividly painted whore waved to him. John waved back and grinned. "They sure aren't bashful, are they?" he said.

"They couldn't be bashful and earn their way," Pike said. "Come on, John. As long as you've insisted that we come here, we might as well see what really goes on." He led them across Little Water Street and up a short hill to where the Americans had built a fort during the Revolutionary War. It had been defended successfully against British troops commanded by General Howe. Recently, the fort had become a popular dueling ground and a site for mass meetings. A week ago, two gangs that had sprung up in New York waged a battle in the fort that left two dead and scores injured.

This night, a war of another sort was to be staged by a man from the Fly Market named Winship. He'd fenced off a large area of the fort. Inside the fence he'd chained a live bull on a swivel ring. Once a crowd had gathered and paid two cents admission, Winship would release a pack of dogs to torment the bull. The crowd wagered on which dogs would be gored by the bull. Winship, a hard-drinking butcher, was becoming rich with his bullbaiting contests.

Winship stood at a break in the fence and collected the admission charges. When he saw Barrigan and Pike approaching, he pegged them as uptowners out slumming. "Evening, gentlemen," he said. "You look like wagering men to me."

"I bet now and again," John Barrigan said. "What do we wager on here?"

"Bullbaiting."

"I've never heard of that," John said.

Winship laughed, which sent his corpulent belly into spasms beneath a bloodstained white apron. "One of the most popular sports in the city," he said. "It'll be ten cents each, gentlemen."

"For what?" asked Pike.

"Admission. I'll tell you what I'll do for you gents." He became conspiratorial in tone. "I know the big bettors inside. I'll see that you are put with them. A couple of smart fellows like you should do right well."

"What's bullbaiting?" John asked.

Again, a hearty laugh. Winship explained the event.

"Let's be leaving," John said to Zeb.

"Leaving?" Winship asked. "Why?"

"Because I don't believe animals were put here on earth, sir, to be tormented and made sport of."

"Nor do I," Pike said.

Winship's laughter turned to a scowl. "You'd best be careful around here," he said. "Two pantywaists like you might not be leaving with everything you arrived with." A smile returned to his round face, but this time it was menacing. He looked over at a group of six men and pointed his thumb at John and Zeb. "A couple of uptown high types. They don't believe in tormenting animals. How do you like that?"

The men laughed.

Zeb and John started down the hill. Their passage was slowed by the crowd moving toward the fort. A burly man deliberately ran into Zeb with his elbow. John found himself being stared at by everyone he passed. A shrill female voice called to him from the first-floor window of a red brick building. He looked at her, then back to where Winship was standing. Some of the men Winship had spoken to were on their way down the hill, their eyes trained upon Zeb and John.

"I think we've got trouble after us," John said.

"We can handle it," Zeb said. "At least that's what you said when you decided to come here."

They reached the bottom of the hill and looked back. Winship's friends were still on their way, their passage also hindered by the crowd.

The sound of a fiddle and a piano originated from inside a dance hall located in the building in front of which they stood. Zeb looked in the window and saw men and women milling about. "In here," he said, indicating a battered doorway. He pushed through it with John at his heels just as Winship's friends reached the corner. One of the men made a gesture to the others indicating it wasn't worth pursuing them

58

further. They laughed and rejoined the crowd on its way up the hill to where bullbaiting was about to begin.

Once inside the dance hall, John and Zeb relaxed for a moment and took in their new surroundings. Red bombazine curtains hung at the windows. The floor was rough wood that had been sanded to better accommodate the dancers. Long wooden benches lined each wall. A makeshift bar occupied one corner of the room. The only illumination was provided by hoop chandeliers filled with candles.

Although it was early in the evening, the dance hall was doing a brisk business. A dozen hostesses dressed in low black satin bodices, scarlet satin skirts and long black stockings and wearing red boots with bells attached to the ankles flirted with the male customers. Two bartenders dispensed whiskey and malt beverages from behind a small bar.

"Are you a drinkin' man, Zeb?"

"On occasion. I know you are."

"Then let's see what the gentleman has to offer."

They went to the bar and ordered, whiskey for John, swan gin for Zeb. The band continued to play for dancing. One of the establishment's girls approached John and suggested they dance.

"I'm not much on my feet, ma'am," he said. "Just a reel now and then."

The girl giggled. "A reel? What's that?"

"Maybe later," John said, smiling at Zeb.

The girl pouted and walked away.

"Pretty thing she is," Zeb said.

"I've seen prettier back in Massachusetts."

"Have you?" Zeb made a face indicating he was not impressed.

"Massachusetts women are the prettiest in the land, Zeb. You should have seen my mother. She was a beauty."

"I'm certain she was, John. But if we're not going to dance, what's the sense in being here?"

"Better than out there with the fat man's crew."

"Oh, that's right. I forgot about them."

Zeb and John found space in a far corner of the room. They leaned against the wall and sipped their drinks. Five sailors, already drunk, staggered through the door and immediately pursued some of the hostesses. The girls put up a mock protest, but two of them quickly disappeared upstairs with two of the sailors.

The two-man band had been playing music for dancing. It was now time to accompany one of the hostesses, a short, buxom redhead who quieted everyone with outstretched arms, smiled demurely at the piano player and began to sing.

There's a little side street such as often you meet,
Where the boys of a Sunday night rally;
Though it's not very wide, and it's dismal beside,
Yet they call the place Paradise Alley.

But a maiden so sweet lives in that little street,
She's the daughter of Widow McNally:
She has bright golden hair, and the boys all declare,
She's the sunshine of Paradise Alley.

She's had offers to wed by the dozens, 'tis said,
Still she's always refused them politely;
But of late she's been seen with young Tommy Killeen,
Going out for a promenade nightly.

We can all guess the rest, for the boy she loves best,
Will soon change her name from McNally;
Tho' he may change her name, she'll be known just the
    same,
As the sunshine of Paradise Alley.

John looked over at Zeb Pike and thought he detected moist eyes.

"She's a fine voice," Zeb said. "Very gentle."

"That it is," said John.

"Why would she be in a place like this?"

"Circumstances, Zeb. Everybody does what circumstances tells 'em to do."

The girl had sung the final two verses of the song directly at Zeb. After drunken applause had died down, she walked away from the band, placed her hand on Zeb's and said, "Would you like to dance with me?"

Zeb was flustered. He looked at John, then into the girl's green eyes. "My name is Zeb," he said.

"My name is Margie. Dance? Or would you like to come upstairs with me?"

"Go ahead," John urged, aware of the spell the girl was casting over his new friend.

"I'll dance," Zeb replied.

Zeb and the girl walked to the center of the large dance floor. He was hesitant at first to put his arms around her. She took the initiative and soon they were moving to the uncertain rhythm of the music.

"I've not seen you before," she said in a light Irish brogue.

"No, you haven't. I'm only visiting New York."

Margie moved closer. "Why would you come to a place like this?" she asked. "You look like you have a bit of money."

Zeb was embarrassed. He glanced about at others on the floor. A sailor had lifted the skirt of one of the hostesses and had jammed his hand between her thighs.

They continued to dance. Finally, Zeb managed to speak. He asked, "Do you like working here?"

"No," she said. "But I'm the only one who brings home anything to pay the man with."

"You haven't a father?"

"Oh, yes, but the rum has hold of him. My mother is dead."

Zeb saw John talking with one of the hostesses. She was twisting her finger in the lock of hair on his forehead and smiling coquettishly.

Margie pressed her pelvis tightly against Zeb's and moved it in a slow circle. Her action had the predictable effect of arousing him into an erection.

"We could go upstairs now," Margie said. "I'm really good at it and it would only cost you . . ." She was about to quote her usual fee, fifteen cents, of which the house would take a nickel. Instead, because Zeb obviously had more money than the usual customers, she said, "Fifty cents, and worth every penny of it."

Zeb was tempted. It had been a long time since he'd been with a woman. He found Margie appealing. But the thought of having sex with someone who sold herself so cheaply to what was probably a succession of drunken, unclean men deterred him. He stopped dancing, reached into his pocket and extracted almost a dollar in change.

"Here," he said.

"Upstairs. You can give it to me upstairs."

"I'm not coming upstairs with you, Margie. But I want you to have this."

Zeb did not notice the commotion at the front door right

away. When he did realize something was going on and turned to see what it was, he was confronted by the sight of a drunken, burly Irishman carrying a length of iron pipe. The Irishman came straight at him, the pipe held over his head like a club. "You slimy bastard," the Irishman roared as he pushed his way through the crowded dance floor. "You turn my Margie into a whore, will you?"

Zeb's reflexes were faster than Margie's father's swing of the pipe. He managed to duck to the side and took a glancing blow on his forearm. Margie shrieked as her father, who'd toppled forward because of the momentum of his swing, spun around and prepared to attack once again. He lunged at Zeb. Zeb grabbed the man's wrist and twisted it while simultaneously delivering a chop across his bulbous nose with the heel of his hand. The nose audibly broke and the Irishman slumped to the floor, blood dripping from his nose onto the sanded timbers, his eyes glazed over from whiskey and from the potency of Zeb's blow.

From John Barrigan's vantage point, the fight was over. It seemed unlikely that the Irishman would try again. But John realized his prognosis was wrong when he saw Margie kneel over her father, then look up at other customers and scream, "Look what he's done to my poor daddy." She pointed up at Zeb. Zeb, too, instantly sized up the situation. He was about to be attacked by a roomful of drunken brawlers, friends of Margie's father as well as a dozen or more sailors, fishermen and local roustabouts joining in for the hell of it.

"Look out, Zeb!"

Pike turned just in time to avoid being cracked over the skull by a brick wielded by one of the Irishman's friends. A sailor tackled Zeb from his blind side and sent him sprawling into the crowd.

John Barrigan grabbed a small table and charged the crowd with it. He reached Zeb and together they fought their way to a corner of the room. They turned and tensed for the mass attack that was certain to come. It appeared that the amateurs in the fray had stepped aside in favor of a particularly menacing group of men, each carrying a weapon. John saw a long dagger in the hand of one attacker. Another held up an iron poker. Still another waved a Hessian bayonet that had found a home behind the bar since the Revolutionary War.

"What do you think?" John asked Zeb as they moved closer together, backs against the wall.

"I think I'd rather be at Fraunces Tavern."

"This is better," John said. "It's good training for New Spain."

"You're mad," Zeb said, laughing.

The man with the sword lunged at Zeb. Zeb sidestepped the thrust, the point of the weapon sticking into the wall. A short uppercut to the bottom of the man's chin brought him to his knees.

"That for you," John yelped as he smashed his fist into an advancing face.

As long as they had room to maneuver, Pike and Barrigan were in command of the situation despite the overwhelming odds against them. Their attackers seemed to have a healthy respect for their youthful physicality and fitness, and for their sobriety.

But as the crowd surged closer and backed the boys into the corner, the tide turned. Zeb was more aware of their predicament than John. In the years ahead he would come to learn that John Barrigan never even considered the possibility of losing a battle, no matter what the odds against him.

Two sailors who'd joined in the fray with the hope of sharing in any money taken from Zeb and John attacked simultaneously. John landed a hard, straight right to the one who came at him. Zeb wasn't as quick. The other sailor lowered his head and caught Zeb full force in the gut. As Zeb doubled over, others in the crowd suddenly sensed easy victory. A dozen men charged. A flurry of blows sent John reeling into a wall. He could no longer strike back. He could only use his arms and hands to protect himself. The attacker carrying the iron poker brought it back and swung with all his strength. It caught John on his left wrist and cracked the bone. He grunted and slumped to the floor.

Three men had leaped upon Zeb and he'd collapsed beneath their weight. They scrambled on top of him, fists flying.

The deafening blast of a pistol discharging brought all action to a halt. Zeb couldn't believe the pounding on him had stopped. John sat up. He held his left wrist gingerly in his right hand. He tried to look through the crowd to see what the source of the gunshot had been. Eventually, the people parted and a woman standing well over six feet tall sauntered through the aisle that had been made for her. She'd stuck a smoking pistol back in her belt. A long, heavy bludgeon was strapped to her right wrist. She wore a floor-length skirt that was held up with suspenders, or galluses as she preferred to call them. That's where she got her name, Gallus Mag, trusted lieutenant and bouncer for One-Armed Charlie Monell, the owner of the dance hall.

"Much obliged, ma'am," John said, standing. An intense pain radiated through his arm. He felt faint.

"Get your bloody asses up and over here," Mag barked in a cockney accent. She turned and pushed through the crowd toward the bar. Zeb was still sitting on the floor shaking his head.

"You heard the lady, Zeb," John said. "Let's go."

Zeb nodded and managed to stand. Blood ran from his nose. One eye had already turned black and blue. He stumbled after John.

"What in hell do you two think you're doing in my place?" Gallus Mag asked. She snapped her fingers and the bartender handed her a large glass filled to the brim with rum.

"Dancin', ma'am," John said.

Mag roared with laughter. "Bloody fops like the two of you do your dancing uptown where the fancy ladies are."

Zeb Pike eyed the door and the relative peace and safety of the sidewalk. "Look, ma'am, if it's all the same with you, we'll just be leaving."

"In a pig's ass you will," she said. "You come in here in your fancy clothes and cause trouble and think you're just going to bloody walk out?"

John's teeth were clenched against the pain of his broken wrist as he asked, "What then, ma'am?"

"You pay your way out, mates." The men at the bar laughed.

"Pay?" John asked. "What do we get for the money?"

"Your ears."

John and Zeb looked at each other. "Pardon, ma'am?" John asked.

"You've got your choice, boys. Either you pay me something for the trouble you've caused or your ears end up with the others." She pointed to a row of jars on a shelf behind the bar. Zeb and John squinted to see their contents. Each jar was filled with liquid in which an unidentifiable object floated.

"Ears?" Zeb asked.

Gallus Mag nodded.

A drunk slapped his hand on the bar and giggled. "That's

right," he slurred. "Ol' Mag here bites 'em off iffen you make any trouble for her."

John, who'd forgotten about the pain in his wrist, looked down at the floor and drew a deep breath. He looked at Mag, who'd unstrapped the bludgeon from her wrist and was weighing it in her hand.

Although they hadn't had the opportunity to plan anything, Zeb and John reacted in concert. Zeb hauled off and floored the nearest man standing between him and the door. John's path was partially blocked by Gallus Mag. He let go of his broken left wrist and drove his right fist into Mag's stomach. It was like hitting a boulder, but the impact was sufficient to stun her long enough for him to break past her, catch another man in the face with his elbow and join Zeb in a race for the door.

The street was filled with people. Zeb took a step to the left, down Anthony Street, but John went right and up Little Water Street, toward the old fort. Zeb caught him and yelled as they ran, "We got trouble up there, too."

John knew Zeb was right. He stopped and looked back toward the dance hall. A small group of men led by Gallus Mag came out of the hall, looked left, then right, spotted the boys and started after them.

"Too late now," John said. He resumed his run up the hill with Zeb at his side.

A loud roar came from inside the fort. A dog had just been spectacularly gored by the tethered bull and the crowd was showing its appreciation.

"We goin' in?" Zeb asked.

John stopped and tried to catch his breath. Both of them looked back down the hill. Gallus Mag was halfway up it. She waved the bludgeon over her head like a flag being carried into battle.

Another roar from the crowd inside the fort. One of the men who'd followed the boys down the hill on Winship's instructions spotted them. Zeb noticed him and smacked John on the shoulder. "Down there," he said, indicating another hill that culminated in a narrow alley next to Coulter's Brewery. They skirted a crowd of men standing in front of Winship's makeshift entrance to the fort and ran down the hill until they reached the alley. John's broken wrist now ached severely. He leaned against the brick wall of the brewery and forced a smile. "Don't ever listen to me again, captain," he said, panting.

Zeb, too, leaned against the wall. "I decided that earlier this evening, Mr. Barrigan."

An especially loud roar rose up from the fort. John looked in its direction. "I'll be damned," he muttered.

Zeb, too, looked up the hill. Gallus Mag and the men with her, after having momentarily lost the boys at the fort, had spotted them resting against the brewery. They were now on their way down the hill, and had even gathered additional forces.

Zeb and John looked at each other. There was no need to say anything, anymore than there was a choice to be made. They were so outnumbered that taking a stand was out of the question, particularly with John's broken wrist. That left running again as the only alternative.

"Let's go," Zeb said.

"I'm bushed," John said.

Zeb grabbed John's left wrist. The spasm of pain that radiated through his body snapped him out of his exhaustion. "Come on," Zeb urged, glancing up at the advancing Gallus Mag.

"All right, captain. Yes, sir."

The alley ran straight for a hundred yards, then branched right and left. They ran to the left, and after progressing fifty yards found themselves in a cul-de-sac, two sides of it formed by walls of the brewery, the third side consisting of a row of two-story tenements.

Zeb tried a door to the brewery. It was locked. A door across the alley leading into one of the tenements was also locked.

They stood in the darkness of the cul-de-sac and looked at each other, their ears cocked toward the sound of many pairs of feet approaching the alley's junction. Gallus Mag and her crew were suddenly visible. They looked to their left, then ran to their right.

Zeb's instinct was to make a run for the junction with the hope that they could reach it before Mag's gang returned. But it appeared to be impossible.

"Hot corn! Hot corn! Here's your lily white corn."

The youthful, plaintive voice that came from a tenement doorway startled both boys. They peered into the doorway's blackness and saw the figure of a young blond girl. She took a step forward and was now slightly more illuminated by the moon above. *"Hot corn!"* she repeated. *"Here's your lily white corn. All you that's got money, poor me that's got none. Buy my lily white corn and let me go home."*

The girl, who was one of many hot corn girls in New York City, was dressed in spotted calico and had a plaid shawl wrapped about her shoulders. A cedar-staved bucket hung from each arm, filled with piping hot ears of roasting corn. She lived in the tenement and had just replenished her supply of corn. About to go out to the street, she'd heard Zeb and John's footsteps and had come into the alley to see who was there.

"Hot corn! Lily white . . ."

John interrupted her singsong spiel by pushing her back inside the doorway. Zeb followed. They no sooner reached the inner recesses of the tenement's hallway when Gallus Mag and her henchmen came roaring into the alley's left fork. Zeb placed his finger against the girl's lips.

Outside, Gallus Mag screamed orders at the men. They could be heard trying every door on the alley. The corn girl pulled away from the boys and quietly slipped a bolt into place on her door. She'd acted just in time. A hand grabbed the door's knob and pulled on it.

Another minute passed. Finally, Mag yelled, "The bloody hell with it. You can be sure we lost a good sum of cash lettin' those two fops get away. Come on."

Zeb, John and the girl remained silent in the hallway. Zeb then asked, "Can we go out the front way, to the street?"

"Yes," she said.

"Then let's do it."

Zeb reached in his pocket, drew out what money was there and gave it to the girl. "Much obliged," he said.

They took off at a trot and continued the pace until well clear of Five points. A public carriage carried them the rest of the way uptown. Zeb wanted to find a doctor for John's arm but his offer was declined. "My daddy's pretty good fixin' things like this," John said. "But much obliged, Zeb."

As the carriage pulled up in front of the Aaron Burr campaign headquarters, Zeb looked at John and started to laugh.

"You always laugh at a man in pain, Zeb?"

"No, no," Zeb said, still laughing. "It's just that after

tonight, anything that happens in Mexico will be like going on a picnic.''

John laughed, too. ''I believe you're right. I can understand Indians, but not these city folks. I'm lookin' forward to travelin' with you, Zeb.''

''The same here, John.'' Pike slapped Barrigan on the shoulder, scrambled down from the carriage and disappeared inside the house.

Later that night, after John's father had set his broken wrist, he asked his son, ''How'd it happen?''

''Local Indians, pa. Strange breed of local Indians.''

His father grunted.

''Know what I decided tonight, pa?''

''No.''

''I decided I'd like to take Mr. Burr up on his offer.''

Robert Barrigan grinned. ''I was thinking along the same lines, son.''

CHAPTER NINE

May 1804

"How do I look, woman?" Manuel Soltura asked his wife as he entered the kitchen.

"Good," Margarita said. "Coffee?"

"Sí, por favor."

He sat at the table and patted the front of his waistcoat. "Tell me, Margarita, do I look important enough to greet the viceroy?"

Margarita, who'd been listening for days to her husband's concerns about the viceroy's pending visit, sighed and poured hot, black coffee into a cup. "Yes, my husband, you look very important. The viceroy will be impressed."

"Good," Manuel said. He sat up straight and attempted to pull in his stomach.

As Margarita placed the cup in front of him, he was patting strands of black hair that were plastered close to the sides of his head. His elbow caught the cup and tipped it over. Some of the coffee ran off the table and dripped onto his pants.

Margarita winced against her husband's string of curses. He jumped up and tried to soak up the coffee with his napkin, but the large, irregular dark stain could not be removed. He swore louder and stormed about the kitchen. "My best pants," he growled. "What will I wear now?"

"Other pants, Manuel. You have other handsome pants."

"Not like these. The white ones are best with this coat." He continued cursing and left the kitchen.

Gordo came into the kitchen from outdoors. He'd been preparing for the calf roundup, an annual event that took place in the spring on every hacienda in the valley. Usually, it took place a month or six weeks earlier, when the grasses had become full and good, and when the calves had matured enough for branding. But this spring had been unusually cold and wet, and Gordo had decided to delay cutting the calves away from the herd until now.

It hadn't been an easy decision. Of all the chores demanded of him as the foreman of his father's hacienda, calf cutting was his favorite. His love for it set him apart from most other young men in the valley. The annual calf roundup meant six or seven days of hard riding and Spartan living out on the plains. The dust would fill the nostrils and eyes and threaten to choke all air from the lungs. Hair and faces would be coated with white alkali. Food would be gritty. The danger of being trampled by a stampeding herd would be constant.

Still, there were those true vaqueros who found greater discomfort in the cleanliness of a bunkhouse bed. For them, food prepared in a kitchen could never taste as good as food cooked over a roaring fire on the plain. Gordo shared the vaquero's love of the range. For that reason, he was as good or better than almost anyone else in the valley at roundup time.

"When do you begin?" his mother asked as she poured him coffee.

"After lunch, mother, *if* I can get these lazy louts to move faster." He sat at the table and stuffed corn bread into his mouth. "I told papa last week that we need to find new workers. Those we have now are a disgrace."

"What did he say?" Margarita asked.

"He said he had no time to think about such things."

Margarita laughed. "Of course not, Gordo. Ever since he learned that the viceroy would visit Valladolid he can do nothing but plan what to say when he meets him." She shook her head. "Your father has great ambition, Gordo."

"Which is good, mother. A criollo without ambition has nothing in Mexico."

Gordo's comment had some truth behind it. While the gachupines, those born in Spain, automatically held virtually every position of power, it was the majority criollo class that had managed to amass most of the wealth in the country.

Once, when asked why he aspired to power when he already had plenty of money, Manuel Soltura said, "Money is only the beginning of happiness. Once a man has his money, to fail to pursue power is to fail at life."

Manuel's philosophy was lost on Margarita, but not on

Gordo. He understood what his father had said, and how accurately his words reflected life in New Spain since Cortés conquered it in the early 1500s. Since that time, and despite the freedom to achieve wealth, almost every criollo aspired to positions held by the gachupines. Their aspirations were not based upon practical need. Rather, it was a matter of having lived as inferior people by virtue of birth far too long. Every Spanish colony around the globe was ruled on the assumption that only Spanish-born subjects possessed sufficient loyalty to be trusted to positions of power. It was a matter of racial purity, argued the privileged gachupines. Most criollos did not seriously debate this precept. They respected the concept of racial purity and forever suffered from a feeling of distinct inferiority.

The criollo argument was for a new breed of racially pure citizens to assume control of New Spain, a breed of native-born Mexicans, sons of the land to be governed.

Margarita Soltura joined Gordo at the table. She watched him eat. "How handsome," she thought. Gordo's courage and strength were a source of considerable pride to her and to his father, although she would have to admit, were she pressed, that it was Juan, the priest, who especially filled her heart with joy. There was a hardness about Gordo that could, at times, cause his mother's heart to trip with fear. Gordo was arrogant and became more so each day. Was it an arrogance that would one day destroy him?

She dismissed those thoughts and shifted to the subject of María. "Your father and I talked last night of María Jardinero," she said.

Gordo grinned and wiped crumbs from his mouth. "She is beautiful, mother, is she not?"

"Of course. Perhaps the most beautiful *señorita* in the valley."

"There is no debate. She *is* the most beautiful."

"What are your intentions, Gordo? You have been seeing her for a year now."

Gordo refrained from telling his mother what his true intentions had been all along. All he'd ever wanted was to make love to María, to taste her sweet flesh in his mouth and to experience the joy of being inside her. It had not happened, and Gordo's frustration was real. Each time he'd courted her, the chaperone was near. Last night, he'd left her home and gone directly to town where his favorite *puta,* a half-caste girl named Jola, relieved his sexual tensions. He'd returned home, drained of the tangible evidence of his manly frustration but bitter at it not having been María who'd relieved him.

His mother asked again what his intentions with María were.

"To marry her," he said, not looking up.

Margarita's brow furrowed. "Your father and I spoke of that possibility, Gordo. It seemed logical that you would wish to marry her."

"Yes, it is logical, mother." Gordo didn't wish to discuss it any further. He was uncomfortable speaking of marriage, especially with his mother. He didn't wish to marry anyone yet, and was surprised at what he'd said. It was the frustration. He would have to marry María if he were to enjoy her sexually. That had become painfully obvious.

Gordo started to leave the table but his mother placed her hand upon his arm and urged him to stay. "Gordo, you know that María's father does not wish a marriage between you and her to take place."

Gordo looked his mother in the eye. "Because she is a gachupin and I am a criollo?"

"Perhaps."

"You have discussed this with him?"

"No, but your father has. As it became obvious that you and María might one day plan to marry, her father took it upon himself to speak with your father."

"And?"

"Her father has said that he will prohibit such a marriage."

Gordo slammed his large hand on the table. "Hypocrite!" he snarled. "He claims not to have feelings of gachupine superiority and yet he protects his precious daughter from a criollo."

Margarita stiffened. "No, Gordo, perhaps you are wrong. Perhaps it is not a matter of a gachupine father protecting his daughter from criollos. If it were, who could blame him? To be Spanish-born holds special meaning in New Spain. But that is not the only reason he forbids María to marry you. He has told your father that your wildness concerns him. He sees you carouse in the village, hears the stories of your nights in the cabarets. That is not the life he wishes for his only daughter, and such a wonderful one at that. Have you considered the possibility that you are the cause of his displeasure at your interest in María, Gordo? If you are serious about María

Jardinero, then it is time for you to settle down and present to her family a suitor worthy of her upbringing.''

"I've heard enough," Gordo said, pulling free from his mother's grip and going to the door. "Father is right. No matter what a gachupín says, he looks upon us with scorn." He was breathing heavily now. His nostrils flared and his eyes widened with anger. He turned and pointed his finger at his mother. "I pledge something to you, mother. I will marry María Jardinero whether her father approves or does not. And if he stands in my way, then that will be his mistake."

When Gordo was gone, Margarita stood for a long while, then went to a long mahogany cupboard and lightly touched a porcelain figure of the Virgin of Guadalupe that her son, Juan, the priest, had given her a week earlier.

CHAPTER TEN

The arrival in Valladolid of New Spain's viceroy, Iturrigaray, was cause for considerable official preparation. Iturrigary arrived in Valladolid at precisely noon, as he'd planned. He was accompanied by a hundred armed soldiers, a contingent of personal servants and a logistics unit consisting of pack mules, horses and covered wagons.

Manuel Soltura had managed to join the town's gachupine leaders in the official welcoming party. The plaza was packed with people from the valley. Women wore their finest dresses, vividly colored outfits that gave the square the look of a large artist's palette. The brilliant noon sun glistened off the white fronts and red roofs of the buildings surrounding the plaza. The sky was navy blue and clear; puffy white clouds hovered over the mountains far in the distance.

Manuel Soltura was perspiring freely. He ran his stubby fingers beneath the tight collar of his shirt and nervously glanced about at those with whom he stood. He'd thought he was the only criollo in the welcoming party and was disappointed when he saw two other criollo men, also large landowners, move through the main mass of onlookers and join the greeters in front of the town hall.

"Buenos días," they said to him.

"Buenos días," he replied, wishing they weren't there.

He looked to where Margarita stood with other wives. She noticed him and smiled. His eyes asked for reassurance that his attire was proper and presentable. She nodded and smiled again.

The military musicians with Iturrigaray's party began playing a spirited march. Iturrigaray sat up straighter in his saddle and waved to the crowd. His path through the plaza was fifteen feet wide. It was lined on both sides with gachupine and criollo citizens. Behind them stood the mestizos and sambos and mulattoes. They outnumbered the more privileged classes tenfold. Scattered throughout their ranks were a few Indians. Small children sat on the shoulders of their fathers, their eyes wide with wonder at the spectacle being played out before them.

Juan Soltura stood with Father Gomez in front of the church. They'd been invited to join the official welcoming committee but had declined, suggesting that it would be more appropriate for the town's clergy to remain aloof from any political involvement, as tangential as it might be. Manuel had argued with his son but to no avail. Juan had said to his father, "No, Papa, you stand proudly with those of importance in the town. I wish to represent my church. That is all."

Iturrigaray brought his horse to a halt directly in front of the welcoming party. The musicians raggedly stopped playing and looked to the officer in charge for further orders.

The ranking member of Valladolid's cabildo cleared his throat and took two tentative steps out of the safety of the crowd and toward the viceroy. "Welcome," he said. "I welcome you to Valladolid."

Iturrigaray removed his hat and waved it to the man. He twisted in his saddle and looked right and left. *"Buenos días,"* he said. A few in the crowd returned his greeting. He broke into a broad grin. This time he shouted his greeting to everyone in the plaza.

"Welcome," many shouted.

"Buenos días, Iturrigaray," said others.

Iturrigaray returned his attention to the man who'd represented the greeters. "It is good to be here in Valladolid. The people here are loyal to the king, of that I am certain."

"Most assuredly, my viceroy." It was Manuel who said it, and he suffered intense embarrassment as all eyes turned to him. He would have been happy had someone else added something, but when no one did, he was compelled to say, "You honor us this day, viceroy. I, Manuel de Soltura, join all others in welcoming you to our town."

Juan Soltura couldn't help but smile at his father. He loved him deeply and knew that he was a good and decent family man who'd worked hard to provide a rich life in New Spain.

But his love for his father was tempered by mild disgust at his blatant attempt to curry favor. He was glad when the viceroy diverted his attention from Manuel and focused upon the group of women of which his mother was a part. María de Jardinero was in that group, too. Iturrigaray drank in her beauty. He smiled and bowed forward from the waist. María coyly lowered her eyes.

The viceroy dismounted. He waved away soldiers who were attempting to control the crowd and greeted those citizens who stepped forward. He then approached the group of women in which María stood. She looked up at him and smiled.

"Buenos días, señorita," he said.

María curtsied. Her father, José, who'd been with the official greeting party, pushed through the crowd and stood at the side of his wife and daughter. He introduced his family to Iturrigaray, then introduced himself. Iturrigaray's relatively liberal posture after years of arch-conservative viceroys had always impressed José, and he vigorously shook the visitor's hand.

"Gachupine?" Iturrigaray asked.

"Sí."

The viceroy looked around the plaza. "Valladolid is beautiful. You are blessed in this valley."

"We count those blessings," said José.

"You are also blessed with a beautiful daughter."

"She inherits her mother's beauty, your excellency."

María did not show any embarrassment at the conversation. She felt, at that moment, as beautiful as the sky above, as regal as the ruling head of New Spain.

Others from the greeting party joined José and his family in a circle around Iturrigaray. The viceroy shook each man's hand and uttered some words of pleasure at being there. Finally, the ranking member of the town council suggested that it was time for Iturrigaray to attend a luncheon that had been prepared for him.

"Good," he said. "I am hungry."

"Then come with us," Manuel Soltura said, "A feast awaits you."

"I feel as though I have already feasted," Iturrigaray said to María.

"The most beautiful señorita in the valley," Manuel said hurriedly, casting a nervous glance at José. My son, Gordo, courts her. He would have been here to greet you, my vice-roy, but he rounds up the calves for his father.''

''Your son is indeed a fortunate caballero to court such a beauty.''

''*Gracias*,'' said María.

Iturrigaray turned his attention to Manuel. ''Your name again, señor.''

''Soltura, my viceroy. Manuel de Soltura at your service, and at the service of our king.'' Manuel was sweating profusely. The perspiration had come through his shirt and jacket and formed large dark rings beneath his arms.

The cabildo's leader motioned for Manuel to join him on the fringe of the group.

''*Perdóneme*, viceroy,'' Manuel said, bowing. He moved through the crowd and joined the cabildo leader, ''*Sí?*'' he asked.

''Manuel, you must remove yourself now. The luncheon for the viceroy is small and the list of invited guests does not include you.''

Manuel's face reflected his pain. ''*Por qué?*'' he asked. ''I was asked to join in the greeting party, was I not?''

''*Sí*, but the luncheon is reserved for gachupines only.''

''Then I protest. It is the criollo who makes this land grow. We are the majority, and to keep the viceroy from listening to us is ridiculous, a slap in our face.''

The cabildo leader tried to calm Manuel. He smiled and placed his hand on his shoulder. ''Manuel, tonight there is the festival at which everyone will speak with Iturrigaray, gachupin and criollo alike. But the luncheon will involve discussions of state, political matters that only a gachupin is privileged to partake in. Please, accept it. It is better.''

Manuel was close to tears. He looked to where his wife stood and wanted desperately for her not to be aware of the slight being inflicted upon him.

''Señor Soltura!'' It was Iturrigaray. Manuel turned in the direction of his voice. ''Señor Soltura, come here, *por favor*.''

Manuel gestured at himself. ''*Sí?* Me?''

''*Sí*,'' Iturrigaray said. ''Come here.''

Manuel was flustered. He fussed with the collar of his shirt as he moved through the crowd and stood in front of the viceroy. ''*Sí*, my viceroy?''

''You will join us at luncheon?''

''Well, I . . .'' Manuel was aware of the angry stares of

77

his gachupine friends. He look at José de Jardinero for guidance. José smiled, which was enough for Manuel. "Oh, yes, my viceroy, I would be honored. There was some mistake in the invitations for the luncheon. I was just correcting them when you called me. Yes, of course I will attend. There are many things I wish to bring up concerning the future of New Spain and the role of . . ."

"Come!" José said, anxious to spare Iturrigaray further speeches. "The food is plentiful and it awaits us."

Iturrigaray turned to María. "Señorita, perhaps I shall have the pleasure of seeing you later in the day."

"Of course," María said, curtsying.

"*Bueno*. Then let us eat. This servant of the king is a hungry one."

Iturrigaray walked briskly toward the tented area at the far end of the plaza. As he came abreast of the church he stopped and greeted Juan Soltura and Father Gomez.

"*Buenos días, padres*. I am Iturrigaray, viceroy of New Spain."

"*Sí*," said Juan. "Your arrival has excited Valladolid."

"I am pleased to hear that. You are the priests for this parish?"

"*Sí*."

"You must represent our God with skill," the viceroy said. "Your flock appears to be contented."

"We do our best," Juan said.

"I am sure of that, padre. The role of the church in New Spain is a vital one. Without it, we would still be dealing with savages."

Juan was tempted to respond but thought better of it.

Father Gómez said, "Their culture simply was different from ours, viceroy, in many ways superior."

Iturrigaray was taken back for a moment. Then he smiled and said, "Of course. The artists among the Indians are very talented. I, myself, have many of their art treasures. They inspire me."

Juan and Gomez said nothing.

"You are joining us at the luncheon?" Iturrigaray asked.

Juan shook his head.

"*Por qué?*"

Juan grinned. "We were not invited, viceroy. But had we been, we would not have accepted. The luncheon, as we understand it, will be spent discussing political matters. And, as parish priests, we are not political, as you know.''

The irony of Juan's comment was not lost on the viceroy. He frowned before saying, ''The church of New Spain is an extension of our king. Your work with the savages of this land benefits all, including our king. I insist that you join me for lunch.''

''Please, viceroy, it would be inappropriate,'' Father Gomez said.

''Nonsense! I wish you there to add your comments to what the politicians will have to say.'' He chuckled. ''I already know what they will say. Perhaps you can offer a different insight into the problems that face us all.''

Juan knew there was no sense in arguing further. He also knew that their comments were not really sought. The viceroy was constantly counseled by the church's hierarchy in all matters of state. The viceroy was simply being a shrewd politician. To exclude the local clergy would cause some citizens to question the viceroy's wisdom and intentions. And although Juan and Gomez did not wish to be used to enhance the viceroy's reputation in Valladolid, there seemed little choice. Even if Juan had decided to balk and to confront the viceroy with his refusal, that option was taken away when Juan's father, Manuel, proudly said to the Iturrigaray, ''This young priest is my son, Juan. He brings great pride to my household.''

Iturrigaray looked at Manuel and nodded. ''You are a man with much to be proud of, Señor Soltura. To have a son serving his god, and a son courting a beautiful gachupine señorita is more than most criollo men could ask for.''

Manuel didn't like the reference to his heritage but smiled and enthusiastically agreed with Iturrigaray. The viceroy turned on his heel and led everyone to the tent where Indian women waited to serve the meal.

At Iturrigaray's table were the leading members of the town cabildo. At his order, Juan and Father Gomez were also seated there.

''You will bless our meal, father?'' Iturrigaray asked Juan.

''Of course.'' Heads were bowed as Juan began. ''Father in heaven, we ask you to join us in this feast that you have provided. And, we ask that those less fortunate than those of us seated at this rich table be especially blessed by you and looked after.''

79

"Amen."

There was little talk of substance as the courses of the meal were served. A clear lamb broth was followed by a rich and thick tomato stew. Beef that had been braised in huge pans over roaring fires was heaped upon everyone's plate, the bubbling juices from the pans spooned over the meat by young Indian boys.

"Excellent, excellent," Iturrigaray said many times.

After the wineglasses had been refilled and mounds of sweet pastries on silver platters had been placed upon each table, the cabildo leader turned the discussion to more weighty matters.

"Viceroy," he said, "there is much speculation here in Valladolid on what will occur in the future in the north."

The viceroy shrugged. "What is there to be concerned about?"

José Jardinero said, "There are rumors that the Yankees plan to invade the northern territory, viceroy. It is said that spies have been sent from the United States under the guise of explorers."

"Nonsense," Iturrigaray said. "It is my policy that all of New Spain, including the northern territories, shall remain secure. I am committed to this and stand ready to send all the troops necessary to insure such a result. One day, it is possible that the Yankees shall be allowed to enter our nation and to settle there. But they shall do so only with my official blessing, and only if they become full citizens, observing our traditions and laws."

"That is good to hear," Manuel Soltura said from his chair at an adjoining table. "Allowing foreigners to live here could reap rewards for New Spain. To bring Yankee commerce into the north would create wealth for everyone."

"And problems," José Jardinero added.

Iturrigaray glanced at both men. He finally fixed on José. "What problems, señor?"

José drew a deep breath, then talked in slow, measured tones. "It would be a matter of new problems compounding old ones, viceroy. We live in a vast land and are spread very thin. The problems that face us here in the central and southern areas need considerable attention. To be faced with new problems to the north would, in my opinion, make it more difficult to proceed forward with solutions here."

Manuel stood at his place. "I disagree, viceroy. The future

of New Spain demands the settling of *all* areas. The future of the country is to the north, if I might be so bold to say so. I am not alone in this belief. I stand ready to serve our king, and you, should you decide to appoint loyal citizens to explore the potentials of the north."

The viceroy drained his glass. He was already slightly intoxicated. He ordered more wine from an Indian servant and asked José, "What problems occur here in New Spain that are so urgent, señor?"

José, too, had had too much to drink. Although his words were not garbled and his mind was clear, his inhibitions were sufficiently lowered to say things to Iturrigaray that might not have been said under different circumstances. He cleared his throat, collected his thoughts and began. "Viceroy, there will come a day when New Spain will achieve true independence. A wave of nationalism will wash over this land and unite us all into a common and unified people. Differences will be erased between Indian and Spaniard, gachupin and criollo."

Manuel was pleased to hear his gachupine neighbor spout off on such matters to the viceroy. He knew José's sentiments only too well and was confident that they would displease Iturrigaray. He lighted a long, black cigar and sat back as José continued.

"To this day, viceroy," José said, "there exists in New Spain a gulf so wide between its people as to appear impossible to close. And yet, this cannot be. Those who are born to this earth upon which we feast continue to exclaim the virtues of Cuauhtémoc. Those who have conquered this land remain true to the memory of Cortés. Neither of those men is alive today and yet their deeds remain imbedded in the hearts of those who would unify this nation."

Iturrigaray scoffed and asked for a cigar. It was given him by a servant. "Cuauhtémoc? Cortés? They are of ancient history. Yes, people love to sit in the cafes and debate the wisdom and deeds of those men who lived so long ago. But to point to them as being indicative of the problems of today's New Spain? Nonsense. We prosper here. The crops grow, the mines give up wealth beyond the dreams of most people. Our might grows daily, along with that of our mother country. No, señor, the only problem we face here in New Spain is to maintain order."

Juan couldn't constrain himself. "Exactly," he sputtered. "To keep order means to rid ourselves of the causes of discontent. It is not enough, viceroy, to quell unrest. The roots of the unrest must be hacked from the ground and burned before a nation can truly achieve greatness.''

Iturrigaray's annoyance at being attacked on two sides was evident. He drew the corners of his lips down and traced a pattern on the table with his index finger. Manuel Soltura sensed his discomfort and stood in back of his son. "This is a mistake," he said, his hands on Juan's shoulders. "This is a festive occasion to celebrate our good fortune in having the ruler of all New Spain visit us in Valladolid. Everyone! Raise your glasses in a toast to Iturrigaray." Manuel raised his glass and a number of the men beneath the tent followed suit. Iturrigaray looked up at Manuel with an expression of gratitude.

"To Iturrigaray," Manuel proclaimed. "To the future of New Spain."

It all happened so quickly that it wasn't until later, when everyone who'd witnessed what had occurred had had a chance to discuss it, that a relatively clear picture could be pieced together. As Manuel toasted the viceroy, an Indian boy of fifteen who'd been part of the crew serving the meal came around behind Iturrigaray, a long pointed dagger in his hand. No one noticed the dagger except Juan. He knew the boy, had given him Communion on many a Sunday morning, knew his mother who worked as a servant to the owner of one of the town's cafes, knew his sister who'd been inducted into the cafe owner's brothel.

Juan's reactions were involuntary. There was no time to think. He spun around, knocking the glass from his father's hand as he did. His grip on the Indian boy's wrist was sure and powerful, but not quick enough to prevent the dagger from sinking into Iturrigaray's shoulder. Had Juan not acted, the dagger would have found its mark squarely in the viceroy's back.

Chaos suddenly broke out as Iturrigaray fell forward from the impact and from the pain of the knife. Juan sprung from his chair and toppled the boy to the ground. Iturrigaray's soldiers raced under the tent, guns drawn, and formed a circle around the viceroy. Others reached down for the boy, who was covered by Juan. There were shouts of dismay from the men at the luncheon. Some called for the boy to be executed immediately.

The soldiers allowed Juan to help the boy to his feet. As

they looked at each other, Juan's eyes filled with even greater sadness than the boy's.

"Por qué?" Juan asked. He already knew the answer. The boy had reached the end of his patience. He'd been conquered, enslaved, reduced to animal status in a land that promised so much. Here was a living example of what José Jardinero had spoken of. The boy had done what he felt he must do, and Juan knew that no matter what his fate, it would be, in the boy's eyes and heart, far better than silently succcumbing to yet another Spanish master.

"May God bestow kindness on you, my son." Juan said, his fingertips resting lightly on the boy's forehead.

"Forgive me, father," the boy muttered as the soldiers grabbed him and dragged him from the tent.

CHAPTER ELEVEN

May 1805

María's mother stepped back and scrutinized her daughter's wedding gown. "The bodice is wrong," she told the Indian seamstress. "Look. The drawstring is visible. It bunches the silk about the bosom."

The seamstress, the hacienda's finest, protested but to no avail. The gown had been four months in the making. She had no desire to perform a last minute adjustment.

María was impatient with the bickering over what she considered to be insignificant details. She said, "If I thought there would be all this fuss, mama, I would have said 'no' to Gordo when he asked me to marry him."

"Nonsense," her mother said with a chuckle. "You have been fawning over Gordo Soltura since you were a young girl. I knew that one day you would marry him."

"You knew it, mama, and papa feared it."

"He has accepted it, María. Gordo has matured. He is now a settled young man."

María smiled. She knew better. Gordo had returned from the calf roundup determined to win María's hand. He told her he wanted to marry her. María's father, José, had accepted Gordo's charade of respectability and eventually gave his blessing to the marriage. As far as he could determine, Gordo Soltura had discarded his wild ways and had dedicated himself to establishing a solid base upon which he and María could build a married life. María, on the other hand, had few illusions about Gordo. He was, and probably always would be, a man in search of adventure. That need would probably include the pursuit of other women. Yet this realization had not deterred María from accepting Gordo's proposal. Her physical attraction to him was too strong to be tempered by reality. She would marry him and become the mother of his children. Problems could be dealt with later. Now, there was only the joy of a wedding day and the anticipation of the passion of that night. She felt it in her loins, a warmth and tingling that could, and often did, reach almost unbearable proportions.

The seamstress and María's mother began a spirited argument over the dress. Her mother finally said to María, "I still do not know why you refused to wear my wedding dress. I would have been so proud."

María knew how hurt her mother had been when she'd refused to wear her mother's wedding gown, which had also been the wedding dress of her grandmother and great-grandmother. María had almost relented, but something kept her from doing so. She felt the need for a fresh start, a desire to establish her own identity at her wedding to Gordo. She viewed this wedding day as the beginning of a new life, an entrance into a fresh new cycle of womanhood, adulthood. She wanted her dress to reflect it.

The seamstress helped María remove the gown. It had been copied from a design from England. It looked Grecian, although it was properly called an English chemise gown. Made of white embroidered lawn, it was cut low and had a longer train than the design called for, a creative touch by the seamstress. The waist was brought up close to the bosom, which accented the breasts to such an extent that José, María's father, had exclaimed upon first seeing it, "No daughter of mine will wear such a thing. It is disgraceful."

But María's mother intervened and the matter was forgotten in the hustle-bustle of preparations.

At the Soltura household, excitement rivaled that found in the Jardinero home. Gordo had been given a bachelor party the night before. It had been hosted by one of his friends from town, and although Gordo had promised himself not to become involved with another woman on the eve of his wedding, he succumbed to the charms of a prostitute who'd been imported to Valladolid for the occasion.

"Well, my son, how do you feel on this day?" Manuel Soltura asked Gordo.

Gordo had just gotten up. He wore a gold silk robe that had been a gift to him from his bachelor friends. His hair was tousled; he rubbed the sleep from his eyes and yawned as he took an apple from the table and inspected it for defects. "I feel splendid, papa. But I will feel better when all the ceremonies are over and I am alone with my bride."

Manuel laughed. "I don't blame you, Gordo. Every man in the valley envies you that." He quickly looked over his shoulder to make sure Señora Soltura hadn't heard.

Gordo bit into his apple and stretched. "And you, papa, you are happy this day?"

"Of course. Such good fortune has fallen upon all of us that only a fool would not be happy."

"Have you heard definitely about the assignment as empresario to the north?"

"No, but it is certain to come any day now. Juan has assured me that Iturrigaray favors me over all others for such an assignment."

Gordo smiled and took a large piece of fruit that had been picked that morning from a gigantic pitahaya cactus plant that grew behind the house.

"Life is ironic, is it not, Gordo?" Manuel asked, his face rounded into a broad grin. "To think that one could have a son who, because of fate, saves the life of a viceroy." He now laughed out loud. "And to think that that same son should be a priest. I don't know why this criollo, this fat criollo, has been so blessed, but I won't argue with it."

"I wouldn't argue with it either, papa, anymore than I would argue with having been born next door to the most beautiful woman in New Spain."

"In New Spain? It used to be just the valley."

"No matter. Will Juan come here before the ceremony?"

"No. He said he will remain at the church and insure that everything is taken care of. How do you feel, Gordo, being married by your brother?"

Gordo shrugged. "A priest is a priest, father. Just as long as he says the right things and doesn't take too long with it."

Señora Soltura entered the kitchen. She went to Gordo and hugged him. "Ah, the proud groom. Did you have a good time last night?"

"Yes." Visions of the whore writhing beneath him flashed through, and out of his head.

Margarita called for one of the servants to join her in the kitchen. "Have breakfast," she said. "A groom needs strength."

Manuel chuckled. He sat back and wiped his mouth. "Tell

me, Margarita, how do you feel about all the changes in our family?"

"Gordo's marriage? I am thrilled, of course, as I know you are."

"Yes, of course I am pleased. It isn't every criollo family that is blessed with the marriage of a son to a gachupine woman."

Margarita flung out her hands and made a sound of disgust. "All you talk of is gachupine and criollo. No wonder there are problems. If we stopped talking about them there would be no problems."

Manuel looked to Gordo. He shook his head at the stupidity displayed by Margarita. "Woman," he said, "the longer the differences are ignored, the longer they will remain. Tell me, have your views of moving to the Texas Province changed?"

"No."

"They had better. When my assignment of empresario comes through from the viceroy, you will have no choice."

"I know that, Manuel, but until the assignment does come through, I prefer to think of this as my home."

Manuel got up from the table and put his arms about his wife. "This will always be your home, Margarita. The home we establish in the north will only be temporary, until I have been able to effectively build an empire there. Then, we shall return."

"How are things at the sala?" Gordo asked his mother.

"*Bueno*. It will be a wedding feast that will be talked about for years to come."

Gordo yawned and excused himself. "I'd better begin to dress," he said.

"That's a good idea, Gordo," Manuel said. "Time flies by on a day such as this."

When Gordo was gone, Manuel asked Margarita, "You will happily accept a move to Texas, will you not?"

She turned and looked into his eyes. "I am your wife, Manuel. I go where you go. But I am concerned about such a move. I hear so many stories about life to the north, about the dangers."

Manuel hugged her. "And I hear stories about the wealth to be made there. Besides, to receive an appointment from the viceroy for so important a mission brings great glory to every criollo in New Spain."

Margarita wanted to say more about her husband's plans and ambitions but decided not to. She wanted nothing to upset the wedding day, especially since her one son would be married by her other son. In all honesty, Margarita Soltura was more excited about Juan's role than she was over Gordo's marriage to María. But she would never acknowledge such feelings, to others or even to herself. "Go," she told Manuel. "Dress. The father of the groom, especially such a successful criollo father, must look good." She kissed him on the cheek and watched him leave the kitchen. Then anxiety gripped her and she touched a countertop to support herself against it. Margarita suddenly felt that the rich, happy life she'd known for so long in the valley would change dramatically into one of sorrow.

"Foolishness," she muttered to herself. "Christine, *adelante!*" she shouted to a servant. "There is much to do."

"You look beautiful," María's mother said to her as she gave a final inspection before leaving for the church. "Just like a painting."

María's maid of honor, Cortina, agreed. "Gordo is a lucky man," she told the bride.

"I hope he feels that way," said María.

"Of course he does," said her mother. "All he does these days is brag about you."

María smiled and picked up a fan she would carry. It was made of whalebone and delicate white lace. "To think, too, that I shall be married by my husband's brother. It makes it more special somehow."

Cortina giggled. "If Father Juan weren't a priest he would have every girl in Valladolid after him."

María stifled a smile. What her friend had said was true. Much gossip revolved around Juan Soltura. Young girls who sat in the congregation during his sermons found it difficult to concentrate upon his words. Standing there in the pulpit, he seemed to exude an aura of intense masculinity, of thoughtful sexuality. The thoughts behind his words were fueled by a divine wisdom and insight into the core of everyone's existence. The congregation, so used to sermons full of abstract Catholic dogma, had trouble initially adjusting to the more humanistic approach of Father Juan de Soltura. But once they did, there was a general consensus that the Mass carried more meaning. At least, people joked, fewer people slept during the sermon.

And always, there were the pretty young girls who were infatuated with Valladolid's newest priest.

María's mother said, "Come now, María, we must leave. The carriage is waiting."

"María said, "I would rather ride Tormenta."

"That would be a fine thing," said her mother. "A bride in her gown riding into town on such a horse."

María's maid of honor giggled. "It would be funny," she said.

María, too, giggled. "Yes, it would. Imagine, riding up to the front steps of the church on Tormenta. I could wear my riding hat with the gown." Cortina laughed even harder, and María kept pace. "Can you see Gordo's face?"

Even María's mother managed a smile despite her annoyance. "Come, come," she urged, pushing María toward the door. "It is time to go. You mustn't be late for your wedding. It's bad luck."

María and Cortina looked at each other and tried to stop laughing. It was hopeless, and they left the room holding their sides.

María rode in the carriage with her mother and father. Other carriages followed carrying various members of the wedding party. As the carriages reached the plaza of Valladolid and came to a stop in front of the church, Father Juan de Soltura was standing on the steps to greet them. He wore the priest's traditional marriage vestments, surplice and white stole. He offered his hand to María. She took it and gracefully stepped down to the ground.

"You look lovely, María," Juan said.

María looked into his deep blue eyes and wondered, for a moment, whether a force hadn't been exerted that would physically draw her into his arms. Ashamed of her thoughts, she thanked him for the compliment and turned to watch the others alighting from their carriages.

"Gordo is a proud and happy bridegroom," Juan said. "He waits inside."

"But he musn't see her," María's mother said. "Not until she comes down the aisle."

Juan laughed. "Gordo has been told not to look into the church until it is time for him to approach the altar."

María's mother breathed a sigh of relief. "Thank you,

Father Juan. It is so good to have you here in Valladolid so that you might marry María."

"It is my honor, Señora Jardinero. Our families have been close for many years. It is good to keep things within families."

Manuel Soltura joined his son and the Jardinero women. "A beautiful day for a wedding," he said, looking up into a pristine blue sky.

"Yes, God has blessed us with such weather," Juan said. "Well, I must return inside. Father Gomez will assist me in the ceremony."

"Yes, my son, go inside and hasten this wedding. I am anxious to get to the feast. The food will be the finest in the valley, I'm told."

"He thinks of his belly at a time like this," Señora Soltura said as she joined them.

Manuel laughed and patted his stomach.

Everyone entered behind Father Juan and took seats on the appropriate side of the church. Manuel couldn't help but notice that as the church filled, the division of the bride and groom's families created an almost perfect split of gachupin and criollo.

José Jardinero, too, noticed it, and wished he'd asked that the families be mingled. With the bride and groom crossing over class distinctions, it would have seemed appropriate for everyone to mix. But it was too late, thought José, and probably just as well. As long as the day went smoothly for María. That was all that counted.

The church organist, a young gachupin who'd arrived from Spain less than a year ago, began to play a theme by the Spanish composer, Padre Antonio Soler. It was a slow sonata heavily influenced by Alessandro Scarlatti, who'd been one of Soler's teachers. The sounds of the pipe organ filled the church and could be heard far across the plaza. Juan, who had just finished preparing items to be used in serving Communion, closed his eyes for a moment and allowed the rich organ sound to wash over him.

He opened his eyes and looked into the gold chalice he held in his hands. The pained face of the young Indian boy who'd attempted to kill the viceroy appeared, undulating in the claret. Juan forced the image from his mind and turned his attention to what was occurring inside the church. The bridal party was poised at the back. To the right of the altar stood Gordo, his father and his best man.

The organist played a processional and María, her gown's train held up by a six-year-old flower girl from a neighboring hacienda, took slow and tentative steps down the aisle. Juan stood at the Communion rail and awaited her arrival. He didn't want to think about her beauty and the effect it was having upon him, but to stop the thought process was like telling oneself not to think of purple donkeys.

María's father stood at her side as Juan softly spoke secular words of welcome to the house of Christ. He turned and motioned for Gordo to join María. Gordo said something to his best man and they both laughed. Then, with a smile upon his broad and handsome face, Gordo joined his bride-to-be.

CHAPTER TWELVE

The fiesta began at eight. As was the custom, the bride and groom stayed apart for the afternoon and early evening. María napped, then joined her mother in the kitchen for what José termed, "women-talk."

Gordo entertained his male friends in his home. They drank wine and played cards. By the time the fiesta began, Gordo was quite drunk and, as was usually the case, the alcohol heightened his bravado.

The sala was packed from the beginning. The orchestra played spirited rhythms and rich melodies from the bandstand. They were the finest musicians available for hundreds of miles, and José Jardinero had spared no expense in hiring them.

When the orchestra had completed its first set, a flamenco guitarist and a singer mounted the stage. They were from the city of Chilpancingo and were considered the best in New Spain. The guitarist, a thick-necked, stocky native of southern Spain, began with a customary prelude consisting of a flourish of running notes and rich arpeggios. The effect was dark and somber, gypsy music based upon the *cante hondo*, Spain's traditional deep, tragic song. He continued to build the prelude, note upon note, chord upon chord, until he'd created a musical tension that had captured everyone in the sala. People moved closer, so spellbinding was his music.

Then, as the guitarist complimented the strength of the music by adding a thumping, rhythmic pattern on the instrument's wooden neck, the singer, a tall, aristocratic woman dressed in flaming red and carrying a black fan, began a long, drawn-out melody using only the syllable *"Ay!"* Her voice was resonant and flexible. She swooped up to exquisite highs and down to booming lows, the guitarist following her to perfection, every note and chord enhancing her vocal magic. Their duet, seemingly without pattern and yet so closely knit as to seem a single voice, continued until the singer suddenly broke off the duet with an ending phrase of great finality.

"*Ole!*" every guest in the sala shouted.

Slowly, plaintively, the guitarist and singer moved into the main body of the cante hondo. Her voice was filled with passion. When she would stop for breath, the guitarist filled in the spaces with short cadenzas. There was, in the performance, all the pain of lost love, the intensity of Moorish passion and conquest, the history of all Spain.

María, who'd learned the cante hondo at school, found the urge to dance almost irresistible. Her feet tapped along with the pulsating rhythms of the guitar. She looked around the crowded sala. Juan and Father Gomez were close to her. So were her mother and father.

Her husband as of that day, Gordo Soltura, stood at the front of the crowd, a bottle of wine in one hand, a large slab of lamb in the other.

"*Caramba!*" he yelled. He handed the lamb to a friend standing next to him and moved to a small space in front of the flamenco performers. He looked at María and beckoned for her to join him. She shook her head. He was too drunk. His steps were hesitant, his gait awkward and lumbering.

José Jardinero looked on with disgust. His new son-in-law was making a spectacle of himself at his own wedding feast. José winced as Gordo tripped and had to be propped up by other guests. A silly smile was painted on his face. He raised the bottle above his head and resumed his pitiful attempts to dance the flamenco.

María, too, was unhappy at seeing the man she'd married carrying on so. She'd wanted to be with him at their feast, dance with him, share in the joy of the day. But he'd arrived drunk, and had continued to drink from the moment he walked into the sala.

"The bride! The bride!" some people called. "The bride must dance."

A woman next to María urged her to join Gordo but María shook her head.

"Come on," Gordo called to his wife. "Get up here." He

took a swig from the wine bottle. It was now empty and he threw it to the crowd.

José turned away and walked to a corner of the sala. Two of Gordo's friends who'd been drinking with him all afternoon joined him on the dance floor. They presented a comic threesome as they bumped into each other, giggling and strutting, one of them assuming the role of a woman and thrusting his pelvis at Gordo. Gordo laughed and mirrored the pelvic thrust.

"Excuse me," María said to those around her. She pushed through the crowd and left the sala. The night air was cool. The stars were obscured by low gray clouds. It would rain before daybreak.

María walked to a tree that grew off to the side of the building, leaned against it and allowed the tears to flow. Her weakness made her angry. She was not the first bride to stand by and watch a new husband drink too much at the celebration. It happened all the time. Some of her friends told her such stories of their wedding days.

It would be different for her, she had thought. Gordo would not disappoint her, not after having pursued her with such ardor for so many months. And yet, he had.

She wiped her eyes with a handkerchief and was about to return to the sala when Juan walked up behind her. He startled her, and she let out a tiny, involuntary gasp.

"I didn't mean to disturb you, María. Are you all right?"

"All right? Yes, of course. It's a wonderful party."

"Yes. Would you like some water?"

"No, *gracias*, father. I . . ."

"Oh, my goodness, María, you still insist upon calling me father. I am Juan de Soltura and, for the Jardinero family, always will be."

María managed a smile. "I'm sorry, but I don't think I could call the man who'd married me by his first name."

"Well, you must, or I shall never marry you again."

María looked at him, then laughed.

"Seriously, María, you must forgive my brother. He has a spirit for life that sometimes goes beyond its boundaries. He celebrates his marriage to a beautiful and wonderful señorita and drinks too much. It will be better in the morning." Juan stopped. He didn't have the heart at that moment to explain away his brother's actions to María. What he wanted to do was to tell her that his brother was unworthy of her, that she deserved far better than a cruel and drunken carouser, some-

94

one with sensitivity and commitment, someone whose love for her would be deep and abiding.

Himself!

"I know," María said. "Gordo has always been and, I suppose, always will be a boy. But how I would have loved to have danced tonight. Yes, this night of all nights in my life. I love to dance."

"Then dance."

"I'm afraid. He might stumble and knock me down."

Juan smiled. "Yes, there is a danger in dancing with one as big as Gordo." More danger than just in dancing, he thought.

María placed her hand upon Juan's arm and looked warmly at him. "May I tell you something, Juan?"

"Sí."

"Today, at the altar, I had thoughts that I had no business having."

"Sí? What thoughts?"

"Of you."

"Of me?" He forced a laugh. "I would hope so. I was, after all, conducting your marriage ceremony, was I not? How could you not think of me?"

"I didn't mean that. I meant . . ."

"Wait, María, don't say what is obviously difficult for you to say. Leave such things unsaid."

"I'm sorry, Juan. I must go back to my wedding feast."

"Of course. Enjoy it, María. Dance by yourself if you must, but dance. Moments must not be lost in one's life. Our lives here on earth are too transitory to be wasted."

María stood up straight and placed both hands on Juan's arm. She felt it tense beneath her touch. "Thank you, Juan," she said.

"For what?"

"For being here. Are you coming in with me?"

"No. I think I shall retire for the night. I leave tomorrow, you know, for Dolores."

"Por qué?"

"I will meet there with other priests."

"About what?"

"Church matters, María. And you? I never did ask Gordo what your plans were after tonight."

"The house built by Martego, on the Cruz hacienda, will

95

be ours until we build our own here. We go there in the morning.''

"I shall miss you."

"And I shall miss you, Juan. Father Juan."

Her lips brushed his. "Good night."

"Buenas noches, María. Sleep well."

As María walked back toward the sala, Juan had to forcibly control himself from calling after her. The vision of his drunken brother climbing into bed with her twisted his stomach in knots. He closed his eyes and muttered, "Forgive me, Father, for I sin. I lust after my brother's wife. Forgive me, forgive me."

He walked toward the house, intending to seek the familiar and comfortable refuge of the basement where as a boy he'd been able to escape the harshness of the real world. But before he reached it, the sound of a multitude of horses' hoofs approaching from the west brought him to a standstill. Juan turned to see who approached at such speed and in such numbers. In minutes, a column of mounted soldiers passed through a clump of trees and proceeded directly toward him. Juan waited until they came abreast of him. The officer-in-charge halted the column and looked down from his horse.

"Hola! Qué tal, padre?"

"Bien, gracias."

"You are from this area?"

"Sí. This is my home, and my parish."

"You can help me then, padre. I look for Señor Manuel de Soltura."

"Oh, *sí*. It is my father. He is over there, in the sala. My brother celebrates his wedding tonight."

The officer looked toward the sala and grinned. *"Bueno, bueno, padre. Muchas gracias."*

Juan asked, "Pardon, señor, but for what reason do you wish my father?"

"I bring him good news, padre. Viceroy Iturrigaray has personally approved him to become empresario to the north. I also carry personal greetings to your brother on his wedding day." The officer leaned closer to Juan. *"Sí, sí,* I am sorry padre. You are the priest who saved the viceroy's life."

Juan nodded.

"What a pleasure. Please, padre, you must join us when we give your father his good news and read the greeting to your brother and his bride."

Juan protested but the officer insisted. Juan did not want to return to the sala but he saw little choice. It would be wrong not to share in his father's joy at receiving the news, or to avoid the pleasure his entire family would experience in having a personal message of congratulations delivered to Gordo and María.

"Sí," Juan told the officer. "I will come."

The arrival of the soldiers brought everything to a standstill in the sala. The officer-in-charge was introduced to Manuel.

"Welcome, welcome," Manuel said, his round face beaming. "What an honor. You bless this feast."

The officer strode to the bandstand and raised his hands for quiet. Gordo tried to collect his wits. He staggered to where María stood with her father and put his arm around her.

"Atención! Atención!" shouted the officer. Some of his men called for order, too. "I am here as personal representative of the viceroy of New Spain, Iturrigaray. *Uno.* The viceroy sends his personal regards to the newlyweds . . ." he consulted a piece of paper, ". . . María de Jardinero and Gordo de Soltura."

Everyone applauded.

"Dos. The viceroy wishes me to inform Manuel de Soltura that he has been appointed empresario to the province of Texas, in the colony of New Spain."

Manuel was surrounded by well-wishers. They hugged him, slapped his back and guided him to the bandstand where he joined the officer.

After most people had stopped talking, Manuel said, "My friends, this is the most important day of my life. I stand here before you the happiest man on earth. My son has married a fine woman. My other son lives his life as a messenger of our Lord and, because he walks with Christ, has been given the courage and strength to have saved the life of New Spain's viceroy, the honorable Iturrigaray. Finally, I thank my God for the generosity of the viceroy in choosing me to be empresario to where the future greatness of New Spain lies, the vast northern province of Texas." Manuel suddenly turned and hugged the officer-in-charge. Tears ran freely from his eyes. He was joined on the bandstand by his wife and by Gordo, who stumbled as he attempted to scale the platform.

Manuel hugged Gordo, then beckoned for María to join them. She shook her head but those next to her physically lifted her off the floor and carried her up onto the platform. She stood next to Gordon and smiled at the crowd.

"*Atención! Atención!*" Gordo cried. "I wish to say something."

Juan winced as his brother grabbed his father's shoulder for support.

"Yes, give us a speech, Gordo," a friend called.

"I need wine."

Gordo took a bottle that was handed up to him and drank from it. Some of the wine ran from the corner of his mouth and dripped onto his black velvet jacket that was already stained.

"Amigos, listen to me," Gordo shouted. "Tonight, you have heard of the great honor bestowed upon my father. He has been given it because he is known as a man of daring and courage."

The crowd roared its approval.

"Well, tonight I wish to make an announcement of my own. Until tonight, until it was known for certain that my father would become empresario to the north, we could not speak of what plans he would make. Always, my father asked me to join him in the north. And tonight, amigos, I tell you that I will!"

María was stunned. She looked at Gordo, then at her father-in-law. Valiantly trying to hold back her tears, she turned to the crowd and forced a smile. There, directly in front of her, was Juan. It was obvious to him that Gordo had never discussed the possibility of accompanying Manuel to Texas. Gordo and María were to build a house and remain in the valley. Juan looked at María and tried to give her courage and hope, but he knew it was futile.

María stayed at Gordo's side until he, Manuel and the officer had descended from the bandstand. The orchestra started playing again and everyone began dancing.

Gordo wrapped his arms around María and tried to lift her from the floor but she resisted. He laughed. "We leave here in a few minutes, my wife. We go to bed." He tried to kiss her but she turned her face away.

He roared with laughter and said to one of his friends, "See? See how my bridge is modest with me? But wait until later."

The officer who'd brought the messages from Iturrigaray

accepted Manuel's offer of wine and food for him and for his men. "Juan," Manuel called to his son. "Come. Join us."

"*Sí*," the officer said. "I wish to drink with the man who saved the life of the viceroy."

"*No, por favor*," Juan said. "I am very tired and must journey to Dolores tomorrow."

"Dolores?" the officer said, his bushy black eyebrows raised. "Be careful in Dolores, padre. There is much trouble there."

Juan knew of what the officer was speaking. Reports had filtered back from Dolores from Father Hidalgo. The local authorities were beginning to clamp down on his activities with the Indians and mestizos. The porcelain factory was in full operation, and the authorities saw it as a threat to civil order. Recently, Hidalgo had been brought up on charges of fomenting unrest among the citizens of Dolores. Unable to prove it, the authorities worked through the church and resurrected charges that had been made against Hidalgo in 1800. At that time he'd been accused of having perverted his spirit and vision by reading heretical works.

This time, he was severely warned that unless he contented himself with simple parish work and ceased to become involved with matters outside his religious purview, he would be suspended.

Juan thanked the officer for his advice. He said good night to those around him and went to the house. He found in the basement the stub of the candle he'd burned during his farewell party years ago. The small mirror, too, was still there. He lighted the candle and looked into the mirror. The image that looked back at him was vastly different than it had been before he'd gone off to study for the priesthood. The face in the mirror was hard and determined. His eyes appeared to be aflame, as was his soul.

A surge of strength caused him to tense. His body seemed to contract, every muscle ready to carry out his mind's order.

"We will act!" he said to the mirror. "In your name, my Father, we will act to right injustice. The time is near."

Having said it, he relaxed his body. He sighed, took one last look at himself in the mirror and blew out the candle.

CHAPTER THIRTEEN

July 1806

Manuel Soltura sat beside his wife on the bench seat of their horse-drawn wagon. Behind them in another wagon rode Gordo and María. A succession of wagons carried other residents of New Spain who'd joined the Solturas on their trek to the northern provinces. Oxcarts hauled supplies needed for the long journey. A small contingent of soldiers assigned to the north territory rode beside the caravan on sturdy horses of assorted coloring and marking.

"Look, Margarita, ahead of us, on the river," Manuel said. He pointed to a long, thin line of burros and mules being driven across a shallow portion of the Río Grande.

"*Qué es?*" Manuel shouted to one of the soldiers. His voice snapped the soldier to attention, who'd been dozing as his horse matched the slow progress of the wagon train.

"*Qué?*" asked the soldier.

"There," said Manuel, pointing.

The soldier followed the direction of Manuel's finger. "*Conducta,*" he said.

"For Santa Rita?" Manuel asked.

"*Sí, señor.* It brings supplies from Chihuahua. Everything comes from Chihuahua. I have escorted it in the past."

Manuel nodded. He looked at Margarita, whose face was grave. "To protect against the Indians," she murmured.

"There is nothing to worry about, woman," Manuel said, not at all certain of his convictions. He turned to the soldier, whose head had slumped forward again. "*Gracias.*"

"*De nada, señor,*" the soldier replied, not looking up.

Manuel and Margarita watched as the convoy completed its river crossing and moved upstream, in the same direction as the Soltura wagon train. Both would eventually end up in the mining town of Santa Rita. The Solturas would remain there overnight before proceeding to their destination, Santa Fe, in the foothills of the Sangre de Cristo Mountains, where the Rio Grande and the Pecos came together.

Santa Fe had become the commercial center for the southwest. Traders, trappers and adventurers from the east had blazed a well-worn trail to Santa Fe from the booming towns of Kansas—Leavenworth, St. Joseph, Weston and Martin—an 800-mile journey through arid plans and windswept mountains, across swollen rivers and icy lakes. Many had died on the trail as hostile Indians vented their rage at having their sacred territory intruded upon, and as the ravages of nature often attacked with all the potency and surprise of an Indian raiding party.

But these factors did not deter those whose lives were ruled by the desire for adventure, and the promise of riches. Each year had seen a greater number of travelers on the trail, and their proliferation was one of the reasons Iturrigaray had granted empresario status to such men as Manuel de Soltura. If it was inevitable that foreigners would seek their fortunes in New Spain, then it was only prudent to see to it that they did so under the supervision and control of Spanish authority.

In the second wagon, Gordo Soltura stood and peered at the convoy in the distance. The slowness of the journey had taken its toll on his nerves. When Manuel had begun making plans for the trip, Gordo had wanted to be sent ahead. He'd estimated that he could make the 1,400-mile journey in two months or less if not encumbered by wagons and oxcarts and the needs of women and children.

But Manuel had overruled him. He'd explained to Gordo that he wanted his son with him, not only out of fatherly pride but because Gordo's strength and experience would benefit everyone. What Manuel did not tell his son, however, was that there was also an element of jealousy involved in his decision. Manuel wanted to be the first Soltura into Santa Fe. It was he, after all, who'd received the assignment from the viceroy; not Gordo. When the members of the Santa Fe greeting party stepped forward to offer their hands, which they surely would, it would be Manuel's hand that would be shaken first.

Gordo looked over at María, who sat next to him. She appeared tired and drawn. Black circles had begun to appear below her eyes over the course of the long trip. She'd said little and had not complained, but Gordo knew that she'd wanted to stay in the valley, in Valladolid, and raise a family. One child had been conceived almost immediately after the wedding. It hadn't happened on the wedding night. Gordo had been too drunk to consumate the marriage and had fallen asleep after feeble, impotent attempts to penetrate his bride. But the next night found him fully potent and erect.

It had not been the pleasurable sexual experience María had anticipated. Although Gordo's physical appearance was arousing, his perfunctory lovemaking left María frustrated and angry. There had been no tenderness that first time, no gentle loving and stroking, only hard kisses and almost instant penetration into a dry socket that was painful for her.

Nor had it improved over the ensuing months. Of course, her pregnancy had interfered to some extent. Gordo had become angry upon hearing of his wife's pregnancy because it directly interfered with plans for the trip to the north. The physician who tended the citizens of the valley advised María not to travel while in her condition, and she took his advice. Manuel and Gordo tried to change her mind. They assured her that the trip would be leisurely and without physical hardship. She'd almost agreed in order to appease her husband, but her mother and father, along with Margarita Soltura, insisted the trip be postponed. It was, until María miscarried in her fourth month.

María's pregnancy had not been the only cause for delay. Another time the trip was postponed because of Indian uprisings in the north. A third delay had to do with anticipated weather conditions.

Now the trip was almost completed. María Soltura sat beside her husband and silently considered what had occurred in her life. So much, and yet so little. No joy. Where was the joy, she wondered? There should have been joy in marrying the valley's most handsome caballero.

She looked at him as he shifted on the seat, the reins held loosely in his large, calloused hands. She knew how impatient he was with the trip and had tried to comfort him, but to no avail. Their lovemaking had become even more unpleasant. At night, in the back of their wagon or on blankets in the tents they carried, he roughly handled her and used her to release his passions and frustrations. He'd consumed much of the whiskey that had been loaded onto the wagons for trading purposes with Indians who might be encountered along the way, and was drunk a good deal of the time.

The wagon train reached Santa Rita at sunset.

A group of ragged Indian and mestizo children greeted the travelers with pleas for money. A few of them had been deliberately maimed and disfigured in order to enhance their appeal.

Manuel Soltura brought his wagon to a stop on the edge of town, and he and Margarita looked around them. Santa Rita consisted of one long, wide dirt road that separated two rows of dilapidated shacks. The ramshackle dwellings were constructed of logs and odd-sized pieces of lumber, grass and mud. Their roofs were dirt and clay. It had rained the night before and portions of some roofs had slid to the ground.

Large puddles covered the road. A clapboard saloon stood at the far end. It was the largest structure in town. Behind it was a clump of tiny shacks in which prostitutes, who'd been imported to service the miners, plied their trade. Unlike the puddles on the main road, the pools of water in front of the whores' shacks were always there. The women emptied their douche buckets by tossing the water out their front doors.

"*Éste pueblo es un asco,*" said Margarita, her face emphasizing the disgust she felt at what she saw.

"*Sí,*" Manuel said. He placed his hand on her shoulder in an attempt to soften her revulsion.

Gordo leaped down from his wagon, stretched and called to his mother and father. "Over there," he said, pointing to an open area next to the saloon. "They play *el gallo.*"

"*Qué es?*" Margarita asked.

"A game. We play it on the range," Gordo said. "Come, we'll watch."

María remained seated on the wagon. "Come, María," Gordo said, offering his hand.

"No," María said. "I don't feel well."

"Nonsense. I want you to see it. I am the best el gallo player in the valley. Perhaps I will join them and you can see for yourself."

"Leave her, Gordo," his mother said. "She's pale. Besides, I would rather prepare for the night. We are all tired."

Gordo would not be put off. He grabbed María's hand and almost yanked her to the ground. "I want you to see."

They walked toward the saloon, past the shacks where the copper miners lived. Some of the soldiers who'd accompanied them from Valladolid walked with them, their destination the saloon where the sound of tinkling music and raucous laughter could be heard. Two drunken miners, bottles in hand, staggered from one of the shacks and almost knocked María over.

"Watch it," Gordo snarled at them.

"Please, Gordo," María said. "Let's go back to the wagon and prepare dinner."

Gordo laughed and waved his hand at the miners, who'd stopped and waited for him to make a move against them. "Have a good night," he said. The miners smiled and continued on their way.

It wasn't until the Soltura family had almost reached the scene of the action that María realized what the game of el gallo was. The men on horseback were taking turns at making passes at the head of a terrified rooster who'd been buried up to the neck in the dirt. One after another the men raced by, leaned over and reached for the rooster's head.

"Caramba, caramba!" Gordo yelled.

One of the riders took a long swig from a bottle, then tossed it to a vividly painted whore who stood beside his horse. He sat back in his saddle and measured the distance to the rooster. He then dug his heels into his horse's flanks and raced toward his target. Swiftly, deftly, he leaned over, one hand holding on to his saddle's horn, and yanked the rooster from the ground with his other hand. Without breaking stride he turned in a tight circle, raised the rooster above his head and violently swung it around and around. Its neck snapped. The horseman returned to the whore and tossed the dead bird to her. She giggled and allowed it to drop to the ground.

"El gallo, el gallo!" some of the bystanders shouted. "More, more."

A flurry of betting activity sprung up among the bystanders. The bets were placed on individual horsemen and whether they could pluck the next rooster from the ground in a single pass.

The horseman who'd succeeded moments earlier was a favorite. He'd dismounted and embraced the whore. She held the bottle up to his lips and he drank much of what was left in it in a long, continuous swig.

Gordo looked around the crowd. An older miner held the reins of a speckled mare. The horse's saddle was light and simple, as opposed to the heavier gear Gordo was accustomed to. Gordo went to the miner and whispered something to him. The miner nodded and handed the reins to Gordo.

"What are you doing?" Manuel asked his son.

"I will play the game, papa. Place a large wager on me."

María winced as she watched another rooster being placed into the ground, its head barely visible. She said to Gordo, "Please, let's go back."

"Not now, woman. I will show you how el gallo is really played."

María looked away as Gordo mounted the mare and rode to where the other men waited for the next round to begin. They eyed him with suspicion. One of the riders asked him who he was.

"Gordo de Soltura. I am from Valladolid."

The man looked to a companion and grinned, exposing a mouth filled with gold. "From the south," he told his friend. "Where the women tell the men what to do." They giggled.

Gordo controlled his urge to strike out at the man. Instead, he said, "Do you wish to bet me?"

"Bet you? Of course."

When they'd agreed upon a price, Gordo turned his attention to the rooster. It was almost dark now. Faint magenta streaks on the horizon were all that was left of the daylight.

Another prostitute who'd emerged from her shack to watch the game openly flirted with Gordo. He returned her attention, oblivious to María's eyes that were trained upon him. The whore approached Gordo and held up a bottle of whiskey. He took it, drank from it and handed it back. *"Gracias, señorita,"* he said, wiping his mouth with the back of his hand.

Someone lighted a pile of dry brush and tree limbs near the rooster. The flickering, yellow flames illuminated the bird and magnified the terror in its eyes.

"Vayase al cuerno!" an impatient spectator shouted.

The winner of the previous game looked at Gordo and nodded. "You first, señor."

"Sí," said another contestant. "You can have first chance."

Gordo said, *"Sí."*

The rooster had been buried deeper than the previous one. Gordo knew he would have to literally scrape his hand along the ground if he were to have any chance of grabbing the exposed head. And he'd have only one pass. If he missed, he would lose. If he succeeded, other roosters would be buried until everyone had had a chance. Those who succeeded would then be matched up until one remained victorious.

"Let's go," Gordo was told.

"*Sí,*" he replied. He dug his heels into the horse's sides and moved toward the rooster. The mare was not swift but she held a straight and steady course toward the target. Gordo leaned to his right and allowed himself to slide from the saddle and to hang close to the ground. His left hand gripped the reins; his powerful legs were locked around the mare's torso.

His hand made contact with the ground just before he reached the rooster. His fingers clamped together, the rooster's head between them. The impact of being torn from the ground instantly snapped the bird's neck.

A roar welled up from the crowd.

Gordo proudly rode to where his father, mother and wife stood. He was grinning broadly. He held the dead rooster out in front of him, like an offering. Margarita and María looked away. Even Manuel found something uncomfortable in the situation. "Well done, Gordo," he said quietly.

"Collect your money, papa. I will win, no matter how many passes it takes." He looked down at María. "What's the matter, woman? Your man is the best here. Why don't you praise him?"

María looked up at him. "To snatch a helpless bird from the ground, Gordo, and to break its neck does not please me. What would please me is to have dinner with my husband and to talk of pleasant things."

"Then go, María. Go cook. Your husband will have dinner with you after he has won el gallo." Gordo turned the mare and rode to where the other riders stood in anticipation of the next pass. The woman who'd given Gordo a drink winked at him and pouted her lips. He laughed and tossed the dead rooster to her.

No other rider managed to grab the bird during that round of el gallo, which left Gordo the winner. He collected some bets he'd wagered on himself, returned the mare to its owner and looked into the darkness for his family. Only Manuel remained.

"Well, papa," Gordo said as they walked along the dirt road through town, "what did you think?"

"You ride very well, Gordo. I have always known that."

"Did you see me grab the head? I have done it so many

106

times on the range. Most men are afraid to hang so low from the horse, but it does not frighten me."

"*Sí*, Gordo." Manuel stopped and placed his hand on his son's arm. "My son, I must say something to you."

"*Sí*, papa?"

"Soon we will all be in Santa Fe, which will be our new home for a long time. It is there that the Soltura name will gain prominence. We will be looked up to in the community, even though we are criollos."

Gordo nodded and looked over to where a prostitute was being carried on the shoulders of two drunken miners. They'd come out of one of the miner's shacks and were headed for the saloon.

"Gordo, listen to me."

"*Sí*, papa."

"You have a fine and beautiful wife. She will bear you fine sons and make you proud."

Gordo looked down at his father. "So?"

"So, Gordo, treat her better than you have. She deserves to be treated with respect and love, just as I treat your own mother."

"María is treated the way a woman should be treated, papa," Gordo snapped. "Besides, it is my business how I deal with my wife, not yours."

Gordo went to step away but Manuel grabbed him. "No, Gordo, it is my business. What happens to you and María reflects upon me in my new position in Santa Fe. I do not wish to be embarrassed by a son who leaves his wife at night for a whore, or a son who drinks too much whiskey and makes a fool of himself."

Gordo shook off his father's hand and guffawed. "Nonsense," he said. "María is tired, that is all. She loves this caballero and I love her. Do not worry, papa. You son will make you a proud criollo."

Manuel said nothing. He turned and walked to where the wagons had been drawn into a loose circle at the edge of town. Behind the wagons were the mines of Santa Rita, caves dug into the low hills from which an abundant amount of copper was taken daily.

Fires burned brightly in the wagon circle. The women of the caravan were busily preparing the evening's meal. It would consist of corn cakes, the last pork from a barrel and a large portion of wet beans.

A chill was in the air. The night's stillness was intruded upon by the plaintive howl of a wolf somewhere in the hills. The faint sounds of music and laughter from the saloon drifted in and out of the camp.

The soldiers had set up their own fires and were cooking their own dinner. A few of them had been positioned on sentry duty but they dozed as they sat on the ground and leaned against the wagon wheels.

Gordo looked for María in the cluster of women around the fires but didn't see her. He went to their wagon and pulled open the flaps of its cloth top. María lay upon a makeshift bed that took up most of the wagon's covered interior. Gordo scrambled through the flaps and roughly fell on top of her.

"Please, Gordo, you hurt me."

Gordo laughed and reached into a crevice between the bed and the wall where he kept whiskey and wine. There was a half-filled bottle of wine. He pulled the cork from it with his teeth and took a long, slow drink. "You want some?" he asked María.

"No."

Gordo dropped the bottle to the floor of the wagon and fondled María's breast. She murmured a protest but he squeezed harder. His other hand ran up her thigh and pressed against her crotch.

"Please, Gordo, I do not feel well."

He grunted and tried to pull her skirt up to her hips. She struggled beneath his weight, her head twisting to avoid his kiss.

"La puta," he growled.

Having her husband call her a whore lit a fire within María. She brought up her arms beneath his chin and jerked them into a rigid barrier. As Gordo's head snapped back, María managed to free her right leg. She brought her knee up into his groin and held it there.

"La puta, la puta," Gordo snarled as he continued to try to kiss her. His lips found hers. She bared her teeth and bit into the fleshiness of his upper lip. He yelled in pain. María felt a trickle of his warm blood on her face.

Gordo sprang up on all fours and glared down at the face of his wife. "Bitch," he said as he brought back his hand and slapped her across the face. He hit her again, and again. Blood ran freely from her lip. Tears flowed down her cheeks but she did not make a sound. She lay there, a placid, almost angelic expression on her face.

Eventually, Gordo climbed off her and left the wagon.

María drew deep breaths and closed her eyes against the pain of her face. She placed her fingertips on her belly and pressed lightly. There was again life in there. She knew it, had known it for over a month. A son. Perhaps a daughter. She desperately wanted to touch what was inside her, to stroke it and comfort it against the pain it might have suffered in concert with its mother.

María's tears had flowed silently while Gordo had struck her. Now, they gushed forth. Her sobs racked her body and shook the wagon. An ache radiated from her heart. She sat up and clenched the heavy cotton comforter beneath her. Still clutching it, she slid across the bed and out the flap of the wagon's covering.

It was now totally dark; the only illumination was provided by the campfires.

"María!" Margarita Soltura had come to the back of Gordo and María's wagon because she was worried about her daughter-in-law.

María didn't respond. She ran to where the horses had been tethered and fed. Tormenta, her favorite since childhood, stood in the midst of the other animals and ate from a mound of wild desert grass that had been gathered by Indian servants.

"María!" Margarita called again.

María continued to ignore her mother-in-law. She yanked Tormenta's reins free and flung herself up onto his bare back. She dug her heels into his sides and urged him from the pack. Margarita, who was out of breath from running, reached the horses just as Tormenta carried María free of the pack. She could only stand and watch as her daughter-in-law disappeared into the distance, past the mines and toward a vast plain of barren land to the west.

María never looked back. She urged Tormenta to greater speed across the black, hard ground. She knew it was dangerous to ride with such abandon across unfamiliar, unlighted territory but she didn't care what happened to her. She wanted only to be alone and free. The contemplation of injury and even death did not frighten her. She desperately needed peace at the moment; and to be alone with her beloved horse, with an endless black blanket of sky above, helped to wipe away the tears and the lingering pain of Gordo's blows.

Alone? Who dwelled inside her as she rode? The thought of carrying another child as the result of Gordo's brutal love-making filled her with disgust that caught in her throat and threatened to make her vomit. She emitted a long, woeful cry as she deliberately headed the horse toward a low rise of rock and gravel. As Tormenta stumbled up it, Maria's body slammed against his massive back, harder and harder, up and down, the impact of rider and horse audible above the noise of his hoofs on the gravel.

They reached the top of the rise. Maria pulled on the reins and Tormenta came to a halt. He snorted; his breath shimmered upon the moon's rays.

And then María felt it, a warm expansion within her groin, a letting go of something, detachment, fluid movement of blood and tissue.

She slumped forward and wrapped her arms around Tormenta's neck. What had been inside her was out now. A life had been ended before it had had an opportunity to grow.

"Forgive me," María said to the sky above her. She thought of Juan, Gordo's brother, and her vision of him in his clerical robes caused her to weep.

She turned at the sound of horses approaching. Gordo was on one, a soldier on the other.

"María, what are you doing?" Gordo asked.

"Leave me alone," she said.

"Come home. Stop this nonsense. It is time for dinner."

A wolf howled from somewhere far away.

"Do not disobey me, woman," Gordo snapped, concerned at the soldier's reaction to seeing his wife defy him.

María sat up, turned to Gordo and smiled. "Yes, Gordo, I will come home for dinner." She turned Tormenta and they descended the long, gradual hill. The wet warmth between her legs no longer upset her. She felt she had spared a child a life of anger and cruelty at the hands of its father. "No," she told herself, "my child will be born to someone loving and gentle, someone who is not so much a coward as my husband."

The campfires and the aroma of food greeted her as María returned Tormenta to the pack of horses. Once he was secured, she went to her wagon and disposed of her loss. Then, her head high, she joined her family for dinner.

CHAPTER FOURTEEN

August 9, 1806

The expedition into the uncharted territory of New Spain, led by Captain Zebulon Pike, was now a reality.

In the expeditionary force were three noncoms, sixteen privates, an interpreter named Baronet Vasquez, a physician, Dr. John H. Robinson, Lieutenant James B. Wilkinson, the son of General James Wilkinson, now governor of the Louisiana Territory, and Robert and John Barrigan, father and son.

It had been more than two years since the Barrigans had been summoned to New York City to meet with Aaron Burr. As promised, Bob Barrigan had advised Pike within two weeks of his intentions concerning the proposed expedition. He'd put it simply: "Me and my son would be right pleased to go with you, captain."

But as the delays mounted, the elder Barrigan began to doubt seriously whether the expedition would ever get underway.

Two events occurred during the two-year delay that threatened to confirm Barrigan's pessimism.

The first one had to do with Aaron Burr's defeat in his run for the governorship of New York. As predicted, the role played in Burr's defeat by Alexander Hamilton proved to be significant. More than that, Hamilton seemed to enjoy crowing about it in public, and in the press.

Burr was infuriated with Hamilton's behavior. He wrote to him and demanded both a public apology and a retraction in the newspapers of certain statements Hamilton had made. Hamilton refused on both counts and Burr challenged him to a duel.

The duel between the former vice-president and Hamilton

took place late on the afternoon of July 11, 1804, in Weehawken, New Jersey. Hamilton was mortally wounded by Burr and died ten hours later, on July 12.

Burr was naturally ebullient over his personal victory, but public reaction did not support his joy. Dealing with the public reaction to the death of Hamilton took an inordinate amount of Burr's time, and kept him from focusing on the mission to New Spain. Burr began to worry that he would lose President Jefferson's support for the expedition. He went to Washington and convinced the president to send Zebulon Pike and the force Pike had assembled on another expedition, this one to explore the headwaters of the Mississippi River. Burr was afraid that the long delay would result in losing the services of Pike and his men. Better to have them intact and working for him than scattered about and involved in other projects.

Pike did undertake an exploration of the Mississippi. He never did find the mighty river's headwaters, but he returned with a force both hardened and experienced. The president was disappointed in Pike's failure to accomplish the mission and almost balked at allowing Burr to launch the New Spain expedition. But by this time Burr had become even more determined to establish a personal stake in the vast southwest. Public life was no longer viable for him. His only hope of reestablishing a power base was to create his own empire. New Spain would be that empire.

Eventually, after much persuasion, President Jefferson relented and told Burr to proceed with the plan to explore the commercial potentials of New Spain. Pike's force, including the Barrigans, gathered in St. Louis and, on August 9, 1806, headed west up the Missouri River and the Osage until arriving at the Grand Osage Indian village on the Little Osage River. They'd picked up along the way a party of Osage Indians returning to their home on the Verdigris River. Despite Lieutenant Wilkinson's objections, Zeb Pike agreed to travel with them. His decision was supported by Bob Barrigan, who dismissed Wilkinson's protestations by saying, "Hell, lieutenant, since they're goin' the same way we are, might just as well join up with 'em. I reckon we'll be spendin' lots of time with these sort of folk before this trip is over."

The Grand Osage village on the Little Osage River consisted of over one hundred dwellings of various sizes and shapes, which housed close to 2,000 people. Five miles to the southwest sat what was called Little Osage village. It, too, was a sprawling complex in which approximately 1,500 Osage lived, a fourth of them warriors.

The Indians traveling with the Pike party agreed to enter the Grand Osage village first and to assure the chieftains that the white men were peaceful and wished only to sit in council and to trade.

But Bob Barrigan felt it would be prudent to have once of the Pike expedition accompany the Indians into the village. "I'd feel a little better knowing just what it was they were sayin'," he told Pike.

"I'll go," said his son, John.

"Nope," Bob said. "I've picked up a pretty fair amount of their language by now. Let me put it to use."

Pike and his men waited a mile upriver. They dispersed in the midst of an abundance of wild grapes, berries and roses that grew along the riverbank.

Zeb Pike and John Barrigan slipped out of the packs they'd carried and sprawled out in soft, green grass. The ten-day journey from St. Louis had been uneventful and relatively easy. The weather had been warm and gentle, with only a single day of rain to interfere with the normal progress of the trip.

John looked up into a sky that had begun to cloud over and said, "I reckon we can't have this weather all the way, Zeb. We'll be hitting north country just about the time the snow sets in."

Zeb stretched and laid his head upon the ground. "Can't choose the weather, John. Can't choose lots of things in life."

John was silent for a few moments. Then, he began to laugh heartily.

"What's so funny?" Zeb asked.

"I was just thinking about that night in New York City. We sure didn't choose much of what happened then, did we?"

Zeb, too, laughed. "That's for certain. Do you know what I've been thinking for the past few days, John?"

"Tell me."

"I've been thinking about that little Irish lass in the dance hall. I liked her, John. I truly did."

"Her pa liked you, too, Zeb."

Pike sat up and rubbed the stubble on his chin. "Sad folks, weren't they?"

"Oh, I don't know, Zeb. There are lots of sadder folks in other places."

Zeb nodded and again laid his head upon the soft grass. He said nothing for five minutes. Then, with a resigned sigh, he muttered, "I do hope the Spaniards don't misjudge us when we get there."

John, who'd also been resting, lifted his head and asked, "In what way, Zeb?"

Zeb shrugged. "Oh, I don't know. It's just that I've had some strange thoughts recently about this mission. It all sounds so nice and easy, just a simple expeditionary force to evaluate trade possibilities in a new part of the land. But a few things came up back in Washington with Mr. Burr that make me wonder about just why we're on our way to New Spain."

"What sort of things?"

Pike laughed. "I'm talking too much, I guess. And please don't get me wrong, John. I'm not questioning Mr. Burr. He was our vice-president, after all."

John Barrigan did not allow his cynicism about public officials to surface. But his curiosity had been piqued. What had come up in Washington to cause this dedicated young officer to question the integrity of the mission? He asked.

Pike waved his hand against the question. "Just forget I said anything, John."

John sat up and looked across the river to a dense field of fruit-bearing pitahaya bushes that grew wild along the bank. For a moment he considered dropping the subject. But he couldn't.

"Come on, Zeb, level with me. What things happened back east?"

Pike looked around. Lieutenant Wilkinson was far away, out of hearing distance. Zeb leaned on an elbow and said, "The general has been making a few comments back east that worry me. I'm not supposed to have heard about them, John, but I did and I can't change that."

"What sort of comments?"

"Well, he's said to a few people that this mission is more than a commercial venture for Mr. Burr. He claims, as I hear it, that Mr. Burr just wants to set up his own little private empire down in New Spain."

Barrigan sat up and whistled. "I don't reckon Mr. Jefferson would take kindly to that scheme."

"That's for certain. Of course, John, this might all be nothing but rumor. Folks in government seem to love rumors. That's all some of them seem to do, pass rumors."

John Barrigan laughed. "Well, all I can say, Zeb, is that if those rumors are correct, there might be some fireworks upcomin'."

"Worse than that," said Zeb, standing and brushing off his clothes. "It could amount to treason, and that's not calculated to advance this soldier's career."

Barrigan stood and looked toward the Osage village to which his father had accompanied their Indian traveling companions. The village was hidden behind low, rolling hills. A brilliant, setting orange sun melted into the hills and cast a warm glow over the countryside. Ripples in the river caught its rays and appeared to be flickering streaks of fire.

"Look, Zeb, here they come."

Pike looked in the direction of the village. A dozen men on horseback rode over the crest of a distant hill, then disappeared behind the next rise, only to reappear on its crest ten minutes later. Eventually, Bob Barrigan led the others with him, all Osage Indians, to where the Pike party waited.

"Howdy, pa," John yelled.

Barrigan nodded at his son. "Captain," he said to Zeb Pike, "this here is White Hair, the chief of the Great Osage village."

John and Zeb looked up at the chief. He sat regally upon a painted horse. A heavy deerskin robe, decorated with streaks of vivid color and studded with tinted shells and stones, flowed from his broad shoulders. He was obviously older than the others with him, although it was difficult to judge his age. His eyes were piercing beneath a headdress of multicolored feathers. He was expressionless. Not a muscle in his face moved.

"It's an honor," Zeb Pike said.

"This here's my son, John," Bob Barrigan told White Hair.

John nodded. "Thank you for havin' us in your village."

Bob Barrigan coughed and cast a discreet glance at John. "We might have a bit of a problem there, son." He looked to where Baronet Vasquez, the translator, stood against a tree. Vasquez was angry at having been left behind when Barrigan went to the village, and had sulked the entire time. "Mr. Vasquez, come on over here."

Vasquez didn't move. He looked at Lieutenant Wilkinson who, like the translator, was annoyed at having to take orders from Barrigan.

"Mr. Vasquez, front and center," Pike ordered.

The translator stood in front of Bob Barrigan and White Hair. Barrigan told him, "We're on good terms, the chief and me, but there seems to some problem with having us stay in the village overnight. I really don't understand enough of what he says to figure it out. Maybe you can."

Vasquez, whose primary mission was to translate from Spanish into English but who possessed a working knowledge of Indian dialects, nodded and asked some questions of the chief.

Finally, after the chief had answered Vasquez's questions, the translator said to Barrigan, "He says that since we are to proceed to the west and will probably meet with the Kansas tribes, that we will tell his enemies of his strength here in the village."

Barrigan shrugged. "Why would we do a thing like that?"

"It doesn't matter, Mr. Barrigan. That is his fear."

"How much do you figure it'd cost, pa, to get him over that fear?" John asked.

Bob Barrigan smiled. "Let's ask. Hate to admit it but every man does have his price, don't he?"

Vasquez asked White Hair whether adding to the gifts the group had already planned to give him would change his mind.

White Hair turned and muttered something to another Indian, a young and imposing warrior named Yellow Feather. He then said to Barrigan, "Weapons. If we have weapons it would make it less important that the Kansas know about us."

The older Barrigan looked at Zeb Pike.

Pike shook his head. "We can't tell just what we're going to need along the way in firepower, Mr. Barrigan. We're not overloaded with weapons as it is."

"Spare a few?"

"Certainly. Three or four rifles."

Barrigan instructed Vasquez to tell the chief that if the group could remain in the village, the tribe would receive three rifles.

"Three?" White Hair turned to Yellow Feather.

The young warrior shook his head.

"More," White Hair said.

"Can't," Barrigan said emphatically.

During the conversation, the physician traveling with the Pike contingent, John Robinson, had remained in the rear, with the noncoms and privates. Bob Barrigan spotted him and motioned for him to come forward. He said to White Hair, "Four rifles, chief, and the use of our doc here to treat any sick folks in the tribe."

"Doc?"

"Doctor."

Vasquez used the Osage word for medicine man.

White Hair indicated that the tribe was already blessed with a fine medicine man.

"Not as fine as Doc Robinson here," said Barrigan. He looked at Robinson. "Hey, doc, how about showing White Hair here what you carry in your bag of tricks."

Dr. Robinson looked at Barrigan for some indication of what it was he was supposed to produce.

"Go on, doc, show him," Barrigan again urged. "You know, the little doll and the thermometer." The doll to which Barrigan referred was a small model of a naked human male body on which the major arteries and veins had been painted in red. It had been copied from the original by the British physican, William Harvey who, in 1628, had discovered the body's circulatory system.

The thermometer was an old centigrade model.

Robinson stepped forward, opened his little black bag and withdrew the thermometer. He handed it up to Chief White Hair who scowled as he turned it over in his fingers. Yellow Feather came abreast of the chief and stared at the thermometer. He said something to White Hair, who nodded in agreement.

"What's the problem?" Dr. Robinson asked.

"We have seen this before," the chief said.

"Go on, go on, give him the doll," Barrigan said. He'd been fascinated with it since the night the doctor showed it to him early in the trip.

The doctor did what Barrigan asked and handed the six-inch mannequin to White Hair. This time the chief's face did not show displeasure at the item from the bag. His eyes clearly showed him to be fascinated with the doll, and when he handed it to Yellow Feather, his face, too, reflected interest.

The chief asked what the red lines represented on the doll. Dr. Robinson started to reply through the translator but Barrigan shut him off. "Let us spend the night in the village, chief, and we'll explain it all to you. And, remember, there'll be three rifles to go with it."

"Four," Yellow Feather said.

Barrigan shrugged and looked at Pike. The captain smiled and nodded.

"Four it is," said Barrigan.

Without another word White Hair turned his painted horse and led the entire Pike force into the Great Osage village. Their arrival caused much commotion within the village's population. Men, women and children lined the wide spaces between dwellings and chattered in singsong, high-pitched voices.

Pike's men were told to make camp on the outskirts of the village, near where the river narrowed and hooked around its northernmost perimeter. While camp was being created, Pike, Wilkinson, Dr. Robinson, Vasquez and John and Bob Barrigan followed White Hair to his home, an adobe, one-story building with a roof of buffalo hides. They were told to wait outside. The chief returned with two women and two men. One of the women was old and stooped. The other was young, no more than eighteen. Her hair was jet black and pulled tightly behind her head. She wore a deerskin dress that hung gracefully from her neck. The outline of full breasts could be distinguished against the deerskin, and both John and Zeb shared an instant appreciation of her charms.

Nor were those charms lost on Lieutenant Wilkinson. He'd married shortly before embarking on the trip to New Spain. His decision to marry had been based upon the same pessimism shared by Bob and John Barrigan, that the mission would never get off the ground. When it finally did, Wilkinson was forced to abandon his wife of one month to the care of her family. He ached for her, and nights spent sleeping alone on the hard ground often found him wide awake and engaged in whispered conversations with her.

White Hair introduced those he'd brought from his house. The woman was his wife, the young girl his daughter. Fleet Fire was the daughter's name. Her black eyes blazed with life as they took in the white men.

The two men were the chief's sons. He told the younger one to fetch the medicine man, whom he called Spirit Stick.

To his older son he said, "Go to the Little Osage village and bring The Wind to me."

As the son ran off, Barrigan asked who The Wind was.

"Chief of other village to the south. I am *his* chief, but he rules those who live there."

"Looking forward to making his acquaintance," Bob Barrigan said, spitting tobacco juice on the ground.

"You have brought food with you?" White Hair asked.

"Yes," the translator replied.

"It is yours to share with us," John Barrigan said.

White Hair shook his head. "You are our guests this night. You will share our food."

"Much obliged," Bob Barrigan said.

"What's for grub?" John Barrigan asked, which caused Zeb Pike to grin.

"My son wishes to know what food we will share with you," his father said.

"Meat from the mighty beast. And the red fruit from the ground."

"Red fruit?" John asked.

"Must mean squash," Pike said, his eyes never leaving the gentle rise and fall of Fleet Fire's bosom.

When The Wind, chief of the Little Osage village, arrived, White Hair and the leaders of Pike's group joined him for dinner. Buffalo meat was grilled over buffalo "chips," buffalo dung, long a favorite fuel on the plains because of its quick kindling properties, and its ability to retain heat. The taste of meat cooked over it was not unlike meat seared over hickory coals.

The squash had been cooked in a huge stoneware vat and was firm and tasty.

Everyone sat on the ground around a brightly burning fire that was continually fed by young Indian boys. White Hair, as the senior and ranking member of the large combined Osage tribe of that area, was served first. When he had tasted the food and was satisfied that it was of good enough quality, he allowed his guests to be served.

Fleet Fire, White Hair's daughter, sat with her mother and a half dozen other female members of the tribe in the shadows of the tent in which the food had been prepared. Although they tried to appear disinterested in the men's conversation, their occasional giggles at a comment, or their increased attention when a subject was introduced that especially caught their interest, gave them away.

One of the Indian woman, who was only slightly older than Fleet Fire, whispered to her, "The tall white man makes your heart wander, doesn't he?" She was referring to John Barrigan.

Fleet Fire smiled. "Yes," she said, "he has a strength I have not seen in other white men."

The other girl grinned. "Yellow Feather would not approve of your interest in him."

Fleet Fire gave her friend a stern look. "You cheapen me with such talk. I am to marry Yellow Feather because it is my father's wish. I will obey my father, although it is not my desire to marry Yellow Feather. You should watch your tongue. My father, who is chief, would not appreciate your interest in Yellow Feather, the man to whom I am promised."

After dinner, White Hair's medicine man, a wizened Indian with a tuft of hair on his chin and a disoriented look in his green eyes, handed out tiny pieces of an unidentified root to each person around the fire.

"What's this?" Bob Barrigan asked.

"It soothes one after dinner," said the chief. "Chew on it and you will relax."

The root did have a mild narcotic effect, and a general calm pervaded the gathering. White Hair asked to see the magic doll he'd been shown by Dr. Robinson. He scrutinized it, then handed it to the medicine man.

"What is this?" asked the Indian healer.

"The human body," Zeb Pike said. "Inside. You and me. All of us. Those red lines are the blood."

The medicine man held the doll close to his face. He turned it slowly, over and over. Finally, he dropped it to the ground and muttered a string of what sounded to be Osage courses.

Chief White Hair said something to the medicine man that was harsh and obviously critical of what he'd said. The medicine man stood and glared at Dr. Robinson. He uttered one final malediction and left the campfire.

"Not a very pleasant fella," John muttered to his father.

"A man hates to have his territory invaded," the elder Barrigan said.

Bob Barrigan turned to White Hair. "Chief, I know I speak for Captain Pike, Lieutenant Wilkinson and everyone else when I say that all we want is to be able to stay here a spell, rest up and do a few things President Jefferson would like to see done."

White Hair grunted and put another root into his mouth. "What things?" he asked.

Zeb Pike said, "Make some maps, take a census, things like that, chief. President Jefferson has sent us here for only one reason and that's to see about opening trade with everyone in this territory. He sees the west as being the future of America, for white men and Indians alike."

Yellow Feather snorted and spit the remains of his root to the ground. His position as a member of White Hair's inner council was secured by past bravery in battle, and by the fact that he was to marry Fleet Fire. Of all the members of the council, Yellow Feather was the most militant. His distrust of the white man was well known among Osage tribes, and it was only the moderating instincts of the tribe's elders that kept Yellow Feather and those who followed him from waging all-out war against what they considered unwelcome, untrustworthy invaders.

It took two days for White Hair, The Wind and the other members of the council to decide to allow Pike's force to remain in the village and to take a census and develop maps of the region. It was not a unanimous decison. A dissenting faction led by Yellow Feather argued vehemently against it, but they were voted down.

Yellow Feather's attitude toward Pike and his men was not mitigated by the obvious appeal John Barrigan had for his intended, Fleet Fire. The girl's eyes seldom strayed from John, and when the tribe's women were called upon to serve food or to help in other ways, Fleet Fire made it an obvious point to serve the younger Barrigan.

One night after dinner, after Pike's force had been in the Great Osage village for a week, John decided to bathe in the river. Fleet Fire, who'd been busy washing dinner utensils, noticed him walk away from where he and Zeb Pike had been working on maps.

After he'd been gone ten minutes, Fleet Fire hurriedly completed her assigned chore and slipped from the circle of women who'd now begun their nightly ritual of gossip. She looked over her shoulder to see that no one was watching her, then moved through a clump of pine trees that stood between the village and the river.

The moon was full. The previous evenings had been cool;

this night had seen a moderation in temperature, and a heavy, humid air mass had settled over the village.

Fleet Fire paused at the far edge of the trees. Below her was the river, tranquil and shimmering in the light of an almost full moon. Ten yards from the bank stood John Barrigan. The water came up to his waist. The sculpture of his upper torso, muscular, taut and void of any excess flesh, was further defined by the moon's illumination.

Fleet Fire watched as John bent over, cupped water in his hands and poured it over his head. A cake of soap made from sotol stalks provided a thin lather which he worked into his chest and shoulders.

Fleet Fire knew she shouldn't move any closer to him, knew she should go back to the village. But it was as though a magnetic force pulled her through the mesquite grass, down a gentle, rocky path leading to the riverbank. Within minutes she was standing next to the pile of clothing John had dropped on the ground before entering the river.

He didn't notice her for a few moments. When he realized someone was watching him, he turned, saw that it was her and smiled. "Good evening, ma'am," he said, not the least bit embarrassed at his nakedness.

"Hello," Fleet Fire said, averting her eyes as he took a few steps toward her. The water dropped a little lower on his body, but his hips and legs remained covered.

"Nice night, ma'am."

Fleet Fire looked up at the moon. She felt a tremor pulse through her body, and although it was sensual, she refused to acknowledge sensuality as its source.

It suddenly occurred to John that the situation was more awkward than it might have been had the girl been white. The fact that this girl was of another culture, one at increasing odds with his own, caused him to pause before coming any closer. His father had always told him not to become involved with any of the Indian girls they'd met in their travels, "Touchy business," his father had said. "Injuns don't like white men messin' around with their women. Problem is, son, that with some tribes, you touch 'em, you keep 'em."

John Barrigan had always heeded his father's advice. But this Indian girl was different. He'd come to that conclusion days earlier. She was the most beautiful Indian girl he'd ever seen. No, even more than that, she was more beautiful than any girl, Indian or white, he'd ever laid eyes on. She exuded a quiet, serene sensuality that had caused his blood to boil on more than one occasion. Once, Zeb Pike had noticed and had made a joke about it.

It was happening again, and John mentally checked that the water covered his erection.

"I was dirty," he said sheepishly.

Fleet Fire, whose English had been honed by a Baptist missionary in the village during her teenage years, suppressed a giggle.

"The water is warm," John said.

"I know," she said. "This is where I, too, bathe."

John could only fantasize at what Fleet Fire looked like in the river, naked, flanked by dozens of other female members of the tribe. There was an unstated but clear-cut understanding within the tribe about the day designated for females to bathe. Every male in the village went about his daily routine as usual, except that no one ventured near the trees that separated the village from the river. The intent was clear: to view a female from the tribe while she bathed was to dishonor her. Those young braves who violated the tradition were punished by being tied to a stake in the center of camp, their hands behind their backs, clothing stripped from them, eyes blindfolded while various members of the tribe, male and female, walked past and taunted them, physically and verbally. Sticks were poked into their bellies, their genitals were swatted with leafy branches and their names were linked to the most vile of the tribe's historical figures.

"It's a beautiful night," John said.

"Yes."

"If I come out and get dressed, could we talk?"

Fleet Fire looked back toward the village. She saw no one. "Yes," she said.

John started toward the bank. When the water dropped to his genitals, he bent his knees and laughed. "You turn around," he said.

Fleet Fire turned her back as John left the river, quickly dried himself with his shirt and slipped into his pants.

"All right," he said.

Fleet Fire was startled that his voice was so close to her. She turned and was only a yard away from him. His physical presence, naked to the waist, drops of river water beaded on his shoulders and chest, excited her. She feared her excitement showed in some overt way, and she lowered her eyes.

"You got nothin' to be afraid of with me," John Barrigan said. He reached out and touched her cheek with his fingertips. Her skin was warm and smooth.

"I should not be here," Fleet Fire said.

"It's all right. We're just talking."

She shook her head. "No, you do not understand. I am to be married."

"I know. To Yellow Feather."

"That is right."

"Do you love him?"

"Love? That is not important. Yellow Feather is a brave and respected warrior. I have been pledged to him by my father, which is my father's right."

Barrigan whistled. "I don't agree with that thinking," he said. "Seems to me a woman should marry who she wants."

"You are not an Osage. We have different customs than you."

"I'm certainly aware of that, Fleet Fire. But we're not doing anything wrong standing here and talking. Tell you what. Let's sit down over there, under that tree. If anybody bothers us I'll explain. No one will think anything bad about the two of us talking."

Barrigan slipped into his shirt, picked up his boots and led Fleet Fire to a gnarled fruit tree that stood alone on the edge of a pine grove. The sweet smell of wild roses filled the still night air and added to the sensuousness of the moment.

At first, Fleet Fire hesitated. Then, she reached out and accepted John's outstretched hand.

They sat next to each other under the fruit tree, their bodies touching, not looking at each other. A wolf's plaintive cry from the nearby hills was, at once, painful and erotic. Two vampire bats fluttered up from the tall grass and disappeared into the pine grove. A few tribe members in the village had begun to chant and to make music. Their sound could barely be heard, but it was enough to remind John and Fleet Fire that they were not alone.

"I don't reckon Yellow Feather thinks too highly of us," John said.

"I do not understand."

"Your fiance. He doesn't like white folks much."

"That is correct. He sees all white men as enemies who come here to drive us from the land."

"That's not true, Fleet Fire." John turned and looked into

her dark eyes. "All white men aren't the same, and the same goes for Indians. You've got to judge a man individually."

"Yellow Feather is young," Fleet Fire said. "He will gain wisdom when he is older."

John didn't want to sound so skeptical but it came out that way. "Sure," he said, placing his hand on top of her hand, "but by that time you'll have been married for years to a man you don't love."

Fleet Fire made a move to leave. John held her wrist and said, "Please, don't go. I'm sorry. I've got no right to talk about things that ain't my business. I'm sorry."

"I should return to the village. They will be looking for me."

As hard as John fought the urge, his lips were drawn to hers. They touched, gently, tentatively, then pressed together until their lips parted and their tongues melded into a soft, warm and wet core of pleasure. John's hand found her breast beneath her deerskin dress. Fleet Fire moaned. She turned and pressed her body tight against his.

The fire within each of them had flared until it singed their senses, clouded their reason with the smoke of passion. Their hands moved over each other in a desperate search for their respective inner cores of pleasure. John had pulled her dress up to her hips. She was naked beneath it, and his fingers brushed her thick, coarse pubic hair. As he probed through the hair and touched the outer lips of her sexual being, her moan joined that of a distant jackal in heat, and her hand gripped his fully engorged manhood through his trousers.

It took every fiber of strength in John's body to disengage from her and to sit back against the tree. His breathing was heavy. His heart raced.

Fleet Fire pulled down her skirt.

"Look, Fleet Fire, I . . . I want you more than I've ever wanted any woman in my life. The only problem is that some big trouble could come out of this. I've got a job to do here and it's an important one. Captain Pike and my pa wouldn't take too kindly to having me mess things up by . . . *falling in love with you.*"

Fleet Fire stood and smoothed her dress. She reached down, took John's hand and helped him to his feet.

"Take me with you," she said, her fingers laced tightly with his.

"You? With me? I don't think I could . . ."

Fleet Fire was the first to hear the sound of feet on the gravel path. Then John heard it, too. They turned and saw Yellow Feather and two other young braves standing twenty feet from them.

John braced for an attack that did not occur. Without a word, Fleet Fire walked up the trail and joined the braves. The four of them turned and walked toward the village, leaving John Barrigan alone. Their passivity left him confused, and more apprehensive than had they attacked him. He slowly put on his boots, drew a deep breath and climbed up the trail to the unknown fate awaiting him and everyone else in the Pike expedition.

"Be a man about it," he muttered to himself. "It's done. Just be a man."

CHAPTER FIFTEEN·

The first thing John Barrigan did upon returning to camp was to inform his father and Zeb Pike about what had happened at the river. He didn't want any surprises sprung on them.

The following day went smoothly. Members of the Pike camp went about their tasks of mapping the region in which the Osage tribe lived, and in trying to take an accurate census of the residents of that region. It wasn't until late in the afternoon, about an hour before dinner, that the elder Barrigan and Zeb Pike were summoned to White Hair's residence. The chief appeared troubled. He sat rigidly in a chair behind a homemade table and fixed his visitors in an icy stare.

"I reckon you wanted to see us because of my son," Barrigan said.

"Yes, that is true," the chief said.

"My boy told me all about it, White Hair, and the way I figure it, there weren't anything that happened to make anybody mad."

"You are not one of us, Mr. Barrigan. Your ways and culture are not ours. It is for me to decide whether your son has brought dishonor to my daughter, to me and to her people."

Pike, who'd taken a seat in the corner of the room, stood and walked to the only window. He looked out over the activity of the Osage village and gathered his thoughts. He turned and said to White Hair, "No one, especially my friend, John Barrigan, meant any offense to you or to your people, chief. Talking to your daughter should not be a cause for anyone to be unduly upset."

White Hair slammed his fist on the tabletop, stood, and leaned on it. "I allowed you into my village because I trusted your intentions. When a man is a visitor to another man's house, he respects and obeys the laws of that house, even if they are not his own laws." He looked at Bob Barrigan. "Your son has violated my daughter's honor and integrity. Yellow Feather, one of my bravest and most trusted warriors, was to marry Fleet Fire. It was Yellow Feather who observed what took place between your son and my daughter near the river. Your son touched my daughter in her most private parts, and kissed her as a husband would kiss a wife. It was seen and observed by Yellow Feather, and I do not doubt his word."

Barrigan had not expected such a vehement response from White Hair. While he had anticipated some trouble stemming from John's brief moments with Fleet Fire, he assumed the meeting with the chief would result in only a reprimand and a stern warning that it not occur again. But it was becoming obvious that there were to be more ramifications then a simple verbal scolding.

"I can't do a thing, chief, except to apologize for my son and to ask him to personally do the same to you, to your daughter and to Yellow Feather. Back where we come from, a man's apology is respected. My son feels badly that this happened and I can assure you that for as long as we remain here as your guests, nothing of this sort will happen again."

"And, as captain of this expedition, I give you my word as an officer and a gentleman," Pike added.

It appeared for a moment that White Hair was appeased. The rigidity with which he had held himself seemed to relax somewhat. His face softened and he sat in his chair with weary resignation.

Bob Barrigan said, "If you would like to summon your daughter and Yellow Feather here, I'll see that John is here to apologize to everyone."

"I am an old man, Mr. Barrigan," said White Hair. "My days are filled with the problems of the survival of my people as other tribes wage war with us, and as the white men from the east scheme to take our land from us. The affairs of the heart are of little concern to me at my age. Were I free to follow my own instincts, I would accept your son's apology as sufficient payment for his wrongdoing. But my people live under very strict laws that have been handed down from our ancestors. As chief of this tribe, I am responsible for seeing that those laws are obeyed, and that those who would violate them are punished, no matter who they are and no matter what culture they come from. According to our laws, my daughter has violated her trust as a woman. She has committed adultery and must be punished for that. To do less would dishonor her further in the eyes of the man who is to be her husband, a man I personally chose for her. I have spoken with Yellow Feather and he has informed me that he will decide by the time of the full moon tonight what punishment shall be inflicted upon Fleet Fire.''

Zeb Pike felt his anger rising. The idea that a simple kiss and caress could so dishonor a young woman that she would be punished for it went against every moral fiber he possessed. He came to the table, placed his hands upon it and looked White Hair straight in the eye. "Chief, I ask you as the leader of this tribe to reconsider any question of punishing your daughter. She did nothing, nor did John Barrigan. We are moral men, and cannot tolerate an unjust punishment inflicted upon someone for a momentary indiscretion on the part of one of our people.''

Neither Zeb Pike nor Bob Barrigan had seen Chief White Hair smile during their entire stay in the Osage village. Now, however, a faint smile crossed his parched lips. "Are you suggesting, captain, that you would attempt to interfere with our ways?''

"I simply wish you to know, White Hair, how strongly we feel about this.''

White Hair stood and pointed to the door. "It is enough that you have violated our laws and have brought dishonor to my daughter. I will not tolerate your further interference into the ways of my people. Tonight, on the sacred council ground, it will be decided. You, Mr. Barrigan, you, Captain Pike, and the young Barrigan will be there. That is all I wish to say. Leave!''

A gentle rain fell during dinner. It was the first dinner that had not been shared by the leaders of the Pike expedition and the leadership of the village. The members of the expeditionary group huddled together and ate in silence. Pike, anticipating trouble, had quietly rearranged the perimeter of their camp so that it could be more easily defended should the villagers decide to attack.

The whole question of the punishment of Fleet Fire had been discussed in detail between Pike, the two Barrigans, Lieutenant Wilkinson and Dr. Robinson. It was decided that nothing could be decided until the terms of the punishment were more clearly spelled out by White Hair. John Barrigan was appalled at the thought of any punishment being inflicted, and proclaimed that if it came to that, he would be forced, as a man of honor, to interfere with the proceedings in any way he could. His father understood his passionate feelings about this, and though he secretly admired and respected him for having such a view, he did what he could to calm his son down.

When the evening meal was finished, John said to those around him, "I'm sorry for the trouble I've caused. I don't understand all the fuss being made but nobody ever said I was supposed to understand the way other people feel, 'specially Indians. No matter how I feel as a man, I'll do whatever is suggested and make sure this mission doesn't get sidetracked."

Lieutenant Wilkinson snickered. "I don't know what in hell you had to mess around with that damn woman for anyway," he said. "I left a wife back home and no matter how much I yearned for a woman, some dirty damn Indian slut wouldn't interest me."

John tensed. He started to get up from his squatting position on the ground but his father grabbed his arm and kept him where he was. "Lieutenant Wilkinson's view of women hasn't got a thing to do with any of this," he said. "Besides, I'd say my son has right good taste in women. That Fleet Fire is the prettiest damn thing I've seen in a long time. Right now the thing that we've got to do is stick together and act as one. Chances are there won't be any big fuss made out of this as long as we all stay calm and try to understand the other person's point of view. I think we can work this out without anybody getting their feathers ruffled." Barrigan looked at Wilkinson and said, "And you keep your damn comments to yourself if you know what's good for you, lieutenant."

Wilkinson glared at Pike. "Are you going to allow a civilian to talk that way to a commissioned officer of the army?"

Pike stood and yawned. "I think so," he said. He looked up at the full moon. "Time for us to be getting to the council meeting. I don't think being late would add anything to our case."

When Pike and the Barrigans arrived at the sacred council grounds, they were met with a contingent of more than thirty Indian leaders. White Hair and The Wind sat on the ground in the center of the other tribesmen. The area was illuminated by a small fire in front of them, and by a dim, eerie light from a moon that was almost totally obscured by storm clouds. A contingent of armed warriors formed a semicircle around the perimeter of the council ground. Pike and the two Barrigans sat on the ground across the fire from White Hair and The Wind. Yellow Feather stood with the other village leaders and scowled at the Americans as they made their formal greetings to the two Osage chieftains.

A member of White Hair's inner council stepped forward and issued a long, fervent prayer that divine wisdom be granted those who would decide the issues of that particular meeting. He stepped back into the crowd and a silence fell over the group.

When no one spoke, Zeb Pike broke the silence by saying, "We have come here as friends, Chief White Hair, and to attempt to settle the differences that have arisen between us as a result of an unfortunate incident involving one of our people. We are here in peace, and we seek to gain from your wisdom a peaceful solution to this problem."

White Hair leaned over to The Wind and whispered something in his ear. The Wind nodded, turned and beckoned for Yellow Feather to sit at his side. The young warrior stepped forward and sat cross-legged next to the two Indian chiefs.

The Wind spoke. "The dishonor you have placed upon the chieftain of all our people through his daughter, Fleet Fire, has caused us much grief. Because it involves White Hair's family, he has asked that I sit in his place as leader of the sacred council meeting. It has been decided that the daughter of White Hair shall be punished for adultery. This punishment is written into our ancient laws, and is the same whether it is applied to the most common and lowest of women, or to the daughter of the chief of our village."

John decided to speak. "You speak of punishment of Fleet Fire because she sat with me by the riverbank," John said. "Your daughter has done nothing wrong. She meant no offense to you or to your people. To punish her would be to inflict a cruelty upon a human being that would not reflect favorably upon the bravery and honor of such a fine people as the Osage. I sit here before you and apologize if I have offended anyone. That was not my intention. I ask only that my apology be accepted as it is done between men of honor, and that no harm befall Fleet Fire. Should there be some need according to your ancient tradition to punish someone for what has occurred, let the punishment be administered to me."

John's father coughed and put his hand on his son's shoulder. "There's no need for anyone to be punished, son. Let's not start being a martyr at this point."

The Wind said to Yellow Feather, "Dishonor has been placed upon you as well as upon the family of White Hair. The adultery has been directed at you, Yellow Feather, since it was to you that Fleet Fire was pledged. It is time that you spoke to those of us in this council meeting, Indian and white man alike."

There was no mistaking the hatred in Yellow Feather's eyes. They burned a brilliant yellow. His nostrils flared, and there was a tension in his thick, muscular body that was unmistakable. He wore the traditional headdress that all Osage warriors wore into battle, a band of long yellow feathers that trailed down his back. Yellow Feather's reputation as a warrior was well-known to everyone in the village, Indian and visitor alike. His heroic feats in battle were the topic of many conversations, and his marriage to Fleet Fire would insure, according to the tribe's sages, that he would one day become chieftain of all the Osage.

Yellow Feather looked across the fire at John Barrigan as he spoke. "It was against my will and advice that you were allowed to enter this village in the first place. The white man possesses no honor, and his word is to be trusted as much as the intentions of a snake. The woman who had been pledged to me as my wife was violated and dishonored by you because that is your natural way. But it has happened in our village, and your ways are not tolerated here even by the most cowardly of my people. My honor is at stake, too, and because Fleet Fire has dishonored me in the eyes of my people, I am the one to determine that punishment shall be given her."

Zeb Pike was getting nervous. He could sense the anger in John Barrigan and was anxious that it not erupt during the meeting. He said quickly, "Have you determined what that punishment will be, Yellow Feather?"

Yellow Feather nodded. "She shall be publicly stoned, and

then shall remain unmarried for the rest of her days. No man would want her after what she has done."

"Stoned? That is barbaric," said Bob Barrigan, getting to his feet.

"It is just," said The Wind. "Yellow Feather has considered wisely the action to take with Fleet Fire, and although the heart of my chieftain, White Hair, is heavy with grief because it is his own flesh and blood to receive this punishment, he agrees with it because he is a man of his people."

"Is there nothing we can do to prevent this?" Pike asked.

"No," replied The Wind. "Unless, of course, Yellow Feather would listen to your words and change his mind."

John Barrigan stood beside his father. "Well, Yellow Feather?" he asked, his jaw set, his eyes filled with determination. "Will you listen to reason and change your views of what is to happen to Fleet Fire?"

Yellow Feather, too, stood and walked toward John until they were no more than two feet away from each other. "You speak of honor, white man, and yet you act dishonorably. You ask for me to change my mind and yet you offer no good reason for me to do that. My disgust with you and those with you has not been disguised by me. The fact that Fleet Fire saw fit to allow you to touch her makes my heart sick and my skin crawl. But my real rage is not with Fleet Fire. It is with you, and my most passionate wish is to punish you for taking from me the woman pledged to me by White Hair."

Bob Barrigan asked that the three of them be excused for a few moments so that they might talk. The Wind nodded, and the three Americans moved out of earshot. They spoke in hushed tones.

"I can't let this happen to her," John said.

"It doesn't look as though you have any choice," said Zeb.

"The captain is right, son. There is no way to interfere with what a whole Indian nation wants to do without losing our scalps."

John looked over his shoulder to make sure no one was listening. He leaned closer to Zeb and to his father and said, "What if I offered to buy Fleet Fire from the tribe. Maybe if we pay enough, they'll go for it. After all, Yellow Feather says that she could never marry anyone for the rest of her life, including him. I don't see why they wouldn't be happy to get her out of the village. All they can do is say no."

The elder Barrigan nodded. "Sounds sensible to me."

"I agree," Pike said. "But don't go making promises we can't keep, John."

"The only promises I'll be makin' are ones that I intend to live up to. Let's go."

The three men returned to the council area.

"My son has a proposition to make, chief," Bob Barrigan said.

John stepped forward and addressed his words to The Wind and to Yellow Feather, who had resumed his place on the ground next to the chieftain. "Since I have dishonored Fleet Fire in your eyes, I wish to have her as my wife."

"Jesus," Pike muttered under his breath.

"If you will let me, I will buy her from you," John continued. "Since Yellow Feather here has decided that she isn't fit to marry anybody in the tribe, I can't see any reason why he wouldn't let her marry this dirty white man who soiled her by touching her."

Had there been more light, John Barrigan would have seen a faint smile of satisfaction come over Yellow Feather's face. The young brave asked that he be allowed to speak in private with The Wind and with White Hair. He was granted the privilege, and the three men spoke in whispers. When their conversation was ended, both chiefs nodded solemnly and indicated that Yellow Feather should speak.

"You wish to marry Fleet Fire. This does not surprise me. Only a white man would find pleasure in being close to a woman whose honor has been destroyed. You speak of paying for her like a common whore. Although she has become that in my eyes and in the eyes of the rest of the tribe, simple payment of goods will not erase the anger you have caused me or the embarrassment you have brought to me. Yes, you may have Fleet Fire for your wife and may take her from this village, but only after I have been allowed to show you and all those like you that the Osage have pride and respect that you evidently do not. If you wish her, you must win her from me in battle. This is what I ask, and Fleet Fire's father has seen fit to grant me this in his wisdom."

It was Bob Barrigan's turn to speak.

He turned to his son. "What's to be gained by fighting with this warrior, John? I reckon' that something else could be worked out with a man as wise as White Hair."

Pike, John and Bob looked to the aged Osage chief. His

response was to simply shake his head and lower his eyes to the ground.

"What sort of contest are you contemplating?" Zeb Pike asked.

"Knives," Yellow Feather replied. "The two of us will fight with knives. Should your friend win, he will be free to take Fleet Fire with him. Should he lose, he will be dead and Fleet Fire will remain here to suffer the punishment that is just and proper."

John Barrigan stepped forward, his fists clenched. "I accept."

His father held up his hands and forced a laugh. "Now hold on a second, son. Let's not be to rambunctious." He looked at White Hair. "I'd like to have an opportunity to talk this over with my son. Could a decision be made on this in the morning?"

White Hair looked up at Yellow Feather for his response. "Yes, you have until the dawn," the warrior said. "At that time we will either engage in our battle, or the punishment of stoning will be inflicted upon Fleet Fire."

John said to his father, "I don't see what's to be gained by waiting. Might as well get it over with right now."

"Keep your damned hot head on, John, and let's do it my way. You've already got us in enough trouble without flyin' off the handle. I think some talking is in order, and if you don't listen to your father I'm goin' to break your head before Yellow Feather gets a chance to do it."

John knew there was no sense in arguing with his father at this point. There were few times when the elder Barrigan threatened physical violence against his own son, and when he did, John knew he was perfectly able and ready to carry it out.

"All right, pa, let's go talk. But right now my blood is boilin', and I'd just as soon get into this while it is. It might just cool down over the night."

"Maybe that's the best thing could happen," his father said. "Come on, let's get back to our camp."

CHAPTER SIXTEEN

The clouds dissipated and the sky became a brilliantly clear, inky black scrim against which thousands of stars flickered. The full moon was like a searchlight that illuminated the Osage village.

The young warriors of the tribe gathered together in an open area to the south of the village and proceeded to worship the gods that would protect Yellow Feather in his combat the following day. The sound from Indian drummers filled the night and set everyone in the Pike camp on edge. Pike instructed Lt. Wilkinson to have the men brought to full battle preparedness. The number of guards were doubled, weapons were checked and the livestock and horses were made ready to be moved at a moment's notice.

Captain Pike wanted to be part of the conversation that was to take place between the two Barrigans, but the elder Barrigan suggested that it might be better for him to spend time alone with his son. As he told Pike, "No matter what I say, captain, it ain't gonna make a damn bit of difference with John. That's the kind of man he is. When he's got his mind set on something there ain't nothin' in this world, including his father, who can sway him from it. All I want to do is to make sure that his thinking is right before he goes through with this dumb damn fight with Yellow Feather. If it's got to be, at least I want to make sure he's got a fair chance of walking away from it."

Pike replied, "I've spent some interesting time with your son, Mr. Barrigan, and I'd say his chances of walking away from any fight are damn good. My only concern is that if he does walk away, the rest of village isn't going to let him walk very far.''

"That's one thing about Injuns, captain, they generally keep their word. Of course, the Apaches don't put much stock in a man's word, including their own, but the Osage are a different breed, I believe. I'm not worried about what's going to happen after John and Yellow Feather get into their scrap. I'm just worried about the scrap itself. That is one tough, fierce-looking Injun.''

Father and son walked together through the pine grove to where John and Fleet Fire had spent their moments together the previous night. They said nothing to each other as they stood on the crest of the rise and looked out over the river as it twisted and turned toward its ultimate union with the Verdigris and Neosho.

Bob Barrigan said, "This is where all the trouble started, son.''

"That's right, pa, and you know what? I'm glad it did. You might find this difficult to understand but I want that woman, and I want her so bad that I figure Yellow Feather is goin' to have his hands full with me.''

"I don't doubt that, son.'' Had he been totally honest, though, Bob Barrigan would have had to temper that confidence with the twisting that was going on in his stomach at the moment. The use of knives concerned him. Obviously, Yellow Feather had spent his entire young adult life becoming expert in the use of a knife, and although John had had a fair exposure to knives and their use in battle, he certainly would have to be considered an amateur compared to the Indian. Still, Bob Barrigan had always known that his son's fierce and iron-willed resolve had put him in good stead in many previous fights. It was that certainty that he was determined to transmit to his son, not the fears and apprehensions he himself felt about what might occur the next day.

"No matter what happens, pa, I want you to know that I love you, and that I'm downright sorry for putting this whole mission in such a mess.''

The older Barrigan had to fight back tears at his son's words. John hadn't told him he loved him since he was a little boy, since the time John's mother died. The older Barrigan coughed, ran his hand across his eyes as though he were wiping away perspiration and forced a laugh. "You never have to tell me that, John. Everything you do proves that to me time and time again.''

Father and son said little to each other until Bob asked, ''Do you really want to take an Indian for a wife?''

''If you'd asked me that a week ago, pa, I would have said no. I believe that people should stick to their own kind. Seems to cause less trouble. But this woman is different. It wouldn't make any difference to me whether she was an Indian or an Arab. Something about her makes me think that she is the right woman for me. It may not go over so big back east, but then again I'm not that anxious to be back there anyway. I like it out here, pa, and as long as I'm out here I'd like to have that woman next to me.''

Bob Barrigan's only response was to nod. He understood. And even if he hadn't, he would have respected his son's feelings in the matter. They spent the next few minutes discussing the strategy of the battle that would take place. Bob Barrigan felt that John should start slowly and feel his foe out before launching his own attack. John disagreed, although he did not express this to his father. He had a healthy respect for Yellow Feather, and decided that if he were to have a chance to win, he would have to be brazen and bold. He would take the offensive immediately.

''A good sleep wouldn't be a bad idea for you, John,'' Bob said.

''I agree with you, pa, but there is someone I would like to see before I go to bed.''

''Fleet Fire?''

''Yup.''

It was the first sincere laugh Bob Barrigan could muster all evening. He said, ''I reckon seeing that young Indian lady doesn't make any difference now. Hell, you could go to bed with her in the middle of the village at this point and not get anybody more upset than they already are.''

John Barrigan found Fleet Fire sitting alone on the outskirts of the village. A chicozapote tree, from which the tribe extracted *chicle,* had been uprooted and formed a bench of sorts upon which Fleet Fire sat. John approached slowly, and when he saw she would not be offended, sat beside her.

''I am sorry,'' she said.

''Me, too.''

Fleet Fire drew a deep breath and stared off into the distance where a low ridge of mountains was silhouetted against the horizon. The presence of a jaguar caused the horses in the tribe's corral to whinny and to shuffle about in panic. The Indian drummers continued their incessant, monotonous playing as a prelude to Yellow Feather's going into battle with the white man. Somewhere else in the village a group of women giggled, and the sound of them caused sadness in Fleet Fire.

"I have made you sad," John said.

Fleet Fire said, without looking at him, "No, you have made me happy. I told you that I wish to go with you and I meant that. The fact that you want me fills my heart with a joy I have never known before."

John tentatively placed his hand upon her shoulder. She flinched, then relaxed and allowed it to remain. "If I've made you happy, Fleet Fire, that pleases me. I shall take you with me as my wife."

Although Fleet Fire's profile was to him, he saw a tear run from her left eye and down her copper cheek.

"Why do you cry?" he asked.

"I cry because my happiness shall last for such a short time."

"What do you mean?"

"Yellow Feather has used me to arrange to fight you with knifes. It was his wish when you first arrived to gather the warriors together and to kill all of you. Only my father's position and wisdom kept him from doing that. Now, because of me, he has gained my father's approval to kill you."

John removed his hand and sat up straight on the uprooted tree. "I wish you wouldn't be so sure about my being killed," he said. "After all, this is going to be a fair fight, and that means that I've got every bit as much chance as Yellow Feather does."

"Were that so, I would not cry. But Yellow Feather is the strongest and most daring of all of the braves in my village. Although I am sure that you are strong and fearless, I fear Yellow Feather will emerge victorious."

John turned, grabbed her shoulders and twisted her so that she was facing him. "Now you listen to me, Miss Fleet Fire. If I felt the way you did I wouldn't be sitting here talking to you like this. I'd be back in my camp shaking like a little child and saying my prayers. I'm sure that Yellow Feather is one hell of a fighter, but so am I. And I know one thing for certain. I love you, and because of that I'll do anything I have to do to have you. I don't intend to get myself killed, and don't you think that for one more minute."

Fleet Fire wiped the tears from her eyes and managed a smile. "You do not have to say you love me, John Barrigan. I do not expect that. I wish only to be with you and to be away from Yellow Feather."

"A man has to trust his instincts, Fleet Fire. That's one thing my father has taught me since I was a little boy. The only things you have that are worth anything are your instincts, and if you don't follow them you're a damn fool. My instincts tell me that you're the woman who was put on this earth for me and that's why I'll fight like I never fought before so that I can be with you. All I hope is that you'll learn to love me like I love you." There was no need to say anything else. Their lips sought each other and they were soon locked in a warm embrace, mouths joined, bodies pressed tightly together.

They maintained their embrace for what seemed an eternity. Then, without a word, they loosened their desperate grasp on each other, stood and looked deeply into each other's eyes. John Barrigan saw a human being who had brought forth in him feelings of such intensity that he thought he might burst.

Fleet Fire, however, saw something else. She saw a man she respected, perhaps even loved. She also saw a vision of that man lying dead in the dirt of the village in which she had grown, Yellow Feather's knife imbedded in his chest.

"Will you be there in the morning?" John asked.

"No."

"Then I will come for you when it is over."

"I will be here."

She turned and walked toward the house of her father, and although John's confidence in the result of the battle with Yellow Feather was at a peak, he, too, wondered whether he would ever see the woman he loved again.

John went directly back to the camp and tried to sleep, but it was a losing proposition. He tossed and turned, and on more than one occasion sat bolt upright in his bedroll, beads of perspiration on his brow, his right hand clenched around an imaginary knife.

The first hint of dawn found John wide awake and staring up at the black, star-studded sky. A magenta glow on the horizon was like a bugler's call to battle. He sat up, rubbed his eyes and looked about him. His father, too, was awake and sitting up next to him. To his left was Zeb Pike, who appeared to be asleep, though he had simply closed his eyes against his thoughts.

The rest of the Pike force were awake. Most of them were on sentry duty and cast nervous glances toward John's sleeping bag. They had talked in hushed tones throughout the night about what would occur the next morning, and it was the consensus that as brave a man and as fierce a fighter as John might be, he would be no match for Yellow Feather. Some of the men even wagered on the outcome of the battle.

As the sky lightened and the glow on the horizon turned to orange, then yellow, John stood and surveyed his body. Although he had not slept, he had rested, and his body felt good to him. There were no aches or pains, as sometimes occurred from having been in an awkward sleeping position. In a word, he felt fit, and as the reality of the contest settled over him, some of the fears he had experienced while lying awake during the night disappeared.

"Good morning, son," Bob Barrigan said.

"Good morning, pa. Looks like it's going to be a nice day."

Zeb Pike got up and stretched. "How do you feel, John?"

"Tip-top," he said. "I think I'll get washed up."

The smell of breakfast cooking wafted across camp.

"Feel like some breakfast?" John's father asked.

"I don't think so. I always did fight better on an empty stomach."

Ten minutes later a young Indian boy arrived at the Pike camp and indicated that it was time for John to come to where the battle with Yellow Feather would take place. Although there was much to say between Zeb, John and Bob Barrigan, no one said a word. Words would not help. It was now to be man against man, knife against knife, the sum and total of two human beings locked in mortal combat from which only one would walk away.

John reached into his bedroll and withdrew the knife he would use in the fight. Its blade was six inches long. Its stock was made of silver and was bound tightly with rawhide. He'd killed a man with it before, years ago, an Indian in Massachusetts who'd attacked him and his father as they blazed a new trail for a fur trading company. It was as though it had happened only yesterday, so clear was the memory of it. That previous time, the feeling of the knife pushing into the Indian's body had been both satisfying and disgusting to John. He'd hoped after that incident that he would never again experience such a feeling. Now, if he did not experience it, it would be because a knife was in his body, taking his own life.

The Indian boy led the Barrigans, Zeb Pike, Lt. Wilkinson, Dr. Robinson and the translator, Vasquez, to the perimeter of the village and beyond. Bob Barrigan didn't like the fact that they were moving so far away from their own camp. He'd have felt more secure being in the midst of many people, especially his own.

Soon they reached a small open area of mesquite grass on which the livestock and horses were occasionally allowed to graze. John did not like the tall, calf-high grass. He had decided that one advantage he did possess over Yellow Feather was quickness of foot, and he knew the tall grass would hinder his movement. He realized that Yellow Feather was also aware that John might hold this advantage, and had chosen this area for the fight with precisely that in mind.

"Looks like the whole damn tribe is out here," Bob Barrigan muttered to John as they approached the clearing. It did appear that way. Hundreds of men, women and children surrounded the clearing. Some were in trees, which afforded them a better vantage point. One tree limb threatened to break under the weight of five youngsters.

Pike, Bob and John were greeted by The Wind, the chief of the smaller Osage village, who had the responsibility of representing Yellow Feather. Bob Barrigan had taken it upon himself to act as the mediator for John in setting up the rules of the combat. He approached The Wind, issued greetings and asked to have the rules explained.

The Wind explained simply that there were no rules. Each man would be armed with a knife of his choice, and would fight until one or the other was dead.

"Sounds simple enough to me," Bob Barrigan said, the words sticking in his throat. If ever there were a time in his life that he wanted to run from something, it was from this absurd battle that would take place over a woman that his son barely knew. Bob walked to his son and slapped him on the arm. "You still want to go through with this?" he asked.

"I could think of things I'd rather do, pa, but it looks like the deal has been made. I'm ready."

"It looks like you're completely on your own, son. The only rule is that you are allowed one knife. Remember what I said. Go slow at first. Feel him out."

"I appreciate your advice, pa, but I think I might do better hitting him fast. This damn grass bothers me."

"I was thinkin' the same thing."

A commotion caused the white men to turn and look into the crowd. Through it came Yellow Feather. He was flanked by other braves from the tribe who were acting as his seconds. He wore only a brief loincloth. His face and upper body had been painted in a garish display of color which, according to the medicine man who did the painting, would ward off possible injury. The streaks of paint made him appear even more sinister and menacing. John noticed that he was barefoot, which raised his spirits a bit. The mesquite grass was hard on the feet, and even though Yellow Feather was undoubtedly used to it, it was possible that if the battle went on for a long period of time his feet might feel the effects of the coarse grass.

John slipped out of his shirt. He wore heavy trousers and boots. The knife was in his belt. He turned to Zeb Pike and shook his hand. "Remember what I said back in New York, Zeb. All we went through there was just getting in shape for this."

"I'm not a bit worried," Pike said. "You're too crazy to get killed."

"I thank you for the compliment, captain. Don't go away."

"I'll be here."

As Yellow Feather stepped into the center of the clearing, the tribe's medicine man fell to his knees and went into a series of wild gyrations. He rolled his eyes up and chanted to some unseen God.

John Barrigan stepped into the clearing and stood ten feet away from Yellow Feather. He watched the medicine man complete his prayers and leave the circle. When he was gone, John nodded to Yellow Feather, waved his knife and assumed the stance of preparedness.

The knife which Yellow Feather held was slightly shorter than John's, but had a wider, thicker blade. John noted that Yellow Feather's left hand had been wrapped in deerskin to ward off any thrusts John might make with his weapon.

The two men slowly began to circle each other. The high, coarse grass proved somewhat of a hindrance for John, but he forced himself to ignore its effect upon his movement. He tried to block all thoughts from his mind so that he might concentrate totally on his opponent. One lapse of concentration and it could be over for him.

The two combatants maintained the distance between them as they circled. Yellow Feather made a few random thrusts with his knife, but the distance between the men insured that no damage could be inflicted. It was more a matter of loosening up, of gaining familiarity with time and place.

Many of the members of the tribe who circled the clearing began to cheer for Yellow Feather. John saw his father and Zeb Pike watching the action. He could not remember ever having seen his father look so concerned. Zeb, on the other hand, looked more enthusiastic than worried. He was crouched in a fighting position himself, and seemed to be moving with John's every step. Pike even had his right hand clenched about an imaginary weapon.

The cheers and chants from the crowd grew in volume. The sun was now fully above the horizon, and although the morning air was cool, perspiration began to run down John's body. He never took his eyes from Yellow Feather's navel. That was something his father had told him years ago. "A man might fake you, John, but you can bet he is going to end up going where his stomach goes."

John decided that it was time to take the offensive, as he had planned. He waited until Yellow Feather had moved to a point where the sun, so low in the sky, was directly in his face. The moment that position was reached, John lunged, his knife at gut level. Yellow Feather grabbed his wrist with his leather-bound left hand and made his own move with his knife. The strength of his grip upon John's wrist was startling. John twisted his hand free and stepped back. The one simple contact between them left little doubt in John's mind that he was in a match-up with the most formidable opponent of his life.

John heard his father yell, "Come on, boy. Git him."

Zeb Pike called, "Easy, John, easy. Take your time."

Although John had made a decision to attack Yellow Feather when the sun was in the brave's eyes, he forgot for a moment that he would be at the same disadvantage when he came to that position in the circle. He was not to forget it very long, however, because the next time he was facing the rising sun, Yellow Feather leaped at him, the knife held above his head, his left hand in front of him like a small shield. His movement took John by surprise, and it was only the young Barrigan's quick reflexes that allowed him to parry the downward thrust of Yellow Feather's knife with his left forearm. The knife blade slashed John's wrist and his blood ran freely onto the grass.

Barrigan and Yellow Feather stepped back and looked at each other. There was a smile on Yellow Feather's lips as he watched the blood run down John's arm. John didn't feel any pain in the arm, so intense was his concentration on what he was sure would be another quick attack. He pressed his left arm against his stomach to try and stem the flow of blood, and continued to circle to his left. He then shifted the direction and moved to his right, his action appearing to momentarily confuse his Indian adversary.

Bob Barrigan's instructions to his son were drowned out by the intensity of the Indian cheers for Yellow Feather. He wanted John to act quickly before the loss of blood drained him of strength. But although his instructions were not heard, the same thought was going through John's head. He drew a deep breath, tensed every muscle in his body, let out a piercing scream and attacked Yellow Feather with abandon. He held his knife at waist level. Yellow feather caught the underside of John's wrist with his left hand and deflected the blade upward, the point of it catching his shoulder and drawing blood. John's weakened left hand grasped Yellow Feather's right wrist. John twisted his body and both men fell to the ground, John on top. It now became a question of relative physical strength as they rolled over and over, each man attempting to control the other's knife-wielding hand. John had trouble maintaining a grip because not only had Yellow Feather been painted in preparation for the battle, his body had been oiled. A violent series of wrenching motions disengaged the two combatants, and they rolled free of each other. John scrambled to his knees, but by the time he had, Yellow Feather had regained his feet and had leaped for the kill. John darted to his right and Yellow Feather's knife sunk deep into the ground where John's body had been. Yellow Feather was on all fours as John spun around and brought his boot into the Indian's buttocks. The force of the kick sent Yellow Feather sprawling forward into the grass. John's reactions were sure and quick. He leaped on the Indian's back and brought his boot heel sharply down into the brave's upper right arm. Yellow Feather's fingers involuntarily relaxed their grip on the knife handle. John stomped his boot on the brave's right hand and brought his knife to his throat.

"Let go of that knife or you're dead," Barrigan said.

Yellow Feather knew the fight was over and that under the terms of it, he would die. His head was turned to one side and John looked down into his face. There was no fear in it, no sudden shift in emotion that would indicate Yellow Feather would plead for his life. He was ready to die, and John felt immense respect for him.

John heard his father yell, "Finish him, boy."

But John couldn't do it. He reached to where Yellow Feather's knife lay beneath his fingertips on the grass, picked it up and threw it to the side of the clearing. He stood, pressed his arm to his stomach to control the bleeding from his wound and slowly walked to where his father and Zeb Pike were waiting.

Bob Barrigan did not look at his son as he approached. His eyes were trained on Yellow Feather and on the other braves for fear that one of them might attack his son from the rear. It did not happen. Yellow Feather got up and simply walked through the crowd and disappeared beyond it.

"Damn, you had me worried, son," John's father said.

"I was a little worried myself, pa. Come on, let's get this arm of mine patched up."

At noon, the Barrigans and Zeb Pike were summoned once again to White Hair's residence. The aging Osage chieftain greeted them formally and without emotion. He said in a monotone, "My daughter belongs to you."

"Yes, that's right," John said. "But what about the rest of us? We would like to stay and finish our work."

"My daughter's dishonor has nothing to do with the bargain we made," White Hair said. "You may stay as long as we agreed upon."

"Thank you, White Hair," Bob Barrigan said. "You're a man of honor and of your word."

"An Osage always keeps his word, Mr. Barrigan. But do not be misled by that. Our distrust for the white man grows with each passing day. Your ways are different from ours, and those differences will one day, I fear, lead us to a war in which no one will be victorious."

"I hope that day never comes," Zeb Pike said.

"It is written," White Hair said.

The chief motioned for them to leave. As they were about to comply, he added, "You have taken from me one of my bravest warriors. But we have many more to take his place."

Bob Barrigan turned and said, "I don't understand, White Hair. My son spared Yellow Feather's life."

"That is not true. By not using your knife on Yellow Feather you shamed him in the eyes of the village. He has taken his own life."

The Barrigans looked at each other, then at Zeb Pike. "I don't understand," Pike said.

"The white man will never understand the Indian," White Hair said.

That night, before a small gathering of the members of Pike's force, John Barrigan and the Indian girl, Fleet Fire, were wed. The service was performed by Captain Zebulon Pike. John's father, Bob, served as his son's best man. The brief, informal ceremony had no meaning for Fleet Fire, except that she understood that it was the way the white man united man and women in marriage.

Just prior to the ceremony, John had approached his father and asked his permission to give a Christian name to Fleet Fire.

"Of course, son," his father replied. "What name were you considering?"

"Susan." It was the name of John's deceased mother.

"It seems to me that you wouldn't have to ask me a question like that," Bob Barrigan said.

"She's an Indian, pa. I didn't want you to think I was giving mom's name to someone you didn't feel deserved it."

"That's the last time I want to hear that kind of talk, John. Fleet Fire is to be your wife, and she'll always have my respect because she is. I'm right proud to have your mother's name given to her."

"Thanks, pa."

John and Susan were given a tent in which to share their wedding night. The events of the day had left John drained of emotion, and until his bride removed her clothing and snuggled in next to him in their wedding bed, he had thought of nothing but sleep. But her presence, the smell of her, the intensely pleasurable feeling of her warm skin against his, revived him. Her brown body, so full and pliable, filled him with desire. Their marriage was consumated in an intensely

pleasurable mutual release of their passion. And after they
had slept a few hours, they again made love, John's young
Indian wife's gasps of pleasure muffled by the press of his
mouth to hers.

"I love you, Susan," John said, his fingers tracing the
contour of her breast and nipple.

"I am yours to love, my husband. I am your wife."

On September 1, 1806, Zebulon Pike and his party moved
west across the Osage trace. They forded the head-waters of
the Little Osage River, moved down the Neosho to the Verdigris and, on September 11, camped on the south fork of the
Cottonwood River. They were accompanied on their journey
by six members of the Osage Tribe who'd expressed a desire
to move west, and who'd been given permission by White
Hair and by The Wind, but only after Pike had compensated
the tribe for their loss with additional weapons.

By the 17th of September they had crossed Smoky Hill and
forded the Saline. That night, a Pawnee hunter entered the
camp and had dinner with them and told Pike that word of
their expedition had spread throughout the southwest.

"We're a peaceful expedition," Pike told the Pawnee hunter.

"The Spaniards consider no one peaceful," the hunter
replied.

"The Spaniards trust no one because they do not trust each
other," Pike said.

CHAPTER SEVENTEEN

September 1806

Santa Fe

Margarita Soltura sat in the tiny parlor of her house in Santa Fe. With her was her daughter-in-law, María.

The Soltura house in Santa Fe was a far cry from what the family had been used to back in Valladolid. Housing proved to be scarce in the bustling trade center of the southwest.

The house was small. Its adobe walls were flaked and crumbled, both inside and out. Numerous leaks in the tile roof had allowed water to drip into virtually every room.

The house had come with some furnishings, and in the few months that they had been in Santa Fe Margarita had managed to secure some other items to make the house more comfortable.

There wasn't a day went by that didn't find Margarita aching to return to Valladolid. But those feelings were tempered by her pleasure at being a supportive and loving wife to her husband in his quest for greater success. She couldn't help but smile as she watched him go about his daily routine as one of New Spain's official empresarios. He held his head high, and a satisfied grin seemed always to be upon his round face.

Margarita's greatest pain had to do with the relationship between her son, Gordo, and María. The dismal state of their young marriage seemed to have stripped from María the youthful beauty she once possessed. The spark, the obvious love of life, was no longer there, and its absence caused Margarita's heart to ache.

Margarita had tried to encourage María to talk about her

problems with Gordo, but she understood María's reluctance. A good wife did not speak poorly of her husband, no matter how unhappy she was. But from Margarita's point of view the situation had gotten sufficiently out of hand to release María from such wifely duty. Perhaps it wouldn't have been so bad had the young couple been able to find their own house, away from María's in-laws. But that proved impossible, and so Gordo and María lived in one room in the Soltura household.

Ever since his arrival in Santa Fe Gordo had virtually abandoned his role as husband. He'd become completely involved in the raucous night life of Santa Fe and with its daily influx of traders, trappers and adventurers who brought with them their dreams, their aspirations and, in some cases, their money. The saloons bustled day and night. The brothels were filled to capacity seven days a week. Both institutions were sufficiently pleasurable to keep Gordo away from the house almost every night. When he returned drunk, his clothes and hair reeking of Spanish whores' perfume, lipstick smeared upon his face, he would go into a rage if he was questioned about his actions. Margarita and Manuel had approached him on a few occasions and had met with his wrath. One night, after they had asked him how he could treat his wife so shabbily, he stormed into the bedroom and struck María.

This particular morning, as Margarita sat sewing a rip in the seam of one of Manuel's trousers, she was especially concerned over what the future held for her daughter-in-law. Gordo had announced that he had decided to join a Spanish army unit that was being quickly assembled to explore the northeast frontier of New Spain, to establish relations with the Comanches, the Pawnees and the Kansas, and to head off any expeditionary forces that might have entered New Spain from America. The latter reason for the expedition was by far the most important. Word had reached Spanish authority of the Pike contingent, and it was feared that unless direct action were taken immediately, Pike might be able to establish a stronghold somewhere within New Spain.

The Santa Fe expedition was under the command of Lt. Facundo Melgares. He was instructed to take with him 100 dragoons, 500 militia and more than 2,000 horses and mules. He was to be equipped for a six-month march.

Gordo and Lt. Melgares had become friendly. Their exploits in the saloons and brothels were the talk of Santa Fe, and when the opportunity presented itself to Gordo to join his friend in his adventure to the northeastern frontier, he readily accepted. As exciting as Santa Fe was for him, his inherent ruthlessness was getting the better of him. María no longer held any appeal for him. They had not shared the bed as man and wife for many months. He wanted to get away, to find new excitement.

Gordo's decision was met with mixed emotions by his family. María said nothing, although she was relieved that Gordo would no longer be with her, even for a limited duration. Margarita was shocked that Gordo would leave his wife so eagerly, and yet she, too, shared some of María's relief. Gordo's father saw it as still another opportunity to spread the influence of the Soltura family in New Spain. He was obsessed with gaining power, and everything that occurred in his life was viewed and judged from that perspective.

Margarita finished sewing the pants and placed them on the back of a wooden chair. She looked at María, who was sitting quietly in another chair in the corner of the room, her hands folded in her lap, and said, ''You say so little, María. It is not good to hold such sorrow inside.''

''What is there to say?'' María asked, rearranging her hands.

Margarita tried again. ''María, although Gordo is my son, my own flesh and blood, his actions disgust me. There is no question that my sympathy lies with you, not with my son. Now that he has elected to leave you for six months, I cannot help but wonder what you will do during that time.''

María stood and went to the door that looked out over a dusty, rutted portion of the road that led into the main town of Santa Fe. A group of naked Indian children played in the road. She looked down the road to where the town itself began. It was almost impossible to see any of the buildings or the plaza because of the dust that was raised by thousands of feet scurrying to and fro. She felt the urge to cry and bit her lip against it. She had promised herself months ago that she would no longer cry because of Gordo. She would never again be hurt by him. He might beat her, he might physically abuse her, but he would never hurt her inner core, her being. She turned and faced her mother-in-law. ''I thought perhaps I might return to the south, to Valladolid.''

Margarita sighed. ''That would bring great sadness to me, although I can understand why you would wish to do that. I, too, would like to return, but my place is at my husband's side."

"I will not have a husband at my side to be concerned about," María said.

"But Gordo will return, María. What then?"

María returned to her chair and sat in it. "As long as I am married to your son, mama, it is my duty to be a supportive and faithful wife. That is the law of our land, and of our God. I cannot conceive of myself being anything else, and that was my heartfelt intention when I married Gordo. I do not wish to return to Valladolid, at least not yet. I have nothing to return to there except my mother and father, and a grown woman should not run home once she has married."

"You received a letter recently from them, didn't you?"

"Yes. Things go well with them, although the unrest grows between the classes. There is much talk of revolution. But hopefully, should such a thing occur, it will not touch them and their lives."

Margarita slapped her palms upon her broad thighs and forced a certain gaiety into her voice. "Well, María, whatever decision you make will be the right one, I'm sure. I would love to have you stay here with me because I find it so lonely. Although Manuel is a fine husband and provider, his work seems to occupy his every moment, and when he is here his mind is elsewhere."

"I've noticed," María said, laughing. "As a criollo he is very proud to have been chosen for this post of empresario."

Margarita got up and straightened her dress. "Pride. Men have such pride."

"Not all men, mama." María also got up and said she would attend to chores in the kitchen. Margarita said she would help, and the two women went into the kitchen, which was the largest room in the house.

Moments later Manuel Soltura came through the front door. He was breathless. He had put on even more weight since arriving in Santa Fe and his collar threatened to strangle him. He held an envelope in one hand, his dusty black hat in the other.

"Margarita, María," he called out, "a letter from Juan."

The women came out of the kitchen and waited as Manuel opened the envelope and read aloud to them.

To my dear family,

Although you have been gone from Valladolid for only a short time, it seems an eternity to me. My work here at the parish keeps me very busy, but there is not a day goes by that I do not think of you, wonder at your life in Santa Fe and yearn for your return.

I, too, will soon be traveling from Valladolid, although my trips will not be for any long duration. I have been asked by certain authorities in the church to travel on their behalf and help establish certain social organizations in nearby towns and villages.

This excites me, for I was beginning to feel trapped serving God in only one parish. I wish very much to go out and touch the people, the children of God who, because of the chance of their birthright, seem to become less and less part of the structure of our society. They seemed to be forgotten children, and it is important to me that they know that God and those who serve him have not forgotten them.

There is great unrest in this part of our nation. it distresses me, and yet I understand it. I only hope and pray that reasonable men will find reasonable solutions for the ills that prevail. I know you share with me this wish.

I visit the hacienda as often as possible, and things go smoothly. I believe your choice of Catano to run the hacienda in your absence was a good one. He seems to be a very capable and trustworthy man, and from what I can see you would be proud of what he has accomplished.

Please tell María that I see her family at least once a week and that they are in good health and good spirits.

Each Sunday I speak to my congregation, and yet when it comes to writing a letter to my family I seem to have so few words to put in it. Therefore, I shall end this letter by simply saying that I love all of you, miss you and anxiously await the day when we will all be together again. My best wishes, papa, to you in your important position as empresario. I know that mama continues to feed you the best food that has ever been prepared in a kitchen in New Spain, and that María has learned a great deal to provide the same sort of service to Gordo.

God bless you.

Your son,
Juan

153

The letter buoyed Margarita's spirits. She took it from Manuel and read it again, then handed it to María who did the same. Of all those who read Juan's letter, it touched María the most. She thought of the handsome young priest, her brother-in-law, so different from the man she had married. Juan was gentle and kind; he had the attributes that could only come from an inner strength that was far superior to the overt physicality of Gordo. She realized that were Juan near she would turn to him for help. It would be Juan to whom she would speak of her problems. But Juan was not near her, and she would have to solve the problems of her life with what she had, and with those who were close to her.

"Well, women, it is time for this empresario to return to his office. I came here only to share the good news of Juan's letter with you. Tonight, at dinner, I wish to discuss with Gordo his expedition with Lt. Malgares. I ask a favor of both of you. I do not wish to have your female sentimentalities interfere in the conversation. This is a fine opportunity for Gordo, and for the Soltura family. Please, do not interfere."

"As you wish, Manuel." Margarita said.

María said nothing. She returned to the kitchen and picked up where she had left off in the cleaning of the breakfast dishes.

One week later the large expedition under the command of Lt. Facundo Melgares departed from Santa Fe. Gordo rode a new horse he had recently purchased, a fine Spanish steed of Arabian origins that had proved itself in recent races that were popular on Sunday morning in the town.

Most of the citizens of Santa Fe turned out to bid the expedition farewell. Margarita, María and Manuel were among them. As the column moved out to the sound of blaring bugles and the cheers of the citizenry, Gordo looked down at María and tipped his hat. They'd made love the night before for the first time in months, and it was the same for Maria as it had always been. Gordo had been drinking and was not interested in love. He simply took her, brutally and without concern for the pain she felt as he plunged into her dry sheath. She had not moved, had not responded and had simply allowed him to discharge into her as though she were an inanimate receptacle for his passion.

As Gordo rode off into the distance at the head of the long, straggling column of men and beasts, a strange calm came over María. For the first time her fears, anxiety and unhappiness were replaced by a sense of resolve. No matter what her role as the traditional Spanish wife, no matter what was expected of her by tradition and law, she would never again subject herself to the cruelty of Gordo Soltura. If he returned, he would return to an empty bed. And if for some reason she was still there upon his return, she would no longer function as a slave to do his bidding.

Manuel had tears in his eyes as he saw his son ride off. He turned to see a smiling María. "Why do you smile at seeing your husband go off?" he asked. "He goes off to perhaps do battle with American military men, and could lose his life."

María turned to her father-in-law and smiled again. "I am proud, papa. I am simply proud of my husband's bravery."

As Gordo and Lt. Malgares rode at the head of the column, Gordo yelled over the sound of thousands of hoofs and the chatter of men, "What do you know of this Captain Pike who leads the American expedition?"

Malgares shouted his reply. "Only that he is a captain in the American army, has a small group of men with him and comes to New Spain to establish an outpost on behalf of his government. We will have no problem with him."

Gordo and the lieutenant laughed heartily and looked ahead to the vast nothingness they would cross before reaching their destination.

CHAPTER EIGHTEEN

By the 23rd of September the Zebulon Pike expedition had crossed the Solomon and had established camp on the west bank of that river.

The following day a small representative group of the Pawnee nation rode in to greet them, and to suggest that a meeting be arranged at which terms of an agreement could be reached between the Americans and the Indians of the area. Pike agreed to the plan, and two days later moved his camp on the banks of the Solomon to the perimeter of the vast Pawnee nation. Pike and Bob and John Barrigan sat on their horses and watched as three hundred mounted Pawnees moved out from their village and officially welcomed the visitors to their land. There was, of course, great interest in the presence of Fleet Fire, now known as Susan Barrigan. Her value to the Pike force quickly became evident. She functioned as a translator in a way that Vasquez could never have hoped to because of his limitations with the Indian languages.

By nightfall a warm relationship had been established between the Pike expedition and the leadership of the Pawnee. Pike chose to establish camp on a high ridge that formed a half moon around the sprawling Pawnee village. Pike and his men had spent days crossing a broad, flat plain. Now, as they sat high atop the ridge and looked over the land below, there was a general feeling of well-being that caused everyone to relax and to view with optimism whatever might lie ahead.

The next few days were spent in council with the leadership of the Pawnee. It was decided that other tribes of the area should be called into council so that a meaningful and all-encompassing set of agreements could be reached. A group of twelve Kansas arrived on September 26 to meet with Captain Pike. Two days later the Osage who traveled with the Pike party, and a delegation from the Kansas tribe met with the Pawnee chieftains and smoked the pipe of peace.

On September 29, a Grand Council was called. It met all day, and by the end of the day, Pike was sufficiently optimistic to demand from the Indian leadership that the Spanish flag that was displayed day and night over the chief's door be replaced by a United States flag.

"I see no reason to do that," the chief said.

"The future of all this land lies with the government of the United States," Pike said through Fleet Fire. "There will come a day in the near future when this territory will no longer belong to Spain. As an official representative of my government, I insist that the flag of Spain be taken down from your doorway and be replaced by the flag I hereby give you." He handed the chieftain the American flag.

Much to Pike's surprise, and to the surprise of Bob and John Barrigan, the chief bowed to Pike's demand. He stood, and without conferring with any of his other leadership, walked to his door, took the flag from above it and replaced it with the flag he had been given by Zebulon Pike.

Bob Barrigan felt that Pike's insistence upon the change of flags was a mistake. There had been no order given to Pike by Aaron Burr or any of his representatives to establish American territory within that area already under Spanish control. Pike's demand seemed arbitrary, and Barrigan considered intervening in the situation. But the obvious pleasure Pike took in seeing such a powerful and populous nation capitulate to his demand indicated to the Barrigans that it was best to stay out of it. Bob Barrigan did, however, suggest to Pike that he return the Spanish flag to the Indians. Pike did so, which seemed to please the tribe's leadership.

Pike and his men remained as guests of the Pawnee nation until the 6th of October when, over the objections of the tribe's leadership to a further push west, Pike instructed his troops to break camp and to prepare for a long march. By this time a tension had developed between the Americans and the Pawnee that threatened to break out in open hostility at any moment. Bob Barrigan chalked it up to the flag incident, although there was obviously much more involved. As in the situation they'd encountered with White Hair and the Osage, the Pawnee leadership was reluctant to see the Americans proceed west to the territory of enemy tribes and to perhaps indicate to those tribes the relative strength of the Pawnee people.

It took intense negotiations for the Pawnee Chief to agree to sell to Pike a fresh supply of horses for the intended trip. As an increasingly disenchanted Lt. Wilkinson noted in his diary: *"On the 6th of October we made some few purchases of miserable horses at the most exorbitant prices, and on the 7th, unmoved by the threats of the chief, we marched in a close and compacted body until we passed their village, and took the large Spanish beaten trace for the Arkansas River."*

It was Pike's intention to continue the march westward to the Arkansas headwaters. He led his party to the southwest along the Spanish trail, but eventually lost the trail where it had been obliterated by buffalo herds.

By mid-October they'd reached the Arkansas River and established a camp along its banks.

The weather had begun to turn cold, and the Pike expedition remained along the banks of the Arkansas for ten days as it made preparations for a further push west into what was sure to be even colder weather.

The ten day stay along the Arkansas River was longer than Pike had intended to remain. He'd originally seen a need for only a three or four day rest, but a growing dissatisfaction within his party resulted in a series of disagreements.

One night, as they sat around a campfire and tried to ward off the chill of the October evening, Lt. Wilkinson announced that he no longer wished to proceed with the journey.

"That's a hell of a thing," Bob Barrigan said. "What do you intend to do?"

"I'm going home," Wilkinson replied.

Zeb Pike was incredulous. He confronted Wilkinson and said, "You're an officer of the American army, lieutenant. I am your commanding officer. This mission will proceed westward until I decide it is no longer viable."

Wilkinson was not to be deterred. He said flatly, "I no longer believe in the purpose of this mission, captain, or in the way it is being conducted. It is my decision to return home as quickly as possible, and I am not alone in this feeling. A number of the men share my views and have agreed to accompany me to the east."

John Barrigan, who was sitting with his arm around Susan, said, "I'm no military man but that seems to be treason."

Wilkinson forced a laugh. "I think this whole trip is treason, gentlemen. I wish no further part of it. I'm sure my father would see things in the same light and I intend to talk to him the moment I reach home. If anyone seriously wishes to stop me I would suggest that they give second thoughts to it. There is nothing to be gained by going further west. If you wish to continue, that is your business."

The next morning Pike called everyone in the force together. He asked for a show of hands from those who wished to accompany Wilkinson home. Five enlisted men raised their hands.

"Are you going to retrace our steps?" Pike asked Wilkinson.

"No, captain, I intend to go down the river in canoes."

Bob Barrigan said, "That doesn't make much sense to me. This river is going to be ice pretty soon. You'd be better off staying with us."

Wilkinson suddenly flared with anger. "I'm sick and tired of taking advice from you, Mr. Barrigan, and from your son. This is a military mission sponsored by the government of the United States. You have no place in it, and I will no longer take your advice or your orders. Is that understood?"

Bob Barrigan shook his head. "Have it your way, son. But I'm telling you that you are in for trouble if you try to go down this river in canoes."

"I'll take responsibility for my decision, Mr. Barrigan." Wilkinson turned to Pike. "Captain Pike, I mean no disrespect to you, nor am I used to disobeying direct orders. But my mind is made up. I wish to begin immediately to build canoes that will carry us down the river toward home."

As much as Pike wanted to continue to fight Wilkinson's treason, and as strong as his inclinations were to use his resources to keep the lieutenant and the other men with him, he realized that to proceed through the difficult winter months with a dissenting faction could only spell disaster. It seemed to Pike it was better to have a smaller group of men working in concert than to constantly be worried about the attitudes of those who did not share their views.

Pike went to Wilkinson and extended his hand. "Lieutenant, I won't try to stop you. I can only wish you well."

Wilkinson breathed a sigh of relief. It had taken every fiber within him to disobey a superior officer, and to follow through on his convictions. He had no idea whether it was feasible to proceed down the Arkansas at that time of year, but his

159

unhappiness with being part of the expedition had become overwhelming. He shook Pike's hand. "Thank you, captain. I wish you success."

And that was all that was said. Wilkinson, two Osage Indians and five enlisted men went to work building the canoes that they hoped would carry them home. They made one canoe from a cottonwood tree. The other was made of buffalo and elk skins and saplings.

On October 28 Wilkinson and his party departed the Pike camp on the Arkansas. Their journey home was to be treacherous and filled with danger, but they did eventually reach St. Louis, the point from which they'd started.

After Wilkinson's party had departed, Pike and Bob and John Barrigan held a meeting.

"Well, gentlemen, what do you think?" Pike asked.

"I never did like the little son-of-a-bitch anyway," Bob Barrigan said. "The hell with him. I say let's get on with the trip because every day we lose just means more snow to contend with further on down the line."

"I agree, Mr. Barrigan," Pike said. He turned to John Barrigan. "Any reservations, John?"

John Barrigan shook his head and smiled. "I've come this far with you, Zeb, and I'll go the rest of the way."

"Good," Pike said. "Let's get moving."

As John Barrigan and his new wife huddled together that night in their tent, he asked her softly, "Are you willing to go further?"

"I do not understand," Susan said.

"There are going to be some very rough days ahead, Susan. It would be possible to find you a home with one of the tribes in this area. I could fetch you when we return."

Susan nuzzled her face into his neck. Her fingertips brushed lightly over his chest and she enjoyed the feeling of his thigh pressed tightly into her pubic area. "I am your wife, John Barrigan. You have named me Susan after your mother. You say you love me. I wish only to be with you and to comfort you in times of trouble."

Barrigan kissed her on the mouth and felt his erection press against her belly. "I love you, Susan."

"And that is why I continue with you, John."

Their lovemaking that night was frenetic and desperate, as though both of them felt that it might be the last time that they were ever to enjoy such exquisite pleasure.

The march as far as the Arkansas River had been conducted at a relatively leisurely pace. Now with the threat of winter, Pike moved the column at an accelerated clip. As they drove westward toward the Stony Mountains, food became critically short and frostbite took its toll on various members of the group. By the end of the first week of November their rations were down to a tin cup of hard corn for each man.

They made camp in a grove of ocote pine. After a fire had been started and everyone had huddled together behind temporary shelters against the wind, John Barrigan asked Zeb Pike for a private conversation. The two young men moved away from the fire and into the pine grove.

"What's up, John?" Zeb asked.

"It's my father, Zeb. He's real sick."

"I can see that, John, but I don't know what to do."

"I talked to Dr. Robinson. He says that nothing can be done except to get him warm and to get some good food into him. How much longer do you figure we have to go before we hit some civilization?"

"I truly don't know, John. I wish I did. All I can see is what you can see, and that's snow and mountains. But somewhere in those mountains there has got to be a settlement of Indians who could save us. If I didn't have that faith I don't think I could go on. My toes are about froze off, and I think I've got a fever, too."

John leaned against a tree and shook his head wearily. "It would be my suggestion that we try to make as comfortable a camp as possible right here for at least another day, Zeb. Maybe we can go out and find us some meat somewhere."

"That's wishful thinking, John. We haven't seen an animal in ten days."

"I don't see we have much choice," John said. "If we push on for another day we're sure to lose some people, including my father. I want one day to look for some food."

Zeb nodded in agreement. "You're right, John. Let's see if we can't hustle up some grub tomorrow. I'm sorry about your father. Maybe we should never have pushed on like this. Maybe Wilkinson was right."

John slapped Zeb on the arm and said in his biggest voice, "What the hell kind of talk is that, captain? What we're going through here can't compare to what we went through back in that wilderness called New York City. Let's get this camp put together and see if we can't get ourselves warm with a few additional fires. Tomorrow, we'll go out and find us some buffalo. I have the feelin' in my bones."

Pike laughed. "John Barrigan, you're as crazy as a loon."

"I accept that as a compliment, captain."

By morning Bob Barrigan's condition had worsened. After feeding him a weak soup which Susan had prepared from pine cones she'd gathered in the grove, John and Zeb left the camp in search of food.

It had begun to snow during the night and visibility lowered dramatically as they forged their way through drifting snow from previous storms and headed for what appeared to be a small valley a mile or two away. Both men suffered from frostbite; there was no feeling in their fingers or toes. The skin on their faces had turned from a fiery red to a sickening gray color. Snow and ice hung from their eyebrows and from the beard John had grown during the journey.

Zeb carried a .69 calliber smoothbore musket. It weighed ten pounds but felt much heavier as they fought their way through the deep snow toward the valley. John's weapon was a solid-framed .44 caliber pistol with an eight-inch barrel. It had been especially made for him back east, and fired a blunt-end rifle cartridge of forty grains of powder. The weapon was his pride and joy, and no matter how fatigued he was at the end of a day he always found time to clean and care for the gun.

After an hour the two young men became concerned that they would not be able to find their way back to the camp, so fierce was the snowstorm that moved in during the early morning hours. There was even a chance that they would lose each other. John Barrigan's pace was faster through the snow than Pike's, and he often stopped and waited for the captain to catch up before continuing.

Once, Pike fell in the snow and lay there for a long time. John went back to him and asked. "Are you all right?"

Pike looked up at him and managed a smile. "Right as can be, John. Just doggin' it a little. Let's go." He got up and continued moving with John toward the valley where they hoped some miracle would occur and a source of food could be found.

It took another hour to reach the valley, which was nothing more than a relatively small, flat area on the other side of the mountain from where they had established camp. They stood together and surveyed the terrain. Visibility was still poor, and what they could see was hardly calculated to raise their spirits. There was nothing but white. It was as though the world had disappeared and had been replaced by a colorless void. The cold was intense. Their eyes had narrowed to slits against the blowing snow.

"What do we do now?" Zeb asked. His words were almost lost in the wind.

"Let's move into the valley a little further," Barrigan said.

As they painfully made their way through thigh-deep snow, Zeb realized that he was losing his grip on reality. There was a surrealistic quality to their situation, and although he realized what was happening to him, he was powerless to fight it. The pain had been replaced by a blissful contemplation of lying down in the snow, closing his eyes and allowing himself to slip from life. Things became reversed in his mind. The blankets of snow that covered the valley floor became warm comforters. Somewhere beneath the snow there seemed to exist a warm, peaceful layer into which he could burrow and once again feel good. He realized he was smiling, his lips split open in a dozen places, the blood instantly frozen into slender red threads over his ice-crusted mouth and chin.

John looked into Zeb's face and saw that something was wrong. He realized that unless something happened quickly and positively, they were doomed, along with the rest of their party back at camp.

John turned away from Zeb and desperately tried to see beyond the blowing, swirling snow. At first, the shape he saw two hundred yards away was only a dark spot. He tried to focus more clearly on the shadowy shape as he did, it seemed to be the form of a large animal. He quickly turned to Zeb and poked him in the arm. "Look," he said.

For a moment Zeb was confused by the simple order. When he realized what John wanted him to do, he summoned his senses and looked in the direction of John's hand.

"What is it?" Zeb asked.

"I don't know," John said, "but if it's what I think it is, that miracle I talked about might be about to happen."

Slowly, awkwardly, they moved through the snow toward the darker form, their guns cocked and ready to fire. As they came closer John's hopes were realized. It was a buffalo, a huge one, that had strayed from its herd that was gathered a half mile further into the valley. The buffalo appeared numb, stunned. It stood like a statue, a monument to nature's wrath.

"Let's fire on three," John whispered to Zeb.

Pike nodded.

"One, two, three."

The sound of their weapons discharging shattered the eerie, frigid stillness of the valley. Both shots found their mark. The beast, without turning its head in the direction of its attackers, swayed slightly to the left, then to the right, and collapsed on its left side.

John and Zeb went to it and looked down. The kill had been instantaneous. The buffalo with its precious meat, was theirs.

It was not until that evening that enough men could be summoned to dismember the buffalo in the valley and to bring the parts of its body back to camp. By the time some of the meat had been cooked and Susan Barrigan could make a warm, life-sustaining stew, the storm had passed, the wind no longer blew and the stomachs of every member of the Pike party were filled.

"We'll leave first thing in the morning," John said to his father. "How are you feeling?"

"Not too good, son, although that buffalo meat could pump life back into any man. I'll be all right. Don't worry about me. I'll be just fine for travelin' by sunup."

They left at dawn and continued west. Bob Barrigan did appear to have gained a little of his health, although he found it difficult to walk and spent most of the journey riding one of the few mules that had survived the trip. As they continued into the Stony Mountains, the snow belt seemed to fade behind them and to the south. Although there was snow on the upper portions of the moutains, there were vast areas that were either without snow or had only a minimal crust. Game was plentiful. Buffalo, elk, deer, antelope and panthers were seen along the way.

One week later, on November 15, the small band of men under the leadership of Captain Zebulon Pike stood at the foot of the tallest mountain in the Stony Mountain range.

Bob Barrigan, who had been propped against a tree, looked up and said to Zebulon Pike, "That's a pretty tall mountain, Zeb. Might be that we're the first white men have ever seen it."

"If that be the case," said John Barrigan, "they ought to call it Pike's Mountain."

After a dinner of venison stew with corn and a mush made of piñon nuts, the exhausted members of the Pike party settled in for a good night's sleep. John and Zeb sat up late into the night. They had bartered for tobacco with a small Indian tribe they'd met along the way, and the heavy smoke from freshly rolled cigarettes filled their lungs.

The sun broke above the horizon bright and brilliant the next morning. John found it pleasurable to linger in the sleeping bag with Susan, and stayed there far beyond the time he normally got up. When he did, he was confronted by a grim Zebulon Pike.

"What's the matter, Zeb?" he asked.

"It's your daddy, John. He's dead."

Robert Barrigan was buried at the foot of the mountain that had become known to the members of the expeditionary force as Pike's Peak. The following day the party departed the foot of the mountain and moved toward the headwaters of the Rio Grande. In doing so it passed into Spanish territory, and once it had, the word quickly reached the Spanish army commanded by Lt. Facundo Melgares, with whom Gordo de Soltura proudly rode.

CHAPTER NINETEEN

Spring, 1807

A meeting between Father Juan de Soltura, Father Miguel Hidalgo and Father José María Morelos had been scheduled to take place in Dolores. The site was changed at the last minute by Hidalgo because of increasing pressure placed upon him in that town by local Spanish officials. The three priests met instead in León, approximately eighty kilometers to the west.

León was a larger town than Dolores. It sat on the border that separated the province of León, and the province of Jalisco. Because of its location, much of the church administration for those two provinces was conducted from the town of León, and the presence of three additional priests would not be nearly as noticeable as it would have been had they gathered in the smaller town of Dolores.

Soltura, Hidalgo and Morelos met at eight o'clock in the morning on a clear, sunny day in April. They sat in the shade of a flowering peach tree on a veranda attached to a small, nondescript home in the center of town. The house belonged to an old friend of Morelos, who had vacated it for the period the priests would be there. Juan had arrived a day earlier and had spent the previous night in the house. Morelos arrived late that evening. Hidalgo made his appearance just moments before the morning meeting.

"Como esta usted?" Morelos asked Hidalgo.

"Quite well, thank you, although these damp days cause the pain in my neck and shoulders to worsen."

Juan noticed what he considered a dramatic change in Father Hidalgo's appearance since the last time he'd seen him. He seemed to have aged considerably, and the lines in his face were longer and deeper than before. Perhaps, he reasoned, it was the constant arthritic pain the older priest suffered. Still, the fire remained in his eyes. Never before had Juan Soltura seen such brilliance and determination in the eyes of any man.

"The porcelain factory?" Juan asked. "It is in full operation?"

"*Sí,*" Hidalgo said. "It provides much work for the mestizos, sambos and Indians."

A matronly mestizo woman who kept house for Morelos's friend served the priests tea with honey, and fresh tortillas. As they enjoyed their breakfast on the veranda, talk turned to the significant events that had recently taken place in New Spain, and in the world. News from the United States that the scheme hatched by Aaron Burr, General James Wilkinson and Harman Blennerhassett had been exposed to President Jefferson by Wilkinson, and that Burr had been arrested in the Mississippi Territory on charges of treason, had piqued the interest of every citizen. It also had prompted the government to dispatch troops to various points along the United States border in an attempt to head off any further exploration into the territory. Burr had been taken to Richmond, Virginia, where he was to be indicted.

The paranoia within New Spain caused by the exposure of Burr's plot to establish a foothold in the Spanish Territory was heightened by news from Santa Fe that a Spanish force led by Lt. Facundo Melgares had interecepted and captured one of the forces that had been dispatched on Burr's behalf, and that was led by an American army captain, Zebulon Pike. Juan Soltura actually knew more of the details of that capture than most citizens of New Spain because of the correspondence he had received from his father. Manuel Soltura had sung the praises of Gordo and his role in capturing Pike and his men. Of course, Manuel could only repeat the story that he had been told by Gordo upon his return, in which Gordo captured Pike under great duress and threat of life. In reality, Pike, John Barrigan, Dr. Robinson and the translator, Vasquez, and the men under their command had offered no resistance to the superior Spanish army. Pike and Barrigan had established a fort on the upper Rio Grande and had begun developing a community within it, made up primarily of other Americans who had ventured into the Spanish Territory in search of furs. Pike, Barrigan and Dr. Robinson had been escorted from the fort to Santa Fe where they were presented to the governor of the province, Joaquín del Real Alencaster. Alencaster interviewed them at length and ordered them detained in the military stockade. He instructed the jailers to treat them with the utmost respect and courtesy, and he assured Pike that he would come to a decision about what to do with them within the near future.

The return of the force led by Lt. Melgares brought the Santa Fe garrison back to full strength, which pleased Governor Alencaster. The Apache tribes of the area had become increasingly hostile, and their random raids upon individual haciendas had intensified, both in frequence and in viciousness.

But Alencaster's comfort at having a full military contingent was to be short-lived. He received orders from the viceroy to dispatch as many men as possible to the borders of the Louisiana Territory along the Arkansas and Red Rivers. Because Gordo Soltura was held in such high regard by Lt. Melgares, he was given a permanent commission and dispatched at the head of a column to a point where the rivers joined.

"How goes it with your family?" Father Hidalgo asked Juan.

"Quite well, I believe, although I cannot say that with any conviction about the marriage of my brother to María Jardinero. Although the letters from my mother and father do not specify trouble, it is obvious if one reads between the lines."

"I am sorry to hear that," Hidalgo said.

"Yes. Well, enough of this. What of news of Spain?" Juan asked.

Morelos, who'd recently spent time with a young priest who'd arrived only months ago from France, reported that there was growing fear within Spain of an invasion by the troops of Napoleon. Charles IV, King of Spain, had ordered a gradual mobilization of Spanish forces to combat such a threat, but the French priest indicated that no one seriously believed that Spain could withstand an invasion by France. The Spanish empire was so far-flung that the ability of the mother country to preserve its independence had been considerably weakened.

The three men sat in silence for a few moments. They were all aware of the destruction which Napoleon's takeover of Spain would bring about within the Spanish Catholic Church. Napoleon's 1801 Concordat with the Pope under which church lands could be confiscated and sold to secular persons could become a distinct reality in Spain and in its colonies, should the French dictator's invasion prove successful. The fear of such an event occupied the thoughts and conversations of most of the church hierarchy in New Spain. For the three priests sitting in León, however, the contemplation of turmoil within the offical church was of less concern than more immediate matters, and when the discussion of national and world affairs was concluded, they turned to what was most pressing to them.

Father Hidalgo made sure that the mestizo woman was gone. He leaned on the table and said, "Gentlemen, the time is drawing near for the revolution to take place."

Juan wanted to say something but Hidalgo asked him to wait until he had finished with what he had to say.

"There is little doubt Viceroy Iturrigaray will be forced from office by the gachupines. Although he has proved to be more liberal than previous viceroys, which is encouraging to those of us in sympathy with the criollo cause, his very liberal stance seems certain to bring about his downfall. I hear much talk of a movement already underway to force him from New Spain." Hidalgo shook his head and closed his eyes. "It is amazing, is it not, how much a tiny minority of people can have such power within a vast nation such as this. Of ten million people, the gachupines comprise less than one percent, and yet they continue to rule, and to benefit from their rule."

"As little sympathy as I have for Iturrigaray, I am concerned at the thought of who might be sent by Spain to take his place," Juan said.

"Yes, the chances are the king will send someone less liberal than Iturrigaray in order to appease the gachupines. However, my brothers, I consider such problems to be irrelevant when viewed against the greatest problem of social injustice within this nation. The choice of a viceroy is not important. What is important is the dream, which I know you share, that one day this land shall be ruled by its citizens and shall not have imposed upon it the whims of any viceroy sent to us by a mother country."

Morelos and Juan nodded in agreement.

Father Morelos looked across the table at Hidalgo and asked, "You say the revolution is near, father. How near?"

Hidalgo started to explain the timetable he had tentatively

set up when the sound of footsteps on the other side of the wall caused all three men to tense and stop speaking. Juan got up and walked to a wooden gate that led from the veranda to a narrow winding street. He opened the gate and saw two older priests standing together, their ears cocked toward the wall. Juan startled them. They flashed broad smiles and uttered greetings.

"Buenos días, padres," Juan said. "May I be of service?"

"No, no," one of the priests said. "We were just taking a stroll."

"It is a lovely day for a stroll," Juan said.

Juan remained at the gate until the two priests had disappeared around a bend in the road. He closed the gate and returned to the table where he told Hidalgo and Morelos of what had occurred.

"I'm not surprised we are spied upon," Hidalgo said heavily. "We have as many enemies within the church as we do within the government."

"Doesn't anyone high up in the church care about the people it serves?" Juan asked, his voice rising with indignation.

Hidalgo hushed him by pressing his finger to his lips. "Speak softly, my son, lest we lose you at a time when we cannot afford to lose anyone. Yes, we have friends high up in the church structure, but they must remain unknown to all but a few of us in order to protect their positions."

Juan reached into the folds of his robe and withdrew an envelope. He handed it to Hidalgo saying, "I almost forgot, Father Hidalgo. Father Gomez sends this to you."

Hidalgo hit the side of his head with the heel of his hand. "How insensitive of me to forget that our dear friend, Gomez, is ill. How does he fare?"

Juan shook his head gravely. "Not well, although the physician who treats him does not seem to be overly concerned. He wished very much to be here for this meeting."

"Yes, I am sure he wanted that," Hidalgo said.

Hidalgo stood. "I must meet with someone of great importance now," he said. "Please join me back here at three and I will tell you in as much detail as possible what plans have been formulated to carry out our cause."

Juan and Morelos watched the older priest walk from the veranda and exit through the gate. There was no doubt that time was taking its toll upon him. He now walked with a slight limp, and his back seemed hunched, almost as though it were in constant battle against the pain in his body.

When he was gone, Juan and Morelos stood and joined hands.

"A game of cards, father?" Morelos asked.

"Yes, of course," Juan said.

Juan had no interest in cards except to pass the time until their next meeting with the man who would become the spiritual leader of the oppressed in New Spain. Had Juan been able to choose what he would do at that moment, it would have been to see his family again, to laugh with his father and to feel the undemanding love of his mother. Juan felt a twinge of desire to see his brother, Gordo. But most of all, it was María Jardinero that he wanted to see again and be close to. Not a day had gone by in his life that he did not think of her, did not revel in the memories of her beauty and in the potent and warm feeling she had given him simply by being close. Daily thoughts of María eventually turned into sexual fantasy, and Juan found himself asking forgiveness of his Lord each time such fantasies overcame him. But recently, he no longer asked for forgiveness. To think of loving a beautiful woman seened right and moral compared to the sickness of poverty. He'd decided only a month ago that his prayers would no longer be for forgiveness for loving. He would devote his prayers to a call for strength, so that the inevitable confrontation with the social injustice that he so hated could be met with honor, and result in victory.

The two older priests who had been listening outside the wall entered the central administrative offices of the Catholic Church of New Spain in León and went directly to the office of Internal Church Affairs.

The secular head of the office dutifully made notes as one of the priests said, "Hidalgo was there, and Father Morelos. There was a third priest present, whose name I do not know."

The administrative head of the office looked up and said quietly, "Find out who he is."

The other priest said, "Of course," and both men of the cloth left the room, their black robes flowing behind them.

CHAPTER TWENTY

Fall 1807

"If I knew being a prisoner was this good," Zeb Pike said to John Barrigan, "I'd have done something bad a long time ago."

Since being arrested on the Rio Grande by Lt. Melgares, Pike, Barrigan and other members of Pike's group had been treated royally by their Spanish captors. They'd been detained in the military stockade for only a short period of time. Then, after numerous conferences with Governor Alencaster, they were allowed to roam free based upon their word to the governor that they would not attempt to leave Santa Fe. Alencaster had nothing to fear. After the long and arduous trek that had almost taken the lives of everyone in the party, the warm sun and pleasant atmosphere of the Spanish town was too appealing to even consider leaving. Not that Pike and Barrigan did not intend at some point to return to the their homes. It was just that a long vacation seemed in order, and as long as Pike was officially a prisoner of the Spanish government, no one in army headquarters could question his absence.

Barrigan's Indian wife, Susan, had become a temporary resident of the Soltura household. Manuel had been promising Margarita that he would find someone to help her with the household chores, and when the young Osage woman arrived in Santa Fe, Manuel readily secured permission from Governor Alencaster to have the girl placed under his supervision. It had worked out extremely well. Susan and María seemed to strike an instant rapport, and it wasn't long before their relationship was more that of sisters than of servant and household mistress.

John Barrigan had desperately missed the companionship of his wife during his internment in the stockade. But now that he was free, he was able to spend many nights with her, either in María's bedroom in the Soltura home while María discreetly vacated it, or in Barrigan's room at the stockade which he shared with Zeb Pike. John had asked permission to set up a household of his own while in Santa Fe so that he and Susan could be together full-time, but his request was denied. As Governor Alencaster had said, "Be thankful you are free to leave the stockade to see your Indian wife, Mr. Barrigan. Please do not strain my generosity."

This night, Zeb and John dressed to attend a reception to be given by the governor at his home in the center of Santa Fe. They'd purchased black cutaway coats, white trousers and ruffled white cotton shirts for the occasion. It felt good dressing up, at least for Pike. Barrigan, as usual, found anything other than roughshod work clothes uncomfortable.

"I wish Susan could be there with me," John said as he struggled into the coat that had been cut a little too small for his frame. "She's my wife, even if she is an Indian."

Zeb didn't respond. He didn't want to feed John's anger at the treatment Susan had been receiving in Santa Fe because of her birth. Nor did he want to upset an obviously delicate situation and perhaps strip away from them the privileges they'd been granted. "Besides," he had told John, "Susan is doing just fine. She seems very happy with the Soltura family. From the looks of the other Indians around here, I'd say she's living like a queen."

John knew Zeb was right and never pressed the issue with him. But it chewed away at his insides, and he realized that it was time for him to take some action to shed his prisoner status, either by virtue of obtaining such a change through official channels, or by escaping from Santa Fe.

Pike changed the subject. "You know, John," he said, "I've never known of prisoners being invited to official receptions at a governor's mansion, have you?"

Barrigan knew the subject was being changed, but went along with it. "Can't say that I have, Zeb. Well, how do I look?"

"Like a man in pain," Zeb replied, laughing heartily. "I guess there is just no way you can ever be made to look comfortable in decent clothes."

"My pa was the same way," John said. The words stuck

in his throat. He desperately wished his father were there with them.

The reception at the governor's house had created a general air of festivity in Santa Fe. The plaza and the streets leading into it were filled with armed, uniformed militiamen whose job it was to insure a level of peace, calm and decorum for the length of time the reception would run. Many citizens who ordinarily would not have ventured out into the center of town after dark found themselves doing just that. Couples walked arm-in-arm. The brothels had been ordered closed for the night. The word was spread that anyone who became drunk and rowdy in the saloons or on the streets would be arrested. Some of the prostitutes had dressed in their finest clothing and walked arm-in-arm with the same young men who, under ordinary circumstances, would have been in their places of business paying them for their services.

Governor Alencaster was in an expansive mood as he stood in a reception line and greeted each of his guests. When Zeb and John reached him, he heartily embraced them and asked that they stand with him to be introduced to the other guests. The governor obviously had a sense of humor. He introduced the two young men to everyone as, "My favorite Yankee prisoners."

After the long reception line passed, the governor led Zeb and John to a lavishly set table on the other side of which Indian servants dressed in white served a vast array of the best food the area had to offer. While Zeb and John filled their plates, Margarita Soltura and her husband, Manuel, came to the table and asked how they were faring.

"Just fine, ma'am," John said.

"It is a shame your wife cannot be here with you," Margarita said.

John knew from past conversations with Margarita that her words were sincere. He thanked her for the sentiment and asked what Susan was doing that night.

"She is at home." Margarita smiled. "Perhaps you should slip away from the reception and join her there."

Zeb grinned. "I suspect, Señora Soltura, that my friend here intended to do precisely that."

John was a little embarrassed. He said, "It would be nice to see her tonight, ma'am. Much obliged."

The dialogue between his wife and John Barrigan annoyed Manuel Soltura. He said, "I am not sure it would be proper to leave the governor's reception for such a reason. It would be disrespectful. Perhaps if your wife were not Indian, things would be better.''

Zeb lightly touched John on the arm to keep him from responding.

Margarita's face lighted up as she looked toward the door and saw María enter the room. Manuel had been angry that María was not ready in time to accompany them to the reception. Susan had helped María dress, and it seemed to Manuel that they were deliberately dallying. They'd even had words about it. He'd said to her, ''To be late to a governor's reception is a disgrace, María. As part of my household I insist you be ready on time.''

María had quietly ignored his words and by the time Manuel and Margarita were ready to leave, she had still not finished dressing.

Now, looking stunning in a turquoise silk skirt embroidered with multicolored flowers, a silver brocade jacket that was fitted closely to her fine figure and a black lace mantilla that hung gracefully from a high, carved bone comb in her rich, black hair, she caused many conversations to stop. Since Gordo had left Santa Fe, first to accompany the Melgares force in search of the Pike expedition, and then to lead the border patrol, vitality and spirit had returned to María. She was, of course, unavailable to the multitude of swooning young men because she was married to Gordo. But there was little debate that María Soltura was among the most beautiful women in the area.

Zeb Pike had never been introduced to María before, and he enthusiastically accepted her outstretched hand and held it as she curtsied. John, who'd been introduced to her the first night he spent with Susan, also extended his hand and María took it. Both men had been taken with her beauty when they'd seen her in town, but the potency of it screamed out at them at that moment in the governor's house.

''You look lovely, María,'' Margarita said.

''She should. It took her long enough,'' Manuel said, giving María a hard stare to indicate his displeasure at her late arrival.

The eight-piece orchestra struck up a tune, and couples quickly filled the dance floor. Zeb and John both looked at María, and it was just a question of who would overcome his shyness first and ask her to dance.

As it turned out, María saved both of them from having to make such a choice. She looked at John Barrigan and said, "Would you care to dance, Mr. Barrigan?"

John was a little flustered, and cast a quick sidelong glance at Zeb.

"Well?" María asked.

"Oh, yes, ma'am, I'd be right flattered." John and María went to the dance floor and joined the other couples. John felt intensely awkward. He had never learned to dance, and he had the feeling he was making a total fool of himself on the floor. María put his fears to rest by smiling reassuringly, and by engaging him in a conversation that took his mind off the music and off the feeling that his feet had turned to blocks of wood.

When the dance was half over, María asked, "Do you know what I think, Mr. Barrigan?"

"No, ma'am."

"I think that no one would miss you if you left here and went to Susan."

"Well, to be truthful, I've been thinkin' of that but I didn't want to offend anybody. After all, I am a prisoner here."

María laughed with gusto. "And probably the most unique prisoner in the history of New Spain," she said. "Please go to Susan. She misses you terribly, and I told her before I left that I would arrange for you to spend most of the evening there. The house is empty except for her, and it would be a shame to waste the night at one of these dull official affairs."

John thought of Susan alone in the Soltura household, and he made up his mind that he would follow María's advice and go to Susan at the first convenient moment.

John led María back to where her mother and father stood chatting with Zebulon Pike.

"I guess you noticed I'm not much of a dancer," John said.

"It was no secret to anybody," Zeb said good-naturedly.

The band launched into another tune. Zeb looked to John to see whether he intended to dance again with María. When it was obvious he did not, he asked María if she would join him on the dance floor.

"I'd be delighted, captain," María said, holding out her arm to Zeb.

As Zeb and María danced, John Barrigan looked around to size up the situation. Manuel and Margarita Soltura had gone off to join friends, which left Barrigan quite alone. "Might as well be now," he told himself as he slowly skirted the perimeter of the large room. But before he could get very far, Governor Alencaster intercepted him and insisted he join a group of civic leaders in a discussion of the potentials of the deteriorating relationship between New Spain and the United States. John realized that to protest would be a waste of time. He followed the governor from the reception hall to a small study where three of Santa Fe's leading politicians had gathered. They were soon joined by Manuel Soltura and another man. John told the men repeatedly that he had little interest in or knowledge of politics and was in Santa Fe because he and his father had been hired by the Pike expedition because of their background and experience as woodsmen. But his words were dismissed as false modesty, and he was soon settled in a comfortable stuffed leather chair, a glass of whiskey in one hand, a long thin black cigar in the other.

As Zeb and María left the dance floor and availed themselves to some punch, they surveyed the room in search of John.

"I don't see my friend," Zeb said.

"I should hope not, captain," María said. "I suspect that at this moment he is where he should be, with his wife."

"That's good news," Zeb said. He ladled punch from a silver bowl into María's glass and asked some questions about her life. She answered them candidly, and they were soon into the sort of discussion that one usually expects from friends of longer duration. Two other young couples joined them, and Zeb soon forgot about John and had settled comfortably into a pleasant evening of dancing, dining and good conversation.

Susan Barrigan sat in the Soltura parlor and anxiously awaited the arrival of her husband. She'd been elated when María assured her that she would see to it that John escaped the reception in order that he might spend time with her, and each minute seemed an eternity, so keen was her anticipation. She was pleased to be alone in the house so that she and John might have some moments together as husband and wife.

After some time had passed and John had not arrived, Susan got up and went to the kitchen where she sliced off a piece of melon. She was washing the knife when she heard a sound at the front door. Her heart tripped, and she went from the kitchen to the parlor. She'd changed from the work dress she wore around the house to a frilly and revealing gown given her by María. It had been a long time since she'd made love with John, and she wanted to greet him as attractively as possible.

She stopped just inside the parlor and touched her hair to make sure it was still in place. María had created a style for her that was different from the way she usually wore it, loose and straight.

The heavy, black wrought-iron handle on the front door turned and the door opened.

The sight of a man other than John so jarred Susan that she let out an involuntary gasp. Gordo Soltura came through the door, slammed it behind him and tossed his hat across the room where it landed in a corner. He was very drunk, and it took him a minute to realize that there was another person in the room. When he did, the vision of feminine loveliness which Susan presented startled him as much as his entrance had startled her.

"Who the hell are you?" he asked.

"I am . . ." Susan turned and went to her bedroom. She started to close the door behind her but Gordo had moved quickly across the parlor and blocked the doorway.

"Hey, goddamn it, I asked you who you were."

Susan's hands fluttered in front of her breasts which were seductively displayed by her gown. She felt very naked, and frightened of the large drunken stranger.

Gordo entered the room and smiled. "Where's everybody?"

Susan moved to take a quilt from the bed that she might hold in front of her. Gordo stepped forward, grabbed the quilt from her hand and tossed it on the floor. "Damn, you're a pretty thing. You look Indian."

"Por favor, señor, I am the servant here. Please excuse me while I dress. The members of the household are at a reception for the governor."

"Is my wife there?" Gordo asked.

"María?" It was the first time Susan had even thought that the man in the bedroom might be María's husband. María had said little about Gordo to Susan, but Susan had instinctively realized that there were problems between them.

Gordo started to unbutton his shirt. He said. "That's right, María. She's at this reception, too?"

178

"Yes." Susan was becoming progressively frightened of Gordo. "Please," she said, "please leave the room."

Gordo unbuttoned the last button, stripped the shirt from his muscular body and tossed it on the bed. His chest hair was coated with alkali from the long ride into Santa Fe. The border patrol he'd commanded had come up with nothing more than an occasional wildcatting trapper or hunter, and when he'd become sufficiently bored with the assignment, Gordo decided to return with the small group of men under his command to Santa Fe. He had been too long without a woman, too long without good whiskey. He'd intended upon arriving home to take care of both needs, although not necessarily in that order. Whiskey would wash the dust from his mouth. Then, he'd thought during the long ride, he would have his way with María.

But this situation reversed his priorities. He grinned, stepped forward and tore the front of Susan's gown to her waist. Her large, firm breasts fell loose, and the sight of them excited Gordo in a way he hadn't felt in months.

"No, no," Susan protested. Gordo ignored her. She made a move toward the door but it was a simple matter for him to take one step to the side and block her path.

"Indian, huh? Good Indian ass is just what I need."

Susan was becoming desperate. She attempted to cover her nakedness with her arms, as her eyes frantically darted about the room in search of an escape route. It was hopeless. The room was small, and there was no way she could get around Gordo and through the door.

Gordo leaned back against the doorjamb and pulled off one of his boots. He was unsteady on one leg and almost fell. It flashed through Susan's mind that she could perhaps push him off balance and out of the way, but she was afraid to touch him, to come close to him.

"Come on, you Indian bitch, get undressed and into bed. We don't have all night."

Gordo struggled with his other boot. Susan realized it was her only chance. She lunged at him and pushed with all her strength. It almost worked, but Gordo managed to catch himself before falling and grasped her arm in an iron grip. He flung her away from him and she landed on the bed. Her action had angered him. The grin was replaced by a scowl. He stood up straight, unbuckled his belt, unbuttoned his trousers and slipped them down over his thighs. Despite the

179

excitement Susan generated, Gordo's penis had achieved only a partial erection. The more he drank the more pronounced the threat of impotence was with him.

He stepped out of his trousers and was naked. He closed the gap between himself and the bed, reached down and tore the rest of the gown free from Susan's body. She scrambled across the bed to its far side and planted her feet squarely on the floor. Her terror was now replaced with anger, and with a determination that no matter what happened, she would not allow this drunken monster to violate her.

"La puta," Gordo growled. "You don't come over here, you Indian bitch, and I'll break your goddamn heathen neck. You understand?"

Susan's reply was a long, pronounced scream of defiance. Gordo had never heard such a scream before. It was not born of fright. Rather it was a clear declaration of intent. Gordo realized that he was face-to-face with a wild animal, and although there was a certain element of fear inherent in the animal's declaration, there was also a heightened sexuality that Gordo responded to.

Gordo was not the only one to hear Susan's scream. John Barrigan had managed to break away from the meeting in Governor's Alencaster's study, and had run across the plaza to capture whatever moments he could with his bride before the Soltura family returned. He had reached the front door when he heard his wife's agony. He flung open the front door, ran through the parlor and burst into the bedroom. The scene that confronted him set off a series of visceral responses over which he had no control. He lunged at Gordo and hurtled him into a wall. His blows were quick and sure. His fists felt the pleasure of driving into the face of his wife's attacker. He brought the heel of his hand sharply against Gordo's Adam's apple and felt the mechanism of Gordo's neck give way beneath the blow.

Gordo slowly slid down the wall and came to rest on the floor. John turned to Susan and told her to get dressed.

"He tried to attack me," Susan said.

"I know, Susan. It doesn't matter. It's time we were gone from here. Put on your clothes and come with me."

John looked down at Gordo. He was motionless. He reached and groped for a sign of a pulse in Gordo's neck. There was none.

"Is he dead?" Susan asked.

"I think so," John said. "Hurry."

Moments later John and Susan were outside the Soltura house, John saddled up two of the horses belonging to the family.

"John, is that you?" a voice asked.

John turned and saw Zeb and María approaching the house.

"Don't get in my way, Zeb. I'm doin' what I have to do."

Zeb broke away from María and ran to John. He looked up at his friend and asked, "What happened? What are you doing?"

"Susan was attacked by a man, Zeb. I think I killed him. We have to leave."

Zeb reached up and grabbed the reins of John's horse. "Whatever happened, John, it can be explained. Don't do anything foolish."

By this time María had joined Zeb at the side of John's horse. "What's happened?" she asked.

"He's inside, ma'am. I think I've killed him, and I did it because he attacked my wife. Please thank your family for all they've done for Susan. We just don't belong here."

"Gordo?" María asked.

Susan looked down at María and nodded. "I am sorry, my sister. I did nothing to bring this about. Please believe me."

María looked up into Susan's eyes and understood. "I'm sorry, Susan."

"Someday we shall meet again, my sister," Susan said. "Thank you."

Zeb and María stood back as John and Susan galloped away toward the center of town.

CHAPTER TWENTY-ONE

John and Susan Barrigan rode through the town of Santa Fe until they reached the Rio Grande river. They paused, and John indicated they would ride south, along the riverbank.

Had Barrigan known that he had not, in fact, killed Gordo, he probably wouldn't have made the impetuous decision to flee from Santa Fe. Certainly, he could have made a case for having attacked Gordo. The Spaniard had attempted to rape his wife.

But John knew that the fact his wife was an Indian would prejudice such a case. As far as John was concerned, there hadn't been any choice but to run.

After they'd ridden for an hour along the river, John came to a halt, climbed down off his horse and ran up a hill that afforded him a relatively unobscured view north. Susan remained on her horse and watched as her husband peered into the distance in search of pursuers. There was nothing on the horizon to indicate anyone was following them. He ran down the hill, helped Susan from her horse and led her and their mounts along an arid creek bed to a point where rocks shielded them from anyone who might pass by. John tethered the horses to a sapling and sat upon the ground next to his wife. They leaned back against a large boulder. John placed his arm around Susan's shoulders and held her close.

"I am sorry," Susan said. Her voice was void of emotion.

"Sorry about what?" John asked.

"For causing you this trouble. Were I not an Indian, you would not have to run like this."

John squeezed her tight and turned her face with his hand so that she was looking directly at him. "It don't make any difference at all, Susan, what you are. You're my wife and I love you."

A large tear ran silently and freely from one of her eyes. "I was dressed in a way to arouse the Spaniard's passion," she said. "I was dressed that way because I waited for you, my husband. María had said you would come to me."

John was angry that Susan should even consider that she had contributed to what had occurred in the Soltura home. He realized he was glad that he'd killed his wife's attacker, and knew he'd do it again if the same situation arose.

"Where will we go?" Susan asked.

"Further south until we hook up with some friendly folk. Then, I don't know. I'd like to head back east where we could live the way decent folk do, but that may take awhile. You and I have never had a proper honeymoon, Susan. Every day since we got married has been full of problems. I promise you that I'll do everything I can to get us back home, and to provide you with the kind of life a man wants his woman to have."

Susan wiped the tear from her cheek and smiled at her husband. "There are no problems as long as I am with you, John. We share what problems we face, and my only hope is that I'll be able to help you when trouble does strike."

John kissed her lightly on the cheek and ran one of his hands through her thick, black hair. "Just havin' you with me is all the help I could ever need, Susan. Just always be with me."

Susan nodded and returned his kiss. Although neither of them said it, they were once again together, and no matter how trying and troublesome the circumstances, it would take all the forces of man, government and God to ever separate them again.

Once John and Susan had left, Zeb had gone into the Soltura house and checked on Gordo. María followed him into the bedroom and uttered a disgusted moan upon seeing her drunken husband naked and slumped in the corner of the room. It was obvious what had occurred, and she shared the rage that John Barrigan must have felt.

Zeb looked up at María after have searched Gordo's neck and wrist for a pulse. "He's not dead," Pike said. "There was no need for John to run."

María said nothing. Her only thought was that she wished

she were with John and Susan. As certain as the sun would rise in the morning and set in the evening, María knew that she could no longer live with Gordo. It did not matter where she went as long as it was away from this man she had grown to hate with such vengeance. She walked from the bedroom, left the house and went to the governor's reception, where she told her in-laws what had happened. They ran from the governor's house, a doctor at their side. When they were gone, María left the reception hall and walked up one of the narrow, dirt roads that led into the Santa Fe plaza. She eventually stopped at the side of a small, clear stream that had been dammed and which provided Santa Fe with most of its water supply. A light breeze rippled the surface of the water, and María's reflection undulated in front of her.

"Home," she said softly, watching her lips as they were distorted by the movement of the water. "I must go home."

John and Susan resumed their ride south until the first rays of dawn broke over the Río Grande. They'd reached a point where the river widened, and where the low hills that had paralleled their journey on their left had given way to an expanse of plain that led into a vast desert area to the east. In the distance was another range of hills, and it was in that direction that John now led them. He knew they needed to stop and rest, to eat and drink. He was reluctant to stay too close to the river for fear that any pursuers would naturally follow that route, just as they had in escaping. They rode at a quick pace for an hour, then slowed to a walk until they reached the foot of the hills that were their destination. A well-worn trail led them to the right. It circumvented the first hill of the range until it reached a thick forest. Beyond the forest was more rugged terrain, and after John had surveyed the area on the other side of the forest, he returned to where Susan waited and said they would make camp there.

"How long will we stay?"

"Until darkness," John said. "It would be better to ride by night until we are further from Santa Fe." He made a bed for them of pine needles, leafy branches and grass. There was no need to build a shelter. The sun had risen to its midday zenith, and the day promised to be warm and dry. It was cool and still in the forest, the silence broken only by the occasional scurrying of small animals, and the cry of birds as they fluttered from limb to limb.

184

John and Susan drifted into a blissful sleep. John had promised to search for food after they'd rested.

Two hours later John awoke with a start. He sat bolt upright and rubbed his eyes. He didn't know specifically what had wakened him. It was more a sense than a sound or disturbance. He looked over at Susan who slept peacefully, a look of serene contentment upon her lovely face.

The sound of John getting to his knees woke her. She looked up at him and asked, "What's the matter?"

"Nothing, nothing. Go back to sleep. I just want to check on the horses."

John had secured the horses in an area one hundred yards from where they slept. He'd chosen the spot because of an abundance of wild grass upon which they could feed, and because of the presence of an underground spring that gurgled up from deep within the earth and formed a small pool of clear, cold water.

John gently patted his wife on the hip, smiled reassuringly and walked toward where he'd left the horses.

When he was thirty yards away from where he'd tied them, he stopped and peered through the foliage. They were gone. His first thought was that they might have broken loose and wandered away, but he knew that the knots he'd tied were too secure for that to have happened. Someone had taken them, and that realization put every one of his senses on alert.

He crept to his right until he had circled the feeding area and had reached a point almost on the opposite side from where he'd first realized the horses were gone. He moved closer to the grazing area and paused just at its perimeter.

He had no chance to react, no chance to defend himself from the attack that took place with such speed and power. Four members of the Faraon tribe, survivors of the Comanche massacres of the Great Plains, jumped him from behind. He fell beneath their weight and was hopelessly pinned to the ground. One of them held a long hunting knife to his neck. A fifth warrior stood above him and poked a long spear into his back.

John wanted to scream to warn Susan, but he realized that would be futile. She, too, was probably captured at that very moment. He twisted his head and looked up into the eyes of his captors.

"Friend," he said. "I am your friend."

His statement was answered by a further twisting of his

arms. The knife at his throat pricked the skin and a thin trickle of blood ran from the wound.

Minutes later John heard the sound of people moving through the woods. Six braves emerged, some members of the Faraon tribe, others of the Mescalero, close relatives of the Faraon. They had Susan with them. Her hands had been tied behind her back. A rope had been attached to her neck and was held by one of the braves.

Other tribe members emerged from the trees. John was allowed to stand. His hands, too, were fastened behind his back and a rope was looped around his neck.

"We come in peace," Susan said in an Indian dialect.

"With a white man?" one of the braves asked.

"He is my husband," Susan said. "We wish no harm to anyone."

The brave issued an order to those with him. Moments later John and Susan were being led to a camp that had been established deep in the hills, and from which the braves had been raiding Spanish settlements to the north and south for months.

Book Two

CHAPTER TWENTY-TWO

August 1810

Father Juan de Soltura settled into a comfortable chair in the spacious living room of the family home in Valladolid. He'd poured himself a glass of red wine and it sat upon a table next to his chair. It was early morning. The temperature outside had already risen to eighty degrees, and it was obvious that a week-long heat spell would not be broken that August day.

Juan sipped the wine and enjoyed the feel of it as it slid down his throat and warmed his stomach. He'd spent the last three days on the family hacienda, having left the daily duties of the Valladolid parish to Father Gomez. Gomez had understood when Juan asked that he be relieved of his duties for a few days. The previous months had been intense ones, and what they would lead to in the immediate future would demand everything the young priest possessed. Juan knew he needed a few days to relax and contemplate the future, and Gomez had agreed.

Juan closed his eyes and allowed his thoughts to wander. The hacienda had functioned smoothly since his family's departure for the northern province. Juan had enjoyed wandering about the property, sometimes on foot, sometimes on horseback. Conditions had not changed for the Indian and mestizo help, but there did not seem to be the open defiance in their eyes that Juan had noticed when his father and Gordo were in day-to-day charge of the operation.

At night, when the scorching sun had set and the air had become cool with breezes from the west, Juan had taken great pleasure in sitting alone on a porch to the side of the house. There, he was able to put into perspective all that had happened to him in his short life, and what he would face in the days to come.

He opened his eyes when one of the Indian house servants came into the room. She asked whether he wished anything.

"No, gracias. You may have the day to yourself," he said.

"Por qué?" the servant asked.

"There is really nothing for you to do," Juan said, smiling. "I just wish to be alone for the day."

"Sí padre," the servant said, backing from the room.

"Enjoy your day," Juan called after her. "Go home to your children and enjoy them."

When the servant was gone, Juan picked up an envelope that was on the table next to his wine, opened it and spread the pages on his lap. It was a letter from his family in Santa Fe, and although he had received it yesterday, he had not wished to open it and read it until now.

> *Dear Juan,*
> *I write this letter to you knowing that I should not be doing it. It is not my place to make comments about the family that I chose to marry into.*

Juan quickly shuffled through the pages and saw that the letter was not, as he had anticipated, from his mother and father, but from María. He returned to the first page and resumed reading.

> *Much has happened to us in recent months, some of it good because it has pleased your father, some of it bad because it has created such unhappiness for your mother and me. Your mother is such a wonderful woman, Juan, and it breaks my heart to see her so heavy with grief over some of the events that have occurred in her life, and in mine.*
> *Life in the northern provinces is not what it was in Valladolid. The traditions and values that were so much a part of growing up in the valley are not part of the daily life here in the north. Greed, corruption and self-ishness seem to dominate everyone's thoughts. It saddens your mother, and me, to see this become such an impor-tant part of your father's life. He remains, of course, a good and decent man, but his ambition has driven him to discard many of the positive traits that your mother loved*

189

him for. Every action is justified by what it will bring in terms of increased power and material reward.

But while it saddens me to see the effect of a place like Santa Fe on the people I love so much, the direct influence it has had upon my life is the real reason I am writing you this letter. It was not long ago that two Americans were brought to Santa Fe as prisoners because they had ventured into Spanish territory. Gordo, your brother and my husband, was part of the force that captured them and brought them here. One of the Americans, whose name was John Barrigan, had married an Indian girl during his long journey from the east, and she became a part of our household during his confinement. It is misleading to use the term confinement, because both Americans were treated with great dignity and respect and were allowed a certain amount of freedom while a decision was being made as to what to do with them.

One night, while your mother and father and I attended a reception at the governor's house, Gordo returned from a patrol and attempted to rape Susan, the young Indian wife of John Barrigan. John came upon the scene and struck Gordo with such force that he feared he had killed him. He was frightened of what would happen to him because of his attack on a Spaniard of some reputation in Santa Fe, so he and Susan rode off into the night.

Gordo was not killed, Juan. His neck had been broken but he survived and after a long convalesence has regained total use of his body, although he suffers considerable pain in his neck and back from time to time. It was the decision of your mother and father not to tell you this story because of the circumstances surrounding Gordo's injury. They felt it would upset you and interfere with the inspired work you do as a priest in Vallodolid.

I agreed to keep this secret from you, until now. Had I not made a certain decision about myself and my life, I would have continued to keep this secret in honor of your mother and father, and because of the embarrassment it causes me to admit that the man I married could turn out to be such a vicious and immoral person. It is not easy to admit that I could be so blind and so careless in falling in love. But I was young and passion blinded my reason. This does not excuse such a decision, for I do believe that if there is one thing each person must do in their *life, it is to take full responsibility for their actions. But I can no longer continue to live as a victim of my youthful indiscretion. It is time for me to act, for I feel that any action I might take would be better than the life of quiet pain and humiliation I endure here in Santa Fe.*

I have decided to leave Santa Fe, Juan, and to return to Valladolid. I have discussed this with your mother, and although it makes her very sad to think of my leaving, she understands and agrees with me. Your father has not been told, nor has Gordo. Gordo and I continue to share a house and bed as man and wife, but our relationship is not conducted as one would expect of a man and woman who have been married under the eyes and blessing of God. I felt it was my duty to nurse Gordo until he regained his health, and I have done that to the best of my ability. Now, as he returns to his former ways, I realize I must follow my heart which demands that I leave him, and return to the land I love in search of fulfillment and peace.

The other American, whose name was Captain Zebulon Pike, was eventually taken to jail in Chihuahua. After spending a month there he was released and escorted out of Spanish territory. We received a letter from him from Washington, the capital of the United States, and he has resumed his career as a military officer. He was a fine young man, as was his friend, John Barrigan.

As for John, the talk is that he and his wife have become part of an Indian tribe to the southeast of Santa Fe. Although no one can determine this for certain, it is reported that he has taken part in numerous Indian raids upon Spanish settlements in the region. There is a large reward for his capture or death, and Gordo's latest plan for adventure is to mount a force to go in search of Barrigan. Of course, it is not the reward that fuels Gordo's passion for this adventure. He has harbored a hatred for Barrigan ever since the night John attacked him, even though the attack was justified because of the assault that Gordo was attempting upon Susan. Gordo is not the sort of person who could understand that. He plans to leave with a group of men in search of Barrigan the day after tomorrow. I plan to leave Santa Fe two days after that. I will join a wagon train that arrived in Santa Fe three weeks ago, and which now plans to

*proceed south to an area near Vallodolid. The people
with whom I will travel are fine, decent Spaniards, and I
know my journey will be a safe one.*

*I will bring with me some things your mother wishes
you to have. I have not told my own mother and father of
my plans to return. It would upset them to think of my
traveling such a long distance without the benefit of
family around me, and I would prefer to surprise them
with my arrival. Please respect my wishes and do not tell
them that I am returning home.*

*Juan, you've been in my thoughts every day since I left
Valladolid. I ask forgiveness of our God whenever my
hatred for your brother enters my heart. We should not
hate, especially those to whom we have pledged ourselves, but my feelings are beyond my control in this
regard.*

*I hope you are well and that your work for our God
fills you with love and fulfillment.*

*I look forward to once again seeing you and benefiting
from the warmth you radiate to everyone around you.*

Thank you.

> *Fondly,*
> *María.*

María's letter caused a heavy sadness to settle on Juan. He
allowed the pages of the letter to drop to the floor and he
finished the wine in his glass. The letter left him confused
too. Confusion had ruled his life lately. The goodness that he
had always assumed was part of the fiber of most men and
women with whom he shared the earth no longer seemed a
reality. He'd ceased to trust the motivations of those with
whom he came into contact on a daily basis. Love and
respect, responsibility and commitment seemed to have given
way to a frantic drive for personal gain. The values assigned
to man in the Bible, the faith in man that Christ had demon-
strated on so many occasions, all seemed misplaced to the
young priest.

It was not the first time that the intensity of these feelings
had caused Juan to physically shake with rage. He found it
happening again as he sat in the chair in his family home. The
thought of Gordo, his own flesh and blood, so blatantly
violating the vows that Juan himself had spoken during the

wedding ceremony caused everything in front of him to turn blood red. His father's ambition distressed him.

Juan picked up the pages of María's letter and noticed the date on the top. It had been written slightly more than a month ago, which meant that she should now be more than halfway through her journey. The contemplation of seeing her again excited him. He was relieved that she would no longer be subjected to the life of Santa Fe as she described it, and to the brutality of his brother. He wished to comfort her. The contemplation of that caused him to smile. Yes, he would comfort her as a priest and, perhaps, as a man. The vision of holding María in his arms and providing her with the warmth and security she so obviously needed had a powerful effect on him.

The pleasure he felt in thinking about María's return was tempered by the thoughts that had previously occupied him that morning. In a few days he would return to the parish where he and Father Gomez would actively put into action the revolutionary plans of Father Miguel Hidalgo. The time had come for the revolution to take place, and Juan's role in it would be large and important.

Father Hidalgo had chosen December 8 as the date for the revolution to begin. He would personally launch it at the fair of San Juan de los Lagos. Once the initial blow against Spanish oppression had been struck at the fair, it would be a signal for Juan to launch the revolution in Valladolid. Father Morelos had already been dispatched to Acapulco where he, too, waited for a signal from Hidalgo. The revolutionary leader had decided that a symbol was needed around which the Indians and mestizos could rally. He had told Morelos and Juan during their meeting in León, "Every revolution has had its symbol. It is not enough to suffer from oppression and wish to challenge it. There must be some mysterious quality that can sustain a prolonged rebellion, and I believe Our Lady of Guadalupe can provide such a rallying point."

While Juan had agreed that a symbol would be needed above and beyond the mere magnetism and charisma of Hidalgo, he quietly questioned the choice of Our Lady of Guadalupe. It had occurred to him during the frustrating years of waiting for Hidalgo to act that if the revolution were truly to accomplish its goal, it would have to be based upon love and a sincere desire that all men of New Spain achieve equal status. If the Indians who would march behind them in the battle for justice took the opportunity to heap revenge upon those who had oppressed them for so many years, it would accomplish nothing more than to shift the cruelty from one side to the other. The choice of Our Lady of Guadalupe could, Juan believed, lead to exactly that end.

The story of Our Lady of Guadalupe began in 1531 when an Indian named Juan Diego was walking up what was known as Tepeya Hill. The virgin appeared and told him that she wished to have a church built on that spot in her honor. The Indian raced home and told a bishop of what had occurred. The bishop called the Indian a liar and dismissed him.

The Indian returned to the spot where he had seen the Virgin and was visited by her a second time. During the second visit she told him to pick some roses. Roses had never grown in that location, and the Virgin said that by bringing roses to the bishop who'd doubted him, the Indian would prove what had occurred.

Roses suddenly dotted the hillside. The Indian picked them, put them in his cloak and took them to the bishop. When the Indian kneeled before the bishop and opened his cloak, the bishop's response was a gasp. Not only did the Indian have roses, but there was a magnificent picture of the Virgin upon the cloth of his cloak. The bishop was convinced, and directed that a shrine be built on the hill.

Years later, in 1754, the Pope gave official recognition to the miracle of Our Lady of Guadalupe. In the shrine that was built, the original cloak with the picture of the Virgin upon it was hung over the altar. Indians of the area flocked to the shrine, stopping outside the wall that surrounded it and then walking on their knees through the courtyard and into the shrine.

At the bottom of the hill where the shrine was built, a natural spring bubbled forth, and its waters were believed to have curative powers. Our Lady of Guadalupe had become, in New Spain, the most important shrine for all Christian Indians. Because the Virgin had revealed herself to an Indian, it was believed that she had bestowed upon all of them a special blessing and challenge for the future. This was what worried Juan. His readings of other historical revolutions were filled with tales of the oppressed rising up and not only seeking their freedom, but punishing those who had oppressed them. Millions had died throughout the ages in the name of a religious metaphor, and Juan did not want to see Our Lady of Guadalupe associated with such destruction.

He'd mentioned his reservations to Hidalgo, but the older priest had dismissed them. Hidalgo had said, "No one, Juan, wishes to see blood spilled on any side. But often, the pendulum must swing to an extreme position before it can return to a natural balance. To win independence from the Spanish will require the use of force. Those who give their lives in the battle will have done so in the name of justice. Their lives are insignificant compared to the greater good that will result."

Juan had realized over the years of waiting that the choice of Our Lady of Guadalupe was not the only aspect of Hidalgo's plan that he questioned. But he also recognized that if justice were to be obtained in New Spain, it would only be through a man like Hidalgo. He had obviously been blessed from above, and to question that blessing was to inject negativism into a situation in which only optimism could be allowed.

Juan left the house and stood in front of the porch. Across the field was the sala in which so many festive occasions had been celebrated. Far in the distance was the home of José Jardinero, María's father. Juan had not spoken to María's parents for the three days he'd been at the hacienda. Now he felt drawn to them.

As he walked toward the Jardinero home it occurred to him that the revolution in which he would take part was directed at José Jardinero, as well as at all other gachupines in New Spain. The realization caused Juan to wince, for José Jardinero was not at all like the guchupine ruling class of the nation.

When Viceroy Iturrigaray had been deposed that year by the gachupines because they felt his views were becoming increasingly liberal, José had argued against it in the cabildo meeting. His protests had little impact upon the meeting, however, and it was agreed that Iturrigaray must go. His successor was General de Garibay, an arch-conservative, a loyal subject of the king of Spain and vehemently pro-gachupine.

The choice of General de Garibay as viceroy of New Spain, while appearing to be a setback for liberal criollo causes, actually heightened the determination of the criollos to overthrow everything that represented Spanish domination. A thirty-year-old captain of the Queen's Dragoons, Ignacio

Allende, had approached local criollo leaders and offered his services in whatever protests might take place in the future. Once he had gained the confidence of the criollo leaders, they asked him go to to the town of Querétaro, where anti-gachupine sentiments were deeply entrenched. Allende and some of his friends formed what was known as a literary and social club there. Included in that club were other criollo army officers, and the membership quickly grew in numbers. Their meetings, while ostensibly to discuss literary and social matters, were actually spent in plotting an insurrection in Querétaro. Once the club was firmly established and its purposes clearly defined, Father Hidalgo had been brought in to coordinate his activities with the Querétaro group.

Groups similiar to the one established by Allende had been formed in other towns in the provinces of Michoacán, Guanajuato and Querétaro. Juan, Father Morelos and other priests who had been recruited in the movement had functioned as liaisons with these groups, just as Hidalgo had done in Querétaro.

In the past, any attempts by the criollo class to rise against the gachupine rulers had met with quick and sure defeat, primarily because of a lack of organization. The years between the time Juan was first approached by Hidalgo to take part in the revolution, and this point in time, when the revolution was about to take place, had been spent in establishing just such coordination. The result was a network of groups throughout central New Spain who shared a common purpose and goal, that of achieving independence from Spain.

The replacement of Iturrigaray as viceroy of New Spain with a more conservative man was not the only event to spread the cry for independence.

On March 19, 1808, the French troops of Napoleon had marched into Madrid, and King Charles IV of Spain had abdicated in favor of his son, Ferdinand VII. Napoleon had refused to recognize Ferdinand. He managed to persuade King Charles to surrender all claims to the Spanish throne to himself, claiming that he was the only man capable of restoring order to Spain. As a result of this move, Ferdinand lost the crown before he'd ever had a chance to wear it.

Napoleon pushed ahead to establish a regency council in order to install his older brother, Joseph, as the new king of Spain.

Napoleon's actions virtually destroyed Spanish authority in

New Spain. The ruling government of New Spain had been able to maintain its power only because of a fierce loyalty to the crown of the mother country. But if the throne in Spain were occupied by a foreigner, who could expect a colony to remain loyal? Certainly, no one intended to pledge allegiance to a commoner such as Joseph Bonaparte.

Liberals in Spain had set up juntas in Sevilla and in Ovido, and each of these groups attempted to reestablish control over the affairs of the colonies. But their power within Spain itself was shaky, and their attempts were feeble.

Adding to the conviction on the part of the criollos in New Spain that independence could be won, was the example of the United States and its revolution. As hard as the ruling gachupine class had attempted to keep literature that reported what had occurred in the United States out of the country, it was a losing battle. The criollo and mestizo classes identified with those in America who had overthrown the British yoke, and took great strength from their brothers to the north and east.

On October 22, 1808, President Jefferson put the question of a Mexico policy to his cabinet. It was Jefferson's desire that New Spain remain under the control of Spain. He believed that it would be preferable for American interests to have Spain continue to rule such a large tract of land in North America, rather than have it possibly fall into French or English hands. At the same time, Jefferson realized that the possibility that Spanish domination would be overthrown was real. So the official position of the United States government was that it would be friendly to any new government that resulted from such an overthrow, but would do nothing to actively aid such an effort.

In 1809, Napoleon suppressed the "Council of Castile," the Inquisition and two-thirds of the convents. He imposed upon Spain his 1801 Concordat with the Pope, and church lands were confiscated and sold to secular interests. These moves only further strengthened the resolve of the clergy of New Spain to join hands with the criollos in a revolution.

Furthermore, many of New Spain's merchants feared that Napoleon might destroy their monopoly with Spain by opening up their ports to French trade. Some of these merchants joined hands with the clergy and with the mass of criollos, who by this time had become dedicated to the concept of freedom from Spain.

All of this had been discussed thoroughly by the leaders of the revolution, including Juan Soltura. There was so much to consider, so many things to question. But now all of the planning and questioning were over. It was time for action. December 8 would be a grand moment not only in the life of New Spain, but in the life of Juan Soltura. There was also the added excitement at the thought of having María there at his side, as he took the action that he knew he must in order to fulfill his destiny as a man of God.

CHAPTER TWENTY-THREE

September 3, 1810

The wagon train with which María Soltura had been traveling arrived in Valladolid at noon. Most of the members of the party intended to proceed further south to Cuernavaca, but those who intended to remain in the Valladolid region dropped her at her parent's hacienda.

As they approached the house, María began to question the wisdom of surprising her parents with her return. Perhaps the shock would be too great. But she realized that she had little choice. She was there, and there was no way now to soften the impact of her return.

María's parents were eating lunch when she knocked on the door. José Jardinero opened the door and stared at his daughter. He was speechless. It took what seemed an eternity for him to collect his thoughts and to blurt out her name.

"María!" her father said. "It is you, María."

María's mother let out a shriek from the dining room. She knocked over her chair in her haste to leave the table and to join her husband at the front door. José still searched for words. María's mother didn't bother trying to speak. She simply rushed through the door and embraced her daughter. Señora Jardinero began to cry, and so did María.

"Come in, come in," José said, standing back to allow the women to enter the house.

"*Por qué?*" María's mother asked through her tears.

María disengaged from her mother's bear hug and wearily sat upon a high-backed, wooden settee that was covered with cushions of varied and vivid colors. "It will take so long to explain, mama," María said, allowing her head to rest against the back of the settee. "But now I will have time to explain everything because I am home to stay."

"But what of Gordo?" José asked. "He is not with you?"

María slowly shook her head and the tears again flowed. "That, too, will be explained as soon as I have rested. It has been a long journey from Santa Fe."

José asked more questions but his wife quietly indicated to him that it would be best to withhold them for the moment. "Let me get you something to drink, to eat," María's mother said.

"Yes, that would be wonderful. The wagon train with which I traveled ran out of food a week ago. Some of the men managed to kill some game along the way but it was barely enough to feed everyone. I am hungry and thirsty."

María's mother motioned José to follow her into the kitchen. When they were inside and out of María's earshot, Señora Jardinero said to her husband, "Whatever brings her home, it is a blessing. She has been through much, José. One look at her assures me of that. Let her eat and drink and rest. Tomorrow will be time enough to find out what brings her to Valladolid."

José nodded his agreement. His wife prepared a plate of fruit, cheese and bread. She asked María, "Wine or water?" Maria indicated that she would like some of both, which made her mother smile as she dispatched José to the wine cellar.

An hour later, when María's plate and glasses were empty and a sense of peace had replaced the anxiety over seeing her parents for the first time in so long, María closed her eyes and sighed contentedly.

"Why don't you go to your room and sleep?" her mother suggested. "A good sleep is what you need. Then, tonight, we can talk if you wish."

María opened her eyes and smiled. "It is so good to be home, mama. So good to be with the two of you. I love you."

María got up, kissed her mother and father and went to the room that had been hers since she was a little girl. Nothing had changed. The canopied bed had been freshly made twice a week ever since María had departed for Santa Fe. Soft, delicate blue and white lace fringed the canopy. A pale blue, yellow and white comforter was soft and inviting.

María closed the door and surveyed the rest of the room.

Nothing had changed. It was as though her mother knew this day would come, and had been in constant readiness for it. A wooden rocking chair that had been imported from Spain occupied one corner. Two small, hand-carved dressers lined one wall. A large mirror hung above them, its frame made of white birch that was flecked with blue.

María went to the window and looked outside. It was a brilliantly sunny day. She drew the curtains closed and removed her clothing. One of the servants had brought the two trunks containing her belongings to the room. She opened one of them and removed a long, sheer, lavender nightgown that she had worn on her wedding night. She was about to slip it over her head when the vision of that night caused her to drop the garment to the floor. She kicked it across the room, found another nightgown, put it on and slipped between the cool, fresh sheets. She was asleep within minutes.

Father Juan de Soltura was alone in his church in Valladolid. He knelt in the first pew and allowed the cool calm of the church's interior to wash over him and to soothe his thoughts. Earlier, he had prayed. Now, he simply enjoyed the peace his prayers had brought to him.

The air inside the church was cool in contrast to the heat outside. The silence of the church was immensely pleasing to him. Father Gomez had gone to the town of Zitácuaro to attend a meeting of that town's revolutionary group. He would not return until morning.

Juan thought of María as he remained on his knees on a low wooden bench in the pew. According to the date on her letter, she would arrive any day, unless some unforeseen circumstance had occurred during the journey that would delay her. A spasm of fear shook him. To travel through New Spain in those days was to invite danger. The various Indian tribes of the northern provinces had erupted into almost constant warfare with the Spaniards. The violence that accompanied that warfare had spread south, and raids upon individual haciendas and rancheros in the valley had become more frequent.

Juan again prayed. "Bring her safely home, Father," he whispered. "Wrap her in your arms and protect her from any harm. I ask this in the name of your son, Jesus Christ."

It was late afternoon. Juan stood in the pew and focused upon the altar. What magic it represented to him, what quiet and powerful dignity surrounded it. He fervently wished at that moment that he could in some way be swallowed up by the altar and what it represented, to be transported into the very mystery that was at the root of all he believed. He had sought his entire life to escape from the ugly realities of the world. Entering the priesthood was not, as most would have believed, a positive move toward something. Rather, it had been a means for him to retreat from the life he had found so painful. His intellect did battle with his emotions. Emotionally, that desperate need to escape was still very much a part of him. Intellectually, he detested himself for the weakness it represented, and he knew that his commitment to the oppressed must be honored and acted upon.

The date, December 8, took center-stage in his thoughts. How long he had waited for the day of action to arrive. Now, it was only three months until his convictions, courage and commitment would be tested.

The young priest walked slowly up the aisle, paused at the front door and considered going outside into the plaza. He decided against it and moved into the other half of the church structure in which he and Father Gomez lived in small, separate rooms. He climbed the stone stairs to the second floor and went to his room. He lay on his cot and closed his eyes, but sleep would not come. He heard the sounds of footsteps on the stone stairs, then the voices of nuns as they proceeded to the roof where they would sit and gossip.

"You must sleep," Juan told himself. He decided that after a nap, he would journey to the home of José Jardinero and perhaps spend a pleasant evening talking with his neighbors of so many years. Perhaps, by chance, they had heard something from María. He had a strange sense that she was very near, and her presence filled the room. He closed his eyes and allowed himself to sink into the cot's mattress.

While María Jardinero slept, her mother spent the afternoon preparing a special meal that they could enjoy together that evening. A freshly slaughtered hog provided pork that Señora Jardinero marinated in wine. She prepared an olla, knowing that María had always had a special liking for the heavily spiced mutton stew. Fresh vegetables from the garden were picked by a servant and brought to the kitchen where María's mother combined them in a salad. José chose the finest wine in the cellar. The dining room table was set with the best silverware and linen the family possessed. Tall, slender white candles surrounded a centerpiece of roses that the gardener had created especially for the arrival of the family's only child.

The stablehands were all excited about María's return. María had brought Tormenta, her favorite horse, with her from Santa Fe. The animal had drawn up lame when they were a hundred miles from Valladolid, and María had nursed him along the final portion of the journey. He'd been fed and brushed down, and salve made from bear fat had been rubbed into his lame leg.

Although José and his wife had agreed not to press María for any details of her decision to return home, the temptation caused José distress during the meal. At his wife's suggestion, he tried to limit the table conversation to the events that had taken place in Valladolid, rather than asking about Santa Fe.

"These are very troubled times in New Spain," José said. "The new viceroy is a cruel and ruthless man. As a gachupin, I should be pleased that one so in tune with my social class now leads the nation. But I'm sure you know, María, that your father has never embraced the philosophy of most gachupines. I fear that the presence of such a man as Garibay will only hasten what is inevitable."

María looked up at her father, a quizzical expression on her face. "And what is that, father?"

"A revolution that will forever change this land."

María returned her attention to the food on her plate. After more silence she again looked up at her father and asked, "Who will lead such a revolution?"

"The criollos."

"That is understood," María said. "But every revolution must have special men who lead it. Who are those men in New Spain?"

"No one is certain, my daughter, although there seems little doubt that the clergy will be deeply involved in whatever happens."

The mention of the clergy naturally caused María to think of Juan. The very thought of him seemed to brighten her spirits at the table, and she asked about him.

"He visited us not too long ago," her mother said. "He is very much loved here in Valladolid, although there are many who now feel that his views are too liberal."

José nodded. "There was a time when his sermons regarding social injustice were met with approval. I suppose that is because they were nothing more than sermons, and there did not seem to be a real threat of revolution. But now that revolution seems a reality, his words from the pulpit strike fear in the hearts of those who would have the most to lose should there be a revolution."

"I look forward to seeing Father Juan again," María said. It was obvious that Juan had not said anything to her parents about the letter he'd received from her, if he'd received it at all. It was common in New Spain for letters not to reach their destination.

Señora Jardinero seemed to lose the glow of excitement that had lit her face throughout the dinner.

"What's the matter, mama?" María asked.

"I was thinking of the two Soltura brothers, and how much better it would have been if Juan had not entered the priesthood but had married you instead."

María started to say something but her mother shook her off. "No, no, forgive me for saying that. It is good that Juan became a priest. Only those with the qualities he possesses should serve God on such a level."

José could no longer contain his questions. He asked bluntly, "What of Gordo, María? What is the standing between you and your husband?"

María knew she could no longer put off her parents on this issue. The traditions of behavior for a woman in New Spain prohibited her from too energetically condemning her husband. Instead, she had mentally prepared during her journey from Santa Fe the characterization of Gordo she would present to her mother and father. She lowered her eyes from her father's gaze and said, "I honor my husband as all good wives must do, but . . ."

A knock on the front door interrupted her.

"Who could that be?" José asked.

Señora Jardinero suggested he go to the door and see. Moments later, José walked into the dining room, his arm around the shoulders of Father Juan de Soltura.

"*Buenas noches*," Señora Jardinero said, standing and offering her hand. "What a coincidence. We were sitting here speaking of you only moments before."

Juan didn't hear her words. The sight of María sitting at the dining room table rendered him mute. She, too, was flustered at his sudden appearance.

Finally, Juan spoke, "Welcome, María." He went to her and extended his hand.

María took his hand and smiled. A warmth spread throughout her body. The pleasure at seeing him once again was intense. "It is good to be home," she said. "So good."

Juan realized that he and María were staring at each other and that it was embarrassing to her mother and father. He withdrew his hand and said, in a forced, matter-of-fact tone, "Well now, María, you must tell me everything about Santa Fe."

María's father started to say that was precisely what he was anxious to hear, but again, Señora Jardinero came to the rescue by saying, "We have established a rule this evening, Father Juan. That rule is to leave all such conversation for the future. For now, our daughter is home, has eaten good food, has rested and blesses us by being here."

Juan nodded. "Of course," he said. "Too much talk can be more fatiguing than a long journey." José Jardinero pulled out a chair and Juan sat in it. He was to María's left, and although he tried to share his attention among everyone at the table, it was almost impossible, so radiant was her beauty, so potent was her effect upon him.

They sat at the table for a half hour. Then, María's mother asked her what she wished to do for the rest of the evening.

María sat back in her chair and stretched her arms out in front of her. "Only to enjoy being home, that is all,"

José suggested that he send a servant to bring some of the neighbors to the house to celebrate María's return.

María shook her head, "Not tonight, father. I'm not ready for that."

"What of you, Juan?" José asked. "Will you honor us by staying here this evening?"

"Oh, no, thank you," Juan replied. "I will stay at my parents' home, and must leave very early in the morning to return to the church. Father Gomez has been away, but will return at dawn. We have much to do to prepare for the coming feasts."

"I understand," José said.

Juan stood and avoided María's eyes. He said, "In fact, I must go to the house now. There are things there I must do before retiring."

There was no hesitation in María. She said, "Let me go there with you, Father Juan. I have not seen your family's home in a long time. It would be good just to see it, if only for a moment. It would make me feel even more at home to be in still other familiar surroundings."

Juan looked at her and said, "That sounds like a good idea, María."

María asked her family if she might be excused. Her mother said, "Of course. It has been a long and exciting day. I think I, too, need a good, long sleep."

José agreed, although María's suggestion that she accompany Juan to his home caused him a certain discomfort. Perhaps it was what his wife had said at the table about how much better it would have been had María married Juan. José, although deeply religious, did not harbor any misconceptions about the celibate life of many priests in New Spain. As ashamed as he was for even thinking that something might occur between Juan and María, the practical side of his nature would not allow his misgivings to be summarily dismissed. However, to express such concern would be to embarrass and dishonor everyone in his home. He shook Juan's hand and said to María, "Do not be long. You need sleep as much as anyone."

María smiled her broadest smile of the day. "Yes, father, I know that. But the rest this afternoon did wonders for me, just as mother's cooking always does. I feel very good. I won't be long."

When Juan and María were gone, José let out a sigh that he had been containing for the last few minutes.

"You look troubled, my husband," his wife said.

"I fear that there is nothing but trouble in the future, my dear. So much trouble that it will try even the best of men."

"I hope you are wrong, José. Come, come to bed."

"Yes, I suddenly feel very tired."

CHAPTER TWENTY-FOUR

The Soltura house was dark when Juan and María reached it. The servants had finished for the evening and had gone home to their families in the ramshackle huts a mile to the north of the main house.

Juan lighted a candelabra just inside the front door, then moved into the living room where he lighted a variety of candles.

María stood in the middle of the living room and laughed. "It is so good to be here again," she said, pirouetting about the room as she took in its familiar sights. "I spent so many happy times in your house, Juan."

"I know," said Juan. "But it makes me sad every time I come here. This house is the house of my family, and my family should be here."

María nodded and went to the mantel over the huge stone fireplace. On the mantel was a three-inch-high sterling silver horse that her father had given the Solturas. María picked up the horse and said, "I always loved this. It reminds me of Tormenta."

"How is your horse?" Juan asked.

"Fine, although he came up lame. I know the men at the stable will have him back in good health in no time."

"Wine?" Juan asked.

"I shouldn't. I had wine at dinner. But I would love some."

Juan went to the kitchen and looked for a bottle of wine. There was none. He called to María, "I'll be back in a moment. I have to go to the wine cellar."

María entered the kitchen and said, "There was always

something about this cellar that was important to you, wasn't there?"

Juan didn't answer.

"You used to spend so much time there. I remember hearing your mother and father talk about it."

Juan leaned on the kitchen table and looked at María. He smiled. "Yes, I did spend a great deal of time in the cellar. It was where I escaped from everything I disliked. In some ways I think becoming a priest offered the same escape."

María's face reflected the pain she felt at hearing that from him. She said, "You shouldn't talk that way, Juan. As a priest you do so much good, bring so much comfort."

Juan sat heavily in a chair at the table and shook his head. "Ministering to the spiritual needs of starving, abused people most certainly is an escape from reality, María. The belly has to be full before God's message can get through. No, I have hidden in my church and in these robes for too long." He lowered his head, and the rest of his words were barely audible. "But that will change soon."

María wanted to ask what he meant but decided not to. She became animated as she asked, "Could I see your cellar?"

Juan looked up and raised his eyebrows. *"Por qué?"*

"I don't know," said María, laughing. "But if the cellar was so important to you I would like to see it."

Juan shrugged. "There is nothing to see. It is a cellar like any other cellar, including the one in your house. The fruits and vegetables are stored there, the wine is kept there and . . ."

María, who had taken a chair next to Juan, placed her hand on top of his and said softly, "Please."

The feel of María's fingers upon his hand sent shivers up Juan's arm, so warm and gentle was her touch. All those years of thinking about her had now resulted in their sitting together, alone, touching. Confusion overwhelmed Juan. All he could manage to say was, "Of course. Come."

Juan took a lighted candle and led María through a door at the rear of the kitchen and down worn stone steps to the cellar. Directly ahead of him was a vegetable storage room. To its right was a large wine cellar. And to the extreme right was the largest part of the cellar, a huge open room in which furniture was stored.

María squinted until she became more accustomed to the darkness. The flickering candle cast bizarre shadows on the rough stone walls. The cellar was cold and damp, and yet

María felt pleasantly warm and comfortable as she stood next to Juan, their arms and shoulders touching. She asked, "Where did you spend your time when you were down here?"

Juan was now embarrassed. He was no longer a young boy, and the pain he'd felt as he sat in the cellar while everyone else was out in the healthy, invigorating air and sun of New Spain returned to him. He pointed to the large room to the right. María took a few steps into it. Juan quickly caught up with her and provided light so that she would not stumble.

They reached a long, thick wooden table upon which a candle, burned almost to its base, and a small mirror lay side by side.

"I used to sit here, María, and think."

María ran her fingertips over the top of the table. "I used to think, too, but probably never about the things you did, Juan. I thought the things that all young girls think of, of clothes and beauty, of romance. I wish I had been mature enough to think of more meaningful matters."

"Oh, no, María, I wasn't a weighty thinker. I was more afraid than wise."

"Afraid of what?"

"Of life, of love, of you."

María laughed. "Of me? Why would you have ever been afraid of me?"

Juan was no longer concerned at censoring his thoughts or the words that expressed them. He turned and faced María directly. "Because you are so beautiful, María. Young girls are not the only ones who think of love and romance. I spent so many hours thinking of you as a woman, wanting you, wondering why I had been born such a frail and weak man."

Their eyes were locked together. María's heart ached at hearing those words from him. How painful it must have been for him, how unnecessary. She wanted to say something, to do something to comfort him, to wipe away all the pain of those years and to make him realize that if he still wanted her, she was his. She would give herself to him without question, and despite the black robe he wore.

Juan ignored the discomfort his words had caused her and continued talking. "I always resented Gordo, María, because he was everything I wanted to be, and was everything I knew you would find attractive in a man. It was very difficult for me to see you look at him with such admiration. I used to hear the chatter about how handsome you thought he was, how dashing and strong and adventurous. God, I wanted to be all those things and more and have you talk about me in the same way. But I hid from the physically attractive world that I was not part of. And now . . .''

María moved closer to him. Their bodies almost touched. Juan held the candle to one side. He could feel the heat radiating from her, hear her breathing, see deeply into her eyes that seemed clouded over with love and life.

"And now?" María asked, the breath from her lips reaching his.

"And now I no longer hide, María, from life and . . ." he had to say it, ". . . and from you."

The final inches between them were closed and their lips met. María's full body pressed against Juan and he shuddered at the sensation. For a moment, they remained that way. But then the passion that had brought them this far moved them hard against each other, bodies tightly pressed, their mouths eagerly working over each other in search of some central, sensual core that would become their mutuality. Juan felt María's tongue against his lips, against his teeth and then against his own tongue. He managed to place the candle on the table and brought his arms around her. His fingers brushed the top of her buttocks. He then lowered his hand and grasped them firmly and pulled her to him as though to merge their bodies.

María pulled back a little and whispered, "Can we go upstairs?"

"Upstairs?" Juan asked.

"Yes."

"Yes," Juan said.

He led them from the cellar to the kitchen, through the living room and up a broad oak staircase to the second floor where the bedrooms were located. He initially led her into his parents' bedroom but stopped. Instead, he took her hand and led her down the hallway to the room at the end that was his. Once inside he closed the door and again took her in his arms. The rush of emotion and sensation was something he'd never experienced before. As he fumbled to remove her clothing he was consumed with the power of the moment. It was as though, for the first time, he had been allowed to enter into life. There was no thought involved now. Everything was raw emotion, the stuff of which life was made.

María's clothes lay in a heap on the floor. Juan removed

his robe and the underwear he wore beneath it and he and María were soon locked in a desperate, naked embrace. They moved to Juan's bed. It was warm and inviting. Juan stripped the covers from it and they lay down together, their legs entwined, their kisses even more urgent.

Juan pulled back and began to explore the wonderful body he'd only dreamed of. His fingers, his lips tasted María's flesh with the same reverence Juan always felt when receiving Communion. *This is my body and my blood. A gift from the Creator.* María's hand found Juan's hardness and her grasp caused him to moan.

"I love you," he said, his lips encircling her nipple.

"Yes, yes, Juan."

A flood of thoughts rushed through Juan's head. He thought of Gordo with María. Had there been other men? What kind of man was he in her eyes? Then nothing mattered except the exquisite pleasure of the moment. He could hear the powerful music of the church organ as his hand plunged between her thighs, fingers wildly searching out the mystery that made her a woman. María writhed and moaned. This was what love should have been, and never was with Gordo. She cried out, in passion and in gratitude for what was happening.

Juan moved on top of her. She spread her legs and he entered her easily, smoothly, on her natural spring of lubrication. Their movements were involuntary, natural and urgent. María shuddered as her orgasm reached her, and Juan's own climax brought from him a cry of joy and relief. The bed had become a puffy white cloud and he sank through it, experiencing spasm upon spasm until he again reached the reality of the bed and room.

They lay side by side for minutes and said nothing. Each of them had found fulfillment that had eluded them throughout their lives. Their lives would never be the same, and both realized it.

Finally, María said, "I must go home, Juan. My father will worry."

"We have so much to talk of, María. So much."

"Yes, I know, but not now. I must go."

"I know."

When they were dressed and downstairs, Juan said, "I know not what the future holds for us, María. Soon, my life will change, hopefully because the life of all New Spain will change."

"What do you mean?" María asked.

"The revolution is near, María."

María stepped close to Juan and took his face in her hands. "And you are part of it?"

"Yes."

"When?"

"December. The eighth. The time is set."

María's face was filled with horror. Her eyes pleaded with Juan. "You will be killed."

"Perhaps."

"Please, no. I couldn't bear that."

"There comes a time in every man's life, María, when he must act upon what is deep inside him. To not act, to not offer myself up in the name of the God I serve and in the interest of justice would forever leave me only half a man. Were I not involved in the revolution, what happened tonight between us could never have occurred. I no longer hide from life. I am now part of life. Perhaps tonight represented my own personal revolution."

María lowered her eyes and her body went limp. Finally, she looked up at him and said, "Could we talk more of this tomorrow?"

"Of course, although it would not be good for you to know too much, to be involved."

María stood up straight and fire came into her eyes. She said flatly, calmly, "Each of us has within us his or her own revolution, and perhaps mine, too, started tonight. I have seen much in my life. Cruelty and hatred is not alien to me. If you will risk yourself, offer yourself, as you say you plan to, then I wish to be at your side."

Juan shook his head vigorously. "No, María, it is not for a woman to become involved in such things."

María stepped back, her hands on her hips, and she cocked her head defiantly. "Not for a woman? It is women who have given birth to the oppressed people of New Spain, and it is women who have given birth to those who would free the oppressed. You underestimate us, Juan. There is strength in women that men will never know, and I offer that strength to you and to the thing you hold so dear."

Juan took her arm and opened the front door. "We will talk more of this tomorrow, María, in the church."

As they left Juan's house and walked down the road leading to the Jardinero house, neither of them noticed the men in the bushes. The men, three of them, had come around from the rear of the house where one of them had climbed a tree and observed through the half-open curtains what had taken place in Juan's room.

After Juan and María had safely passed, the men went to where they had tethered their horses and rode swiftly into Valladolid where a captain of the Valladolid military force and a representative from the church offices in León awaited their report.

CHAPTER TWENTY-FIVE

The next day, at noon, as Juan was about to leave the church with Father Gomez to meet with members of Valladolid's revolutionary council, José Jardinero burst into the church and asked if he could speak with Juan privately.

Juan led José into the secular portion of the church building where they stood alone at the foot of the stairs.

"What's the matter?" Juan asked.

"They've arrested María," José said breathlessly.

"Arrested her? For what?"

"I don't know. They will only tell me that she is being held for questioning."

"That's ridiculous. Why would they want to question María?"

"I was hoping you could find that answer, Father Juan, and intervene in this matter."

Juan sat on the edge of one of the stone steps and tried to sort out his thoughts. He said to José, "I can't imagine them doing this to the daughter of a gachupin."

José snorted. *"This* gachupin is not in favor in Valladolid. Because I expressed sentiments favorable to Viceroy Iturrigaray, they consider me a potential enemy."

Juan asked, "How is María? Did you see her?"

"No. I was not allowed to see her. Please, Father Juan, do something. There must be a great mistake."

Juan agreed with José and promised he would go immediately to army headquarters. But when José left the church, a feeling of helplessness and hopelessness settled over him. He wondered whether he would vomit. María had been arrested because of him, and he wished he were dead.

* * *

María sat ramrod straight in a wooden chair in the army captain's office. Her lips were set in defiance. Her dark eyes followed him as he paced behind his desk, a forced smiled upon his lips. He slapped a riding crop against his thigh and constantly played with the scraggly black hair on his chin.

"I ask you again, Señorita Jardinero, of what you and Father Soltura spoke of last night."

"And I have told you, captain, that it is Señora Soltura. I have also told you that what I spoke of with the priest last night is none of your business."

Up until this point the captain had been relatively pleasant. He now pivoted and slapped the riding crop on his desk. "When a man and woman make love they speak of many things, *Señora*. A man tells a woman of his inner thoughts and plans when consumed with passion. In this case, it is even more likely because such a great sin has been involved. Father Soltura has disgraced himself and his church by breaking his vow of celibacy, and you, *Señora*, are nothing more than a common slut despite your gachupine birth. I warn you, *Señora*, that if you do not tell me what the priest spoke of with you last night, I shall use methods that will loosen your tongue."

He stood up and the smile returned to his face. "Personally, I detest these methods, especially when I consider that a woman will be the victim of them. But I have little choice. There is no doubt that a revolution is about to take place and it will be led by the members of the clergy, including your beloved Father Soltura."

The captain came around the desk and perched on its corner. He leaned close to María's face and lightly flicked the tip of the riding crop against her cheek.

"I will give you a little time, Señora. Then, we will do what we must. There is more at stake here than you. The future of this entire nation is in the balance."

CHAPTER TWENTY-SIX

John Barrigan and thirty braves from the Faraon and Mescalero tribes with whom he and Susan had been living for many months, moved stealthily through a field of tall, mature maize. The field led to the edge of a tiny Spanish settlement just outside the town of San Luis Potosí. The settlement was primarily made up of fur traders. They trapped along the Río Pánuco and moved the furs they had gathered along that river to the Gulf of Mexico, where they were placed on ships for transport to Europe.

John and the braves stopped at the edge of the field and peered through the tall, green stalks. There was little activity in the settlement. Bales of beaver and buffalo peltry, each of which would bring about ten dollars when delivered to the buyers on the Gulf, hung from the side of the dozen houses that made up the settlement.

One of the braves pointed to a group of six men who entered the village after having checked traps along the river. Barrigan nodded and looked around to make sure that the full contingent of warriors was present and ready for the attack.

The brave next to John carefully weighed the long spear he carried, turned it in his hands and tested his grip upon the shaft. All was ready. Another small Spanish settlement would fall to the vengeance of the tribesmen with whom John and Susan Barrigan had placed their lot.

It had been a number of months since Spanish soldiers from Santa Fe had driven the Faraon and Mescalero tribes from their headquarters in the hills to the east of the Rio Grande. The Spanish had assumed they had surrounded the hills, but had not covered every escape route. The Indians and

John and Susan had slipped away in the night and headed south. Their original intent was to find another secure area in which they could establish a village. But the pressure put upon them by pursuing Spanish military forces proved to be too intense for anything permanent to be established. A series of skirmishes had left more than twenty of the braves dead. Some Indian women and children had also fallen to Spanish armored might, and after a month of fleeing, thoughts of finding a permanent settlement had been replaced with a fierce and dedicated commitment to waging all-out war against those who had taken their land from them, and who would turn them into slaves.

John had been caught up in the spirit of the Faraon and Mescalero as they became a renegade band, committed to no tribal order. He often wondered whether he would feel as strongly in concert with their cause had he not married an Indian woman. But the answer to that didn't seem to make any difference. He was now a warrior engaged in warfare, and although many of the vicious and cruel acts his Indian brothers perpetrated upon the Spaniards upset him, he understood the boiling anger inside each brave that led them to openly massacre everything Spanish with which they came in contact.

John had attempted to mitigate some of their policies, particularly where they pertained to women and children. It was the custom to kill the men of a settlement and to scalp them. The women and children were invariably taken captive and forced to move with the tribe until their numbers became too cumbersome. During these periods the Spanish women were often raped. When it was time to sever the women and children from the Indian contingent, they were simply left to fend for themselves. Occasionally, the more volatile of the braves murdered some of the women and children, and it was this practice that had brought John in direct confrontation and conflict with the band's leadership.

Now, as John and the braves posed for yet another attack, the doubts that had built up in his mind regarding his role with the renegades was more pressing than ever. He had spoken with Susan only that night about whether they should leave their Indian family and strike out on their own. They could go to the coast where they could travel by sea away from New Spain and back to the United States, or they could go deeper south into New Spain, in search of a more peaceful and

217

fulfilling life together. John's sentiments were for going to the coast. Susan, however, seemed reluctant to leave New Spain. John understood her feelings. She was, after all, an Indian. Even more than John, Susan felt an affinity for the Indians with whom they had lived for so long, and understood their rage at those who had conquered them. Talk of revolution was everywhere, and although Susan did not understand the politics that might result from a successful revolution, there was something inside that told her that John could find great success and happiness by being there when it occurred.

John, too, had such feelings. If the revolution succeeded in establishing a nation independent from Spain, it would mean that those Americans who were there at the moment of victory might well play an important role in the future relationship between the new country and the United States.

But Susan had another consideration that she did not express to John. Word had reached the tribe with which they traveled that María de Soltura had left Santa Fe and was returning home. Susan had hoped that they might run across the wagon train with which María was traveling. The young Indian woman wanted to once again see the woman whom she had felt to be such a kindred spirit. María had often talked to Susan about Valladolid, about the lush valley in which it was situated, the crops, the magnificent weather, the joy of rising in the morning to days filled with promise. It sounded idyllic to Susan, and she yearned to experience the things María had spoken of.

It was time to strike the fur traders in the Spanish settlement. John knew this and was prepared to play his part. But he didn't want to. He'd had enough of slaughter, no matter how justified it might be from the Indians' point of view. He wanted only to settle down somewhere with his wife, raise the children that would result from their union and find peace and happiness.

"It's time," he told the brave next to him, as he rose from his knees and prepared to assault the settlement. "It is time."

The young brave in charge of the raiding party gave the signal and everyone burst through the remaining cover of the field of maize and headed for the men who had just returned from checking traps. The braves' voices shrieked Indian pledges of retribution against the enemy. Some of the braves had circled to the right through the maize field, and attacked the trappers' flank. The Spaniards were greatly outnumbered.

There appeared to be only a dozen men in the entire settlement. Their wives let out cries of horror and attempted to gather up children and to seek safety in the small houses.

John and the braves did not know that on the other side of the settlement, hidden in another field of maize, was a force of more than two hundred Spanish army troops. The leadership of the army had been alerted to the movement of the marauding Indians, and had guessed right. They had established their position before dawn and had received constant word of the Indians' movements throughout the morning. The moment the attack was sprung on the settlement, the troops launched their own attack. Half of the soldiers were on horseback. Everyone was armed heavily with bayoneted muskets. The surprise factor on the side of the Spaniards, coupled with their obvious superiority of manpower and weapons, rendered the attacking Indians defenseless. Panic set in; it gripped everyone in the Indian party, and within moments they were no longer a unified force. Each man was left to survive or to perish on his own.

The air was filled with the sounds of the muskets and the acrid smell of spent powder. The bodies of the Indians who'd been hit by the fire went through individual dances of death, some falling heavily and finally, others spinning and writhing until the thrust of a bayonet completed the job.

The leader of the Spanish force spotted Barrigan. There had been much talk of the white man who'd joined the Indian raids, and a handsome reward had been placed upon his head. The Spanish commander wanted very much to capture him alive and to bring him in as proof that the reward belonged to him. He had issued orders to his men not to fire upon the white man unless it was absolutely necessary. This order, and the hesitation it caused on the part of those soldiers who saw John, provided him with the few seconds he needed to make his break for safety. His instinct was to return to the field of maize and hope that he could outdistance his pursuers. But instead of that, he found himself veering to the left and running full speed and parallel to the advancing Spanish line. It was a good decision, some houses in that direction provided cover for him and allowed him to make another left and head into the perimeter of the field of maize where it abutted a forest of fruit trees, beyond which was the Rio Pánuco.

John's heart threatened to burst from his chest. His legs felt like lead as he entered the grove of trees and made his way as quickly as possible to the river. Behind him, he heard the shouts of pursuing soldiers. He paused for only a moment to draw a deep breath and to bend over, his hands upon his knees. Then, with another deep breath, he ran along the riverbank until reaching a rocky rise. He followed a break in the rocks, scrambled over some large limestone formations and tumbled down the other side. The fall scraped him in a dozen places. He got to his feet and continued to run until he reached the Indian camp that was located in the hills between the towns of María del Río and Ríoverde. As he approached the camp he saw nothing in it that would cause him to be suspicious. But his guts were gripped with a powerful sense of danger, and he stopped two hundred yards from the camp and hid behind a broad oak tree. Nothing seemed changed in the camp as far as he could see. He had to make up his mind quickly. He either had to enter the camp and warn the women and children who waited there for the men to return, or continue his race alone from the Spanish soldiers, the sounds of whom came closer with each passing moment. He realized he didn't really have a choice. He had to find Susan.

"John!"

John wheeled around in the direction of the voice. "John." He moved into the trees and saw Susan huddled behind one, her eyes wild with fright. He went to her and wrapped his arms about her.

"What's wrong?" he asked.

"Soldiers," she said breathlessly. "They are in the village waiting for you to return."

"How did you . . .?" John asked.

"I was gathering nuts in the forest when they arrived," she said.

"But we have no time."

John stood up straight and listened. The soldiers who'd attacked the braves in the fur trading settlement were very close now. There wasn't a moment to lose.

John looked at Susan and asked, "What of the women and children?"

"Most are dead. The others have been raped and tortured."

They didn't speak another word to each other. John took her hand and led her deeper into the trees in a direction that carried them away from both the Indian camp and from the pursuing Spanish army. They didn't stop moving for two hours, until John felt confident that they could rest for ten minutes without fear of being overtaken. They lay on their backs in a field of tall grass, their breath so labored that it threatened to burst their chests, their bodies drenched with perspiration. Above them a merciless sun beat down upon them. Insects they'd stirred up in the grass stung their flesh. But there was no feeling of discomfort for either of them. It was as though this was the life they were destined to lead. Fugitives, always running from something, someone. John reached over and took Susan's hand and squeezed it.

After ten minutes John turned to Susan and said, "I'm sorry. I did not mean this life for you."

Susan sat up and placed her index finger against her husband's lips. "We must go," she said softly. "We must not stop for too long."

They followed the same pattern they'd followed when escaping from Sante Fe. They traveled by night, slowly, cautiously, staying away from main roads and populated areas, living off what food they could find along their route.

Forty-eight hours later they stood on the outskirts of Dolores. The name of the town had been carved into a piece of wood that was secured to a tree along the road leading into the small town.

"I know of this place," Susan said. "María spoke of it. The brother of her husband is a Catholic priest, and often spoke of a wonderful man who is the priest here.

"What was his name?" John asked.

"Hidalgo."

"You're sure?" John asked.

Susan nodded. "María told me his name means, in Spanish, a noble man. I could not forget that."

John led Susan a little closer to town and looked around. Like most Spanish towns, it was dominated by the church, large, white, serene. There was danger in seeking out this priest whom neither of them knew, but by that time the threat of danger held little meaning. They needed to rest, to make contact with someone who could help them in their lonely quest for safety in such a large and alien land. "Hidalgo," John said under his breath. "Let's find this noble man."

John and Susan approached the church from the rear and hugged its walls until they reached the front door. They stepped inside and tried to become accustomed to the darkness that was broken only by four candles flickering on the altar. There wasn't a sound. John and Susan stood quietly in the shadows at the rear of the church, their hands joined, their senses on the alert for any signal of impending danger.

"There is no one here, Susan," John said.

"Let us ask someone."

"No, we cannot risk that," John said. "Maybe we can lay down on a couple of those benches until we can get some rest and figure out what to do next." He led her to the front of the church and into a pew. Cushions that had been made by local Indians and donated to the church for use as kneeling pads during the services, served as their pillows as they stretched out on the hard wooden benches and reveled at being inside a solid structure for the first time in a long time. There was a wonderful, welcome spirit of calm and safety in the church, which dispelled their natural fears and anxieties, and John and Susan drifted off into a blissful sleep.

At first, the voices that woke John seemed far away. He wondered if he'd been dreaming. He lay very still on the bench and tried to focus his awareness. Two men were talking. One had obviously just entered the church and had been greeted by the other. Their voices were muffled, their words indistinct.

Susan, too, had heard the voices and was fully awake. Neither of them dared move. They listened as two men moved to a rear pew, sat in it and continued their conversation in hushed tones.

John looked at Susan and indicated she should remain silent and still. He slowly and carefully raised his head and peered over the back of the bench. The first rays of sunrise filtered through tiny stained-glass windows and illuminated the source of the voices. There were two priests, both in clerical robes. One was an older man with tufts of white hair. The other man was younger. The older priest listened to what the younger priest was saying.

John lowered his head and collected his thoughts. They could stay where they were and hope that the priests would leave the church without discovering them. Or they could confront the priests and trust that they would not turn them in to local authorities. One of the priests probably was the Father Hidalgo of whom Susan had spoken.

John decided on the latter course of action. He gently patted

Susan's leg and nodded reassuringly. He sat up, and so did she.

At first the priests didn't notice the visitors. It was only when John stood that he captured their attention and their conversation stopped. John led Susan by the hand up the aisle to the rear pew.

"Buenos días, Señor, Señora," Father Hidalgo said. "May I be of help?"

"Buenos días, padre. My name is John Barrigan. This is my wife, Susan. Would you be Father Hidalgo?"

"Yes, I am. And this is Father Juan de Soltura."

Susan's eyes lighted up at the mention of Juan's name. "You are the brother of Gordo," she said, "who is married to María."

Now it was Juan's turn to react with excitement and surprise. "Yes," he said. "How do you know that?"

Susan and John told the two priests of the experiences in Santa Fe which brought Susan into contact with María. When they were finished, Juan sadly shook his head in recognition of who they were. "Then it was you who attacked my brother."

"Yes, father. He . . ."

"Please, don't feel that you have to explain," Juan said. "My brother is not a source of pride to me."

Father Hidalgo said, "You must be hungry. Would you like some breakfast?"

"If it's no trouble, padre," John said.

"No trouble at all, my son." Hidalgo stood and slipped from the pew. "Follow me," he said. "I suddenly feel very hungry myself. One of the women will prepare us something."

The four of them sat around a small table in the portion of the church set aside as Father Hidalgo's living quarters. They were served fresh melon, tortillas and hot oatmeal, and John and Susan quickly realized just how hungry they were. When they'd finished what had been placed upon the table, Hidalgo asked whether they wished more.

"I'm not a man to abuse good hospitality, padre," John said.

Hidalgo laughed. "Eating more of the food of this parish wouldn't be abusing its hospitality, Mr. Barrigan, it would just be complimenting it." He called for more food, which was quickly served.

They lingered at the table over strong black coffee.

"I suppose you know, Mr. Barrigan, that your exploits with the Indian raiding parties in the north have not gone unnoticed. There are rewards for you throughout New Spain," Hidalgo said.

Barrigan nodded. "I'm well aware of that, Father Hidalgo. I'm not proud of some of the things I've done, but it was a matter of circumstances. I did what I had to do to survive."

Hidalgo looked at Juan. "We all do what we must to survive," he said. "The question now is what will you do from this point on?"

"I'm not sure."

Juan told Susan that María had returned safely to Valladolid and that he had seen her only two days before.

"How is she?" Susan asked. "She was like my sister."

The expression on Juan's face answered the question more eloquently than any words could have. He looked at Hidalgo, who indicated that it was all right for the younger priest to say what was on his mind.

"María has been arrested by Spanish authorities," Juan said. "That is why I came here this morning. She was arrested two days ago."

"Why did they arrest her?" John asked.

"Because she knows me," Juan said. "I'm sure you're aware of the fear the Spaniards have about revolution."

"You'd have to be deaf, dumb and blind not to hear that kind of talk around New Spain," John said. "But is she involved in a revolution?"

Hidalgo shook his head and smiled. "No, John, but anyone who wears these robes is suspected of that kind of activity these days. The fact that María grew up as a neighbor to Father Soltura and sought him out upon her return to Valladolid means to our Spanish friends that she must know something of any revolutionary plans."

Hidalgo turned to Juan. "Father Soltura, you were telling me upon your arrival of the details of María's arrest and detainment. Maybe you should finish what you were saying."

Juan wasn't sure he should in front of John and Susan.

Hidalgo said, "I think we're with sympathic friends here, father. I don't have any question about that."

Juan nodded. "María has been detained because the authorities are convinced she knows of the plans for the revolution. She knows very little, except that plans are under way. How much I had wished I had not seen her, not even mentioned to her anything about what is to occur. It has placed her in grave jeopardy, and I curse myself for the indiscretion that led to it.''

Hidalgo reached over and put his hand on Juan's forearm. "Do not be too hard on yourself, my young friend. What is important now is not to question what we have done, but to plan what we must do in the future to help your friend.''

Barrigan said, "That makes sense to me. I know how much my wife, here, liked María de Soltura, and I'm ready to do anything I can to help. You can count on that.''

Hidalgo asked Juan, "Has she been mistreated?''

Juan shook his head, "Not yet, as far as I can determine. They will not let me see her. She is being held in solitary confinement and not even her own family can visit her. I did receive word from one of the Indians who works inside the prison that although she has not been physically harmed, there are plans to apply torture to make her talk.''

John was aware of the young priest's anguish. Juan's hands were tightly clenched. His mouth was set in a hard, straight line, his teeth jammed against each other. John said, "It might be none of my business, padre, but you said before that there was an indiscretion that led to her being arrested. I don't understand why they'd pick on María for information about any revolution. There must be lots of other folks you know who could tell them as much, or more.''

Juan started to answer John's question but Father Hidalgo cut him off in midsentence. "It doesn't seem to me that any of this is important for the moment. What I would like to know, father, is exactly how much she does know.''

"Almost nothing,'' Juan said. "Yes, I told her that there was to be a revolution and that I was a part of it. I mentioned the date but nothing else. The use of torture on her will be a waste. She will tell them nothing.''

"María is a very strong woman,'' Susan said. "She will resist them to her death.''

Father Hidalgo looked at John Barrigan and asked, "You say you will help us, Mr. Barrigan. Would you be willing to risk your life for us, and for María?''

John Barrigan nodded.

"I am pleased to hear that,'' Hidalgo said. "Many lives will be risked in this revolution, including those of Father Soltura and myself. Your reputation as a man of courage and daring precedes you here. It can only be to our benefit to have you with us.''

''Just tell me what to do and I'll do it,'' Barrigan said, turning to Susan for support. Her clear, dark eyes gave him all the strength he needed. He placed his large, calloused hand on top of hers and gently squeezed it.

Hidalgo sat back and pondered the situation. Then, he said flatly, ''We must rescue María from the prison. We must also move up the date of the revolution. María knows the date. A simple confession by her that a revolution is in the planning, and that it involves a member of the clergy, could be cause for the Spaniards to launch a series of mass arrests. Certainly, Father Soltura, you are in great jeopardy. The Spaniards could use you as a reason for implementing martial law in every province of New Spain. We must not give them that opportunity.''

Juan was dismayed at Hidalgo's analysis of the situation. The need to change plans had been brought about by his own weakness. But he knew that to apologize for it again, and to seek forgiveness, would anger the older priest. What had happened had happened. The moment could not be retrieved. Hidalgo was right. Plans would have to be changed. He stood and suggested that he and the Barrigans leave that night for Valladolid. They would spend the rest of the day planning María's release.

Hidalgo agreed. He told Juan that a meeting of the revolutionary council of Valladolid should be called two nights hence.

''You will be there?'' Juan asked him.

''Yes. We must be ready to strike the moment María has been rescued. The simple act of releasing her will undoubtedly set off the same chain of events as would occur were she to be coerced into confessing a revolutionary plot. We must be ready to act immediately.''

John Barrigan said, ''This here is the tenth of September. How soon do you figure you can put the revolution into the works?''

Hidalgo smiled. ''Almost immediately. Past years have been spent wisely, Mr. Barrigan. We have built a force of sizeable number and dedicated leadership. The oppressed can be rallied within hours. The change of plans may be a blessing, after all. There is no reason to wait until December to launch the revolution. Choosing that date in the future perhaps only reflects my own lingering doubts and fears about its success. We are ready to move now, and that is exactly what we will do." He turned to Juan. "You will arrange the meeting?"

"Yes," Juan said.

"Mr. Barrigan, I welcome you to our cause."

"I'm happy to be here," John said. "Even if I wasn't I wouldn't have much choice. I'm a hunted man with a price on his head in the middle of a hell of a big foreign nation. I'm married to an Indian. I reckon' I've got a lot to gain from being involved in this revolution. But I'll tell you something else, padre. I've seen a lot of what goes on in this country, the way most of the people are treated like slaves. Back in the United States, 'specially where I come from in Massachusetts, we don't take kindly to the thought of a man being a slave to any other man. I'd say that the timing has worked out pretty good for Susan and me. We'll fight down to the wire with you."

Everyone stood and hands were shaken.

Hidalgo said to Barrigan, "You have a mischievous gleam in your eye, Mr. Barrigan."

John broke into a broad grin. "I've been through some tough times, Father Hidalgo, and it looks like this is goin' to be another one. I was just thinkin' that there is one man I'd love to have at my side in the days to come."

"Who's that?" Juan asked.

"A fella named Zeb Pike."

"The American army captain who was sent by Mr. Burr?" Hidalgo asked.

John raised his eyebrows, "You don't miss much, do you, padre?" he asked.

"We can't afford to," Hidalgo said. "Too much is at stake. By the way, you do know that Mr. Burr jumped bail and fled to Europe, do you not?"

Barrigan shook his head. "I've been out of touch. But it looks like I'm about to be in touch, maybe more than I've ever been in my life."

John and Susan were given a room upstairs where it was suggested they rest until they could meet again early in the afternoon.

Juan and Father Hidalgo returned to the church and sat in a pew.

"I wish you to hear my confession," Juan said.

227

"Of course, my son. But I would suggest that if your confession has to do with the fact that you succumbed to the weakness of the flesh and broke your vow of celibacy with María de Soltura, you not squander the potency of your guilt by confessing it to me. The guilt that you feel should be directed toward the church to whom that vow of celibacy was given, and which works hand-in-hand with a government that keeps nine-tenths of its nation in slavery."

"I love her," Juan said, his eyes fixed upon the back of the next pew.

Hidalgo nodded. "And she is your brother's wife."

"Yes."

"It is your love for her that might sustain you through the dark days ahead, father. You have journeyed all night to bring me important news, and you will retrace that journey again this night. I would suggest you sleep until the meeting this afternoon. And if you have trouble sleeping, allow the joy that love for a beautiful woman provides to help you."

Hidalgo stood. "Until this afternoon, Father Soltura."

"Gracias."

CHAPTER TWENTY-SEVEN

September 13, 1810

María de Soltura sat alone in the tiny cell she had occupied since her arrest. It was located in a long, low adobe building in the northwest corner of the Valladolid Spanish military compound. The building contained twenty cubicles, each equipped to handle two prisoners. A small window high on the wall was barred. The door to each cell contained an equally small barred opening.

The only illumination in the cell came from a candle that burned on a tiny, rough-hewn table. María sat on the edge of her bunk. Her mattress was one-inch thick and filled with straw. She wore the same clothes she had worn throughout her confinement. Her hair was disheveled and damp with sweat. Her shoes and stockings had been taken away from her and her bare feet were cold as they rested upon a plain dirt floor. The sound of rats could be heard as they scurried from cell to cell in search of food. A pot of water sat upon the table next to the candle. A clay pot was on the floor in one corner of the cell. It was the only bathroom facility available to María.

She'd just been visited once again by the commandant of the military prison. His visits had become more frequent. María noticed that he was drunk on the last few occasions. This night, he had obviously vomited because the smell of it was strong upon his clothes. He smoked long black cigars that he rolled himself. His breath reeked of alcohol, and he had to steady himself on a few occasions as he paced the cell.

Although the commandant had made sexual advances to María, he seemed reluctant to press them to the point where she had to physically resist. He shifted back and forth between threats of physical harm to her, and promises of rewards should she cooperate. Usually, he left her cell angry and shouting threats. Tonight had been no different. He'd told her that if she did not decide by morning to confess what she knew about the revolution and about the role of the Catholic clergy, particularly the role of Juan de Soltura, she would be tortured and, if that did not produce the desired results, killed.

Despite the commandant's threats and the physical hardship of life within the prison, María's thoughts did not dwell upon those conditions. Rather, she was consumed with something she had heard that afternoon while sitting in the commandant's office. He'd tried to convince her during that visit that it would be in the best interest of her gachupine family for her to cooperate with the authorities. María was told that her father had fallen into great disfavor and that only her confession could stave off his arrest.

She'd wanted to learn more about the position her father was in and had hinted to the commandant that he might have finally reached her. He seemed pleased with this turn of events and had left the office in search of another officer to be present during what he was certain would be a forthcoming confession. While he was absent from the office, María had gone to the wall and had pressed her ear against it to better hear a conversation that was taking place in the next office. There were three men talking, and although many of the words were lost to her, she'd heard enough to cause her heart to sink. What she'd gotten from the conversation on the other side of the wall was that a meeting of revolutionaries was to take place in Valladolid the next evening, and that a full-scale attack upon that meeting would be launched. Everyone attending it would be arrested and tried as traitors to the state.

María was certain that Juan would be part of that meeting. She had spent the rest of the day in despair. She felt so helpless, unable to warn Juan of what would surely be a disaster for him and for those with whom he was involved.

Now, at ten in the evening, she sat on her cot and stared at the candle as it burned closer to the table. Soon, it would extinguish itself, just as Juan and his revolution would be extinguished.

María's eyes filled with tears. Her life had taken such a dramatic turn downward in such a short period of time. The horror of being married to Gordo, the displacement from her home to Sante Fe, Gordo's attempted rape of Susan, and

María's own decision to leave her husband and to return to Valladolid—all this combined with the love she felt for Juan threatened to break her apart. The quiet tears turned into sobs that increased in their intensity until her entire body shook. She was determined not to make any noise that might entice the solitary guard to her door, but found she could no longer control herself. She let out a long, painful moan and gave vent to the screams that were inside of her.

The prisoner in an adjoining cell cursed her and told her to be quiet.

Her sobs lessened and she was soon left with silent tears again. She lay down upon the straw mattress and pulled her legs up into a fetal position. She thought of Juan and of what would happen to him.

Ten minutes later a voice called her name. It was a girl. María sat up on the cot and looked at the door. Someone's shadow was partially visible beneath it.

"María."

María got up and walked to the door. She had to stand on tiptoe to look through the barred opening. Standing outside the door was Susan Barrigan.

"What are you . . .?"

"Ssh," Susan said, glancing down the hallway to the sentry's station. She'd told the guards at the front gate that she was one of the Indian servants who worked in the kitchens and who cleaned the offices and quarters. Once inside, she'd gone directly to the prison building, entered it and approached the sentry. He was a very young man, and had been dozing in a chair when she entered.

The sight of Susan was at first confusing, then arousing to the young soldier. He asked why she was there, and she told him she'd been sent by his friends to service him sexually.

Susan's claim made no sense to the young soldier, but he was overcome by the sexual passion he felt at seeing the beautiful girl standing before him. He got up from the chair and started to put his arms around her. He gasped, then moaned as she sunk a knife into his abdomen. She quickly placed her hand over his mouth. He slowly sunk to the floor, Susan's hand still firmly planted against his face. She took the keys from his belt and walked down the long corridor until she came to the door upon which María's name had been written.

Susan quickly opened the door with the key and motioned

for María to follow her. They quietly moved down the corridor until they came to the sentry station. María looked down at the man, a pool of his blood growing larger beneath him.

Susan went to the main door of the prison building and looked outside. She turned and said, "Come, María. John is waiting for us."

The military compound was very dark. The moon was but a sliver in the black sky. The only sounds came from a building near the front entrance in which enlisted men were housed. They were having a party, and their loud, drunken talk could occasionally be heard.

The two guards who'd allowed Susan to enter were still at the front gate. Their shift would change at midnight.

Susan and María huddled together in the shadows of the enlisted men's quarters. Susan whispered, "Give me one minute. When I have turned their backs to you, leave quickly."

"What of you?" María asked.

Susan gripped María's wrist. "I will be fine, my sister. We have no time to lose. Just do as I say."

María watched as Susan left the shadows and walked up to the two guards. One of them made a lewd sexual comment to her and she laughed. Her response to the comment prompted other remarks. She giggled when one of the guards suggested they go to a secluded area along the wall and make love.

Susan took one of the guards by the hand and walked with him toward an area that was shielded from the rest of the compound by a low storage hut. The young soldier turned and waved for his companion to come with them. There was much laughter as they moved away from the main gate. The minute they did María left her position and slipped through the gate. Once outside she didn't know where to go. She couldn't leave Susan. She looked around and saw the closest cover was a deserted, ramshackle house fifty yards from the gate. She was about to run to it when, out of the corner of her eye, she saw a figure move from where it had been hiding against the wall of the compound. It was a man. He quickly went through the gate and in the direction Susan had taken the guards. There were the sounds of a scuffle. One of the guards started to yell something but his words trailed off into an agonized moan. Seconds later Susan and John Barrigan emerged through the gate, grabbed María's hand and ran to the deserted house. Behind it were three horses. One of them was Tormenta.

John and Susan mounted the other two horses. María stood

speechless. She started to ask a question but John cut her off. "Quickly!" he said. "We haven't a moment to lose."

María mounted Tormenta and the three of them sped away, first a hundred yards down a road leading into the village, then to an open plain beyond which the haciendas of Soltura and Jardinero were located. The sound of the horses hoofs upon the hard ground were sure and steady. The wind that whipped María's face was like a breath of life to her.

They pulled up in front of María's home. Her mother and father were waiting outside. Their horses had been saddled and provisions had been loaded upon another horse. The Jardineros and María were overwhelmed at seeing each other and wanted desperately to embrace, but there was no time for that. The mother and father mounted their steeds. John took the reins of the packhorse and they all rode away to the north.

An hour later they reached their destination, a thick forest of ahuehuete trees that grew up the slope of a moderate mountain range. They dismounted and walked the horses into the forest until they'd reached a large clearing in which a camp had been set up. María was surprised at how permanent the camp seemed to be. Dozens of men milled about. Tents had been erected, as well as lean-tos and storage areas that were covered by animal hides attached to tree limbs. Two large fires burned over which huge cauldrons of soup and stew were kept constantly hot for those who wished them.

There was now time for María and her family to be reunited. They hugged and kissed. María's mother cried freely.

María was still not over the shock of seeing John and Susan. Although she had often thought of them, she'd assumed they would never meet again. But here they were, her saviors, alive and well. She hugged Susan, hesitated, and then embraced John.

The excitement of her rescue from the prison had temporarily caused her to forget about what she had heard concerning the meeting in Valladolid scheduled for the following night. Then she remembered. Her eyes widened and she told John she must speak with him about something of great urgency.

"Go right ahead, María, although maybe you'd better have some of the good stew that the cook here has whipped up. You must be hungry."

María shook her head. "There is no time for that." She excused herself from her parents and went with John to an area secluded enough to insure their privacy. She told him of

233

what she had heard. When she'd finished, John rubbed his chin and thought for a moment. "It looks like we've got a lot of problems to solve right quick," he said. "Gettin' you out of prison and killin' those guards is likely to bring the whole damn Spanish army out lookin' for us. We'll have to break down this camp immediately and head somewhere else. And the priests are goin' to have to be warned off from that meeting."

"I know," María said. "They should be told right now."

"That's what I was thinkin'," John said. "We'll have to send somebody into town to find them."

"I'll go," María said.

"Don't be ridiculous. If there's three people in this whole damn valley that the Spanish will be looking for it's you, me and Susan."

María looked up at John and pleaded with her eyes. "I know I'll be able to find Juan safely. I can dress differently, and I know my way around Valladolid. Please, John, let me do this. I can't explain it to you, but it is more important to me than anything in my life to be the one to warn him."

John looked over María's shoulder at the men in the camp. "I don't have time to argue with you, María. I reckon you will get through safely. But if you don't, you know what's going to happen to everybody at that meeting."

María nodded gravely. "Don't worry, John. I'll make it." She kissed him on the cheek. "And thank you for getting me out of prison. You and Susan are two of the most wonderful people I've ever known."

"You were good to Susan in Santa Fe, María, and I'll always be grateful for that." He again looked at the activity in the camp. "I don't reckon your folks will take too kindly to your going back into town."

"I know. Don't tell them until I'm gone. I'll get together some sort of disguise and will leave immediately. Where can we meet you after I've warned Juan and Father Hidalgo?"

John shook his head. "I hadn't thought about that. I'm not sure where we ought to move this camp to. I'll tell you what. I'll check with your father about a new location for us. I'll let you know before you leave."

María squeezed his arm and ran off in search of an appropriate disguise for her mission.

José Jardinero, when asked about a possible site to which the group could move, suggested the town of Acambaro, approximately seventy-five kilometers to the northeast. "There is a large ranchero there directly to the west of the plaza. It belongs to a friend of mine, and I know that he has pledged his allegiance to the revolutionaries. He will welcome us there, at least for a short time."

John said he would spread the word to the men to break camp and to depart immediately.

"María?" José asked. "Where is she?"

John shrugged his shoulders, "I'll go find her. I've got to talk to her about a few things anyway. You and the señora just stay here and rest until we're ready to move. I'll bring María back to you."

"Muchas gracias," said José.

John found María just as she was slipping into a heavy shawl of the type generally worn by older Spanish women. A large piece of black cloth was secured over her head. Susan had drawn lines into María's face with a charred end of a stick.

"You certainly have aged, ma'am," John said with a smile.

"I hope the Spanish see me the same way," María replied.

John told her where they would meet.

"I will tell Juan and Father Hidalgo that," she said. "When do you expect to reach there?"

"Sometime tomorrow. We'll wait for you there."

María kissed Susan on the cheek, then embraced her.

"You take care," John said.

"Sí. Until tomorrow."

John and Susan watched as María mounted Tormenta, cast a final look back at them and headed through the trees toward Valladolid. When she was out of sight, John said to Susan, "I hated to lie to her family that way, but I knew that being the one to warn Juan was important to her. I guess I'd better go tell them that she's gone and that they won't see her until tomorrow."

"I pray for her," Susan said.

"Yeah, me, too," John said heavily.

Gordo Soltura arrived in Valladolid less than an hour after María's escape, and after the sentries had been murdered in the military garrison. He and the twenty Spanish soldiers who'd set out from Santa Fe in pursuit of John Barrigan and the renegade Indian tribe had followed their prey all the way

235

to the south. They would pick up their trail, then lose it, then find it again, only to suffer the frustration of arriving at the scene of a massacre a little too late.

San Luis Potosí was no exception. The Spanish army that had ambushed Barrigan and the Indians told Gordo that only one man had escaped, and that it was the tall white man. No one knew exactly in which direction Barrigan had fled, but Gordo had a hunch that it would be further south. The commander of the force in San Luis Potosí had argued that Barrigan would more likely have headed for the coast. That was where he intended to lead his soldiers in search of the elusive American.

Gordo decided to follow his instincts and head south. He led his men into Dolores where they learned that a white man with an Indian woman had been seen there. No one knew for certain where they had gone, but Gordo decided that Valladolid was as good a choice as any. Certainly, Susan must have heard many stories about it from María while she lived in the Soltura home in Santa Fe.

Soon after his arrival in Valladolid, Gordo was told to report to the garrison commander there. The commandant's office was buzzing with activity. Gordo and his men were immediately pressed into service to mount a hunt for María, and for those who might have helped her escape.

The commandant busily barked orders to his aides and ignored Gordo until the name Soltura hit home. He turned and said, ''Soltura? That is the name of the prisoner who escaped.''

''María?'' Gordo gasped. ''She was here?''

''Sí. It is a stroke of good fortune for us that you have arrived. Señor Soltura. Surely, you must know where your wife would go under these circumstances.''

Gordo thought for a moment. ''To our home in the valley, I suppose.''

The commandant smiled. ''If she does, she will be captured immediately. I have dispatched a force to your home, as well as to the home of her parents.''

Gordo turned from the commandant and walked to a wooden chair in which prisoners sat while being interrogated. The front legs of the chair had been sawed off a half-inch so that the prisoner was constantly leaning forward.

Gordo shook his head. The irony of the situation almost

made him grin. He turned and said, "Why was my wife arrested?"

"Because she has knowledge of plans for the revolution?"

"Where would she get such knowledge?"

"From your brother, the priest."

Gordo snorted. "It does not surprise me. The clergy of New Spain, my brother included, are dedicated to the overthrow of everything that is good and decent here. It matters not to me whether those who betray our king include my brother or my wife. I am loyal to you and to all officials of New Spain, and I am ready to do what I must to insure that order is maintained."

The commandant suggested that Gordo gather up the men with whom he'd arrived and ready them to join the search for María and for those who'd rescued her. He then added, "We have knowledge of a meeting of revolutionaries that is to be held tomorrow night here in Valladolid. It will include your brother, Father Soltura. However, because of the events that have occurred here this evening, our plans have changed. I intend to immediately dispatch troops into the village to arrest your brother and any others who might be part of his plan to mount a revolution."

"Let me join that force," Gordo said.

The commandant scowled. "I am not sure it would be wise to pit brother against brother. Certainly, you would have feelings for him that might get in your way."

Gordo shook his head and approached the desk. He hit the top of it with his fist and said angrily, "No, no. My brother is a weakling who was destined to betray his family, his neighbors and his countrymen. I wish only to see justice done. My reputation and record as a loyal subject of our king, and of the army of New Spain is well established." He stood up straight and cracked a crooked smile. "Besides, I could be of great help in persuading my wife to give up this silly infatuation she seems to have developed for renegade priests. I assure you, commandant, that I will be of great value to you."

The commandant sighed and looked outside. Troops had gathered and were awaiting orders. He turned to Gordo and said, "Very well, then. Have your men join with Captain Malevido. He operates under my direct orders and is familiar with what we have planned."

"*Gracias*, commandant."

Gordo left the commandant's office and rejoined the small group of men outside who'd traveled with him from Santa Fe. He commanded them to attention, then walked to where Captain Malevido stood in front of more than one hundred armed Spanish soldiers. Malevido wore a royal blue dress coat with a double row of brass buttons down the front. His epaulettes were gold fringe that hung from brass plates on the shoulders. The collar of the coat was high and snug about his neck. His face was round and pockmarked. It was framed by long, greasy black hair that hung over his ears, and by a blue forage cap with a shiny black visor, upon which a braided gold star had been affixed. A brillant scarlet sash was secured about his waist.

Gordo felt shabby in front of Captain Malevido. He was dressed in the same way as his men, in a coarse shirt, black jacket with two of its buttons missing, coarse gray trousers and black boots that were hopelessly scuffed. Gordo's men wore barracks caps. The only thing that set Gordo apart from them was his wide-brimmed sombrero. He'd discarded the red shako cap that had been issued to him in Santa Fe after he'd joined the army and had received his commission. Once he'd ridden away from the scrutiny of the garrison commander, he'd quickly changed to the sombrero in which he felt infinitely more comfortable.

"Gordo de Soltura reporting as ordered," Gordo said to Malevido. He resented having to go through such formality with a man he was confident was far less daring and able than he was.

Malevido seemed puzzled.

"I operate under direct orders of the commandant," Gordo said. "I have unique qualifications and knowledge of the people we hunt tonight. I am to join your force, although my men and I will operate independently based upon the knowledge that I possess."

Captain Malevido had to keep himself from smiling. A graduate of Mexico's best military academy, he found the oafish Gordo to be amusing. But he wasn't about to get into a discussion over it. The garrison commander had stepped from the building and had shouted an order that everyone move out.

Gordo, too, did not wish to continue the confrontation with Malevido. He simply turned on his heel and returned to his men. "Mount up," he barked. His troops followed his order, and once the main force had ridden from the garrison and entered the road leading into Valladolid, Gordo and his men brought up the rear.

The pain that radiated up and down Gordo's spine and into his neck had worsened over the course of the journey from Santa Fe, and it was particularly acute now. But so intense was his concentration on playing a major role in breaking up the revolution, that the pain was soon filtered out of his existence. He saw María, saw Juan in his mind, and his disgust with them was so overwhelming that he could have become physically ill. He thought, too, of John Barrigan and the Indian girl, Susan. How much he wanted to find them and to repay Barrigan for the damage that had been inflicted upon him by the gringo.

Gordo settled into his saddle and allowed a general sense of satisfaction to settle over him. This was to be an eventful night, one that he would remember for a long time. Of this he was sure, and the realization of it made him feel very good.

Juan, Father Hidalgo and two members of the Valladolid revolutionary council sat upon the roof of the building adjoining the Catholic Church. They were waiting for some sort of signal that the rescue of María had been accomplished. Originally, it had been suggested that María be brought to the church. But Juan had vetoed that idea. He reasoned that the church would be one of the first places they would look for her, and he urged that she be taken to the relative safety of the encampment that had been established two weeks earlier in the countryside.

But there was to be a visit from someone from that encampment to let them know that María was safely there.

"We should have heard by now," Juan said, his voice filled with anguish.

Hidalgo patted him on the back. "It is too soon, my son. Give them time. We might not receive a signal of her safe rescue for hours."

"What if they didn't succeed?" Juan asked. "If the attempt by John and Susan was unsuccessful, María's life would be in much greater danger than it was before."

Hidalgo looked up at the stars and closed his eyes. "Pray, father, Our God is with us this night and will hear your prayers."

Juan felt shame. He bowed his head and silently prayed that María was safe.

One of the members of the revolutionary council, who'd been standing at the wall overlooking the plaza, suddenly tensed as he saw a line of soldiers from the garrison moving up the road toward the plaza. He turned and said, *"Aquí, aquí."*

Juan and Hidalgo went to him and looked over the wall.

"What do you think?" Hidalgo asked.

"I think the rescue was successful, father." Juan said. "I would assume they are out looking for María."

Fortunately, María had seen the advancing troops, too. She had approached the plaza from the east, which afforded her a relatively secluded view of the town. Some instinct had told her to wait among the trees and be certain nothing unusual was occurring before she exposed herself. Those few moments of delay had saved her, because it was during that brief period that the troops came into view.

María's initial response upon seeing the soldiers was to assume that they were looking for her and for the Barrigans. But then it occurred to her that her escape might have prompted the commandant to push up his timetable for the arrest of Juan and the other revolutionary leaders. She mounted Tormenta and moved along the cover of the trees until she was five hundred yards from the rear of the church. She realized that if her hunch was right, she didn't have much time to lose. She sat up straight, drew a deep breath, squinted her eyes and whipped Tormenta on his flank. He shot forward and quickly covered the distance to the church. María looked up to the low wall that ran around the roof and wondered if she dared call out. She didn't have any choice. She could hear the troops coming to a halt in front of the church, and Captain Malevido barking an order to enter it and arrest everyone inside.

"Juan," she called. "Juan. Juan."

Juan had heard Malevido's order too. María's call to him had been lost in the scuffle in front of the church.

"We must go over the wall," Hidalgo said, quickly moving in that direction.

Hidalgo, Juan and the other two men only heard María call when they reached the back wall. Juan looked down and, seeing her, thought his heart might stop. His hands gripped the tops of vines that ran up the sides of the walls. He didn't hesitate. He flung himself up onto the wall and allowed himself to hang until his feet found what appeared to be a secure

240

tangle of vines. He glanced upward and saw that Father Hidalgo was doing the same thing. He was concerned for Hidalgo. The older priest had not been feeling well, and his arthritis had threatened to cripple him at times. But none of that seemed to bother Hidalgo now. All four men safely reached the ground. María had dismounted and she embraced Juan. Everyone listened as the soldiers battered in the front door of the church with boots and musket butts.

"I locked it," Juan said.

"Come," María said, pointing to the trees five hundred yards away.

Hidalgo turned to the two secular members of the council. "They do not know that you are involved in plans for the revolution," he said. "You must tell the others that there will be no meeting tomorrow night."

María hurriedly added, "We will gather tomorrow at a ranchero directly to the west of Acambaro. It is owned by a friend of my father."

"Sí, sí," one of the laymen said.

They all took off on the run toward the trees. María held Tormenta's reins. The horse cantered with them for half the distance, then balked. María spoke to him but the horse continued to balk. His lame leg that had been treated gave him pain again.

"Leave him," Hidalgo said.

"No, I can't," María said.

Tormenta whinnied, reared up and pulled free of María's grip.

Juan put his arm around her shoulder and said, "I know, I know, but there is nothing we can do."

María knew he was right. They resumed their run for cover. When they reached the trees, María looked back. She saw Tormenta limping toward the church. Soldiers could be seen on the rooftop. A seldom-used back door to the church had been kicked open and troops spilled through it.

"We have to keep going," Hidalgo said. He was in great pain. His neck and shoulders ached.

"Look," María said, pointing.

Juan followed the direction of her finger and saw what had captured her attention. Gordo's small contingent of men had circled to the back of the church on horseback and come to a halt two-thirds of the distance from where María and her friends stood.

"Is that Gordo?" María asked.

Juan sighed, "I think so. I looks like my brother."

They continued to watch as Gordo rode up to Tormenta and grabbed the horse's reins.

Without another word Juan, Hidalgo and María turned and made their way through the trees in a direction opposite from that of the church. The two lay members of the council separated from them and ran in a direction that would skirt the main part of the village.

Gordo Soltura sat upon his horse and twisted Tormenta's reins. "She has been here," he muttered.

One of his men who'd been sitting next to him asked, "What did you say?"

"Shut up," Gordo responded.

CHAPTER TWENTY-EIGHT

September 15, 1810

Susan Barrigan leaned over the sleeping body of María Soltura and gently shook her. The women who had gathered at the ranchero belonging to José Jardinero's friend had slept inside the main house, while the men had spent the night taking shifts as sentries and planning the next move.

"Wake up, my sister," Susan said.

María opened her eyes and waited until they adjusted to the rays of morning light that poured through the window. "What time is it?" she asked.

"It is early," Susan said. "Juan and John wish to see you."

María sat up and rubbed her eyes. "How long have you been up?" she asked.

"I did not sleep most of the night. I am glad you did, however."

María looked around the large living room in which the women had huddled together during the night. Some still slept. Others were awake but remained on the floor or on couches.

"Where is my mother?" María asked as she got up and tried to brush the wrinkles out of her heavy, purple velvet dress.

"Outside, with your father." Susan smiled and squeezed María's arm, "Come, there is much to be done in preparation for leaving."

"Leaving? I thought we might stay here a few days."

Susan shook her head. "That would be good, to remain here and rest, but I think Father Hidalgo has decided to move to another location. "I'm sure they will tell you all that."

Susan got up from her knees and made her way through the maze of bodies on the floor. María followed her.

Outside the house, there was much activity.

"*Buenos días*, María," José said when he saw his daughter come through the door.

"*Buenos días*, papa," María replied. She ran her hands through her hair that had been pulled into a tight bun behind her head. "It will be a beautiful day."

María's mother agreed and came to where her daughter stood on a broad, sprawling porch that wrapped around two sides of the house.

"How did you sleep?" María's mother asked.

"Like a baby, mother. I would have slept that way under any circumstances."

José came to where his wife and daughter stood. He shook his head. "It was a foolish thing you did to insist upon being the one to warn Juan and the others," he said. "We are about to enter dark and troublesome days, my daughter. I do not see any outcome but death for everyone involved. While I sympathize with the cause that lights such fire in Father Hidalgo and in those whom he surrounds himself with, I must question the wisdom of mounting a full-fledged revolution at this time. The odds are overwhelmingly against everyone involved in such a folly. I care not for myself. My life approaches its end anyway. But I beg of you, María, that you and your mother escape before it is too late."

María looked deeply into her father's eyes and saw fatigue and worry. He'd aged considerably from the way she remembered him prior to leaving for Santa Fe. She'd noticed it at the dinner table on the night of her return, but the severity of it was now even more apparent. Deep lines creased his long, angular face. His hair seemed even grayer than the day before. His eyes were sunken, and a grayness surrounded them.

"Papa, I love you very much. I know that everything you have ever done in your life has been out of your love for me and wanting the very best things for me in my life. But I also remember you saying on more than one occasion that we often cannot choose the direction our life will take. Yes, had I made a decision not to marry Gordo, things might have been different. But it would not have changed the direction taken by the country to which I was born. The need for revolution obviously has a life of its own, and it is nothing but chance that you and mama and I were born at this time and in this place. There is no turning back for me now. Perhaps more than anyone I have become visible as part of the revolution that seems inevitable. I have been captured, imprisoned, and have already been the cause of blood shed. There is nothing for me now except to continue.''

José wearily shook his head. It was not, however, a denial of what his daughter was saying. He knew she was right. It was just a sign of the profound sadness and weariness he felt.

María forced a smile, wrapped her arms around her father and kissed him on the cheek. She stepped back and said, ''I have never felt more alive and more useful, father. I believe in what Father Hidalgo and Juan are doing, and I can only pray that through my efforts, and those of everyone who would share in those efforts, that New Spain might become a nation of equality and of love, rather than of oppression. I wish to do my part.''

Her father nodded and he, too, managed a smile.

''Because it is no longer possible to predict what tomorrow will bring for any of us,'' María said, ''I wish to tell you something now and pray that you will understand.''

''Qué?''

''I am in love with Juan, father.''

''It is a love that cannot find fulfillment, María. Juan is married to God.''

María closed her eyes. She became aware for the first time of the heat from the sun as it slowly, relentlessly rose higher in the sky. ''It matters not to me what happens with my love for him. It only matters that the love is there.'' She knew she was embarrassing her father, and rather than continue to make him uncomfortable, she again kissed him on the cheek and ran toward the barn where Father Hidalgo, Juan, John Barrigan and the other leaders of the revolutionary force were in conference.

When María entered the barn, everyone stood and warmly greeted her. It was obvious to Hidalgo that Juan wanted to go and embrace her, and yet was reluctant to do that because of what Hidalgo's reaction might be. Hidalgo put his mind at ease by going to María himself and warmly hugging her. Juan did the same, although his embrace lasted much longer than had the elder priest's.

''Come, join us,'' Juan said, taking María's hand and

leading her to where they'd been seated on the floor of the barn. She sat next to Juan and looked around the circle.

"María, I asked that you be allowed to be part of this meeting because of the role you have already played in the events of the past few days," Juan said, reaching and placing his hand upon her's. "Father Hidalgo has made a decision with which we all agree."

Hidalgo nodded. "You see, María, man's best-laid plans often do go awry. Each time a decision is made, events force it to change. That is the situation we are in now. Father Soltura has asked that my decision be explained to you. At first, I saw no reason to do that. But my young priest friend has wisdom beyond his years. It is obvious that the women of New Spain, at least many of them, stand ready to join us in the fight for freedom. Even here, there are many women who, because of circumstances or because of their convictions, are an integral part of whatever we do from this point forward. It was Juan's feeling that you could function as a leader of the women, someone who could instill in them courage and fortitude that will be needed in the hard days ahead, and that you could function as a liaison between those of us who lead the revolution and the women who will carry out our plans."

María was filled with a sense of satisfaction and importance. She looked at each of the men, set her lips in a line of determination and said, "I am flattered that you would think this of me. Yes, of course, I will do whatever I can to aid in this just cause."

"Good," Hidalgo said. "Before I again go over the plan, do any of you gentlemen have any further questions about it?"

"I reckon I don't know enough about it to have questions," John Barrigan said. "All I know is that I believe in what you're doin' and want to help." He laughed. "Hell, padre, I have about as much choice as the women here. I just happen to be here at the right place and right time to take part in something that's goin' to turn a whole nation upside-down. Nope, no questions."

Hidalgo looked at Juan.

"No, father. I have no questions of importance. I have done my questioning in the past. Now, my heart, mind and body are prepared to give unquestioning support to what must be done."

Hidalgo moved his head in a circle and tried to alleviate the pain in his neck and upper back. It had radiated to his shoulders and down one arm. He tried to dismiss the pain from his thoughts and began to explain the plans to María.

"The revolution will begin tomorrow morning," he said.

The power of Hidalgo's simple statement caused María to stiffen. She glanced at Juan, then across the circle at Hidalgo. "Tomorrow?" she asked, her eyes wide. "Can a revolution be mounted on such short notice?"

"Yes," Hidalgo said.

María allowed her body to relax as she answered. "I accept what you say, father. Obviously you have spent many years working toward this moment and for me to question your wisdom would be inappropriate."

Hidalgo beamed broadly. The lines of fatigue, worry and pain disappeared in the glow of his smile. "Your reaction is exactly the one that I received this morning from Mr. Barrigan and from Father Soltura. Again, my answer is yes. We have no choice. By now, every available soldier in the Spanish army is combing this part of New Spain in search of us. We can no longer wait."

María asked, "But if the Spanish soldiers are now mobilized in the valley, how can we possibly start the revolution?"

"That's what I asked, too," John Barrigan said.

"The answer, María, is that the revolution will not begin here in the valley," Juan said, squeezing her hand. "It will occur tomorrow morning in Dolores."

María said nothing. She was aware of Juan's gentle stroking of her fingers, and a warm sensuality filled her.

Hidalgo rubbed his face and tugged on an ear lobe. "We will leave within the hour for Dolores. I have spent much time in that town, María, and have gathered together a force that can be mobilized within hours. I carry to them the spirit of Our Lady of Guadalupe, around which they can rally. There are thousands of them, tens of thousands. They are loyal and fearless, and they will comprise a revolutionary force without parallel in the history of the world."

María nodded. "Then the only thing I ask is what can I do immediately to help?" she asked.

Juan stood and helped María to her feet. Barrigan and Hidalgo also got up, Hidalgo with some difficulty.

"Have the women ready to move," Hidalgo said. "Tell them that the revolution is beginning and that they are needed."

María frowned. "What of those who do not wish to risk their lives alongside the men?"

"There will be those who will make that decision," Hidalgo said. "No one can force them to fight. But they must travel with us to Dolores until the actual moment of revolution. Do not tell them any more than you have to, in case they should fall into the hands of the enemy. Tomorrow morning, once the war has been declared, they will be free to go their own way."

"I am glad of that," said María.

John Barrigan went to the door of the barn and looked outside. He turned and said, "I guess I'd better get out there and make sure everybody's ready to go in an hour. You've got some good men out there, padre, but sometimes they move a little slow." He broke into a smile. "That's one thing I've noticed since I've been in this country. Everything moves a little slower than back home. Maybe that's good." He went through the door and ran toward the main body of men.

Hidalgo went to the door and waited for Juan and María to join him. He realized that they wished some time alone. He stepped outside and closed the door behind him.

Juan took María in his arms. She buried her face in his neck. Juan placed his hand on the back of her head and slowly, gently stroked her auburn hair.

"I love you," María said.

Her words were muffled and Juan did not fully understand what she had said. *"Qué?"* he asked.

María pulled her head back and said clearly, "I love you."

"And I love you, María. I have loved you for many years."

"It is my love for you that gives me strength."

Juan closed his eyes. "I am afraid that to love me should give no one strength. I am a priest, and I am about to take part in a revolution that will undoubtedly cost me my life and the lives of those who stand with me."

María reached up and kissed him on the lips. "I can think of nothing more wonderful than to die with you, Juan. Without you, I do not have a life."

Juan was stern when he said, "Don't talk that way, María. You have much to live for."

María nodded. "Yes, I do. But there is nothing I want more than to be reflected in your love. Do not worry about me, Juan. I am older than my years. I know the risks."

Juan stepped back. He looked at the floor as he spoke. "It is not the risk of death that concerns me, María. The greater risk in loving me is that even if we are successful and victorious, your love for me might not be fulfilled. I am a man of God, and although I disagree with many aspects of the church I serve, I could not leave it."

María's eyes filled with tears and she fought to hold them back. She understood, yet could not accept what Juan had said. Could the love for an unseen God be greater than that for a woman? Often, while with Gordo, María had had to grapple with the emotions brought about by Gordo's infatuation with other women. It was not easy for María to accept Gordo's infidelity, and yet it suddenly seemed insignificant when compared to the difficulty of competing with something as all-encompassing as a man's love for God. There was nothing to fight, nothing to take aim at, no way to win.

María knew she had to leave or would break down in front of Juan. She said to him, "There are many things we must do before the question of our love can be decided. There is a revolution to be won. When that has been accomplished, things might be in better perspective."

Juan wished he hadn't said what he had, although he knew it was the only fair thing to do. Deep down inside he was convinced that should the revolution be successful, he would probably discard the black robes of his faith and pursue the love of this woman. But for now, his faith in God had to remain uppermost in his mind. It was that strength that had carried him this far, and without it he feared himself as doomed as the entire revolution might be. He stepped close to María and took her face between his hands. He kissed her brow, each of her eyes and then her mouth, lightly at first, then with strength and passion.

"I love you, María.

"And that is good enough for me, Juan."

They left the barn and joined the preparation for the move to Dolores.

CHAPTER TWENTY-NINE

The events of the previous night had sent the Valladolid garrison commander into a rage. Nothing had gone as it was supposed to. María had escaped, the Barrigans had obviously aided her, and the attempts to break the back of the revolution by arresting its leaders, particularly Juan de Soltura and Father Miguel Hidalgo, had failed.

The commandant hadn't slept all night. He stormed from his office and across the compound to where his officers had gathered. Hundreds of troops milled about the compound. Some slept, others played cards. The commandant stopped two or three times to scream at some of the enlisted men for their lack of proper uniform and their failure to acknowledge him as a commissioned officer. There had never been much discipline in the army units of New Spain. Military decorum was left to the discretion of each individual area commander. Enlisted men who had been conscripted were never sure of what the appropriate behavior was when confronted by an officer. There were no set guidelines, no long-standing traditions to follow. Everything depended upon the whim of the commissioned officers, and on this morning in September, the Valladolid commandant was not a man to be trifled with.

Gordo and his men had separated themselves from the main body of troops in the compound and were gathered in a far corner. Gordo had been dozing, his chin on his chest, his sombrero pulled down to shade his eyes from the rising morning sun. He heard the commandant yelling at officers in the other corner, and he raised his head and looked in that direction. He saw the commandant flail his arms and stamp his foot on the ground, then strike a lieutenant across the face. The commandant wheeled about and stomped in Gordo's direction.

"Get up," the commandant screamed at Gordo.

Gordo muttered something under his breath and lowered his head.

The commandant kicked Gordo's boot. *"El hijo de la puta madre,"* the commandant shouted.

Being called a son-of-a-bitch brought Gordo to his feet. He glared at the commandant and told him that if he ever called him that again, he would kill him.

The commandant was taken back at Gordo's response. There was something in Gordo's eyes that indicated that he would do exactly what he had promised. But the commandant couldn't back down completely. Many of his men were looking at him, waiting to see what he would do about the challenge Gordo had just presented him.

The commandant breathed heavily. His nostrils flared, his eyes narrowed to slits. Finally, after he and Gordo had stared at each other for what seemed an eternity, he said with deliberately moderated tones, "I wish to speak with you in my office, Señor Soltura."

"Por qué?" Gordo asked.

"Just come with me." The commandant turned and walked with deliberate strides toward the building in which his office was housed. Gordo looked at his men, shrugged and slowly followed in the same direction.

Gordo sat with other officers in the commandant's office and listened to him go into a tirade about the ineffectuality they'd displayed the night before. He talked of his reputation being tarnished because of their inept performance. He called them a national disgrace, and said that if a revolution took place and was successful, the responsibility for the fall of New Spain would rest directly upon their shoulders.

No one said anything as the commandant continued his harangue. The truth was that none of the officers cared very much about the threat of a revolution, and their sentiments in this matter mirrored those of the men who served under them. A potential revolution was of monumental importance to the political leaders of the nation, but its urgency had not filtered down to the rank and file of New Spain's army. The officers and the men they led would have been just as happy to forget about María, the Barrigans and the priests and to get back to their normal routine, going through the motions of a military life and using their military status to enhance their appeal in the cantinas and brothels of Vallodolid.

Had the commandant been candid, he, too, would have admitted a certain lack of concern about the events of the night before. But he couldn't be that cavalier. Two couriers had arrived early that morning carrying messages from army headquarters in Mexico City, and in León. The orders were direct and to the point. They were convinced at headquarters that the revolution was imminent and that it would, in all likelihood, begin in Michoacán Province, in which Valladolid was located. The Valladolid commander was directed to muster every available soldier, and to form as large a militia as possible within twenty-four hours.

The message from León referred specifically to the role the Catholic clergy would play in the revolution. The Valladolid commandant was ordered to place under arrest every member of the clergy within his jurisdiction. There were to be no exceptions. Once under arrest, subsequent interrogation would determine those who had been arrested without cause and those whose arrest was justified in the name of national security.

"What about Dolores?" a young lieutenant asked. He had to fight to keep from yawning.

The commandant cursed the young lieutenant for detouring from the thrust of the meeting. He added, "Dolores is not in my jurisdiction. I do not have time to be concerned about things and places that are not under my control."

Gordo's ears perked up at the mention of Dolores. He knew that his brother had spent considerable time there, and had, in fact, stopped there before returning home from his religious studies. Gordo could not conceive that María, the Barrigans and the priests would remain in Valladolid, considering all that had occurred.

"Maybe the lieutenant is right," Gordo said.

Gordo's suggestion sent the commandant into an even more irrational state. He repeatedly slammed his fists on his desk and reminded the assembled officers that he was in charge because of his proven intellect and wisdom.

It was obvious that there was no sense in offering any suggestions. When the commandant had calmed down to a point where he could issue orders simply and without rancor, he instructed his men to prepare their troops for immediate dispersal to selected areas of the valley. The only separate and special instruction he gave was to Gordo. He told him, "You and your men will remain here for duty should your special knowledge of the area and of the escaped prisoner be required."

Gordo mumbled and filed from the room with the others. He went to where his men were seated, and when one of them asked what they were to do next, he simply said, "Shut up and go to sleep."

Which was exactly what Gordo did.

By noon, most of the troops in the compound had moved out to establish search parties in the areas of the valley selected by the commandant.

At two that afternoon, the commandant came to where Gordo and his men were resting and told Gordo that he was on his way to attend a meeting of the Valladolid cabildo. "You will remain here until I return."

Gordo didn't bother getting up. He muttered under his breath and smiled inwardly at the frustration he knew he was causing the commandant. The commandant wanted to say something else but thought better of it. He mounted his horse and rode from the garrison in the company of four other uniformed officers.

Gordo continued to sit with his back against the wall. His back and neck ached, and he thought of the source of that pain, John Barrigan. The image of Barrigan had never been far from Gordo since the night of the attack. Often he was awakened in the middle of the night by bitter dreams of the Yankee from Massachusetts. And the idea of María as part of the group that planned to overthrow the Spanish government caused his stomach to twist into knots and his mouth to go dry. He didn't know who he hated more, Barrigan or María. Perhaps his brother, Juan. All Gordo knew was that there were many people with whom he had a score to settle, and the urgency of that feeling brought him to his feet. He looked around at his men and barked an order: "On your feet, you lazy dogs. We're moving out."

Some of the men asked where they were going, but Gordo ignored their questions. He sent some of them to the storehouse, from which they returned with a supply of provisions: ammunition and six brass-hilted sabers, three of them short and with slightly curved blades, the others longer and with straight blades.

"That was all you could find?" Gordo asked.

"*Sí.*"

"You took every weapon that was available?"

"*Sí.*"

Gordo spit into the dirt and shook his head. He'd wanted to arm his small contingent with as many weapons and as much ammunition as possible. He sensed that he was not far from an ultimate confrontation with his enemies, and he wanted to be ready.

One of his men again asked where they were going. Gordo said from his horse. "To Dolores."

"*Por qué?*"

"Because I think my beautiful wife and my loving brother are waiting for me there," Gordo said. He slapped his horse on its flank and led his men through the gate of the compound and to the north.

CHAPTER THIRTY

Sunday, September 16, 1810

Father Hidalgo and his revolutionary contingent arrived in Dolores at midnight on Saturday. They'd stopped along the way in Amealco, Celaya, San Miguel and San Luis de la Paz where they'd gathered small forces of sympathizers. By the time they'd reached Dolores, their party numbered in excess of five hundred.

They stopped in the hills directly to the east of Dolores. John Barrigan was left in charge of the group while Hidalgo and Juan rode into town and went directly to the church. During Hidalgo's absence the parish had been in the hands of a young priest who'd been sent to him by the same clerical sympathizer who'd originally recruited Juan. The young priest had been instructed to conduct parish business as usual, but was also told to supervise the completion of a broad, high wooden platform that Hidalgo had ordered built in front of the church. When questioned by local authorities about the purpose of the platform, Hidalgo had explained that it would play a part in the upcoming Dolores fair. The platform was actually a stage from which Hidalgo would rally his local supporters to revolt when the time came. He didn't know, of course, that Dolores would, in fact, be the scene of the first revolt. But he always felt that the small, sleepy town, whose name meant Our Lady of the Sorrows, would play an important early role in the cause.

Now, as he and Juan stood outside the church and looked at the completed platform, Hidalgo took pleasure at having ordered it. He knew that in the morning he would stand upon it and sound the call of freedom and justice for New Spain.

Hidalgo and Juan entered the church and went to the small

room in which the young priest slept. They woke him, and the three of them went into the inner recesses of the church and sat together to the side of the altar.

"Why have you returned, father?" the young priest asked Hidalgo. I thought you were to be gone another week."

Hidalgo shook his head. "There has been a dramatic change in our plans. The revolution will begin in the morning."

The young priest was shocked. He asked, "So soon?"

"Yes," Juan said, leaning back against the side of the altar. "We have been through a great deal and are left with little choice except to begin immediately."

The young priest asked, "Then I am ready, Father Hidalgo. Simply tell me what to do. I am at your bidding."

Hidalgo instructed the young priest to contact those who had been designated leaders of the revolt and to alert them to be at early Mass. "No later than seven," Hidalgo said. "At seven o'clock I wish the plaza to be filled with those who will carry our banner."

The young priest stood. "I will leave immediately. Is there anything else?"

Hidalgo shook his head and sighed. "We have spent too many years preparing for this. It is now a matter of seeing all our plans put into action. The time for thinking and talking is over. It is now time for the oppressed to raise their voices as one and to shed the yoke of Spanish oppression. If God is with us, and I cannot help but feel that He is, we will be victorious."

The young priest started to leave but Hidalgo called him back. "Pray with us, father. An entire nation must now pray so that its cause will be clearly heard by its God."

The three priests knelt at the side of the altar and prayed. They blessed themselves and uttered Amens.

Hidalgo placed his hand upon the young priest's shoulder. "Go now, my son, and spread the word. Be sure that the leaders you contact realize they must swiftly pass the instructions down to each unit that has been established. Remember, no later than seven. The bells will toll at that time and the revolution will begin."

When the young priest had left the church, Juan asked, "Perhaps I should have gone with him, father. He seems so young to carry such an important message."

"No, Father Soltura, I prefer that you stay with me." Hidalgo smiled. "It is interesting that you view him as being so young. You, too, were that young when you first became involved in this grand cause."

Juan couldn't help but smile. "Yes, how quickly passion for a cause ages one."

Hidalgo and Juan stood and walked to the rear of the church and into the small bedroom. Hidalgo lighted a candle and indicated that Juan should sit on the cot.

"I wish you to hear my confession, father," Hidalgo said. Juan was surprised at the request. He only said, "Yes, father. And I ask that you hear mine."

"Of course," Hidalgo said, falling to his knees in front of Juan.

When Hidalgo had finished his confession, he listened to Juan's. In the darkened room illuminated only by the single candle, Juan told Hidalgo in detail what had occurred between him and María.

"When this is over, my son, what will you do?" Hidalgo asked. "Will you leave the church?"

"If only I possessed the wisdom to know the answer to that in advance," Juan said. "I only know that my love is divided between my God and this woman."

Hidalgo lay back on the cot and closed his eyes. He said, "That dilemma is one that I have avoided throughout my entire adult life, Father Soltura. It is one of the benefits of the priesthood. Had I been torn as you are, I could never have focused my attention so completely upon the thing that is most dear to me, the liberation of New Spain. While I do not envy you the decision you must make at some point in the future, I think I understand. I can only ask that until the time arrives, that you dedicate all your thought and energy to the thing we have worked so hard to bring about."

"The revolution," Juan muttered.

"*Sí*, the revolution. Let nothing stand in the way of that."

"I promise you that, father," Juan said. "I promise you my total allegiance and dedication."

"That is all I can ask."

Hidalgo sat up. "I must ask you now to return to our friends in the hills and inform them of what will occur in the morning. They must begin to arrive at the Mass from many different directions. To see a large group of people enter the plaza at one time would arouse too much suspicion. The Barrigans and María must not show themselves until after the actual rebellion has begun. Do you understand?"

"Yes, I do."

"Then go now, my son, and ready our friends for battle. I will see you in the morning."

"Until then," Juan said, quickly leaving the room and passing through the doors of the church. He stood in front of it and looked up at the wooden platform that was silhouetted against a full moon. He shuddered. The moment of truth had arrived, and it filled him with intense excitement and dread.

At seven in the morning on Sunday, September 16, 1810, the bells of the Dolores parish rang loud and clear. The plaza was filled with men and women of mestizo, criollo and sambo birth. Juan, who stood on the raised platform next to Hidalgo, estimated the size of the crowd at over 2,000. He recognized many faces from the group that had remained in the hills until early that morning. He turned and looked down at the door of the church. Inside were María and John and Susan Barrigan. Juan returned his attention to the crowd and saw José Jardinero standing with his arm about his wife.

The crowd was restless. There was much talk. A contingent of Spanish soldiers had ringed the plaza. They were armed. Long bayonets glistened on the ends of their muskets as they caught the first rays of the early morning sun.

There was no mistaking the look of apprehension on the face of each of the infantrymen. They were greatly outnumbered. Most of the citizens in the plaza carried a weapon.

The young priest who'd been assigned to the parish climbed the platform and whispered something to Hidalgo. Hidalgo turned to him and said, "You have done your job well, my son. I thank you."

Juan looked to the rear of the crowd and saw that it continued to grow as the humble and oppressed arrived from their homes in the countryside. The roads leading into the plaza were jammed. The sea of faces extended beyond the town and out into the fields behind the buildings.

Hidalgo said quietly, "It is time." He held up his hands and asked for order. It took a few minutes for everyone to realize that they were to be silent. Finally, the last comments from the crowd were uttered and the plaza of Dolores became remarkably silent.

"My children, this day comes to us as a new dispensation," Hidalgo shouted. "Are you ready to receive it? Will you be free? Will you make the effort to recover from the hated Spaniards the lands stolen from our forefathers three centuries ago?"

There was no response from the crowd. Men, women and children hung on every word of this priest who'd risen from the clergy to lead them in battle. Juan searched for a sign of discontent, an indication on anyone's face of disbelief. He could find no example of it. He looked at the soldiers. They were tense. They appeared ready to move and yet it was obvious there was nowhere for them to go. In order to reach the platform they would have to push through thousands of people, a task that seemed as hopeless to them as it did to Juan.

"The Spaniards are bad enough themselves, but now they have sold our country to the French. Will you become Napoleon's slaves? Or will you, as patriots, defend your religion and your homes?"

A chorus of response welled up from the crowd. "We will defend them!"

"Long live our Lady of Guadalupe!" someone screamed.

"Death to the government! Death to the gachupines!"

The crowd began to chant, "Long live Our Lady of Guadalupe. Long live Our Lady of Guadalupe."

The cries from the crowd sent shivers up Juan's spine. It was as though a giant hand had come down from the heavens and lifted him into the air, so buoyant was his spirit, so passionate was his feeling.

But as the crowd continued to chant, "Death to the gachupines, death to the gachupines," Juan's passion was tempered by fear. As he stood there on that glorious fall morning, he hoped for a moment that it was only a rallying cry, and did not indicate the true sentiments of those who uttered the words. But he did not hold out much hope for that. It would be a revolution in every sense, and blood would flow.

Hidalgo was growing hoarse. He strained as he called upon the crowd to remember its debt to Cuauhtémoc, and to dismiss forever the influence of Cortés.

The officer in charge of the Dolores Spanish troops was helpless to act. The inflammatory words spoken by Father Hidalgo were clearly the words of a traitor. Had the crowd not been so large, he might have attempted to move in upon those who stood on the platform. But it would have been hopeless, and the officer in charge knew it. He stood by with a look of utter frustration upon his face. His men reflected the same feeling of helplessness. They could only watch as Hidalgo finished his speech and called upon everyone in the plaza to follow him as they began their march across New Spain in the pursuit of liberty and freedom for all.

Another group of military men watched the scene from a different vantage point. It was the small group of soldiers led by Gordo Soltura. Had they taken a direct route from Valladolid to Dolores, they would have arrived there the previous evening, perhaps in time to have disrupted the mass rally. It had been Gordo's intention to go directly to the Dolores church in search of his brother, María and Hidalgo. But Gordo hadn't been able to resist stopping off in Celaya where a favorite girl friend lived. He and his men dallied there all afternoon and late into the night, and it was only after they'd slept off their drunk that they proceeded to Dolores. They'd arrived only minutes before the bells had tolled, and suffered the same impotence as the Dolores military.

Gordo seethed with rage as he stood at the rear of the crowd and watched his brother shoulder-to-shoulder with Hidalgo. He was almost driven to attempt an attack upon the platform despite the multitude of sympathizers that stood in his way. But even Gordo's impetuousness was tempered that morning by the spectacle of thousands of aroused and oppressed citizens of New Spain. He could only stand and mutter to himself as Hidalgo finished his call for revolution by calling upon the crowd to take into their hearts the symbol of Our Lady of Guadalupe, and to condemn to obscurity forever the "White" Virgin of Los Remedios that had been embraced by the gachupine ruling class for centuries. Hidalgo instructed the crowd to dedicate itself from that point forward to freeing New Spain. He turned, descended from the platform and moved to the front door of the church.

"What now, Father?" Juan asked.

"Dolores is ours," Hidalgo replied. "We shall make sure it is secure before marching forward to expand our victory. Then we shall march to Guanajuato where our sympathizers eagerly await us."

Juan looked over his shoulder at the crowd. He asked, "What of them, father? They appear anxious to take action. I fear they will not wait peacefully for your next order."

Hidalgo sounded annoyed as he said, "Their leaders have been instructed what to do until we leave here. We must confer inside the church. Come." He turned from Juan and opened the door.

Juan was right. The crowd was becoming unruly. But he was not the only one who sensed it. His brother, Gordo, realized that it would not be long before the crowd turned on anyone who represented Spanish authority. He turned his horse and motioned for his men to follow him out of the town. He'd no sooner gotten clear of the throngs of revolutionaries when a faction of them turned on the remaining members of the Spanish military force. The sounds of muskets filled the air as the soldiers attempted to fight off their attackers. But they were so greatly outnumbered that their shots were but feeble gestures of self-defense. The Indians and mestizos pounced upon the soldiers and butchered them within minutes.

The sound of the slaughter outside could faintly be heard inside the church. Juan said, "Father Hidalgo, what I have feared is evidently happening outside. You must return to the platform and call for order."

"It is too late for that," Hidalgo said. "These people have been brutalized all of their lives, and to ask them to restrain themselves would be not only a folly, it would be unfair. I do not wish to foster violence, but the movement we have launched is a tidal wave. We are helpless to stop it, and our only course of action will be to sustain that rage within them so that they will not flinch when faced with the greater opposition that will certainly appear in the future. I do not wish to discuss this again with you or with anyone else, Father Soltura."

John Barrigan looked back and forth at the two priests. He was torn. On the one hand, he sympathized with Juan. He, too, had felt the same reservations about violence when he and Susan had traveled with the renegade Indian tribe and had slaughtered Spanish settlements south of Santa Fe. Yet, he knew that ultimately Hidalgo was right. It was too late now to question the morality of the revolution. To do so would necessitate pulling back in purpose and action, which would mean certain defeat. He gripped Susan's arm tightly and asked Hidalgo what he should do.

"Go outside, my son, and meet with the Indian leaders." Hidalgo turned to Juan when he said, "Tell them to use only the force necessary to secure the town."

"I'll go with you," Juan told John. He looked at María, whose smile told him that she understood what he was feeling, but also that he must find the strength to overcome his feelings.

"Let's go, padre," Barrigan said.

Father Hidalgo watched the two young men leave the church. He excused himself from María and Susan and went to his living quarters where two men waited for him. Both were dressed in peasant clothing, but their manner of dress did not accurately reflect who they were. One of the men was the third-ranking administrative bishop of the Catholic Church of New Spain, Father Gualdido de Sorentino. The other was an aide. After greeting each other, Father Sorentino quickly briefed Hidalgo on the names of Catholic clergy who, up to that point, had not revealed their involvement with the revolution. They included clergy in an array of towns and villages stretching from Dolores into vitually every province of New Spain.

After the names had been noted by Hidalgo, he asked whether there was any intelligence from within the church hierarchy that might be of help to him now that the revolution had actually begun.

Sorentino shook his head. "There is great pressure upon all of us to bring our weight to bear on those priests who rebel, but that is nothing new. What I must know, however, is your plan of action from this point forward, Father Hidalgo. There mustn't be any surprises."

Hidalgo, who'd given considerable thought to the direction the revolution would take, quickly told Father Sorentino and the aide he'd brought with him of his tentative plans. It was his intention to drive south, through Guanajuato, Celaya, Querétaro, Amealco, Jilotepec, Zumpango and finally into Mexico City.

Father Sorentino's eyebrows went up. "Will you be ready to attack the capital so soon?"

"Yes, I'm certain it is the right thing to do. To wait too long would be to allow the Spaniards to muster their forces in defense of the capital. I wish to strike quickly and surely. I am confident that by doing so it will fall, and from that point forward the rest of New Spain will easily fall into our hands."

Sorentino stood and shook Hidalgo's hand. "I would not presume to argue tactics with you, Miguel. You have worked long and hard to mount this revolution and I am certain its outcome could not be in more capable hands. I must leave now. I congratulate you on an auspicious beginning to a just and noble cause."

"Your words mean much to me, Father Sorentino. You, too, have labored long and hard behind the scenes to provide the revolution with many fine young men. God must look upon you with great pride and joy."

Sorentino shrugged and put on the dusty, beaten sombrero he wore. "I hope so, Miguel. After all, it is for our God that we act. Good day."

Sorentino and his aide left the church, mounted horses and rode to the west, toward León.

CHAPTER THIRTY-ONE

Gordo Soltura and his men rode into the tiny mining settlement of Xlipote, just east of León. Since leaving Dolores, Gordo had grappled with the question of what to do next. The size of the crowd and the savagery with which it had slaughtered the Spanish soldiers had impressed him. He realized that he could do nothing alone. Yet he had no idea which direction would lead him to a sizeable Spanish contingent with which he and his small band of men could hook up. The largest Spanish military contingent that he knew of was in Valladolid. But it didn't make sense to Gordo to return there and to become part of that army again.

In a word, Gordo was confused. The spectacle of Dolores had not been lost on him, and yet he found it impossible to believe that a full-scale revolution had actually begun. He'd held the lower classes of New Spain in such contempt for so long that he couldn't believe that they could actually rally together in an attempt to overthrow Spanish rule. The thought of such pretension filled him with anger.

Gordo and his men went to the only cantina in Xlipote. It was housed in a run-down, board-and-batten shack that stood by itself on the side of a rutted, dusty road that led through the town. Across the street from it stood three similar structures. One housed the mining company's office. A general store and mining supply operation was in the shack to the left. The building to the other side of the mining company was broken up into a series of cubicles in which some of the miners lived, along with two worn and weary prostitutes.

There was little activity inside the cantina. The few miners who had gotten up that Sunday morning and had returned to where they'd partied the night before sat quietly in a stupor. Some slept, their arms folded upon tabletops and their heads resting upon their arms.

The arrival of Gordo and his men caused those in the cantina to look up and take notice, but they soon ignored the visitors. The bartender was a wizened mestizo who dutifully dispensed whiskey to his new customers.

"What now?" Gordo was asked by the only noncommissioned officer under his command.

"You saw," Gordo snapped, downing the contents of his glass and shoving it across the rough bar top toward the bartender. "The animals you saw this morning and the pig priests they rally around think they shall conquer New Spain." Gordo spat on the floor, downed the drink that had just been given him and indicated that he wanted another. He was boiling inside. The more he thought about the gall of the Indians and mestizos, the more inclined he was to take matters into his own hands and to wage a private war against them. As he sat at the bar and gulped whiskey, a sense of bravado developed. He could see himself taking a heroic stand against the revolutionaries and achieving national applause for that stand. Somehow, despite the fact that the crowds in the square of Dolores had numbered in the thousands, they did not seem to be a physical threat to Gordo now. He'd spent his entire adult life ruling over the lower classes who worked on his father's hacienda and with whom he came in contact in the towns and villages of New Spain. They were cowards, pathetic, sniveling cowards who needed only to be kept in their place whenever thoughts of rebellion might creep into their minds.

Gordo suddenly began to laugh.

"What's so funny?" His NCO asked.

"I was just thinking of the minds of the Indians and mestizos. Imagine that? They have no minds, do they?"

His NCO joined his commander in laughter.

Gordo called for more whiskey. He slapped his NCO on the shoulder and said, in a loud voice, "Do you know what, you fool?" he asked.

His NCO grinned. *"Qué?"*

"This band of hoodlums is just beginning to make trouble. The way to stop them is to act immediately, before they have a chance to add more demented animals to their ranks. I have a mind to ride back to Dolores and teach them a lesson."

The NCO stopped grinning and looked across the room to where some of the other soldiers were seated at tables. Gordo's comment didn't make any sense to him. As much as he liked to consider himself a brave soldier, the throng of angry people in the square of Dolores that morning was not one to be confronted by a ragamuffin group of twenty men. It would be suicide to confront such a mob.

Gordo nudged the NCO in ribs and stood up. He was unsteady on his feet and had to lean back against the bar to maintain his balance. "Hey, amigos, listen to me," he yelled.

The other soldiers in the saloon looked at him, then at each other, and resumed drinking.

Gordo stamped his boot upon the floor. "Hey, you bastards, listen. We're going to ride out of here and go back and teach those bastards a lesson."

No one responded. Eventually, a young soldier in the corner who'd felt the effects of the whiskey much too quickly, started to giggle. Gordo glared at him and told him to shut up.

The NCO leaned close to Gordo and suggested they take a siesta before thinking any further about going back to Dolores.

"Shut up!" Gordo said.

"*Sí, sí,* commandant," the NCO said, slowly moving along the bar away from Gordo.

Two Indian mine workers who'd been asleep in the corner of the room for the past hour, had woken up and decided to leave. They slowly stood and made their way toward the door.

Gordo spotted them and ordered them to stop.

The Indians obeyed Gordo's order and stood next to the front door. "*Sí?*" one of them asked.

"Come here, you dogs," Gordo commanded, motioning to them with his index finger.

"*Por qué?*" the other Indian asked.

Gordo exploded with anger. He kicked the bar stool across the room and took a few unsteady steps toward the Indians. "You don't ask me questions," he roared. "I am Gordo de Soltura, an officer of the Spanish army and one of the most feared and respected men of New Spain."

The Indians eagerly agreed with him.

"Come here, I said," Gordo repeated.

The Indians slowly approached him. When they were within arms length, Gordo suddenly struck out with his fist and caught one Indian flush in the face. The bones in his nose cracked audibly, and blood spurted from it. Before the other Indian could react, Gordo caught him on the side of the head with a backhand that sent him sprawling into the middle of the room.

"Get up!" Gordo said to the Indian on the floor.

"Sí, sí," the Indian said as he scrambled to his feet. *"Por favor, señor,"* he said, his right hand over his heart to indicate his sincerity. "We wish no trouble, señor. Please, we are poor Indians who work in the mines. We will leave. We wish no trouble."

Gordo smiled. Striking the two Indians had given him a sense of power, of purpose. He stood at his full height and instructed them to remain in the room until he had decided what to do with them. He turned to his NCO and asked, "These animals will join the revolution, won't they?" His NCO shrugged. "Do you doubt that?" Gordo asked.

"No, no, commandant."

Gordo resumed his smile. "Then what shall we do with them? They will be traitors to the State. Traitors should be executed."

The NCO was becoming increasingly anxious about Gordo's behavior. He looked around the room in search of some wisdom from the other men but received none. Those who were not too drunk had listened and watched the scene with interest, but had no idea what it might lead to. The NCO again turned to Gordo and said, "Whatever you say is right, commandant." He forced a grin that exposed a mouth in which more than half of his teeth were missing.

Gordo was pleased with the answer. He looked at the Indians and was momentarily concerned about what he saw. They seemed enveloped in a haze. There were two heads on each body. Then, he saw two, three and even four identical images in front of him. His head began to spin and he reached back for support from the bar. His glass had been refilled. He picked it up and drank it, then returned his attention to the Indians. "Outside," he ordered, his speech slurred.

The Indians nodded and went for the door. One of them opened it when Gordo yelled, "Halt!" He drew a deep breath in an attempt to ward off the disorientation he was feeling and took unsteady steps toward the door. When he reached it he indicated with his head that the Indians should precede him. They did as they were instructed and Gordo followed them through the door, after first turning and motioning for his men to follow.

It was almost noon. The sun was brilliantly hot and caused a wave of dizziness to come over Gordo. He looked up at the sun and was temporarily blinded by it. He thought he would fall. He looked down at the ground and willed himself to be steady. The pain in his neck and back returned and he winced.

The Indians stood together in the middle of the dirt road. The one with the smashed nose held his hand to his face in an attempt to stem the bleeding. Drops of blood fell to the ground in front of him and on to his bare brown feet.

Gordo turned to his men, who'd straggled out of the cantina and who stood in front of it. He commanded, "Prepare a firing squad for these traitors."

His men looked at each other. No one took him seriously until he cocked his repeating flint-lock pistol by turning a lever on its left side that revolved the breech block, aiming with an unsteady hand at a point just above the heads of his men and pulling the trigger. Most of the men flung themselves to the ground. Their action caused Gordo to laugh. "Get up and follow my orders, or I will have you shot for treason."

The men scurried to their feet. Some of them ran back into the saloon to get their weapons.

Gordo's shot had alerted the sleepy village that there was something worth seeing in the streets. People began to appear from the shacks along the road. Many of the miners lived in tents behind the shacks. Some of them, too, dragged themselves out of their sleeping bags and stumbled toward the scene of the action.

The two Indians shook with fear as Gordo turned to them, his face fixed in a menacing expression.

"Por favor, señor. We have done nothing. We are just servants of you and of the owners of the mine. Let us go, please."

Gordo issued an order to take the Indians to a spot across the road and against the side of the mining office building. His men followed his instructions, and when the Indians were in place, Gordo took uncertain steps toward where they now stood.

"You are going to kill them?" the NCO asked.

"Sí, that is what they deserve."

The NCO was not about to argue with Gordo. There was

no sense in arguing with a crazy man. It would be best to simply get it over with and then return to the cantina where they could continue drinking and sleeping.

Gordo chose four of his men as executioners. He pointed to where he wanted them to stand. They missed his intended mark by a few feet and he angrily stumbled across the ground and drew a line on it with the toe of his boot. The men stepped up to the line and looked at their target, the two Indians who were silhouetted against the white wooden side of the building.

Gordo returned to where he'd originally stood and surveyed the situation. By now, a number of people had gathered and formed a rough circle around the area.

Gordo wanted to make a speech. The vision and the words of Father Hidalgo addressing the throngs in the Dolores plaza were very much with him. He'd been impressed at how totally captivated the audience had been when the priest had spoken, and he wished to make the same impact upon the people gathered before him. He surveyed the scraggly crowd of sleepy miners. One of the two prostitutes had ventured out from her cubicle. She'd wrapped a blanket around her and stood next to the only civilian in the crowd who wore anything that resembled formal Sunday clothing. He was the manager of the mining operation, which gave him unofficial status of mayor of Xlipote. The whore whispered in his ear. He nodded and tentatively approached Gordo. When he was six feet from him, he took off his wide-brimmed white sombrero and held it over his heart. "Señor, I am Martinga de Almonte. I welcome you to our village. I am the mayor."

Gordo tried to focus on the mayor's face but he was still having trouble with his vision. He asked, "So what?"

The mayor displayed a wide, crooked grin. "I do not wish to interfere señor, with an official of our government and an officer of our army. But I wanted to ask why these Indians are to be killed. We have little help here in the mines, and cannot afford to lose ablebodied workers."

"The country is at war, señor," Gordo said in his most imperious tone. "These men are traitors to the king. The revolution has begun and I have been placed in charge of halting it. Go now, leave me alone."

The mayor nodded, replaced his hat upon his head and returned to where he had been standing with the whore.

It took Gordo a few moments to recover from the interruption. The Indians had dropped to their knees and were praying loudly to anyone who might hear them. They'd been converted to Catholicism, and their voices uttering Catholic prayers infuriated Gordo. He thought of his brother. He turned to the Indians and wished Juan was standing there with them, about to be executed upon Gordo's direct order.

"This execution will take place under the direct orders of Gordo de Soltura, commissioned officer of the king of Spain." Gordo spoke as loudly as possible, and tried to give each word a ring of power and wisdom. "This execution is the first official act against the revolutionaries of New Spain. As the commander of this execution, I . . ."

The sound of the horses ridden by Father Gualdido de Sorentino and his aide caught Gordo's attention. He turned and saw the two men as they rode slowly up the street. The two men noticed the crowd and brought their horses to the fringe of it. Gordo assumed they were exactly what they appeared to be, an older and younger man of lower-class origins traveling from one place to another. There would have been no reason for that perception of them to change except that Father Sorentino dismounted his horse and walked up to the mayor of the village. "What is going on here?" the priest asked.

The mayor cast a nervous glance at Gordo and indicated to the priest that he should ask that question of him. Father Sorentino did not hesitate. He walked up to Gordo and asked, "Are these men being executed?"

Ordinarily, given the circumstances of the moment, Gordo would have simply dismissed the intrusion and returned to the task at hand. But there was something in this stranger's eyes that caused Gordo to pause. He asked, "Who are you to question an officer of the king's army?"

Father Sorentino almost divulged his true identity. He held himself in check and said, "I am a concerned citizen, señor. There are laws under which the citizens of this land can be executed. Has there been a trial?"

"A trial?" Gordo laughed. "A revolution has begun, señor, and these are two members of it. They are being shot by my order. Now go away and leave us alone."

Father Sorentino engaged Gordo in a battle of locked eyes until Gordo looked away. Sorentino then walked to where the Indians were on their knees and placed his hands upon their heads. He said softly, "Fear not, my sons. I am a priest. I will do what I can to prevent this from happening."

Sorentino did not realize that Gordo had come up behind him.

"A priest?" Gordo asked.

Sorentino turned and nodded. "Yes, I am Father Gualdido de Sorentino. I hold a high ranking position within the Catholic Church of this nation."

"Then you are a traitor, too," Gordo said.

"Think what you may, but unless there has been a proper trial for these two men, they will not be shot."

. Gordo couldn't believe that he was being confronted in this manner. There was considerable strength and determination in the tone and words uttered by Sorentino, and Gordo found himself confused as to what action to take. His inclination was to shoot the priest, or to command his men to do it, but he couldn't bring himself to issue such an order.

Sorentino ignored Gordo and urged the Indians to regain their feet. When they had, he said to Gordo, "If a revolution has begun, it will be to save wretched souls such as these from the tyranny and cruelty of the king you represent." He led the Indians to where his aide stood with the horses.

The small crowd could not help but observe that Gordo was visibly shaken. He could barely control the tremors in his body, and he held his right wrist with his left hand in an attempt to steady it. He desperately tried to collect his thoughts. If the priest succeeded in interfering with Gordo's official act, Gordo would be subject to the scorn and ridicule of the men under him. He looked at the four-man firing squad, who were looking at him for some indication of what they should do next.

Gordo suddenly acted. He issued a command that Father Sorentino and the other priest be arrested immediately for interfering with the official duty of a commissioned officer of the army of New Spain. His men were slow to react to his order, but they eventually moved to where the priests stood next to their horses. The Indians had mounted the horses and the priests were preparing to take their position behind them.

"You ask for trouble, señor," Sorentino said to Gordo.

"Trouble does not concern me, father. I am holding you for questioning concerning the revolution that has begun in Dolores."

Sorentino looked up into the face of the Indian whose nose

had been broken. He nodded encouragingly to him and said, "It appears we shall be here for a while, my son. Take the horses and feed them and give them drink."

"*Gracias, padre,*" one of the Indians said.

Sorentino's young aide asked the older priest whether there wasn't something they could do.

Sorentino looked at Gordo and managed a smile. "I think this officer will understand the mistake he is making." He slapped his aide on the back to give him courage. To Gordo he said, "Very well, commandant, we will answer your questions. We know nothing of any revolution. You will soon realize this."

Sorentino's quick and easy submission to Gordo's arrest took Gordo off guard. He fumbled for words, then managed to say, "We shall see about that." He led them into the cantina where he ordered everyone to leave except the members of his military party.

"I would like a drink," Sorentino said.

By now, Gordo had sobered up. He felt more in control of the situation. "Give this priest a drink," he told the bartender. "Put the bottles on the bar. Then, leave." The bartender did as he was told.

Gordo and Father Sorentino sat across from each other at a round table.

"Ask me what you wish," Sorentino said.

CHAPTER THIRTY-TWO

The first hour of Gordo's interrogation of Father Sorentino was leisurely, and even included some good-natured bantering between the two men. Gordo was drunk with power. He felt very important sitting with a high-ranking member of the Catholic clergy of New Spain and being in the position of demanding answers to his questions.

Sorentino found the oafish Gordo comical, despite his obvious capacity for violence with the slightest provocation. The priest occasionally wondered whether Gordo's ineffectual, bumbling manner wasn't studied, its purpose to disarm him and cause him to let down his guard. But whenever this thought crossed his mind, Sorentino always came back to the conclusion that he was dealing with a buffoon who was doing a great deal of role playing.

It wasn't until the second hour that Gordo began to toughen up in his his questioning. Frankly, he was becoming bored with the way things were going. He couldn't think of many questions to ask, and each time he repeated them, Sorentino's answer was the same.

Gordo stood and paced the room. The younger priest who'd accompanied Sorentino had sat silently in a far corner where Gordo had directed him to sit. His eyes darted about the room as he watched and listened to the questioning of Sorentino, and his thoughts vacillated between attention to what was happening and to questioning what he would do should physical force be applied during his turn with Gordo. As it turned out, he did not have long to wait to put himself to the test.

"I ask you again, Father Sorentino, why you, as a ranking member of the clergy, are dressed like this."

Sorentino smiled. He'd made it a point of smiling before answering each question, and the pattern was beginning to annoy Gordo. "How many times must I tell you, señor, that when I travel I prefer to dress in the clothing of the working class? I find that it allows me to get closer to those I serve in the name of God."

Gordo swore and kicked a brass spittoon the length of the bar. He snarled, "And I say you are a liar, padre. You were in Dolores this morning, and yet you say you know nothing of what went on there."

Sorentino smiled. "Yes, that is correct. It appeared to me that a fair was about to begin, and that was what Father Hidalgo told me."

Gordo was now losing control of himself. His previous calm, which he felt would establish him in the priest's eyes as an officer of experience and wisdom, was now giving way to the internal rage that he so often felt when frustrated. His voice rose to such a pitch that it startled some of the soldiers who were in the room with him. "You are a liar. You say you serve God and yet you lie in front of Him. If I do not receive honest answers, I will kill you."

Sorentino did not like the direction the conversation was taking. He saw before him an animal who lacked the reason and judgment to make him think twice before physically abusing or killing a member of the church hierarchy. He considered making up a story in an attempt to appease Gordo, but instead he said softly, "Threats to kill me are empty ones, señor. I'm an old man. I have lived my life. I will not be intimidated by you." The moment he said it he wished he could withdraw his words. Gordo immediately turned his attention from Sorentino to the young priest in the corner. Sorentino knew that Gordo had accepted his logic, and was now about to extend it to the younger priest who certainly did have much to lose.

"Take him outside," Gordo said to two of the soldiers who leaned on the bar. He pointed to Father Sorentino.

Sorentino stood. "I warn you, Señor Soltura, that if you harm me or the young man who accompanies me, you will be brought to judgment by . . ."

Gordo laughed wickedly. "By God?" His laugh intensified until he was doubled over and holding his sides. He managed to motion to the soldiers to do what they'd been told. They went to Sorentino, took him by the arms and marched him out of the cantina.

Gordo now turned his attention to the young priest in the corner. "Please, Señor Soltura, I know nothing. Father Sorentino told the truth. And even if he did not, I assure you that I would not know things that he would. I am only a secretary to him. You must believe me."

The obvious fright exhibited by the young priest delighted Gordo. He'd begun to wilt under Sorentino's strength. Now, he had someone over whom he could exert power. He motioned for the young priest to come to the table. Gordo watched as the young man took hesitant steps away from the security of his corner and stood behind the chair in which Father Sorentino had sat.

"Sit down," Gordo said, pointing.

"Sí, señor," the priest said as he took the chair.

Gordo walked close to the priest and towered above him. "You heard the questions I asked Father Sorentino?"

"Sí."

"I am certain you have better answers for me, padre."

The priest looked up with large, round, pleading brown eyes. "Please, señor, believe me, I know nothing."

Gordo screwed his face up into a grimace and brought the back of his hand across the priest's cheek. The force of the blow almost knocked him from the chair. He started to get up but Gordo slammed him back down.

"What do you know of the revolution?" Gordo asked.

The priest began to deny any knowledge when Gordo hit him again, this time on the other side of his head. To Gordo's amazmnt, tears began to run from the priest's eyes. The sight of it filled Gordo with a sense of immense power. He looked around at the soldiers who remained in the room, grinned and again looked down at the priest. He made a fist and held it inches from the priest's face. "What did you learn in Dolores of what the bastard priests intend to do now with the revolution?"

The priest hesitated. Gordo drew back his fist. The priest suddenly began babbling that he had learned some things and would be glad to share them with Gordo.

Gordo hadn't expected it to happen so quickly. He was taken back and was not ready to deal with the information that he was about to be given. He sat across the table and said, "You will tell me?"

The priest's eyes remained on the floor in front of him. He put his hand to his mouth and wiped away a tiny trickle of blood that ran from its corner. *"Sí,* I was present at a meeting with Father Hidalgo, another priest name Soltura and . . ." The priest looked up at Gordo. "He has your name."

Gordo snorted. "Yes, he is my brother, and it will be my pleasure to see him hanged in the name of the king I serve. Go on, tell me of the meeting."

The priest returned his gaze to the floor. He spoke in hushed tones. "The two priests were at the meeting along with a woman named María, an Indian girl named Susan and a tall gringo named Barrigan, I believe." The mention of María and Barrigan hit Gordo in the gut like a hot sword. He wanted to ask more about them but decided to keep the conversation to revolutionary plans before pursuing personal interests. He ordered the priest to continue.

"Father Hidalgo plans to leave Dolores today and proceed to Guanajuato. He will leave some of those who follow him in Dolores to secure the town and to defend it. He plans to march eventually to Mexico City."

Gordo's laugh was spontaneous. He slapped the table and looked around at his men. "Can you imagine that?" he asked uproariously. "Those fools think they can take the capital of New Spain. Lunacy!"

The young priest eagerly agreed with Gordo.

"You say there was a woman named María and a man named Barrigan. Will they march with the revolutionary force?"

"Sí, although Father Hidalgo did talk of sending some people ahead to alert the leaders of the cities they plan to take next."

"Who will these people be?"

"I do not know."

Gordo suddenly picked up the edge of the table and threw it over onto the priest. It knocked him to the floor. He said from where he knelt, "Please, señor, I have told you everything I know. I would not lie to you."

Gordo looked down and found the sight of a priest praying to him to be amusing. He shook his head in disgust and left the cantina.

It had started to rain. Large drops hit the dusty road and skittered about like water in a hot frying pan. The rain felt good on Gordo's head and bare arms. He looked across the road to where some of the citizens of the mining village still stood and discussed what had occurred that day. The whore who'd stood with the unofficial mayor of Xlipote leaned against the door of the building in which she lived.

A sharp pain radiated up Gordo's spine, into his neck, and caused a blinding flash before his eyes. He put his hands to his head and moaned. When the sensation subsided, he again looked across the road and realized that he must take some time out to decide what to do with the information he had just received. What better way to spend that time, he mused, than in bed with a woman, even an old, used whore like the one across the road.

He started across when his NCO ran up to him and asked what his next orders were.

The pain again shot through Gordo's body. He stopped, turned and said to the NCO, "Shoot the priests. And tell the men to be ready to move in two hours."

Gordo withdrew from the whore and rolled over onto his back. The sound of muskets firing and a sharp scream from the young priest broke the stillness of the room.

"Someone is shot," the whore said, rubbing an area on one breast where Gordo had roughly handled it.

"Traitors," Gordo mumbled. "Now shut up. Wake me in one hour."

CHAPTER THIRTY-THREE

It had been Father Hidalgo's intention to personally lead the revolutionary force he'd mustered in Dolores to the next target, the village of Guanajuato. But problems began to crop up in Dolores to alter his plans.

Hidalgo decided to approach each village in three waves. The first wave would be a small group whose mission it would be to coordinate the leadership of the village in preparation for the arrival of the main force. Once that initial mission had been accomplished, the second force, of no more than two hundred men, would establish strategic positions around the village. Then, the main body of armed revolutionaries would sweep in.

After some debate, it was decided that Juan, María and Susan Barrigan would lead the initial group into Guanajuato. Hidalgo had reservations about including María in that group, but she insisted upon being at Juan's side at all times.

The second group would be led by John Barrigan. Hidalgo was increasingly impressed with Barrigan's common sense and daring. He considered himself and the cause he led to be blessed by the presence of the tall, angular Yankee from Massachusetts, and he was quick to let Barrigan know of his faith in him. John responded with a fierce and passionate loyalty to the cause with which he was now involved.

The main body of fighting men would be led by Hidalgo, at least for this next stage of the move toward Mexico City. A force of three hundred men were to remain in Dolores under the leadership of a criollo army officer who'd defected many months ago.

Juan, María and Susan left Dolores at one o'clock that

Sunday afternoon. Riding with them were twenty heavily armed Indian and mestizo patriots. Susan's role was considered crucial. Her Indian origins were a great asset, and Hidalgo had announced that no matter who led the advance teams from that point forward, Susan must always be included.

Juan, María and Susan, along with their group, approached Guanajuato apprehensively. The taking of Dolores was one thing. Now they were venturing into unknown territory and had no way of knowing whether the events in Dolores had triggered a mobilization of Spanish troops between that town and the capital, Mexico City. To their surprise and pleasure, there wasn't a Spanish soldier within miles of Guanajuato. They were met at the outskirts of town by the revolutionary leaders.

"A small force of no more than ten men were here yesterday," the representative from Guanajuato told Juan, "but they left soon after their arrival."

"That is good news," Juan said. "How many men do you have to contribute to the main army that Father Hidalgo will lead into Guanajuato later today."

"Three hundred, perhaps four hundred," was the reply.

"What about arms?" Juan asked, dismounting and stretching.

The revolutionary leader from Guanajuato said, "That is a problem. We have done all we can to find weapons, but most of the citizens have only crude arms."

María looked at Juan and said, "That shouldn't matter."

Juan did not share her optimism. He said, "It might not matter now, but in the days ahead I suspect every weapon will become crucial, particularly when we reach Mexico City."

After Juan dispatched lookouts, the Guanajuato leader, a middle-aged farmer, led Juan and his group into town where they sat in a small cantina and awaited the arrival of the next wave from Dolores, led by John Barrigan.

They drank tequila and ate tortillas that had been wrapped around shredded beef and pork. Their spirits were high. The lack of opposition, while not necessarily indicative of the future, was certainly welcome at that stage.

Juan had changed from his clerical clothing into a faded green chamois shirt and tan twill work pants. He felt free to sit next to María and to hold her hand. On two occasions she leaned over and lightly kissed him on the cheek. It was the warmest and most relaxed Juan had felt in quite a while. It was as though by removing the uniform of the church, the rigid restrictions of that institution were removed along with it. He felt as he did when he was a boy, lying in the cool stream that ran through his family's property in Vallodolid. The tequila had brought about a mellow feeling of well-being and, for that moment, there was no revolution, no church intrigue, only the exquisite pleasure of sitting close to a woman whose love he shared and whose fingers gently stroked the plam of his hand.

María was wearing a frilly white blouse. Her large, firm breasts pressed against its fabric and became the subject of Juan's attention more than once as they sat at the table. He looked down at her lap. She wore a taupe velvet skirt that had fallen into the space between her thighs, causing in Juan a feeling of intense sensuality. He remembered the night in his house, in his room, when they'd made love. He wanted to repeat that scene right now, although he realized it was impossible. Later that evening, however, wherever they might be, he and the woman he loved could again give vent to their passion.

Susan Barrigan had remained outside the cantina for most of the afternoon. She sat with her back against the wall of the building and allowed the heat of New Spain's sun to penetrate her and to soothe the worries and rigor of the past weeks. She'd almost dozed off when the door opened and Juan poked his head out. Susan looked up sleepily.

"I didn't mean to wake you," Juan said.

"I wasn't sleeping," Susan replied. "I was enjoying the peace."

Juan came down from the steps and knelt beside her. "It should be time for John and others to be arriving," he said.

Susan sat up straight and her face became animated, "That's right. They should be here any minute."

"I sent some of the men to look for them. Perhaps you would like to join them and welcome John when he arrives." Susan stretched her arms in front of her. "Yes, I would like that. I miss him so much."

"Go then, Susan. The men are stationed only a few hundred yards outside the village, on the ridge. It would delight John to see you.

Susan stood. The thought of being the one to run to John and to tell him that there was nothing to fear in the village filled her with excitement. She turned to Juan and kissed him on the cheek. "You have been so good to us, father."

Juan looked down at his clothing and smiled. "I don't think you should call me father when I'm dressed like this."

"You will always be father to me," Susan said. She kissed him again on the cheek and took off on the run toward the outskirts of the village.

María joined Juan outside the cantina. She stood next to him and they put their arms around each other's waist. Juan looked into her eyes and said, "I love you."

"Not as deeply as I love you, Juan. I am consumed by my love for you."

Juan looked up into the blazing sun and closed his eyes. He said quietly, "You sustain me as no one has done before, María. I need you."

The sound of those words filled María with love and warmth, and she pressed close to Juan, reveling in the feel of his body.

Susan stopped running after a few yards and proceeded at a slow walk toward the place where she would rendezvous with her husband. She passed a final row of low houses before reaching a vast open field that led to an abrupt rise on which the lookouts had been posted. She stopped when she reached the open area and looked up to the crest of the hills. She saw no one. A thick clump of trees obscured her view of the lookouts. She was about to resume her progress toward the hills when, without warning, three men ran from behind the last house, knocked her to the ground, picked her up and carried her back to the building.

The blow to Susan's head had momentarily stunned her. A hand was clamped over her mouth, another over her eyes. She struggled but was helpless in the grip of the men who'd attacked her. She was thrown roughly to the ground behind the last house. The hands remained upon her eyes and mouth until someone said, "Let her see."

The hand was removed from Susan's eyes and she looked up into the face of Gordo Soltura.

Gordo had led his men into Guanajuato through a mass of boulders and rocks that stretched from the low range of hills surrounding the town to almost the very back of the houses. He'd positioned himself atop one of the boulders and had observed what went on in the town since the arrival of the advance party from Dolores. He'd seen Juan, María and Susan lead the small contingent of men into the town, had watched Susan dozing against the building and had seen his brother and his wife standing side by side, their arms about each other in front of the cantina. When he saw Susan begin walking to where the lookouts were posted, he decided to act. Although he hadn't seen John Barrigan, he was confident that Barrigan would be arriving shortly.

Now, he had in his possession Barrigan's wife.

The sight of Gordo caused Susan to stiffen. She twisted her head and bit viciously into the flesh of the hand that covered her mouth. She drew blood, and the Spanish soldier to whom the hand belonged cursed her and pushed hard against her face.

Gordo was giddy with the way things were proceeding. He grinned as he said, "We meet again, you Indian bitch."

Susan's eyes were wide with terror and hatred. She frantically squirmed against the hands that held her to the ground but could not free herself.

Gordo leaned close to her face and said, "Your husband will be here shortly, will he not?"

Susan's eyes remained fixed upon the face of the man who had attempted to rape her.

"You didn't think you'd ever see me again, did you?" Gordo asked. "Well, my Indian bitch, the glorious plans for a revolution are over. Gordo de Soltura has seen to that." He couldn't contain himself. He broke into a laugh that soon turned into a rasping cough from deep inside him. He closed his eyes against pain that suddenly radiated from his spine up to his head. When the spasm had passed, he looked away from Susan and toward the rest of his men, who were hidden in the rocks and boulders. He waved for them to join him behind the building.

When they were all assembled, Gordo made his next decision. The ease with which Juan's advance group had entered the village had obviously created a false confidence within the revolutionaries. Gordo had expected to see them dispersed around the village as sentries. That had not happened. The Indians and mestizos in the advance party were either relaxing in the cantina, or had found comfortable spots outside it in which to siesta.

Gordo had counted the men dispatched to the ridge as lookouts. There were three.

Gordo told his NCO to take six men to the ridge and to kill those who were there awaiting the arrival of the next contingent from Dolores. He was left with fourteen men. He couldn't believe how smoothly things were going. It would work. He could literally secure the town, capture the revolutionary leaders and single-handedly break the back of the revolution. Such actions were what national heroes were made of. It would mean unlimited glory and wealth. Perhaps he would even be appointed viceroy by a grateful king. The adrenaline flowed through his body. He scrambled to his feet and ran to the other end of the building from which he could see the cantina. Juan and María were still standing in front of it. Gordo returned to his men and issued his next orders. Confident that the sentries who'd been assigned to the ridge were by now dead, he would personally take Susan to that spot and have her there when John Barrigan arrived with the next body of troops. He told his men to use the element of surprise and to attack the cantina, but to do it with as little bloodshed as possible, and to spare the lives of the man and woman who stood in front of it. His order didn't make any sense to some of his men, who didn't like the idea of having their actions curtailed. But when Gordo repeated it, they didn't argue.

As the men under Gordo's command moved along the back of the building and quickly covered the distance between it and the next building, Gordo pulled Susan to her feet and pushed her against the wall. He clasped a hand over her mouth and snarled, "If you make a noise I will kill you on the spot." He reached into the white crossbelt which made one part of a white X across his chest and withdrew a long, straight bayonet that was carried in a black leather scabbard. He held the point of the bayonet to Susan's throat. To make sure she understood, he pressed the tip against her flesh until a thin trickle of blood ran down onto her dress. He removed his left hand from her mouth, grasped her thick, black hair in an iron grip and turned her around. She was now in front of him, the blade of the bayonet against her spine. "Move, and do everything I say," he hissed.

Gordo had been right. Those in and around the cantina did not have a chance to react to the sudden appearance of armed, uniformed Spanish troops. Most of the revolutionary force never had a chance to get off the ground where they'd been napping. They were rudely awakened by the press of muskets in the ribs, and looked up into the faces of smiling Spanish soldiers.

What Gordo had not bargained for was that in the time it took for the men to move into position to make the assault,

Juan and María had left the area. It was María's suggestion that they join Susan on the ridge of the hills and form a welcoming committee for John Barrigan. They'd left the front of the cantina and had turned into an alleyway leading to a beaten path that Juan had noticed earlier in the afternoon. The path wound its way through a grove of giant tuna trees that had turned vivid red and yellow with the approaching autumn season. It presented a more scenic route to the top of the hills, and María had eagerly agreed with Juan's suggestion that they go that way.

They'd no sooner reached the edge of the grove than the Spanish soldiers made their move on the cantina. Although it was a relatively bloodless assault, the soldiers fired two shots when some of the revolutionary forces made an attempt to run.

Juan and María darted into the trees and nervously looked back at the center of the village. They were stunned at how such a peaceful afternoon could be shattered so quickly and with such finality.

"What shall we do?" María asked, as she clung to his arm.

Juan forced himself to shed the confusion of the moment and to think clearly. "We must warn those waiting for John."

"Susan is there," María said.

"Yes, I know. Come." He grabbed her hand and led her quickly through the grove of tuna toward a point at the foot of the hills where they could make their way up the southern slope.

John Barrigan had heard the two shots as he and the group of men under his command approached Guanajuato. He halted the column and waited for further sounds. There were none. He immediately decided to disperse his troops to the left and right, to flank the village. He kept with him a group of forty men, and after scanning the ridge of the hills separating him from town, he slowly led them toward the slope that rose up a hundred yards in front of him.

Gordo had remained hidden on the crest. The three bodies of the revolutionary lookouts were sprawled among rocks and shrubs. He kept his hand firmly clamped over Susan's mouth, the bayonet paused and ready to strike into her back should she make any warning sound. They were alone on the ridge. Gordo had dispatched the six soldiers who'd killed Juan's lookouts back to town to bolster forces there.

He watched intently as the tall, rugged gringo from Massachusetts, the man who'd almost killed him in Santa Fe, crouched low and led the ragged band of Indians and mestizos to the foot of the slope. It wasn't until John had reached a point approximately halfway up the slope that Gordo left the cover of a huge boulder and boldly displayed Susan for her husband to see.

At first, John wasn't sure who stood on top of the hill. He squinted against the rays of the sun and shielded his eyes with his hand. Then, there was no mistake. It was his wife, Susan, and the man who held the bayonet to her back was María's husband, Gordo.

"John, I'm all right," Susan yelled.

Gordo was shielded from John by Susan. John carried his solid-framed .44 caliber pistol, but he was helpless. If he attempted to shoot Gordo he would surely hit Susan.

"I will kill her," Gordo shouted down the slope. "I assure you of that. Drop your gun and tell your men to do the same."

Never before in John Barrigan's life had he felt such confusion and inability to act. The hatred that he'd felt the night Gordo had attempted to rape Susan welled up in him again. He wished he had killed him that night, and not simply injured him.

John looked back at his men, who were sprawled out along the slope awaiting orders from their leader. He thought of Zeb Pike and wished he were there with him now. Zeb had always been able to make a quick and proper decision under stress. While John had also been able to think quickly under difficult circumstances, this situation presented a new set of considerations. He was at the head of a column that was launching one of the great revolutions in the history of the western world. It was obvious to him that defeat at this early juncture could spell failure for the entire cause. Could he sacrifice the success of a national uprising of oppressed people that had been so carefully developed for so many years in order to save one person, even though that one person was the wife he loved so much?

He realized he had no choice. Susan had brought into his life a dimension he'd never dreamed he would ever possess. They'd shared so much together, had faced so many trials and tribulations. He could not sacrifice her, no matter how worthy or lofty the cause. He stood and dropped his weapon to the

285

ground. His men looked up at him and asked with their eyes whether they were expected to do the same. John could not bring himself to command them to give up the dream that had been alive for less than a day. He looked up at Gordo and raised his hands slightly from his sides in a gesture of helplessness.

The ease with which Barrigan had backed down only served to heighten Gordo's already overgrown sense of power. "Tell those miserable animals with you to throw their weapons away and to retreat down the hill," he commanded.

Barrigan said, "You tell them, Gordo. I am no longer their leader."

Gordo shouted to the men with Barrigan to leave their weapons where they were and to move down the slope on their bellies. When no one moved, John turned and told his men to do what they'd been instructed to do. One by one, the Indians and mestizos backed away from their weapons and returned to the bottom of the hill.

"Well, you have won," John said. "I have done what you have asked. Now let my wife free."

"Let her free? Your Indian bitch and I still have unfinished business."

John trembled with rage. The bayonet in Gordo's hand was still pressed against Susan's throat. John wondered for a moment whether help could be expected from the village, but the absurdity of that possibility was quickly evident to him. If Gordo could stand alone so brazenly with Susan, everyone else in the village must either have been captured, or killed.

"I ask you to release her," John said. "She has done no harm to anyone. If you release her, I will willingly give myself to you as a captive."

Gordo laughed. He tightened his grip on Susan's hair and made an overt gesture of ramming the bayonet into her throat.

At first, John couldn't believe what he saw. Juan and María came over the crest from the village side. They paused and then abruptly went into action. Juan dove across the brief span separating him from his brother and flung himself into Gordo's back. The impact knocked both Gordo and Susan to the ground. They rolled down the slope toward John Barrigan, coming to a stop halfway between the ridge and where he stood. Gordo's arms were wrapped around Susan, and the bayonet was still tightly gripped in his hand. Before John could react, or before Juan could get to his feet and launch another attack, Gordo raised the bayonet and plunged it into Susan's abdomen. At first, there was no sound from her. Then, a low, anguished moan came from between her lips. It soon turned into an agonized scream. Then, silence.

Gordo looked up at Juan and sneered. He slowly got to his feet, the bloody bayonet still in his hand, and locked his brother in a battle of eyes.

"Why?" Juan asked. "Why did you kill her?"

Gordo was breathing heavily. He took a few steps toward Juan and said, "That was always your problem, my brother. You never understood the difference between us and Indian trash."

"May God have mercy on your soul," Juan said.

"If God has mercy for anyone, Juan, it had better be for you." He suddenly lunged at his brother, the bayonet held out in front of him as though his arm were a musket. His thrust was stopped only inches away from Juan's chest by the explosion of John Barrigan's musket. He'd picked it up from the ground, taken aim and, when he saw Gordo attack Juan, fired. The musket ball caught Gordo squarely in the back and hurtled him forward, past Juan and onto his face in the soil. Blood oozed from the wound and ran across his broad back. It formed tiny red balls of dust on the ground.

Juan looked down at John Barrigan and held out his hands in a gesture of sympathy.

John did not see Juan at that moment. He could only see his dead wife, the beautiful Indian girl for whom he had fought and to whom he had given the Christian name of his dead, beloved mother. Tears welled up in his eyes, then flowed freely down his cheeks. He felt utterly drained. It was as though life itself had been siphoned from his body along with the life that had left his wife. He fell to his knees and sobbed, his body wracked with convulsions.

Juan went to him, knelt and placed his arms about his shoulders. He murmured the prayers of the Catholic Church that were so much a part of his life as a priest. He had comforted so many people in times of sorrow and travail, mouthing words that had been written centuries ago and that would be repeated for centuries to come. But those words seemed pitifully empty and without meaning at that moment. They were, after all, nothing more than words. He could not muster the courage to pray for Susan's soul and for John to find peace. He could say nothing more than, "I'm sorry."

Juan and John remained on the hillside until the sound of the army led by Father Miguel Hidalgo could be heard as it approached the village of Guanajuato. The men who'd accompanied John had remained at the foot of the hill. They did not wish to impose upon the tragedy that had obviously taken place just above them.

The sight of the dead bodies of Gordo Soltura and Susan Barrigan shocked Father Hidalgo. He looked at Juan, then at John. "How did it happen?" he asked quietly.

"It doesn't matter," Juan replied. María had come to his side and they stood together. Their hands were tightly linked.

Hidalgo carefully knelt upon the ground and administered the last rites to the two bodies in front of him.

An hour later, the village of Guanajuato was secured. A small group was left to defend it, and with swelling ranks, Father Miguel Hidalgo led the revolutionary army of New Spain toward its next destination in its mission of freeing a nation.

CHAPTER THIRTY-FOUR

By the first week of November 1810, Father Miguel Hidalgo stood on the verge of power as he reached Monte de las Cruces, just outside Mexico City. Behind him were more than 200,000 oppressed people. They outnumbered the gachupine defenders by more than ten to one. Despite the urging of Father Juan de Soltura, John Barrigan and other advisors, Hidalgo decided that it was too soon to attack Mexico City. "We must wait until we have more men and arms," he said.

The delay proved to be a fatal mistake. The formidable gachupine general, Félix María Calleja, surprised Hidalgo's army and split it in two. Hidalgo retreated to Guadalajara where, on December 12, a revitalized Spanish army dealt him a smashing defeat. Hilalgo and his rebels retreated once again, this time to Aguascalientes. As the forces of the king's army pressed forward and threatened to annihilate Hidalgo's army, Juan and John Barrigan convinced him to resign as leader of the revolution.

Hidalgo seemed at peace with his decision to resign. He decided to go to Acatita de Baján, just southwest of Nuevo Laredo, on the Río Grande. He took with him three other priests, including Juan Soltura. The purpose of the trip was to convince the church leaders of that area that victory by the revolutionary army was inevitable, and that the church should throw its support behind the criollo cause.

Hidalgo and his friends never reached their destination. A loyal garrison of the interior provinces intercepted and arrested them, and they were tried by a military tribunal. During the trial, which lasted three days, Hidalgo took complete responsibility for the revolution and for every act committed by the rebels.

An ecclesiastical court defrocked the priest on July 29, 1811.

On July 31, 1811, Father Miguel Hidalgo, Father Juan de Soltura and five other priests convicted by the military tribunal were executed by firing squad. The priests stood with crosses in their hands. All of them prayed except Father Juan de Soltura. He could think only of María.

Epilogue

CHAPTER THIRTY-FIVE

September 1821

Violet streaks on the horizon heralded another dawn over the valley of Valladolid. José Jardinero sat in his favorite chair in a corner of his library and pulled a well-worn blue flannel robe tighter around him.

On the table next to him were the letters he and his wife had received from their daughter, María, over the past ten years. The mail had provided the only communication between them. They hadn't seen her since the days immediately following the execution of Fathers Hidalgo and Juan de Soltura. It had been decided at that point that John Barrigan and María would lead a group of survivors from the dwindling Hidalgo force to where Father José María Morelos commanded rebels on the coast. If there were any hope for the revolution to be revived, it would rest with Morelos and his growing army.

José and the Jardinero family had returned to Valladolid and resumed daily life in the valley while the revolution went on around them.

A year after their return to their home, they were joined by the remains of the Soltura family. The death of both Soltura sons, Gordo and Juan, had left Manuel and Margarita shattered. For Manuel, it was more than the loss of his sons. The revolution threatened to strip from him his cherished position as empresario to the north. When the demands of defending the nation against the rebels took priority over all other matters, the borders were shut off to foreigners. There was no longer a need for government land agents, and Manuel was forced to leave Santa Fe.

Two months after he and Margarita reached Valladolid, a massive heart attack took his life.

Margarita de Soltura and the Jardineros found an even greater closeness than had existed between them before the tragic events that had changed their lives. Although they did not combine their rancheros and haciendas legally, José took over the day-to-day management of both tracts of land.

José lighted a pipe that had been a present from his wife upon the occasion of his sixty-third birthday. He inhaled deeply and held the smoke in his lungs. The sound of a pair of redbilled toucans outside the window caused him to pause and smile. He exhaled the blue-gray smoke and watched it float lazily to the ceiling.

As he'd done on so many mornings since María and John had departed to join forces with Father Morelos, José lifted the pile of letters from the table, placed them upon his lap and opened the first envelope. The letters were always kept in a wall safe in the library, and José was careful to keep them in the order of the dates that appeared at the top of each one.

He read from the first one, which was dated February 12, 1912. It said, in part:

> . . . you mustn't worry about me. Since finding Father Morelos and joining his fight on the coast, things have gone rather well. John is now second-in-command to Morelos and the army grows, not only ln number but in dedication and strength. By the time your receive this, the siege of Cuautla will have begun, and all of us are confident it will result in total victory . . .

José replaced the letter in its envelope and closed his eyes. The siege of Cuautla had not been successful, according to a subsequent letter from María and from reports that trickled back to Valladolid. Morelos and his troops had suffered serious reversals, although the clerical leader, John Barrigan and María had not been injured.

In an attempt to defuse revolutionary movements throughout its vast empire, the government of Spain had proclaimed a liberal constitution. The constitution had been passed by the cortes and announced in Mexico on September 28, 1812. It had not brought about its intended result. Members of the revolution saw it as a ploy and reacted accordingly.

Early in 1813, Joseph Bonaparte had been deposed in Spain. A letter from María in the spring of that year indicated that despite problems, the Morelos troops continued to control most coastal areas. Then, in September, Morelos convened what was termed the Congress of Chilpancingo. There he drafted a purely Mexican constitution which formed a legal Mexican government, independent of Spain. By November, the congress had adopted Morelos's constitution. It appeared that independence might have arrived.

But in 1814, Ferdinand VII was restored to the throne in Spain and he immediately abolished the liberal constitution that had been adopted there.

In September 1814, the Jardineros received another letter from María, this one delivered by a private messenger.

My beloved mother and father,

Life these days seems so confused. Each victory, each triumph, is tempered by a defeat. Good news seems always to be fleeting. Bad news rushes in to strip away the joy.

When Ferdinand was restored to the throne of Spain and reinstated his conservative constitution, the future appeared dark for our cause. But eventually, the pessimism within our ranks was replaced by a renewed sense of purpose. Next month Father Morelos and John will convene a second Mexican congress of independence, this time at Apatzingán.

As you are undoubtedly aware, John Barrigan has established himself as a potent and respected force in this battle for a just independence. The pride with which I view him grows each day, and I would be less than honest were I not to admit that I now love him deeply, and that he has expressed a similar love for me. He is such a fine man, so dedicated to a cause that does not even involve his own people. Recently, he received word that his friend, Zebulon Pike, was killed in the war between the Americans and the British. It affected him deeply. His love and respect for Zeb Pike was without bounds. I met Zeb only briefly, yet I can understand John's feelings for him.

I pray that you are receiving my letters. I will assume that you are, and I will continue writing to a mother and father I love very much. And that love extends always to Señora Soltura. Please tell her that for me.

Your loving daughter,
María

P.S. Again, I apologize for never including my address in my letters. It must be that way, as I am sure you understand.

There hadn't been another letter from María until the summer of 1816. Much had happened in New Spain during the intervening period.

A year after Father Morelos had convened his second congress of Mexican independence, he was captured and executed at San Cristóbal Ecatepec. That occured on December 22, 1815. His death created for his followers a magnificent martyr to whom to dedicate their revolutionary efforts.

Early in 1816, 9,000 rebels battled a gachupine force of more than 30,000 men, and won. It was a costly victory, however, and in August of that year, the new viceroy, Juan Ruíz de Apodaca, launched a major effort to subdue the revolutionary forces. By December of 1816, four months after José had received María's most recent letter, it appeared that the rebels had been so splintered that defeat was inevitable, and that Mexico would remain firmly in the grasp of its mother country, Spain.

Again, a long stretch of time went by in which the Jardinero family did not hear from their daughter. Two short letters arrived in 1817, one in 1818 and one again in 1819. By then, significant events within the nation and within Spain had occurred that once again pointed to the possibility of independence. Liberals in Spain had made a major push to gain control of the cortes, and it appeared that their efforts might bear fruit.

But of all the news that sped through New Spain, the most important for the Jardineros was contained in a brief letter they received from María in January of 1820. It said simply:

John and I have been married. I have given birth to a child, a boy, whom we have named John José Barrigan. He is your first grandchild, a healthy and handsome boy of whom we can all be proud. I thank God that events within our land point to freedom and dignity for every citizen. I pray for that for my son more than anything.

Love,
María

By November of 1820, it had become obvious to the gachupine rulers of New Spain that a major effort would have to be launched to destroy the revolution once and for all. The only rebel leader of any importance still operating was an Indian of peasant origins, Vincente Guerrero, who maintained a sizeable force in the mountains to the south. The viceroy felt that if Guerrero were defeated decisively, the back of the revolution would be broken. He dispatched a young criollo officer named Augustín de Iturbide, who'd refused an offer from Father Hidalgo to join the revolution, and who'd played a role in the capture of Father Morelos. Officially retired and short of funds, Iturbide jumped at the chance to lead an army of 2,500 men against Guerrero's smaller force.

Iturbide was surprised at the strength of Guerrero's men during initial skirmishes, and decided to meet with the rebel leader in an attempt to work out a compromise solution. Guerrero was wary at first, then agreed. The two leaders met in the town of Iguala, sixty miles south of Mexico City. Incredibly, Iturbide offered to lend his support and that of his army to independence in New Spain. Guerrero and Iturbide drafted what became known as the Plan of Iguala, which was proclaimed to the nation on February 24, 1821.

Present at the Iguala conference, besides Iturbide and Guerrero, were John and María Barrigan.

The provisions of the plan were simple but sweeping. Mexico was to be independent of all foreign power. Only the Roman Catholic Church would be tolerated.

Race or social status would not be considered for the holding of public office, but property rights and positions would be protected as they stood prior to the agreement. The special privileges of the clergy and military would be upheld, and the throne of the new and independent nation would be offered to the Spanish king, or to a member of the royal family.

The provisions of the Plan of Iguala suited both liberal and conservative interests, although many of the social reforms desired by the liberals would obviously have to be postponed. For them, an immediate declaration of independence was sufficient. The conservative gachupine leaders accepted the plan because of the provisions regarding protection of existing rights and positions, and the offer for the royal family to provide a ruler.

In July 1821, the newly appointed viceroy of New Spain,

Juan O'Donojú, arrived in Córdoba. He was met by members of the new ruling council headed by Iturbide, was detained and forced to sign the Treaty of Córdoba. Its terms were much the same as those of the Plan of Iguala, except that it provided for the throne of the new nation to go to someone other than a member of the royal family, should those suggested for the position not meet with the approval of Iturbide's council. And it gave Iturbide permission to lead his army into Mexico City in order to insure compliance with the new constitutional.

José de Jardinero thumbed through the few remaining envelopes until he came to the most recent letter from María. The letter had arrived a week before. In it, she'd told her parents that it was possible that she, John and their son might soon be coming to Valladolid. It depended, of course, upon a complete resolution of the government turnover. Iturbide had promised that all charges against John and María would be dropped.

Señora Jardinero came down the stairs and entered the den. "Again you sit and read the letters," she said, going to her husband and placing her hand upon his neck.

José looked up and smiled. "They give me great comfort," he said, placing his hand upon hers.

His wife sat upon the arm of the leather chair. "It is interesting to live through this period, is it not?" she asked, pausing to listen to the sound of the birds outside the window. The sun had risen further and the windowpanes were splashed with orange and red.

"*Sí,*" José said. "This is the day when the new emperor of our land rides into Mexico City in triumph. We must pray for him that he possesses wisdom and strength to lead us on the right path."

His wife nodded. "Do you think María truly is coming home?"

"Now that conditions seem settled, I don't see why not. She is married to a national hero, a legend. They must always be careful. A man like John Barrigan will always have enemies."

"*Sí.*"

José sighed and placed the letters on the table. "I suppose there will never be true peace anywhere in the world."

"Why do you say that?"

"To be a large and growing independent nation will tempt others to rob us. There is much talk that the Americans want to wage war with us and take this land for their own."

"Not in our lifetime, José."

"I hope not."

As they sat in silence, the sound of horses' hoofs could be heard in front of the house.

"Are the men ready to work so early?" Señora Jardinero asked.

José shrugged. "I can't believe that."

Footsteps bounded up the stairs to the front porch. The Jardineros got up and went to the door. José opened it and looked down. Staring up at him was a boy about three years of age. His skin was dusky, his eyes blue, his hair brown. Behind him stood John and María Barrigan.

"Hello," María said.

José gulped and wiped a tear from his eye. "Hello," he said. "Come in. Welcome home." He scooped up his grandchild and led everyone into the house.

Bestselling Books for Today's Reader — From Jove!

__**CHASING RAINBOWS** 05849-1/$2.95
Esther Sager

__**FIFTH JADE OF HEAVEN** 04628-0/$2.95
Marilyn Granbeck

__**PHOTO FINISH** 05995-1/$2.50
Ngaio Marsh

__**NIGHTWING** 06241-7/$2.95
Martin Cruz Smith

__**THE MASK** 05695-2/$2.95
Owen West

__**SHIKE: TIME OF THE DRAGON** 06586-2/$3.25
(Book 1)
Robert Shea

__**SHIKE: TIME OF THE DRAGON** 06587-0/$3.25
(Book 2)
Robert Shea

__**THE WOMEN'S ROOM** 05933-1/$3.50
Marilyn French